D0211345

LARGE
PRINT

WITHDRAWN

BEAUTIFUL
LIES

BEAUTIFUL

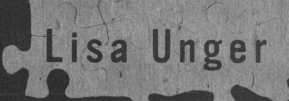

Lisa Unger

LIES

A NOVEL

DOUBLEDAY LARGE PRINT
HOME LIBRARY EDITION
RANDOM HOUSE

3 1901 03941 9918

This is a work of fiction. Names, characters, places, and incidents either are the product of the author's imagination or are used fictitiously. Any resemblance to actual persons, living or dead, events, or locales is entirely coincidental.

Copyright © 2006 by Lisa Unger

All rights reserved.
Published in the United States of America by
Random House Large Print in association
with Shaye Areheart Books, New York.
Distributed by Random House, Inc., New York.

ISBN-13: 978-0-7393-2580-3
ISBN-10: 0-7393-2580-9

This Large Print edition published in accord with
the standards of the N.A.V.H.

For Jeffrey
You're everything. Always.

As he was anonymous, without a name . . . at all orphan, quidam.

CYPRIAN K. NORWID

October 25, 1972

There were times when she wished he were dead. Not that she'd never met him, or that he'd never been born, but that he'd get hit by a car or get himself killed in some other violent way like a bar fight, or his arm would get caught in a machine and he would bleed to death before anyone could save him. And she wished that in those final moments, when he felt his life draining from him, that he'd understand what a bastard he was, what a waste of life. She could envision him, his blood pooling in a black kidney-shaped puddle beneath him as he repented in terror, understanding with a final clarity that he was about to pay for the man he was. In those dark moments he'd be sorry, so sorry. But it would be too late. That's how she felt about him.

She lay alone in the dark, on the old

pilled quilt atop her bed. The radiator was cranking dry, hot air, making an occasional loud bang as if someone were hitting one of the pipes with a metal wrench. She strained to hear the soft, measured breathing of her daughter down the hall. A strong wind rattled the window. She knew it was cold outside, colder than it had been yet this autumn. But she was sweating a little. The heat in her apartment always ran too hot. In the night the baby (though she really wasn't a baby anymore at almost two years old) would kick off her covers. She was listening for that, for the sudden shift the child made in her sleep when she pushed the blankets away. But she was listening, too, for other noises.

Her heart had finally stopped racing and the baby had finally stopped screaming, but she knew he would come back. She lay fully clothed in a gray sweatshirt, jeans, and sneakers, the phone in her hand. A baseball bat lay beside her leg. If he came back, she would call the police again, even though they'd already come once tonight after he'd gone. She had a restraining order. They had to come no matter how many times she called.

She couldn't believe it had come to this, her life. If it weren't for her daughter, she'd think what a mess she'd made of it, how many mistakes, how many broken expectations. At least she knew that she did one thing well, that in spite of everything, her baby was happy and healthy and loved by her mother.

The clock beside her bed cast a green glow and the only sounds now were the child breathing and the hum of the refrigerator down the hall. It was old; there was a low groan and a slight rattle to it. She hardly noticed anymore except when she was listening closely to the darkness, worrying about where he was and what he would try next.

Their relationship had been all but over when she told him she was pregnant. If you could even call it a relationship. They'd gone out a couple of times. He'd pick her up in his Monte Carlo and take her to a pizza place where people seemed to know him. He'd pull out her chair and tell her she was pretty. He'd tell her that a couple of times over dinner, using it as filler for a conversation that faltered more than it flowed.

They'd seen The Candidate with Robert Redford and The Getaway with Steve

McQueen, neither of which she had particularly wanted to see, not that he'd asked. He'd
just drive them to the movie theater and
walk to the ticket window, tell the clerk
what he wanted to see. Maybe that should
have been her first clue. If you're going to
the movies with your date, shouldn't you ask
her what she wants to see? In the darkened
theater with a bucket of popcorn between
her legs, he'd play with her ponytail and
whisper in her ear how pretty she was . . .
again. The second time, during The Getaway,
she'd let him touch her breast and almost
liked it, felt herself go hot between the legs.
That night, he'd come back to her apartment
and they'd slept together. But he didn't stay
the night. She'd slept with him again a few
times after that, but he stopped taking her
out for pizza and movies. And then, just as
she was starting to count on hearing his
voice on the phone, feeling his arm on her
shoulder, he faded out of her life. They all
seemed to do that, didn't they? Seemed like
one week they were together, but by the next
they were strangers. For a while she had
heard from him every night, which turned
into every other night. Then her phone
stopped ringing altogether. She'd look at it,

sitting there on the kitchen counter, pick up the receiver to make sure it was working.

She hadn't been raised to chase a man, to ask him out or ask why he'd stopped calling, so when she didn't hear from him, she never tried to reach him. Of course, she'd not been raised to let a man grope her in a theater and then sleep with him, either.

Anyway, he was nothing to her but a way to pass the time, a way to get over the man before him. How different the two men had seemed on the outside. The one before had been wealthy, treating her to fancy evenings in the city, buying her gifts, dresses and jewelry. He'd spoken French to her, and even though she didn't understand, she was impressed. Her mistake had been that he'd been her boss. And when he'd tired of her, he'd suggested that he'd make it comfortable for her to find another job. They were so different, this one and the one before. But in the end they were all the same, weren't they? They got bored and wanted her to go away. Or they became distant and cold. Or violent like this one.

Her parents, both heavy smokers, had died within two years of each other, far too young. Her mother died slowly and terribly from emphysema and her father from a sudden heart attack. She had no brothers and sisters. So she had no one to shame with her unwed pregnancy, but no one to turn to, either. Maria was her only friend; a woman downstairs known to everyone as Madame Maria. The older woman made her living reading tarot cards in her apartment, giving guidance from "the Goddess," as she liked to say. Madame Maria had told her that a gift was on its way to her. Maria always said that. This time she was right.

When she was sure, she went to see him. He asked her how she knew it was his. She started to really hate him then and wondered how she could have ever given herself so cheaply to someone so undeserving. She assured him that she wanted nothing from him, had just wanted to give him the opportunity to be a father. He left her standing in a dark parking lot. It started to rain, just a light mist, as she listened to the rumble of his Monte Carlo driving off into the distance. It had been a mistake to go see him; she'd misjudged him. Had thought he might do right by her. Wrong again.

Then, maybe it was guilt haunting him, or curiosity, or maybe even some latent capacity to love, but he started coming around when the baby was a few months old. And it seemed as if he might be taking an interest in being a father. But after a while, it was just like the movies: He thought he could start picking the show and the time, and cop a feel while he was at it. The battles started. The police were called. Apologies offered. Forgiveness granted for the sake of the child. Over and over . . . until the unforgivable afternoon. Then the battles really began.

She spent many nights like this since then, lying in the dark fully clothed, waiting. And she'd had so much time to think about why it was happening. She'd gone over every interaction they'd ever had, dissecting and analyzing all her words and actions, wondering what she might have done differently. But the only thing she came up with was that she should have noticed about the movies, how he never asked her what she wanted to see. That should have told her what kind of man he was. Sometimes it's the little things that tell the tale.

She remembered that afternoon; it was seared into her like a brand on her skin. "B" for bad mother. She remembered getting the call from Maria at work, racing home to her apartment, where she'd let the baby stay with him during her shift. She remembered hearing the wailing, unmistakable, heart-wrenching, a connection directly from her child's heart to hers as she took the stairs two at a time. She remembered bursting through the door to see him sitting on the couch, his face slack with fear. The door to the nursery was closed as if he'd shut it against the child's crying. She was sick, every membrane on fire with fear, as she threw open the door. The baby sat in her crib, bright red from crying, her arm bent horribly, unnaturally. She grabbed her child and ran, screaming, "What did you do? What did you do? Look what you've done!" He sat there, mute, his arms outspread. She didn't look at him again as she ran with her screaming, injured child in her arms.

She didn't, she couldn't wait for an ambulance. As gently as she could, she put the baby in her car seat. The little girl's cries felt like knives, cutting and killing her inside. Her own tears felt like they should be blood. She tried to keep her voice measured, cooing as she drove. "It's okay. It's okay, my love. Mommy's here. Mommy's here."

In the emergency room, the doctor took

the child from her arms and she followed him as he rushed her into the belly of the hospital to the pediatric floor. She prayed; she prayed that her baby's doctor, who alternated between the Little Angels clinic and the hospital, would be here today. Her prayers were answered and in minutes her daughter was under his careful hands.

"Oh my, little girl. What has happened to you?" he said quietly. She could do nothing but stand mute beside them.

"Mom," he said gently. He never used her name when he was attending to the baby. "I know this is scary, but I'm going to ask you to go wait outside so that I can fix this little munchkin right up. You're very upset and frightened right now and she knows that, she can feel it. Can you be very brave and wait outside?"

She nodded against her will and allowed herself to be shepherded outside by a nurse. The nurse, a young woman with bright blue eyes behind thick horn-rimmed glasses, looked at her with equal parts sympathy and suspicion. There was judgment there, too. Cold and certain. Could they think I'd hurt my daughter? she wondered through the fog of her fears. Could they think that?

It seemed as if her chest would explode from the sheer force of the emotion churning there as she watched the doors to the examining room. The baby's crying had gone from screams to whimpers and then there was silence. She felt paralyzed, lashed to the orange plastic chair on which she sat, unable to bring herself to investigate the silence. Then, after a hundred years, the doctor emerged.

"She's going to be fine," he said gently, sitting beside her and putting a hand on her knee. He went on about the delicacy of a broken bone in a toddler and all the special considerations they would take when setting it and how they would need to proceed with the healing of it. The words She's going to be fine repeated in a loop in her mind until her heart had accepted the information and started to return to its normal rhythm, until her blood started its passage again, bringing her back to life. She had been suspended in her terror, hovering between life and death, until she knew her child was no longer in pain.

"It's okay," he was saying to her, looking into her eyes. "It's going to be okay."

But there was something else in his eyes,

too. There was worry and there was suspicion in an expression that was normally so kind and warm.

They were at the hospital for most of the night, as the child was sedated and her arm was set in the tiniest cast. The doctor stayed with them until it was time to go home. As she was preparing to leave, the doctor touched her arm and looked at her with an expression she couldn't read.

"You love your child more than anything, don't you?" he asked her, sounding so sad.

"More than anything."

"Are you going to be able to protect her?" It seemed like such an odd question, especially since it was the echo of the question her own aching heart was asking.

"Anybody wants to harm this child, they'll have to kill me first."

He nodded. "Let's see it doesn't come to that. Make sure you follow up on pressing those charges. And I'll see you at the clinic on Thursday—or before, if there's any problem." His voice had gone stern and she nodded obediently.

"I wish," she said as he turned away from her, "that she had a father like you."

He looked at her strangely, seemed about to say something, then decided against it. He smiled at her, a warm, comforting smile full of compassion. "So do I. So do I."

Whenever she thought of that moment, it filled her heart with a renewed hatred for the man who'd hurt her child. It cemented her resolve against his constant begging for forgiveness, his constant pleading for a minute, just a minute with the baby, and then his raging against her when she denied him. It had been an accident, hurting the baby. He'd never meant to hurt her, he claimed. He'd seemed contrite enough. But she kept thinking about what the doctor had asked her. Are you going to be able to protect her? The only way she could be sure the answer was yes is if she kept him out of their lives.

She might have been dozing a bit, but something jarred her and she transferred her grip from the phone to the baseball bat. She lay silent, adrenaline running, listening to the night. The baby shifted in her sleep and sighed. She heard the slightest snap, more like a ping, the sound of a metal spring straining, as if the screen door were opening, ever so quietly.

He'd never been quiet before. He'd always come banging. She felt her throat tighten and she quietly got off the bed, the phone forgotten, the bat heavy in her hand. She walked to the doorjamb and peered out into the small living room of her apartment. From there she could see the front door. The lock looked too flimsy suddenly and she cursed herself for not having installed the dead bolt and chain as the police had recommended. She hadn't been able to afford it. The window beside the door was gated, but it hung over a landing that anyone could reach by a flight of stairs.

Did she just see his shadow move in front of the window? The curtains were drawn but the streetlight in the parking lot shined bright throughout the night and sometimes she could see the shadows of people passing on the way to their own apartments. She listened again and heard nothing. She was about to relax when she heard it again, that straining metal spring. Was he standing outside her door, inside the screen? Her breathing came more quickly and her chest felt heavy.

She looked at the phone she had left on the bed and thought about calling the police. But she couldn't face them coming here for nothing again. He'd already gone by the time they arrived earlier. And even though they took her report again respectfully, she was starting to feel like the little boy who cried wolf. If she called them again, and it really was nothing, she'd be so embarrassed. She gripped the bat with both hands and moved toward the door.

She moved quietly, slowly. He'd always come loudly, she reminded herself. He'd never tried to quietly break in and hurt them. Or her other worst nightmare, steal her baby. In the area, three children had gone missing in the last year. Every night, their little faces looked out at her from the television screen, their bright smiles, their sweet eyes like a haunting. Gone from their homes, each of them. None of them found, not even a trail to be followed. Every once in a while she'd hear on the news that there'd been a sighting in a mall or at a rest stop or an amusement park. But then the lead would go nowhere. She thought more than a little about those parents, the gaping holes in their chests, their lifetime of horrible questions and unspeakable imaginings. Maybe the only thing that kept them alive was hope, the only thing that kept the razors from their wrists and the guns from their mouths was the idea that they'd open their doors one day and see their child again. She couldn't imagine the crippling grief for a child who might be alive somewhere, unreachable, or might be dead . . . never knowing what would be worse.

She was close to the door now, just three feet away, standing beside her secondhand couch. She hadn't heard anything as she crept toward the door, so she stood frozen like a statue with the bat poised.

ONE

It's dark in that awful way that allows you to make out objects but not the black spaces behind them. My breathing comes ragged from exertion and fear. The only person I trust in the world lies on the floor beside me. I lean into him and hear that he's still breathing but it's shallow and hard won. He's hurt, I know. But I can't see how badly. I whisper his name in his ear but he doesn't respond. I feel his body but there's no blood that I can tell. The sound of his body hitting the floor minutes before was the worst thing I've ever heard.

I feel the floor around him, looking for his gun. After a few seconds I feel the cool metal beneath my fingertips and I almost weep with relief. But there's no time for that now.

I can hear the rain falling outside the burned-out building, its loud, heavy drops smacking on canvas. It's falling inside, too, trickling in through gaping holes in the roof down through floors of rotted wood and broken staircases. He moves and issues a low groan. I hear him say my name and I lean in close to him again.

"It's okay. We're going to be okay," I tell him, even though I don't have any reason to believe this is true. Somewhere outside or up above us a man I thought I loved, along with other men whom I couldn't identify, are trying to kill us, to protect an awful truth that I've discovered. I am hurt myself, in so much pain that I might pass out if I didn't know it meant dying here in this condemned building on the Lower East Side of Manhattan. There's something embedded in my right thigh. It's possibly a bullet, or a large spike of wood, or maybe a nail. It's so dark I can just barely see the large hole in my jeans, and the denim is black with my blood. I'm dizzy, the world tilting, but I'm holding on.

I hear them up above us now, see the beams of their flashlights crossing in the dark through the holes in the floors. I try to control my breathing, which to my own ears sounds as loud as an oncoming train. I hear one of the men say to the others, "I think they fell through. They're on the bottom." There was no answer but I can hear them making their way down over creaking wood.

He stirs. "They're coming," he says, his voice little more than a rasp. "Get out of here, Ridley."

I don't answer him. We both know I'm not leaving. I pull at him and he tries to get up, but the pain registers on his face louder than the scream I know he suppressed to protect us for a few minutes more. If we're not walking out of here together, we're not walking out at all. I drag him, even though I know I shouldn't be moving him, over behind an old moldy couch that lies on its back by the wall. It's not far but I can see his face white and gritted in terrible pain. As I move him, he loses consciousness again and in an instant feels fifty pounds heavier. But I've seen all four of his limbs move and that's something. I realize that I'm praying as I pull him, my leg on fire, my strength waning. **Please God, please God, please God,** over and over again like a mantra.

The way the couch is lying, it forms a crawl space against the wall just big enough for the two of us. I pull him in there and lie on my belly beside him. I pull an old crate over toward the edge of the couch and look through the wooden slats. They're closer now and I'm sure they've heard us because they've stopped talking and turned their flashlights off. I hold the gun in both hands and wait. I've never fired a gun before and I don't know how many bullets are left in this one. I think we're going to die here.

"Ridley, please, don't do this." The voice echoes in the dark and comes from up above me. "We can work this out."

I don't answer. I know it's a trick. Nothing about this can be worked out now; we're all too far gone. There have been plenty of chances to close my eyes and go back to the sleep of my life as it was, but I haven't taken any of them. Do I wish now that I had? It's hard to answer that question, as the wraiths move closer.

"Six," he whispers.

"What?"

"You have six bullets left."

TWO

Until recently my life has been fairly uneventful. Which isn't to say I was just plodding along when the single occurrence I am about to share with you turned my world on its axis, but now that you mention it, that's not too far off. And yet I have come to believe that it was not one event precisely but an infinite number of small decisions that led me into the circumstances that have so changed me and those around me. People have died, lives have been altered, the truth has not so much set us free as it has ripped away a carefully constructed facade, leaving us naked to begin again.

My name is Ridley Jones, and when all of this started, I was a thirtyish writer living alone in an East Village apartment I'd rented since I was a student at NYU. It was a third-floor walk-up in a small building on the cor-

ner of First Avenue and Eleventh Street above
a pizzeria called Five Roses. With its black
gated front door, its dim hallways and sagging
floors, its ubiquitous aroma of garlic and olive
oil, it had a certain kind of charm. And beyond that it was miraculously cheap at eight
hundred dollars a month. If you know New
York, you know that rent like that is almost
impossible, even for an eight-hundred-square-
foot "junior" one-bedroom that looks out over
a back courtyard where dogs barked for most
of the day, even when the only view is of the
tenants in another building living their parallel lives with as much self-importance as I
lived my own. But it was a good place and I
was happy there. Even when I could afford
something better, I stayed, just for the comfort
of a familiar space and the proximity to the
best pizza in New York City.

You might be wondering about my first
name. My father, Dr. Benjamin Jones, a New
Jersey pediatrician living in a quaint and comfortable Victorian house with my mother, a
former-dancer-cum-housewife whom he has
loved and who has loved him since the day
they met at Rutgers University in 1960, has
always lamented his plain last name. He
thought of it as a name you give when you

don't want people to know who you are, like
Doe or Smith. Growing up, he was almost
embarrassed by the ordinariness of it. He was
raised in a flat gray suburb of Detroit,
Michigan, by ordinary people who expected
him to live an ordinary life. But he didn't
think he was only ordinary, and when it came
time to name his children he didn't want them
to feel that they were expected to be ordinary,
either. He gave me the name Ridley after
Ridley Scott, the filmmaker . . . he always was
a bit of a film buff. He thought this was a very
unusual first name for a girl, something special, and that it would encourage me to lead
an extraordinary life. And he felt that as a
writer living in New York City, I was doing
just that.

Even before the events that I am going to
share with you, I suppose in my own way I
have been extraordinary, but only in the fact
that I have loved and been loved by my parents, that I have been a happy person for most
of my adult life, that I like pretty much everything about myself (except for my thighs),
love my work, my friends, the place I live. I
have had good relationships with men, though
I couldn't say until recently that I've ever
known true love. When you live in New York

City, you know that these things are indeed extraordinary.

But there was so much I didn't know, so many layers hidden in a past that I wasn't even aware existed. I don't want to think that ignorance is to be held accountable for my relative bliss, but I suppose you'll think that's so. Certainly now something within me has changed. The world is a different place, and happiness, true peace, seems elusive. The woman I was seems hopelessly naive. I envy her.

When I look back on my life, I marvel at how it hasn't been the major decisions that have most impacted its course. It's been the tiny, seemingly inconsequential ones. Think about it. Think about the sudden events that have affected your life. With most of them, wasn't it just a matter of seconds one way or the other? Wasn't it the little decisions that caused you to cross this street or that, to move yourself into or out of harm's way? These are the things that get you in the end. Who you marry, what you choose as your profession, how you were raised—yes, that is the big picture. But, as they say, the devil's in the details.

Well, I'll get to it then.

It was a Monday morning, autumn going on winter in New York City. The Indian summer had passed and the first chill had settled in the air. It was my favorite time of year, when the oppressive heat and humidity trapped within the concrete walls of the city lifted, leaving behind a place that was new in its briskness.

When I woke that Monday, I could tell by the meager amount of light that struggled in through my windows that it was a gray day. I could see that the glass was freckled with raindrops. It was this small detail that affected my next decision. I reached from beneath the down of my comforter for the cordless phone that rested by my bedside, checked my caller ID for the number, and then dialed.

"Dr. Rifkin's office," came a voice as flat and hard as a city sidewalk.

"This is Ridley Jones," I said, faking a hoarseness in my throat. "I've come down with a bad cold. I can still come in, but I don't want to make the dentist sick." I added a pathetic cough for emphasis. Dr. Rifkin was my dentist, a tiny little gnome of a man who'd taken care of my teeth since I was a freshman at NYU. With a long white beard and a potbelly, checkered shirt under suspenders, orthopedic shoes, and an endearing waddle, he always disappointed me with a thick Long

Island accent. He should have been Scottish. He should have called me "lass."

"Let's reschedule," she said officiously, as if she didn't buy it but couldn't care less.

With that I was free. Freedom, I'd have to say, is probably the most important thing to me, more important than youth, beauty, fame, money. I wouldn't say more important than love. But some people who know me well have claimed that it's at least a toss-up deep inside me. One of those people was Zachary.

"Breakfast at Bubby's?" I said when he answered. There was a pause where I heard him turn over in bed. A few months ago, I might have been beside him.

"Don't you have a job?" he asked.

"I'm between assignments at the moment," I said with mock indignation. It was true; I **was** between freelance assignments. But it wasn't an issue for a number of reasons.

"What time?" he said, and in his voice I heard the sad mingling of hope and regret that I often heard when we spoke.

"Give me an hour?"

"Okay, see you then."

Zachary was the man I should have married, the one I was supposed to marry. Our lives have been intertwined since we were children. My parents loved him, maybe more than they did my own brother. My friends loved him, his sandy blond hair and bright eyes, his fit, athletic body, his successful private pediatric practice, the way he treated me. Even **I** really liked him. But when it came down to decision time, I balked. Why? Fear of commitment? A lot of people believe that about me. But I don't think so. All I can say is, forever and Zachary just didn't seem compatible. There was nothing that I could point my finger at precisely. We had a great friendship, good sex, a shared passion for the dinosaur room at the Museum of Natural History and Häagen-Dazs French Vanilla ice cream, among other things. But love is more than the sum of its parts, isn't it? In the end, I cared about him so much that I just thought he deserved someone who loved him more than I did. If that doesn't make a lot of sense to you, you're not alone. My parents and Zack's mother, Esme (whom I sometimes felt closer to than my own), were still floored by my decision. Since we were children they'd harbored a (not so) secret fantasy that Zack and I would be together. So when we started dating, they were nothing short of jubilant. And when we split, I think they had a harder time with it than Zack and I did.

That morning, Zack and I were trying to be friends. I'd ended our relationship a little over six months earlier and we were struggling past his disappointment and injured feelings (and pride, I thought) toward what I hoped would be an enduring friendship. It was awkward but hopeful.

I rolled from my bed and pushed it back against the wall. Remember how I said the building sags? Well, there's literally a dip in the floor of my bedroom. Since my bed is on casters, I occasionally wake up, particularly after a restless night, to find that it has rolled into the middle of the room. It's a small inconvenience. Some might even call it an endearing quirk of East Village living.

I ran the water in the shower and closed the door to steam up my narrow black-and-white-tiled bathroom. Listening to the sound of the rain, I padded into the kitchen and started a pot of coffee. I zoned out, still not quite awake, as the espresso maker hissed, sending the smell of Café Bustelo into the air. I could hear the street noise from First Avenue in the distance and smell the pastries baking in

Veniero's, the bakery behind my building whose venting system released its aromas into the courtyard. I looked across the courtyard: The cute guitar player still had his shades drawn; the gay couple were dressed for work and sitting at their kitchen table with large black cups of coffee, the blond reading **The Village Voice** and his dark-haired lover **The Wall Street Journal;** the young Asian girl was doing her morning yoga stretches while her roommate seemed to be reading aloud from a script in the next room. Because of the cool temperature, all the windows were closed and all of these lives played out before me like muted television screens. They were all accessories to my morning, just as I would be to them if they happened to look out their windows and see me waiting for my coffee to espress.

Like I said, I was between assignments. I had just finished a profile on Rudy Giuliani for **New York** magazine for which I had been paid quite nicely. I had a couple of other irons in the fire, articles I'd pitched to editors who knew me at **Vanity Fair, The New Yorker,** and **The New York Times.** As someone who had been working regularly for nearly seven years, I was confident that one of those ideas would turn into an assignment, though later, I hoped, rather than sooner. I was comfortable that way. At first, the freelance writing gig had been a bit of a struggle. If my parents hadn't subsidized my meager income when I graduated from college, I probably would have had to move back home with them. But as I have a modicum of talent, am a professional who meets deadlines, and am a writer without much of an ego who takes editing well, I made a reputation and some good contacts and the rest is just a lot of hard work.

Even with that, I might not be **as** comfortable if my uncle Max hadn't died nearly two years ago. Max was an uncle who wasn't actually an uncle, but really my father's best friend from Detroit, where they had been boys together. Both sons of autoworkers, my father and Max lived in the same suburb for eighteen years. While my father came from a solid home, my grandparents hardworking blue-collar people, Max's father was an alcoholic and a physically abusive man. One night when Max was sixteen, his father's violence turned deadly. Max's father beat his mother into a coma from which she never awoke. Rather than let him become a ward of the state, my grandparents took Max in and somehow managed to help both him and my father through college.

My father went on to medical school and later became the pediatrician that he is to this day. Max went into real estate and became one of the biggest developers on the East Coast. He never stopped trying to pay back my father and my grandparents. Because my grandparents flat out refused a cash payback, he lavished them and us with Caribbean cruises and outrageous birthday gifts, from bicycles to new cars. Naturally, we adored him. He never married and, without children, treated my brother, Ace, and me like we were his own.

Everyone always thought of him as a happy man, rarely seen without a smile on his face, always ready with a belly laugh. But even as a child, I remember sensing a deep sadness in him. I remember looking into his blue eyes and seeing grief edging his lashes, pulling down at the corner of his mouth. I remember how he'd glaze over, lost in thought, when he thought no one was looking. And I remember the way he always looked at my mother, Grace, as if she were a glittering prize that had been awarded to someone else.

Uncle Max was an alcoholic, but because he was a happy drunk, no one seemed to mind.

The Christmas Eve before last, after leaving my parents' house, where we'd all spent the evening together, he never returned to his home. He'd apparently stopped off at a bar after leaving us, then several hours later got into his black Mercedes sedan and proceeded to drive off a bridge and into the frigid water below. By accident or design, we'll never know, though a lack of skid marks indicated that there was no last-second slamming of the brakes. It was icy that night. That might have been it, the rubber of the tires unable to find purchase on the slick road. Or perhaps he passed out at the wheel, never saw it coming. We prefer to think of it as an accident, since the alternative would haunt us all.

As a family, we were bereft, but my father most of all; he'd lost the person with whom he'd shared most of his life. It still didn't feel quite right to celebrate Christmas Eve, a night we'd always shared with Max and the night we lost him.

In his will, he'd left most of his money to my parents, and to the Maxwell Allen Smiley Foundation. He'd created this foundation long before I was born, and it existed to fund myriad charities that offered assistance and shelter to battered women and abused children. But he also left a large sum of money to me and my brother, Ace. With the help of an accountant, my share of the money had been solidly invested. As a result, I had the freedom I so cherished. My brother, on the other hand, injected that money into his veins. Or so I assumed. But that's something else.

I wasn't thinking about any of this that morning. I was just looking forward to a day that I owned, where I could do anything I wanted. I showered, blew-dry my hair, pulled on my four-year-old Levi's, as faded and soft as memory, a bright red Tommy Hilfiger sweatshirt, Nikes, and a Yankees cap, and headed out the door. If I had known, I would have paused at the door to say goodbye to a perfectly lovely existence, an enviably simple, comfortable, happy life. Not perfect, of course. But pretty close, comparatively speaking.

In the hallway I tried to be as quiet as possible. I strongly suspected Victoria, my elderly neighbor, of waiting by her door to hear when I entered and left my apartment. The knowledge of this caused me to come and go quietly. Not that I disliked her. It was only that because of her loneliness and my compassion for her, an encounter could represent a ten- to twenty-minute delay. But I wasn't quiet enough that morning. As I locked my door, I heard hers open.

"Excuse me," she whispered. "Is anyone there?"

"Hi, Victoria. Good morning," I said, heading toward the stairs.

Victoria was as thin and pale as a slip of paper. Her inevitable flowered housedress hung off her as if it were still on the hanger. At some point, her hair had been replaced by a slate gray wig that looked as if she'd been at it with a pair of scissors. The skin on her face was deeply lined and sagged like melted wax. She claimed proudly, at least once every time I saw her, that she still had her own teeth. Unfortunately, she only had five or six of them. She whispered rather than spoke, as though she was afraid others were waiting at their doors the way she did. I always liked Victoria, though we generally had the same conversation every day and she never from day to day remembered who I was. She'd tell me of her three brothers, all police officers now dead. She'd tell me how she never meant to stay in the apartment that she once shared with her mother, also now dead, but she somehow just never got around to moving.

"Oh, if my brothers were still alive . . ." she said this particular morning, her voice trailing off. "They were police officers, you know."

"They must have been very brave," I answered, looking longingly at the staircase but walking toward her instead. Of all the responses I'd given her over the years, she seemed to like that one the most.

"Oh, yes," she said with a widening smile. "Very."

I could just see a sliver of her through the door she had opened only a few inches, her housedress with tiny purple flowers, her stockinged leg, her gray orthopedic shoe.

Victoria lived in a time capsule of antique furniture and drawn shades. There was not an item in her apartment that wasn't older than I was by at least fifty years, everything worn with time and wear, most of it covered in dust, all of it so heavy, so rooted that it seemed never to have been moved. Heavy oak armoires and bureaus, brocade couches and wing chairs, gilded mirrors, a baby grand topped with a clutter of yellowed photographs. I went in only when I'd gone grocery shopping for her or to change her lightbulbs. I couldn't leave there without carrying out

some of her sadness and loneliness with me
like a cloak. There was a smell that I've come
to think of as life rot. Where a life has spoiled,
gone bad through lack of use.

I used to wonder what choices she'd made
in her life to wind up with no one at the end.
It's something I think about now more than
ever, like I mentioned: choices. The little ones,
the big ones. Maybe once, like me, she had a
perfectly wonderful man in love enough with
her to propose marriage; maybe she, like me,
had turned him down for reasons unclear even
to her. Maybe that was the first choice that led
her to this life.

She had a niece who came in occasionally
from Long Island (feathered hair, three-
quarter-length red wool coat, sensible shoes),
an in-home caregiver who came three times a
week (different people all the time, carrying
themselves with as much energy and enthusiasm as pallbearers), and a couple times I'd seen
people from Meals on Wheels. I lived in that
building for more than ten years, and I'd never
seen her leave the apartment. To me, it seemed
as though she **couldn't** leave. That if she
stepped out of her apartment and onto the tile
floor of the hallway, she'd crumple into a pile
of dust.

"Well, if they were still alive, they certainly wouldn't stand for all the noise coming from upstairs," she warbled, her voice sounding like a top that was about to lose its spin.

I'd heard him, too, the new guy moving his things up the stairs the night before. I hadn't been curious enough to poke my head out.

"He's just moving in, Victoria. Don't worry. I'm sure he'll quiet down soon."

"Did you know I still have all my own teeth?"

"That's wonderful," I said with a smile.

"You seem like such a nice girl," she answered. "What's your name?"

"Ridley. I live right next door if you need anything."

"That's an odd name for a pretty girl," she said, baring her gums. I waved and went on my way.

Gray stone stairs and walls, a red banister, and black-and-white tile floors led me downstairs. On the second floor, the fluorescent light overhead flickered and went black, then came back to life. All the building lighting did this; it was a major electrical problem that my landlord, Zelda, appeared to have no intention of fixing.

"What? You think I got money to have the

goddamn building rewired? Want me to raise your rent?" she said when I complained. That pretty much put an end to that; I just made sure nothing in the apartment blocked my way to the fire escape.

On the ground floor, in the narrow hallway that leads to the gated vestibule, there was a note on my mailbox, which I hadn't visited since Friday out of sheer laziness. **Too many magazines!** chastised the red angry scrawl from my mailman. I could barely open the box because it was stuffed full of envelopes, bills, junk mail, catalogs, copies of **Time, Newsweek, New York** magazine, and **Rolling Stone.** With effort I pulled everything out and ran back up the three flights to my apartment, unlocked the door, and threw everything inside, then locked the door and left again.

You're saying to yourself, Do I need to know all of this, all the minutiae of her leaving the building? But these two encounters, the tiny choices I made heading out to the street, changed everything. If I was a different kind of person, I might not have paused to talk to Victoria. Or perhaps I would have paused longer. I could have walked right by my mailbox, not seen or ignored the note from my mailman. It's all these choices that we could have made, the things we might have done. We see them with perfect clarity only long after the moment has passed. Just thirty seconds either way, and I wouldn't have this story to tell you. I wouldn't be the same person telling it.

More small decisions on the street. I was running late, so instead of making a right and walking to TriBeCa (admittedly a long walk, but definitely doable if you have enough time), I walked to the curb to hail a cab. It was there that I saw them. A young mother with auburn hair pulled into a tight, high ponytail, one baby in a stroller, the other, a toddler, held by the hand, waiting at the light. There was nothing unusual about them really, I mean nothing that most people would notice. It was just the contrast to Victoria that struck me, the beauty and energy of these young lives compared to the sad and lonely twilight of the other I had just encountered.

I watched her. She was a small woman, but there was that strength about her that young mothers seem to possess. It was the ability to push and carry, hold tiny hands and monitor a million needs and movements, the Zen calm of producing a Ziploc bag of Cheerios from the front pocket of a diaper bag just as a little face starts to crumble, the way of molding an expression to communicate compassion and understanding to a toddler who could barely talk. It was musical, a symphony, and I found myself rapt for a moment. Then I turned my attention to the sea of cabs approaching . . . eight-thirty on a rainy Monday morning. Good luck. Not one light signaling availability, and a few anxious commuters looking for the same cab standing on corners all around. I resigned myself to being late, decided to grab a coffee. But as my eyes returned for a moment to the small family across the street, I felt a jangle of alarm. The mother was staring into the stroller, and the toddler, forgotten for maybe a second, had wandered into the street. There had been a brief lull in the flow of traffic, but the little boy, in his faded denim pants, red puffy overcoat, and little black stocking cap, was now directly in the path of an approaching white van. A glance to the van revealed a driver talking heatedly into his cell phone, seemingly oblivious to the road in front of him.

Everyone always says, "It's all a blur." But I remember every second. I was a shot fired from a gun, unthinking and with only one path available to me. I ran into the street. I remember the young mother glancing up from the stroller as people started to yell. I saw her face shift from confused to terrified. I saw the people on the street turning to stare; saw the little boy oblivious, toddling along toward me. I felt the hard concrete beneath my feet, heard the blood rushing in my ears. I was completely focused on the kid, who looked at me suddenly with a confused smile as I bent, arms outstretched, reaching for him as I ran. Everything slowed down but me; time warped and yawned but I was a rocket. I felt the warmth of his body, the softness of his coat as I scooped him up in one arm. I saw the grille of the van, felt the metal of the fender nick my foot as I dove both of us out of its path. I watched the van continue up First Avenue, never slowing, as if the whole drama that had played out before it had gone completely unnoticed by the driver. My body was tense, my teeth gritted with determination and fear, but I relaxed when I heard the little boy cry, saw him looking at me with terror. His mother ran over and grabbed him from me, sobbing into his little jacket. His tears turned from whimpers into a howl as if something primal told him that he'd just averted a great darkness. At least for now. People surrounded me, looked on with concern. Was I all right? Even then the answer still would have been yes.

So you're thinking I did a good deed. Everything turned out all right. Not that big a deal. And I agree. Anyone with half-decent reaction time and a heart would have done what I did. But it's those little things I was talking about. Standing behind me on that corner of First Avenue and Eleventh Street was a photographer for the **New York Post.** On his way back from shooting some high-profile thug's "walk of shame" from the Ninth Precinct, he'd come over to Five Roses to see if they were open, which naturally at 8:30 A.M. they weren't. He'd popped into the Black Forest Pastry Shop on the corner for a coffee and bear claw. These items were now lying on the ground at his feet where he'd dropped them in his haste to get to his camera. He got the whole thing on film.

THREE

It must have been a slow news week. And, okay, that action shot the **Post** photographer captured **was** pretty sensational, if I do say so myself. The combination of those two things, and I got my fifteen minutes. What can I say? I lapped it up. I'm not a shy person and I **do** like to talk, so I did all the interviews: **Good Day New York, The Today Show,** the **Post,** the **Daily News.** My phone was ringing off the hook and it was pretty fun. My parents even got some reflected glory in the New Jersey **Record.** They're not shy, either.

By Friday, my image had been on every local television show and in every newspaper in the tristate area. There was even some national pickup because of a sound bite on CNN. People were stopping me on the street to hug me or shake my hand. New York City is a quirky place in general, but when you're the

"New Yorker of the Moment," it's absolutely surreal. A city that can seem bitterly lonely and aloof even with its throngs of people suddenly seemed to turn its face from the sidewalk and smile. I think when someone does a good deed in New York City, it makes the rest of us feel as though we're not alone, that maybe we **are** looking out for one another in spite of evidence to the contrary.

"I can't believe you, Rid," said Zack over drinks at the NoHo Star. The echoes of a hundred conversations rose up and bounced off the high ceilings of the restaurant, and the aromas of Asian-infused cuisine mingled with the scent of the warm breadbasket on our table. I looked at my good friend, because he had always been that, and was grateful for him.

"What? You didn't think I had it in me?" I asked with a smile.

He shook his head. There was that look again, that mingling of longing and regret and something else I just couldn't put my finger on. I averted my eyes; it made me feel like such a heel.

"Believe me, I know you have it in you. You've been like that since we were kids— defender of the weak, cheerleader for the un-

derdog." Was there the slightest shade of resentment in his voice?

"Someone has to do it," I said, lifting my
Cosmo and taking a sip.

"But why you?" he asked. "That woman
should have had a better eye on her kid. You
both could have been killed."

I gave a shrug. I didn't see the point of
judging and analyzing a single moment in
someone's life. I was just glad to have been
there to mitigate the consequences. He went
on, as he was prone to do.

"And all those pictures of you . . . forget it.
You're going to have psychos crawling out of
the woodwork. You should have just stayed
out of it." He shook his head disapprovingly,
but I could see the caring and the respect that
was behind it. He was a good guy, worried
about my well-being above all things.

"Oh, yeah," I said with a laugh. "And let a
little kid get mowed down by a van."

"Better him than you," he said with eyebrows raised.

"You're so full of it," I said with a smile.
He would have been the first one diving
in front of the van to save that kid—Justin
Wheeler, by the way. Three years old and
counting. Did I mention that Zack was a pe-

diatrician like my father? (And yes, they worked together at some of the clinics where they donated their time. See how complicated this whole breakup was?) He dedicated his whole life to the care of children, and I'd never met anyone, other than my father, who was so passionate about his work.

"Seriously," he said, softening, returning my smile. "Watch out for yourself until all this dies down."

I touched my glass to his.

"To the hero. To **my** hero," he said.

Things did die down, of course, and my life returned to its natural rhythm. By the following Monday, a week to the day since I'd plucked Justin from the path of the van, my phone had stopped ringing for interviews, I noted. I got a call from the features editor at **Vanity Fair** regarding the article I wanted to write on Uma Thurman. We made an appointment to get together on Tuesday afternoon. I went to bed that night still flushed with my fifteen minutes but happy that everything was settling back to normal.

The following day, I got dressed like a grown-up and took a cab uptown to the **Vanity Fair** offices. I had a brief meeting with the features editor, a busy, somewhat tightly wound, impossibly chic older woman who I'd worked successfully with before. Provided that Ms. Thurman agreed to the article, we settled on a fee and a deadline and we were good to go. I took the train back downtown and dawdled some at St. Mark's Bookshop and toyed with the idea of starting a novel. I strolled toward home, picked up some sandalwood incense from a street vendor, and as I passed it on my way back to my apartment, lamented the Gap on the corner of St. Mark's (the mecca of my gothic youth) and Second Avenue. I'm sorry; the Gap has no place on the same street as Trash and Vaudeville.

By the time I got back to my apartment, the afternoon was darkening and I was freezing in my black wool gabardine Tahari suit, my feet screaming in protest of my gorgeous but painful Dolce & Gabbana leather pumps. But I figured I deserved to be uncomfortable in these shamefully expensive (but **so** fabulous) items. It's only right to suffer for fashion. I wrestled another unwieldy pile of mail from my box, took off my shoes, and jogged up the stairs to my apartment.

My apartment was small—okay, minuscule—with a bare minimum of storage space. Actually, it had only one closet at the end of a hallway that ran parallel to my bedroom but went nowhere. But I liked that it kept a limit on the amount of clutter I allowed to accumulate in my life. I had a sense that if I needed to pack up and move in a day, I could, and that thought gave me a significant amount of comfort. Which was strange because I had been there for more than ten years and had no desire to leave. There was something about that apartment that made me feel rooted and free at the same time. It was exactly the way I wanted it, with comfortable, plush furniture, and area rugs to soften the hardwood floors. The walls were freshly painted a subtle cream. It was cozy, familiar . . . **my** space. And yet at the same time, I had no attachment to anything there.

That night I changed into my most comfortable pair of black yoga pants and sweatshirt, pulled my hair up, and settled onto the chenille sofa with my stack of mail to sift through. I made piles: one for magazines, one for garbage, one for bills. And I began to sort.

It was relaxing in its mindlessness, the simple act of sifting through, putting items into their place. Then I came across an eight-by-ten envelope with my name and address handwritten in a black scrawl, no return address. There was something about it, even though it was an utterly innocuous manila envelope. In retrospect, it seemed to radiate a warning, to throb with a kind of malice, which I naturally ignored. I sliced the top open cleanly with a letter opener and removed three pieces of paper. Even now I still find it amazing how these simple items were able to challenge everything I ever thought I knew about my life.

In the envelope there was a clipping of the **Post** article that featured a picture of me. There was also an old, yellowed Polaroid photograph. In it, a young woman in a flowered dress held a little girl on her hip. The woman looked stiff, her expression drawn. The child looked at her with eyes bright with laughter, mouth smiling. A man stood behind them, tall, broad shouldered, incredibly handsome with chiseled features and sharp, intelligent eyes. He had a possessive hand on the woman's shoulder. And there was something about his expression that wasn't quite benevolent, though I couldn't put my finger on it. I couldn't explain the constricting in my throat, the adrenaline suddenly pumping through me, causing my hands to shake. The woman in the photograph bore such a striking resemblance to me that I could have been looking at my own portrait. The child in her arms resembled pictures I'd seen of myself, though at that moment I realized I'd never seen images of myself that young.

And there was a note including a phone number and a question.

It read simply: **Are you my daughter?**

FOUR

It takes only a moment to bring myself back into my childhood completely. I can close my eyes and be overcome with the sense memories of my youth. The aromas from my mother's kitchen, the scent of Old Spice and rainwater on my father when he returned from work in the evenings, my cold fingers because my father's body temperature always ran hot and the house, as a consequence, always cold. I can hear my parents laughing or singing, sometimes arguing, and later outright yelling when things really started to go wrong with my brother, Ace. I can remember my green shag carpet and Laura Ashley wallpaper, tiny pink roses with mint-green stems on a white background. And in all the memories I had of those years, that night with the picture in my hand there was one that stood out vivid and terrifying among all the innocuous and happy ones.

I was fifteen and late coming home from the school paper (I was a little bit of a brain, a dork, in high school). Even though I wasn't supposed to ride with boys in their cars, I had taken a ride from a senior named Frank Alvarez (broad shoulders, long dark hair, kind of a burnout but sexy). When we pulled into my driveway, he'd tried to kiss me. I remember that he had the heat cranking in his car, that Van Halen was playing on the radio, that he exuded a kind of desperate sexual energy and wore way too much cologne. Polo, I think. It wasn't a scary situation, and although I wasn't "into him," as we too-cool adolescents used to say, I was flattered and could barely wait to get out of the car and call my friends.

When I entered the house, my parents were sitting at the kitchen table looking grim. My father held a cup of coffee in his hands and my mother looked as if she'd been crying. It was a bit too early for my father to be home and dinner should have been cooking but the kitchen was cold.

"Oh, Ridley," my mother said, as if she'd forgotten I was expected home. "What time is it?" My mother was a little bird of a woman, really tiny with small, refined features and lustrous auburn hair. She moved with the grace of a dancer and carried those faded aspirations in her impeccably held posture and jutted chin. She looked ten years younger than the other mothers I knew, though she was actually older than most of them.

"Go on upstairs for a while, will you, lullaby?" said my father, getting up. "We'll get you some dinner in just a bit." He was moving into what we would later call his Ernest Hemingway stage, without the drinking. He had a full graying beard and a slight (getting less slight) belly. He stood just over six feet tall and had powerful arms and big hands. He had a way of hugging me that made every childish worry disappear. But he didn't hug me then, just put a hand on my shoulder and ushered me toward the stairs.

When I'd entered and saw them sitting there, I figured I was in some kind of trouble for being in the car with Frank Alvarez, but I realized quickly that they were too upset for a small transgression like the one I'd committed.

"What's going on?" I asked.

Before my father could answer, Ace was thundering down the stairs, a large backpack over his shoulder.

My brother and I were raised in the same house by the same parents and still managed to have completely different childhoods. He is older than I am by three years. He was willful where I was yielding; rebellious where I was obedient; sad, angry where I was happy. For the longest time he was to me the very embodiment of coolness. He was movie-star handsome with jet-black hair and ice-blue eyes, defined muscles and chiseled jaw. All my friends were in love with him, and if you'd told me he got up five minutes before me and put the sun in the sky, I'd have believed you.

"Where are you going?" I asked him, because more than just the backpack, he had a nearly palpable aura of leaving and not coming back. He'd threatened this a million times, and every time he and my parents fought, I felt a nausea that he'd make good on it. Fear and sadness opened in my belly as he pushed passed me.

"The fuck out of here," he said, looking at my father.

"Ridley," my mother said. "Go upstairs." I heard a kind of desperation in her tone. I headed up slowly, lingering with my hand on the banister and looking at these three people whom I loved, so sad and angry at one another that they were barely recognizable. They all looked gray, faces stiff as stones.

I couldn't remember a peaceful moment between Ace and my father. When they were in a room together, it was only a matter of time before an argument erupted, and it had been getting worse in the months before Ace left.

"You're not going anywhere, son," said my father. "We're getting you help."

"I don't want your help. It's too late. And you're **not** my father, so don't call me son."

"Don't talk like that, Ace," said my mother, but her voice was small and her eyes filled with tears.

"Ridley," my father roared. "Get upstairs."

I ran, my heart beating in my chest like a drum. I lay on my four-poster bed in the dark and listened to the echoes of their yelling. Far on the other end of the house, I couldn't hear their words and I didn't want to. When Ace left, he slammed the front door so hard that I felt its vibration in my room. Silence followed and then was broken by the sound of my mother sobbing. Eventually I heard my father's footsteps on the stairs. Ace never crossed that threshold again, and that's the night I realized that every ending is not a happy one.

Somewhere along the line I just blocked

out what Ace had said. Or made myself believe that it was just his anger, his addiction, or maybe both that had led him to say, "You are not my father." When I asked my dad about it later, he'd said, "Ace just meant that he **wished** I wasn't his father. But I am and there's no changing that, no matter what passes between us."

"Well, I'm glad you're **my** father, Daddy," I said, as much to make myself feel better as to comfort him.

As I sat in my apartment with those papers in my hand, I heard Ace's words again, and this time I could not silence them. They were like a key that unlocked a box containing myriad other questions that had hovered in the periphery of my consciousness over the years, but to which I had never actually entertained answers. They were little things that might have been easily explained . . . unless they **couldn't** be. Things like: Why were there no pictures of my mother pregnant? Why were there no photographs of me before the age of two? Why did I resemble no one in my family even a little? These little questions now tapped on my consciousness like moths at a light.

I started to feel a little panicky, a little dramatic. Then I remembered my conversation with Zack. **And all those pictures of you . . . forget it. You're going to have psychos crawling out of the woodwork.**

He was right, of course. This **was** New York City; the crazies don't need much of an excuse to get busy. I held the Polaroid in my hand; maybe the woman didn't look that much like me, after all.

I did what I always do in times of crisis, small or large. I picked up the cordless phone to call my father. The receiver was in my hand before I was even conscious of reaching for it, the keypad burning, waiting for me to punch in the numbers. But my finger hovered there above the glowing numbers as I hesitated, hearing blood rushing in my ears. I stared at the phone, not quite able to will my fingers to move. It was silly, wasn't it? To call over such nonsense. In the distance, over the buzzing of the dial tone, I heard an insistent knocking.

The sound brought me out of my head and it took a second to realize that there was someone at my apartment door. I came back to the present and walked across the room, looked through the peephole. The man standing in the hallway was a stranger but I opened the door a crack. I know what you're thinking. What New Yorker is going to open her door to a strange man, particularly in a moment like this, after receiving a letter like that?

New Yorkers are really no more savvy than anyone else. We're just more paranoid. And I was too distracted to think about protecting my life. Besides, the guy I saw through the peephole interested me. As in: He was **hot.** I opened the door and looked at him. He was frowning, hands on his hips.

You feel the chemistry, you know. It's that little jolt that lets you know the sex would be good, very, very good. You feel it in your lungs and between your legs. It doesn't really have anything to do with looks, but for the record: dark brown hair, almost black, cropped close to his head, so short it was really little more than stubble, deep brown eyes, candy lips I was already imagining in the little dip between my collarbone and my throat. He felt it, too, I could tell. He looked less angry for a moment.

"Look," he said, recovering nicely, "if you have a problem with the noise, how about just knocking on the door and letting me know, instead of running to the landlord."

Everything on him seemed to fit together perfectly into one tight, lean line. But there was meat to him, not bulk, a kind of supple strength. I could see the detail of a tattoo snaking out from his right shirtsleeve.

"You have the wrong door," I said, trying not to smile in anticipation of his embarrassment. "I didn't call the landlord."

He let the information hang between us for a second and then said the only thing that was appropriate. "Oh." Awkward silence and a shifting of weight from one leg to the other. "Sorry."

"No problem," I answered, and shut the door.

He **was** hot. But I was distracted by the mail I'd received. Logical Ridley could see clearly that this could be the bizarre antic of a twisted mind. But there was another Ridley, a little scared, a little anxious, thinking, There are too many questions. Check it out.

I watched him walk away through the peephole. I leaned against the wall across from the door and zoned for a minute. Everything around me seemed weightless and I felt a lightness in my head and my stomach. I couldn't have told you why, maybe it was a mild kind of shock. I'm not sure how long I stood there.

Eventually I returned to the couch and picked up the photos and note again. The interruption had kept me from calling my dad, and now it didn't seem as urgent as it had a minute earlier. I put the pictures and note back on the table and lay on the plush couch that was too big for the room but that I loved because it was as comfortable as an embrace. A surprising hot, wet sadness overcame me. I cried hard but tried not to sob. The walls and doors were thin and I didn't want anyone to hear, especially the yummy tattoo man from upstairs.

FIVE

It's a little-known fact, but parents are like superheroes. With just a few magic words they can make you feel ten feet tall and bulletproof, they can slay the dragons of doubt and worry, they can make problems disappear. But of course, they can only do this as long as you're a child. When you've become an adult, become the master of your own universe, they're not as powerful as they once were. Maybe that's why so many of us take our time growing up.

After a restless night and a seriously unproductive Wednesday where my major accomplishments included doing a load of laundry at the Laundromat downstairs and making a tuna fish sandwich, I left my apartment and headed to the PATH station at Christopher Street. Every Wednesday since I'd come to college in the city, I've taken the train home for dinner with my parents. I'd often go home on the weekends, too, but Wednesday had just become this **thing** that we had. Esme and Zack often joined us, but not since the breakup. And I felt bad about that. But a part of me was guiltily glad, too. I liked having my parents to myself.

"Ridley, how are you doing, hon?" Esme had asked earlier that day over the phone. We still talked relatively often, which was nice. She'd been the nurse in my father's various offices for longer than I'd been alive. She was more like an adored aunt and a close friend than someone who worked for my dad and the mother of my boyfriend. In fact, I'd been almost more concerned about losing my relationship with her than anything else when I ended it with Zack.

"Zack said you seemed a little stressed," she said in a near whisper, as though she were talking about some kind of embarrassing feminine problem. "He's worried about you."

I knew this was well meaning. But I didn't think I had seemed stressed during my dinner with Zack. Isn't it weird when someone tells you something about yourself that's not true? They're utterly certain of their assumption, and the more you try to convince them other-wise, the more they seem to dig their heels in.

"No, Ez," I said, trying to sound light. "I'm fine."

"Really," she said, as if she were talking to a mental patient. "Good. I'm glad he was wrong." She didn't believe me and was letting me off the hook. Then I started thinking, Maybe I **am** really stressed, and the only one who can't see it is me.

This is something I really hate about my-self. I am influenced by people's erroneous as-sumptions about me. Maybe you know what I mean. During my conversation with Esme, I started to feel really stressed out. Another thing I hated was the idea that people were talking about me, deciding how stressed out I was, feeling sorry for me and then telling me about it. It seems very controlling and manipulative. As if they want me to seem weak and frayed so that they can feel strong and together, superior to poor Ridley, who's under so much **stress.**

We chitchatted for a while about my latest article, her worsening rheumatoid arthritis, gift ideas for my mother's approaching birth-day. Maybe it was just my guilt, but I still felt, six months after the fact, that we were tiptoeing around the fact that I had broken her son's heart and laid waste to everyone's dreams of a wedding and grandchildren.

In Hoboken, I got on another train and took the half-hour ride to the town where I grew up. It was about a fifteen-minute walk from the train station to my parents' house. Built in 1919, but gutted and made completely modern in the late eighties, it sat nestled among giant oak and elm trees, an absolute bastion of Americana. It was one of **those** towns. You know. So precious with its general store and original gas lamps, winding tree-lined streets, pretty houses nestled on perfectly manicured lawns, a virtual picture postcard, especially in the fall and at Christmastime. It was about four o'clock when I walked through the front door. I could smell meat loaf.

"Mom," I called, letting the screen door slam behind me.

"Oh, Ridley," said my mother, emerging from the kitchen with a smile. "How are you, dear?"

She embraced me lightly, then pushed me back the length of her arms and scrutinized me for any sign of trouble: circles under my eyes, a breakout on my chin, weight gain or loss, who knows.

"Is something wrong?" she asked, with a narrowing of the eyes.

That was generally one of the first questions my mother asked me when I called, or when I came home. As if I didn't see them all the time. I call my father nearly every day at his office, but to be fair, I talk to my mother more rarely.

"No," I said, hugging her. "Of course not." She nodded but gave me that look that reminded me that she knew me better than I knew myself and that lying was futile. Did everyone **want** something to be wrong with me?

She felt so small to me. Where she was bony and angular through the arms and shoulders, I was muscular and round. Where she was boyish through the hips and chest, I was full. Where the features of her face were small, delicate, fair, mine were softer, slightly rounder. I looked into her face and suddenly thought of the woman in the picture I'd received last night. My mother looked nothing like me; that stranger was my image.

"What **is** it, Ridley?" she asked, putting her head to the side and inspecting me with her ice-blue eyes.

"When's Dad coming home?" I answered, walking away from her into the kitchen and opening the oven door. A meat loaf sizzled happily in tomato sauce and the heat warmed my cheeks. I was glad for a reason to look away from my mother.

"Any minute," she said. When I didn't say anything else, she changed the subject. "So, have you leaped into traffic to save a toddler, rushed into any burning buildings . . . anything exciting like that?"

"Nope. Just that one kid."

"Good. You probably shouldn't make a habit out of it. Your luck might run out," she said, giving me an affectionate pat on the ass.

I sat at the kitchen table and she chatted on about her volunteer work at the local elementary school, Dad's practice and his work at the clinic for underprivileged kids where he donated his time. I didn't hear a word my mother was saying, not that I wasn't interested. I was just eager for the sound of my father's car in the driveway.

"Are you even listening to me?"

"Of course, Mom."

"What did I just say?"

"If it isn't my little heartbreaker," boomed my father as he came in through the back door. He'd taken to calling me that after the breakup.

I got up and went to him, eager to feel

his familiar embrace, the comfort of my father's arms.

"How are you, lullaby?" he said, hugging me hard.

"Good," I said into his shoulder.

"Good," he said with a smile and a pat on my cheek. "You **look** good," he said. I was glad **he** didn't think I looked like there was something wrong.

But I guess there was something wrong, even then. I'd brought the picture and the note with me to the house. I had toyed with the idea of trashing it, just putting it in the bin where it belonged and forgetting it altogether. But for whatever reason, I couldn't bring myself to do it. I left the apartment without the envelope but halfway down the stairs turned around and went back for it. I guess I wanted to show it to them so they could tell me how ridiculous it was and we could all have a good laugh. Ha-ha.

After dinner, we all sat full and quiet under the glow of the old Tiffany lamp that hung over the table.

"Something weird happened to me yesterday," I said, filling a conversational lull.

"I knew there was something," my mother said, satisfied with herself.

"Mom," I said with that tone that I think expresses perfectly how predictable and annoying I find her sometimes.

"What is it, Rid?" asked my father, his face open and concerned.

I slid the photograph and note over to them. I watched both their faces since I figured the tale would be told in the first millisecond after they processed the information in front of them. But their expressions told me nothing. My father and mother put their heads together and squinted at the photo. My father pulled glasses from his shirt pocket. I could hear the refrigerator humming and the blood rushing in my ears. The teapot came to a boil but my mother didn't notice and the clock above the sink ticked quietly.

"What's this?" my father said finally, a confused but benevolent smile on his face. "Some kind of joke?"

"I don't get it," said my mother with a quick shake of her head. "Who are these people?"

I looked at them. It was a perfect innocent reaction and I waited to feel relief, a little stupid for having even brought it to their attention. It was exactly what I had wanted. But instead I felt an inexplicable anger.

"I don't **know** who they are." My voice shook a little and both my parents turned their eyes on me. "This came in my mail yesterday."

"And . . . what?"

"And **look** at it," I said, tapping it with my finger. "That woman looks just like me."

My father made a show of looking more closely at the picture. "Well, she does bear a bit of a resemblance. But so what?" My mother, I noticed, had looked at the photograph once but didn't look at it a second time. Instead, she leaned back and looked at me. I couldn't read her eyes.

"This person believes I'm his daughter."

"How do you know it's a he?" my mother asked pointlessly.

"I just think it is," I said weakly. "The handwriting is masculine. I don't know." Sigh. "I just do."

At this point my father did something I hadn't expected. He laughed, a deep belly laugh. "Honey," he said finally. "That's ridiculous."

"Really, Ridley," said my mother. "This is not funny."

I looked at them, pulled my shoulders

back. "I'm not trying to be funny, Mom. I got this in the mail yesterday and . . . it resonated with me. I have questions."

"Well. What kind of questions?" asked my father, his laughter dying. "You can't possibly be entertaining for a second the idea that you're not our daughter. This person is having a joke at your expense, Ridley."

"You're smarter than this, aren't you?" asked my mother with another quick shake of her head. "I mean, your face has been plastered all over the television and the newspapers for over a week now. Some nutcase thought you resembled someone he knows or used to know. And he's either crazy, thinks you're his daughter . . . or he's trying to mess with you. This is so silly."

I paused, doubt creeping up and tapping me on the shoulder.

"How come there are no pictures of me before I'm two years old?" I asked, sounding more like a child than I would have liked.

"Oh, Christ," said my mother. "Now you're starting to sound like Ace."

I hated when my parents compared me with him, this child who had so injured them, so disappointed them. The one who chose the streets and the life of a junkie over their home and their love. The one who'd caused my parents so much pain over the years. I cringed but I didn't say anything. I kept on looking at her and she finally answered.

"I've **told** you that we used to keep the photographs in the rec-room closet in the basement. The basement flooded and the pictures were ruined. All your pictures from the hospital, taking you home, and much of your infancy."

She **had** told me that, but I had forgotten. I was starting to feel a bit unstable. But something compelled me to press on. "And I suppose all the pictures of your pregnancies were in those albums as well."

"No," she said slowly, drawing out the syllable as though she were talking to an infant. "I got very big during both pregnancies and was self-conscious in front of the camera. I know it seems silly but I was young."

My mother was a beautiful woman with creamy skin and almond-shaped eyes. She had this wide mouth that could curl into a megawatt smile bright enough to light the stars in the sky. But when she was angry, her beauty turned to granite. She had always been one of those mothers who didn't have to say a word to reprimand; just one of those looks froze you in your tracks. She had turned that gaze on me now and it took real courage, dredged from deep inside, for me to keep at it.

I leaned into them. "I don't look like anyone."

My mother looked away from me and made a grunt of disgust. She got up from the table and walked over toward the stove. My father glanced at my mother uneasily. He'd always kowtowed to her temper, and an old resentment about that rose in me but I kept silent. He looked back to me.

"That's just not true, Ridley," said my father. "You look a great deal like my mother. Everyone has always said that, don't you remember?"

Now that he mentioned it, I did. There **was** a resemblance around the eyes. I did share her dark hair and high cheekbones. For a second it dawned on me that perhaps I'd lost my mind. That I was suffering from some form of posttraumatic stress. You always hear about that on shows like **Dateline,** you know. People whom the world regarded as heroes for a few days and then forgot about; how they lose it, get depressed. Maybe that was happening to me. Maybe I was creating a drama because I craved the attention I had had for a short time.

"But what about Ace?" I persisted. "What he said that night."

"How can you ask me to explain the things Ace says?" my father said sadly, and I could see how the mention of Ace pained him. Suddenly the air around us was electric with his grief for a son who lived but chose to be dead to his parents. "I don't even know him anymore."

We were all silent for a moment, my mother standing at the stove with her arms crossed and head down, my father sitting across from me at the table, his eyes on me with a gaze that at once implored and accused, me leaning back in my chair and trying to figure out why I had brought this to them and why I was so passionately pressing them for answers, why I felt my heart thrumming and my throat dry in some kind of adrenaline response.

My father pushed the picture back toward me and I picked it up, looked at it closely. It had lost its power; there was just a couple with their child. Strangers.

"I'm sorry," I said, sticking the photograph back in my pocket. Shame burned at my cheeks and pushed tears into my eyes. "I don't know what I was thinking."

My father reached out to touch my arm. "You've been under some stress, Ridley, with everything that happened last week. Some- one preyed on that. I think you should call the police."

I rolled my eyes. "And tell them what? That some **mail** really freaked me out?"

He shrugged and looked at me with a compassion that I didn't feel I deserved. My mother walked back to the table with our tea mugs. She sat and kept her eyes on me. There was something there I hadn't seen before and then it was gone. I thought it was disdain for my lack of faith, my willingness to hurt them.

"I'm sorry, Mom."

"That's all right, dear. I understand how you could become confused. Especially with all the **stress.**" I heard in her tone that she didn't understand and it wasn't all right.

Later, on the train ride back to the city, I watched burbs roll by me as I sat with my feet up and my head pressed against the glass. I'd shared an awkward dessert of chocolate ice cream with my parents and then left after helping my mother clean the kitchen. My mother had turned cold on me and gave me only the briefest embrace as I left. She was like that. She demanded absolute loyalty; anything less and she would freeze me out until I had made penance.

A metacommunication had passed between us years ago and I had always accepted it on a cellular level. She could accept the loss of one child and blame it on him, blame it on his addiction. But the loss of two children, and she saw any digression on my part as a kind of loss, would cause her to look within herself. And this she was not willing to do. As a child, I feared her anger and disappointment. As an adult, I could accept them but I still didn't like it. I felt bad about the evening, unsure how I'd allowed myself to be so rattled by an anonymous note and a photograph of strangers.

As the upper-middle-class burbs morphed into the urban ruin of Newark, I thought about my brother. I hated him. Hated him like a child hates a fallen hero. I hated him for his unlimited potential and his failure to realize it. I hated him because I could see everything that was wonderful about him, how brilliant, how beautiful he was, and how he had turned his back on everything he could have been, cast it off like a designer suit for which he'd paid an obscene sum and never wore. And I loved him for all those things as well. Pitied him, worried after him, adored him, and despised him. I remembered how it was to be pinched by him, chased by him, teased by him, hugged by him, comforted by him. There was an open wound in my heart for my brother. When I thought of him, a tsunami of emotion always welled and crashed within me.

After all the heartache Ace had caused my parents, the drugs, the petty crimes, the arrests for DUI, and finally his departure from our home at the age of eighteen, I was an absolute angel by comparison. I did the usual stuff, lied, did some minor drinking, once I drove the car with just my learner's permit, got caught with cigarettes. But otherwise I got straight A's, edited and wrote for the school paper, had nice friends whom my parents thought were okay. No major dramas. I felt I owed it to them to be good. Maybe even deeper, I believed that if I caused them any more pain it would destroy them. So I kept myself safe, in line, and out of trouble.

We never talked about Ace after he left. And I mean **never.** I couldn't mention his name without my mother bursting into tears and running from the room. We all pretended he had never lived there. The silence allowed him to grow into this mythic figure in my mind.

This beautiful rebel who was too bright, too sensitive for the normal life we lived. I imagined him a musician or a poet, hanging out in cafés, stoic in the pain of the misunderstood genius. A secret part of me harbored resentment toward my parents for driving him away.

After that horrible night when he left, I didn't see him again until I was a freshman at NYU. I was living in the dorms on Third Avenue and Eleventh Street. I'm not sure how he found me, but when I left the building one morning heading to class, I saw him on the corner. His skin was pasty with raw red patches, and even from a few feet away I could smell the stench of his unwashed body. His face was gaunt. He'd shaved the long dark hair I'd always loved and his skull was a mess of black stubble and tiny scars. His blue eyes, my mother's eyes, were bright and hungry.

"Hey, kid," he said.

I must have just stood there gape-jawed for longer than it seemed because he cringed beneath my gaze and said, "Do I look that bad?"

"No . . ." I managed. I felt so awkward, torn between the urges to run away from this person who wasn't even supposed to exist and to embrace the brother, the hero that I had lost and grieved so desperately.

A stuttering "How are you?" was all I could manage.

"Um . . . **good,**" he said, running his hand self-consciously over his head. As he did this, I saw track marks on his wrist. I took a step back. Remember that Batman episode where everyone thinks he's turned into a criminal, given into the dark side after so many years as the Caped Crusader saving Gotham from the Penguin and the Riddler? That's how I felt about Ace that day. There was disbelief; there was horror. But most of all there was this deep, wrenching sadness that my childhood hero had been brought low by the forces of evil.

"Listen," he said. "Do you have any money? I've had the flu this week and haven't been able to work. I need to get some breakfast."

I gave him all the money I had in my wallet. I think it was twenty-five bucks. And that's pretty much the way it was from that point on with Ace and me. My parents never knew it, but since that day, I usually saw him about once a month. We generally met at Veselka on Second Avenue. He always had a knish and I usually ordered the potato pancakes. We'd sit in the crowded East Village institution and no one paid any attention to the junkie and the

hip (well, I **am**) student (later, urban professional) sitting across from each other. He
talked shit about getting clean. I gave him
money. I knew I shouldn't. What can I say? I
was the classic enabler. But I just loved him so
damn much, and that was the only way he
would let me show him. Besides, I couldn't
even imagine what he'd have done to get cash
if I hadn't given it to him. Actually, yes I
could, and that was another reason.

Sometimes he would disappear for months
and I wouldn't hear from him, not even once.
I rarely had a way to reach him. For a while he
was squatting somewhere up in Spanish
Harlem, or so he said; other times on the
Lower East Side. I never knew for sure. When
I didn't hear from him I would be sick, absolutely haunted with fear. I took out an ad in
the back of **The Village Voice** once, not even
knowing if he ever read it. It was an act of desperation, one that yielded no results. But
eventually he would run out of money or get
lonely and he'd call me again. I never asked
him where he'd been, what he'd done, why he
hadn't even tried to call. I didn't ask because I
was afraid to run him off again.

"When are you going to wise up?" Zachary had wanted to know. "He uses you. He doesn't love you. People like that don't even know what love is."

That's the thing about love that Zachary never seemed to understand. When you love someone, it doesn't really matter if they love you back or not. Having love in your heart for someone is its own reward. Or punishment, depending on the circumstances.

The train screeched into Hoboken and I got out with the crush of people heading into the city. I had to push my way onto the PATH train and it took an eternity to groan its way into Manhattan. I walked from Christopher Street home. The cold air and long walk made me feel better, made the conversation with my parents seem farther away, helped me forget that I still had the photograph in my pocket and doubt in my heart. By the time I reached the building, I was feeling almost normal again. I walked right past my mailbox and didn't even look at it. No mail tonight. I jogged up the stairs and stopped in front of my door. Sitting before me was a bottle of Merlot and two glasses. A note folded into one of the glasses read: **Allow me to apologize properly? Jake, 4E.**

SIX

I walked up the flight to Jake's floor. But at the top of the stairs I hesitated. The fluorescent ceiling light hummed and flickered, casting the hallway in an eerie glow. I looked at the wine bottle and glasses in my hands and thought, Who is this guy? What am I doing? Before I could answer myself, the door opened and he was standing there in a black T-shirt and faded Levi's button-flies. He reached out to take the wine and glasses from my hands and smiled. It was a tentative smile, shy.

"I wasn't sure you'd come."

I'll tell you something about myself. I can get my head turned by a good-looking guy as much as the next girl. But sexy doesn't impress me. Smart impresses me; strength of character impresses me. But most of all, I'm impressed by kindness. Kindness, I think, comes from learning hard lessons well, from falling and picking yourself up. It comes from surviving failure and loss. It implies an understanding of the human condition, forgives its many flaws and quirks. When I see that in someone, it fills me with admiration. I saw it in him. His eyes, a deep brown, almost black, heavily lidded with dark lashes, made me want to confess all my sins and secrets and do penance in his arms.

"You don't have to apologize," I said, nodding toward the note still in the wineglass. "I would have been annoyed, too."

He stepped to the side and held the door open for me and I walked in. He closed the door quietly behind me. I turned to look at him and I must have seemed skittish.

"You want me to leave it open?" he said, concern wrinkling his brow.

"No," I said with a small laugh.

"I'll just pour the wine," he said, disappearing into the kitchen.

Where my apartment looked out on the back of the building, his looked out onto First Avenue. The street noise was not much diminished by the thin windows, and a cold draft made the sills freezing to the touch. He had the heat on high but the room was still uncomfortably cool. He had the same bleached

wood floors as I did but that's where the simi-
larities ended. In my place, I strove for absolute luxury and comfort. Four-hundred-count
cotton sheets, down pillows and comforters,
plush area rugs, warm blankets. I liked bright
colors, fresh flowers, scented candles. Not in
a girlie way, but in a way that indulged the
senses.

Jake's place looked like a prison cell, albeit in
an urban-industrial cool way. A sheet-metal
sculpture, with jagged geometric shapes over-
lapping one another, dominated one wall. A
glass-and-brushed-chrome table was surrounded by six elaborate wrought-iron chairs.
A futon and a few scattered wooden Eames
chairs provided an unwelcoming sitting area.
In the corner a laptop glowed on a spare black
table. There were no photographs, not one object of any personal nature, not even a scrap
of paper out of place. I glanced over at the
door that I imagined led to his bedroom
and wondered if a peek inside would reveal a
bed of nails beneath the glare of an interro-
gation lamp.

"It's a bit spartan, I know," he said, coming out with the wine.

"Just a bit," I said.

"I find I don't need that much," he said.

He handed me a glass and raised his to mine. The tone that sounded when they touched together told me that they were crystal.

"To getting off to a better start," he said.

We looked at each other for a moment and I felt that electricity again. It brought heat to my cheeks. There was a silence between us but it was comfortable. The lighting was low; a few pillar candles were burning and the overhead light was turned down to little more than a glow.

"So where did you move from?"

"Uptown," he said. "I had a cheap place up by Columbia. But the neighborhood was getting so bad that I felt like I was living in a war zone. The gunfire was literally keeping me up at night."

"So you moved to the safety of the East Village?"

"I like a little grit in my neighborhood. I'm not into posh," he said, and that shy smile came back. My heart did a little rumba.

"What do you do?" I asked him, even though I hate the question.

"Do you want to sit down?" he said, leading me by the arm over to the futon. He sat beside me at a polite distance, but still close. I could smell just the lightest scent of his cologne. If I reached out my hand just an inch, I could touch his thigh.

"Was that a stall?" I asked, and he laughed. It was a nice laugh, deep and resonant.

"Maybe. It's just that when I tell people what I do, it seems to dominate the conversation for a while. And it's really not as cool as it sounds."

"What are you . . . a cabaret dancer?"

"I'm a sculptor," he said, pointing to the piece I'd noticed on the wall.

I took a sip of my wine. "That **is** cool," I said, looking at the object with new eyes. Hard lines but with the look of liquid to it, like a steel waterfall. There was a strange power to it and something alienating as well. Metal has that quality, doesn't it? Beautiful to the eye but cool to the touch.

"You make your living that way?"

"That and the furniture," he said, nodding toward the table. "And a few other things here and there. It's not easy to make a living off your art."

I nodded. I understood that.

You know that feeling you get when you step into someone's aura and you feel as though you've known that person all your life, as if their energy is as familiar to you as the sound your refrigerator makes? I didn't have that feeling with Jake. Everything about him felt new and electric. He was utterly unfamiliar, a stranger who intrigued me like a mind-bender. With Zack every new moment was like a memory of a life I'd lived already—I could predict exactly what would happen between us and most of it was pretty nice. But I didn't want my life to be like a riddle to which I already had the answer. Some people find that kind of predictability comforting. I don't.

The conversation flowed easily as we chatted about my work, some about Zack, the usual getting-to-know-you stuff. You show me yours, I'll show you mine. Now that I think back on it, it seems as if I told him a whole lot more than he told me. He kept pouring wine and I kept feeling warmer, more relaxed. We had somehow shifted closer to each other. He'd laid his arm across the back of the couch, and if he'd lowered it, it would have been resting on my shoulders. I could feel the heat of his skin, see the stubble on his jaw. Did I say sexy didn't impress me? Well, maybe a little.

"So you had a pretty big week last week," he said, pouring some more wine.

"Are we still on that first bottle?" I asked. He'd gotten up a couple times to refill my glass and I'd lost track of how much I'd had to drink.

"No," he said. "Not by a long shot." I could see that his skin was flushed. And there was a looseness to him that I found appealing. It made me realize that he had been nervous as well when I first arrived. And I liked that. It made him real. It meant he wasn't arrogant.

"You heard about that?"

"Who didn't? It was all over the papers."

"Yeah . . ." I said. The mention of it brought me crashing back down to earth, remembering the picture, my parents. It must have been all over my face. I'm not so great at hiding my feelings.

"Hey," he said, touching my shoulder. "What did I say?"

He leaned into me and I could see the concern on his face. I looked away from him because somehow his compassion made me want to cry.

"Ridley, I'm sorry," he said, putting his wineglass down. "We don't have to talk about it."

But it was too late. He'd opened the floodgates and the whole story came rushing out in a tumble, everything from leaving my apartment that Monday morning to seeing my parents earlier tonight. I hadn't told anyone except my parents about the picture. He was perfectly present, listening, making all the right affirming noises. He was totally focused on me.

"Wow," he said when I was done.

"I bet you're sorry you asked," I answered with a little laugh.

"No," he said. "I'm not."

He touched my hair lightly, pushing it away from my eyes. It was a gentle gesture, intimate. He held my gaze.

"So you believe your parents. You'll just leave it at that?"

"What's not to believe?" I answered weakly, not really convinced myself. "The whole thing is ridiculous. I know who I am."

He nodded, looking at me with those eyes, seeing something in me that I was distantly aware of but neglecting.

"Still," he said after a moment. "You're not even curious enough to call?"

It's funny when you meet someone who you think is so different from you and then they manage to connect you to a part of yourself you ignore. The curiosity was a flame inside me, one that had flickered in my parents' assurances but which burned still. Jake breathed butane on it.

"I don't think so," I said, standing up.

"I'm sorry," he said, rising with me. "I didn't mean to scare you off."

I smiled. "I don't scare that easily."

He nodded, looked uncertain. I was glad he didn't try to convince me not to leave because it would have been so easy. Every nerve ending in my body was aching to kiss him, to feel that smooth, muscular flesh against me. I wanted to see the rest of that tattoo, the one that snaked out of his collar and curled out of his shirtsleeve. But I felt something for Jake, something too powerful to sleep with him or even kiss him that night. I wanted more. And I wanted to take my time.

I was exhausted when I got into bed, the stress of everything, the wine, Jake. So I fell out quickly, almost as soon as my head hit the pillow. But I dreamed of Ace. I chased him in a darkened urban landscape where shadows moved quickly across my path. Doorways through which I tried to pass warped and disappeared. Then I wasn't chasing Ace but being chased by a dark form. I came to a house that resembled my parents' home, but once inside, I found myself in the lobby of my building. I turned to see the form rattling at the gated door, though I still couldn't see his face. I woke, startled in the dark, my breathing heavy as I tried to get my bearings and shake the dream-terror that still lingered. I sensed a malevolent presence in the apartment and sat paralyzed for a moment, listening for the intruder who I was sure would slip from the shadows any minute. The fear faded as the images from my dream slipped away.

I was wide awake. I got up from bed and rummaged through my pants pockets and found the photograph and the note. I crumpled both in my hand and put them in the garbage. I pulled on a pair of sweatpants and sneakers and left the apartment with the garbage bag. It was after three and the building was asleep, except for the faintest sound of a television I heard somewhere in the distance. I crept down the stairs and through the hallway to the back of the building. I pushed open the dead bolt on the heavy metal door and flipped on the light. Rats skittered away from the sound and the stench of refuse rose up to greet me as I tossed my garbage bag in the nearest can.

I knew that Zelda would come before the sun rose and roll the cans out to the sidewalk, that the garbage would be picked up early in the morning even before I got out of bed, and the note and the photograph would be gone as if they'd never existed. What about this flame of curiosity I was talking about? It wasn't out. It was just that I could not imagine the consequences of knowing the answers. I'll admit it wasn't exactly a noble decision but I chose ignorance.

I headed back up the stairs feeling lighter with relief. I was halfway up when I saw a shadow on the landing above me, the figure just out of the line of my vision. I stopped in my tracks and my heart started to race.

"Is someone there?" I said. I knew everyone in my building and had never once had a moment of feeling unsafe there. Any one of my neighbors with a genuine purpose for being on the stairs would have answered me. I heard a shuffling, someone moving against the wall. I looked behind me and the light on the landing below had started to flicker, then went dark. The sound of my own breathing was loud in my ears, adrenaline started to pump through my veins, and every nerve ending in my body throbbed with fear. I didn't know whether to go forward or backward.

"Who is it?" I said, louder.

I looked around for something to defend myself with but there was nothing. Then I heard footsteps hard and heavy in a run. I pushed myself against the wall, as if I could disappear by making myself very flat. I was about to scream when I realized the footsteps were moving away from me. I crouched down and looked up through the space between the staircases and saw the figure of a man. He had a large build and I saw his gloved hand on the banister. He ran up the last flight and exited the door that led to the roof. I braced myself for the sound of the fire-door alarm but it didn't go off.

I sat weak with relief on the staircase and wondered how he would get off the roof. Then I heard the groaning of the fire escape ladder out front. I wondered if anyone else had heard it, too. But after a minute, the building was silent again, as if none of it had ever happened. I walked cautiously back to my apartment and closed the door. A second later I heard another door close and lock. I couldn't be sure whose door it was, whether it was above or below me.

SEVEN

Obviously, I didn't sleep much the rest of the night. I checked the gates on my windows and double-locked my front door and basically sat in my bed wide-eyed, startling at every little sound until the black sky lightened from charcoal to gray. Another night I might have called Zack or even my father, but since everyone seemed convinced that I was on the verge of a nervous breakdown, I didn't want to give them an incident that might prove them right. After a little while I began to doze until my alarm went off an hour or so later.

I got up and made a pot of coffee. As I listened to the machine's familiar hiss and gurgle and smelled the aromas from Veniero's, I started to feel normal again. Everything about the night before began to seem surreal, as though I might have been dreaming from the moment I got on the train to go to New

Jersey. I'd thrown out the photo and made a decision to consider the whole thing a hoax. In my sunny kitchen, I could halfway believe that I had imagined the whole encounter on the stairs. You know, because the **stress** was causing me to **hallucinate.** Anyway, it was over. It was just me, Ridley, on a normal Thursday morning. Denial . . . it ain't just a river in Egypt. Seriously, I think it's something your mind does when it has too much to handle. It takes a little vacation.

I went into my office—really, it's just a little space I have sectioned off with an Oriental screen where I keep my files and laptop. I rummaged through some papers on my desk and found the business card Uma Thurman's publicist had given me. We'd met at a yoga class and wound up going to Starbucks afterward for some chai. Her name was Tama Puma. She was crunchy, smelled of patchouli. Tall with broad shoulders, had that gray complexion and limp hair that people who eat a macrobiotic diet always seem to. She was impossibly thin and spoke softly but with a lofty self-importance. We'd chatted briefly about the article I wanted to write and I had told her I'd call if the features editor at **Vanity Fair** accepted my pitch. I left a message for Tama and felt glad to be getting back to work, moving forward from a neatly diverted disaster.

When I opened my door, I saw it there on the ground. The sight of it felt like a blow to the solar plexus. Another envelope with my name scratched across in black marker in the same harsh, scrawling hand. I picked it up and went back into my apartment. The whole world seemed to spin around me as I ripped the envelope open. There was a clipping from an October 27, 1972, newspaper. The headline read YOUNG MOTHER FOUND SLAIN; TODDLER MISSING. The rest of the article had been clipped away, but there was a headshot of the young woman from the first picture and another photo of the little girl. Looking at the woman's face again, even in the grainy newsprint, I could have been looking in the mirror. And looking at the child, I noticed something on her face that I hadn't seen in the first picture. She had a small brown birthmark under her left eye, identical to one I had on my own face. There was a note as well.

It said simply, **They lied.**

I was out of my apartment and down the stairs in a shot, racing for the garbage cans. I ran into my landlady, Zelda, in the hallway. "Did the garbage pick up?" I said, running to the front door.

"Ah," she said in disgust, lifting her hands. "Sanitation strike. Lazy sons of bitches, like they don't get enough money. It's still in the back. Goddamn unions."

The garbage bag was on top of the can and the picture and number easy to find. I unwrinkled the photograph and the note and went back upstairs. I stopped at my apartment and picked up the clipping. Then I took everything upstairs to Jake. Why would I do this? I barely knew him. But I think it was precisely because he was a stranger, utterly unconnected to the other people in my life, that I thought he might be the only one with any perspective.

"I'm sorry," I said when he opened the door. "I need some help."

I handed everything to him and pushed past him without being invited in. He looked at me, then down at the papers in his hand.

"This is what you were telling me about last night?"

"Yes. And something I found at my door this morning."

He nodded, his face still and solemn. He

never asked why I'd brought this to him, what I wanted him to do. He sat at the table, started flipping through the items, and I saw lines crease his brow as he frowned down at the papers in his hand.

"This woman could be you," he said after a minute. "She looks just like you."

"I know," I answered.

"Could be someone fucking with you."

"Why? What would anyone have to gain?"

"Some people just like to play with lives. Some psycho sees your picture in the paper, you remind him of someone he used to know, someone who died. You become his target."

"Okay. Explain this," I said, pointing to the tiny mole just below the corner of my left eye. He looked at the photograph and saw an identical mark on the face of the child as I sat across from him.

He nodded slowly and looked over at me. "I'll admit it's weird."

There were things about him that I hadn't noticed the night before. There was something sad around his eyes, lines there that seemed to mark the vision of tragedy. I could see through his white T-shirt that the tattoo, which peeked out of his short shirtsleeve, also worked its way along his chest and over his collarbone. I saw a scar on his neck; it was an inch long, thick and raised as though there were something beneath the skin.

"But what do you want me to do?" he asked gently, coming to sit beside me.

I looked at his hands; they were thick and square, the knuckles calloused, blue veins roping beneath the skin. Something about them simultaneously turned me on and sent a shock of fear through me. In the daylight, he looked harder, tougher, bigger than I remembered him looking last night.

"You know what?" I said, getting up. "Forget it. You're right. I don't even know you. I'm sorry."

He didn't say anything. What an idiot I was. I gathered up the papers. I wished the floor would fall out beneath me.

"I'm overreacting. **And** it has nothing to do with you," I said. He stood and blocked my exit.

"I don't think you're overreacting," he said. I let him take the papers from my hand. He put them down out of my reach, then put his hand in mine.

"It's okay, Ridley. I'm not sure how, but I'll help you figure this out if you want me to."

And we stood like that. The joining of

hands is highly underrated in the acts of intimacy. You kiss acquaintances or colleagues, casually to say hello or good-bye. You might
even kiss a close friend chastely on the lips.
You might quickly hug anyone you knew. You
might even meet someone at a party, take him
home and sleep with him, never to see him or
hear from him again. But to join hands and
stand holding each other that way, with the
electricity of possibilities flowing between
you? The tenderness of it, the promise of it, is
only something you share with a few people in
your life.

His pull was irresistible.

"Really?" I said, feeling a wash of relief and
gratitude.

"Really."

"Okay."

I felt the skin of his hand, hard but warm
against mine. I could see all the facets in the
gems of his eyes and I could feel that gaze
searching me inside. I could sense the many
layers of the stranger before me and I was
afraid, intrigued, and deeply moved. When he
guided me into his arms and held me there,
the lines of our bodies melted into each other.
I placed my cheek to his throat and felt his
pulse throbbing. I was on the precipice of

some yawning darkness, glad to have even this uncertain ally.

I don't know how long we stood like that. A long time, I think.

Finally he said, "So this guy wants you to call him."

"Yeah, I guess," I said, lingering a second in his arms and then pulling away. I sat at the table.

"Doesn't that seem weird to you?"

"Why?"

"Well, think about it," he said, sitting across from me.

"First of all," I said, "why did you assume it was a man?" I had made the same assumption and was wondering what it was that led him to that as well.

He considered it a second. "The handwriting is masculine, for one thing. And the article says the woman in the picture is dead and the little girl missing."

"Okay, why do you think it's weird that he'd send a note?"

He shrugged. "If this guy thinks he's your father and that you're the little girl in this picture, then he's been looking for you for a long, long time. And it means his daughter was **kid-**

napped. If your child was missing, for whatever reason, and you'd spent all these years looking for her and suddenly thought that she might be alive and well, wouldn't you come running, call the police, something more drastic than sending a note and a picture?"

I thought about it a second. "Maybe he's uncertain. Or afraid."

He shook his head slowly. "Maybe," he said. "But maybe he's got something to hide himself."

"Like what?"

"I don't know," he said, picking up the newspaper clipping. He seemed to be considering something but stayed silent.

"What?" I asked finally. "What are you thinking?"

"I have a friend," he said, turning his eyes on me. He seemed suddenly unsure and held up his hands. "Listen. I don't want to overstep my bounds with you."

I figured that he was thinking about last night when I'd scurried away from him, when he thought he'd scared me off.

"If anyone's overstepping their bounds," I said, "it's me dumping all of this on you."

He hesitated another second. Then: "This

friend of mine, he's a detective," he said, not looking at me but at his feet. "Someone I grew up with. He might be able to help."

If you're wondering why he would be helping me, I didn't know. But I was more grateful than curious. Men who are attracted to you will pretty much do anything, right? Right.

EIGHT

I went east toward the river. In this new skin, I couldn't think of anything else to do but wander. Wandering is not new to me. I've done a lot of it and New York City is the perfect place to lose yourself for a while—permanently, if you want to. You could walk a hundred blocks and pass a thousand people and no one would ever notice you, even if, five minutes ago, your face was on everyone's television, on the front page of every paper. That fast, you could become a ghost. I was already losing myself, slipping through the fissures that were suddenly appearing in the facade of my life. I was vapor. I wafted down Eighth Street toward Tompkins Square, past the newly gentrified tenement buildings that held within their walls the energy of generations of strife and poverty, now gutted and newly painted, fitted with picture windows boasting trendy East Village boutiques. In that gleaming glass I caught sight of a woman who didn't know who she was anymore, who didn't know from where or from whom she came.

I stopped to look at her. She looked real enough, like flesh and blood and bone. But if you reached out to touch her, she faded like a hologram.

I'd left my problems with Jake. He told me to take a break, get some distance and get my head together. So I left the question of my very identity at his doorstep like a bag of unwanted clothes at the Salvation Army. For the time being, I wanted to get as far away from the questions as I could. And yet as the East Village morphed into Alphabet City, unfortunately I realized that every time I caught my reflection in the mirror, I'd be reminded that I was suddenly a stranger to myself.

Maybe you think I was overreacting. Did I really have enough information at this point? Hadn't I felt guilty and embarrassed not even twenty-four hours earlier for having entertained these very thoughts? What can I say? This idea had wormed its way into my consciousness and was now burrowing and expanding beneath my skin. I wouldn't say I felt shattered exactly. But I felt like one of those

East Village tenement buildings, stripped to naked wood, gutted, old brass pipes exposed, wires hanging like webs, a shell of myself waiting for reincarnation.

I found myself on Avenue C. This is the real Alphabet City. Not the one on Avenue A before Tompkins Square, packed with trendy shops and cafés, million-dollar co-ops, shabby-chic lofts, all struggling in their new opulence for the look of East Village grit that had seemed so undesirable when it was real. The money hadn't made it down this far yet. It was as though once you passed the park, you'd entered a dead zone, a place that the city had decided to leave to its own devices. It felt lawless and abandoned, except for tiny pockets like the Nuyorican Poets Café, flowers of creativity that had pushed their way through the concrete. Here abandoned buildings stood like limping rebel soldiers against the encroaching wealth that would force the longtime residents of this neighborhood onto the streets. Here empty lots were littered with garbage, old furniture, stripped cars, and barrels filled with fire, surrounded by the city's discarded people. The homeless, the junkies, the runaways, those among us who had somehow lost their way and had stopped groping for a way back. I walked, aware, but with my head down. It's not the place where you want to call attention to yourself. You just move through as though you belong. And today I did belong. I was looking for Ace.

On Avenue D and Fifth Street, I came to the building where he'd told me he'd been squatting the last time I saw him. It looked better than most buildings. After World War II, there'd been a rush to put up as much housing as possible in the East Village for the boys returning home. The result was a great deal of shoddy construction, and now many buildings, like my own, were sagging in the middle, facades crumbling, pieces falling onto the sidewalks below. This one looked pretty solid, heavy white stairs leading to an entryway flanked by Doric columns. A black man the size of a refrigerator sat sentry by the door, his tremendous girth completely enveloping the chair beneath him, making it look as though he were levitating. He wore a New York Rangers jersey and a red baseball cap turned backward. His carefully faded denims were clean and pressed. His sneakers were a riot of color and wound up his ankle; he tapped his foot to an invisible beat. I stood at the bottom of the stairs and looked up at him.

His eyes were already on me. I could see him sizing me up. Was I five-oh? He gave me a nod and his three black chins knocked against one another lazily, his eyes yellow and flat, revealing nothing.

There was a time when I would have judged this man, this gatekeeper to the hell behind him, in his pockets or hidden somewhere near him the stash of crack cocaine or heroin or whatever it was he was selling. I would have felt the hate rise in my throat like bile. But the relationship between the addicted and the dealer was so complicated, so delicate. Who was worse, the people who wanted or the people who supplied? What about the rest of it? The poor parenting, bad socialization, racism, poverty that created the pain that created the junkies and their dealers. Even I had my place in the chain as the enabler; in giving Ace money, didn't I have some part in this? See what I mean? I **did** belong here.

"Whatchu want, girl?" he said, not unkindly. His eyes had narrowed and a smile that was more a reluctant turning up of the corners of his mouth puckered the flesh of his face.

"I'm looking for my brother. Ace." My voice sounded foolish, naive even to my own ears.

He gave a little chuckle and his whole body shook. "If he's in there, he ain't your brother no more."

There was a wisdom in that statement that surprised and hurt me. I felt my face flush at the truth of it. I walked up the stairs and his expression registered a mildly amused surprise, as if he'd expected me to turn away. I looked at him when I reached the top and he shrugged, apathy slackening all the features on his face.

This was not the first time I'd ventured into a building like this looking for my brother; once in a fit of worry I'd taken the train to Spanish Harlem. The streets seem harder above Ninety-sixth Street, the anger and the desperation crowd the sidewalks, dangle like legs from fire escapes. People are out, driving loud cars, hanging out windows, yelling. The danger is like the humidity in the air before a storm, no doubt that the sky will erupt, only a wondering of when and how and who will be left standing. The air in the East Village here seemed less electric, the violence lazier, slower to ignite. Still I felt a flutter of fear as I stepped from the light into the dark vestibule. The air around me turned stale but alive with the odors of human waste, too many bodies in a poorly ventilated area, and a ubiquitous smell of something burning, something chemical and poisonous. In the walls I heard murmurs, low groans, somewhere the sound of a radio or television, the cadence of a measured and professional voice delivering information. I made my way into the semi-darkness and headed toward a staircase.

As children, we'd shared a bedroom wall so thin, I could hear Ace turn or sigh in his sleep. Our bedrooms had once been a much larger room in the old house, and as part of the renovations it had been divided into two smaller rooms with an adjoining bathroom. It was a separate universe from the rest of the house, and the master bedroom where my parents slept on the ground floor, overlooking my mother's garden. A baby monitor left over from my infancy served as an intercom in case I needed my parents in the night. If I needed them, I could turn it on and call out. But when I woke in the night, frightened from dreams or thirsty or just lonely, it was Ace that I wanted.

I would slip out of my bed and walk softly across my carpet in the dark, through the bathroom that adjoined our rooms. I could see the shadow of the great oak tree dancing in front of his window, hear the heavy breathing of his sound sleep, see the outlines of his **Star Wars** action figures on their shelf, the pile of books on his desk; I could smell the scent of Johnson's baby shampoo, which we both used long after we weren't babies anymore. Pushing myself up onto his bed and into the curl of his body, I would always wake him.

"Ridley," he would say, his sleepy voice a combination of annoyance and resignation and love. "Go back to your own bed."

"I will," I'd say as he draped an arm around me and fell back to sleep. "In a minute."

I'm not sure I've ever slept that well again. You get too old for that kind of comfort, you know? That innocent physical closeness where all you want from other bodies is their cozy, gentle warmth, like puppies in a litter. As you approach adolescence and develop a sexual consciousness of your body, contact with other bodies becomes charged. It happened to Ace first, of course. He started closing the bathroom doors when he got up to pee in the night. The first time I heard him do that, I knew on some instinctive level that I couldn't crawl into his bed anymore. Overnight we had lost each other in that way.

On the building's second landing, the floor

creaked beneath my feet in a way that made me feel unsafe. I felt it give just slightly under my weight. With every step I took, I half expected to go crashing through the floor and land in a crumbled pile on the level below. Ace had told me he was staying with a girl on the second floor, that she had a window that looked out onto the street. So I walked toward the door closest to the street side of the building and knocked.

"Ace," I called. "It's Ridley."

There was only silence as the sunlight from outside filtered in through the dirty hall window; its gate was so rusted it looked as though a single touch might dissolve it to dust. A car cruised by outside and I felt the heavy bass of the subwoofers resonate in my chest and fingertips. The murmurs I'd heard on entering the building had quieted in the wake of my relative shouting. The walls and doors around me seemed to hold their breath. I heard a shuffle behind the door and could sense that someone stood tentatively on the other side listening out as I listened in. From the other end of the hall came an unmistakable squeaking, a scratching within a pile of rubbish that I could just make out in the dim light. I pretended not to see the rats as they skittered and rummaged. I knocked on the door again, this time louder.

"Ace," I said, sounding nervous and desperate. "Please."

I startled when the door opened and a wide blue eye peered out through the space allowed by the chain. Long strands of filthy blond hair hung before the eye, a woman's eye that might have been pretty once. But now it was bloodshot and smudged black with fatigue.

"He's gone," she said.

"Where?"

"What do I look like, his wife?"

I shrugged, not sure how to answer. The eye blinked slowly. "Do I know you? You look familiar."

I shrugged again, feeling at a loss for words. I gave a mild shake of my head to indicate that I didn't know if she'd seen me before. The eye looked me up and down. I could see something living in the lashes, in the lines beneath. It was hunger.

"You're the one who saved that kid."

"That's right. Look, do you know where my brother is?"

"**You're** Ridley. That bastard. He never told me that you were his sister."

I opted for shrugging again. It seemed like a useful, noncommittal gesture.

"He talks about you all the time," she said. I heard the crackle of envy. It made me childishly happy to know he thought about me, had told this stranger about me.

"You don't have any idea where he might be?"

She closed the door and I heard the chain release. Then she opened the door again, but not all the way. I could see a painfully thin leg, a sharp hipbone jutting against gray sweatpants that had been cut down into shorts, one breast flat and hard beneath a lavender cotton camisole, a collarbone that looked as if it could snap like a twig, and half of a gaunt gray face, square jaw, and that one wide blue eye. It was as if she wanted me to see exactly half of her, keep me guessing about the other half. Her fingertips, with nails bitten to the quick, snaked around the door. I felt pink and fleshy, conspicuously healthy and well nourished beside this woman who was all right angles, hard luck written on her body in the form of scars and track marks. I searched my memory for her name. Had Ace even told me?

"I haven't seen him in a week," she said.

I listened to her voice, listened for sadness or worry. But it was flat, emotionless. I searched her half face. I'm not sure for what. For something I could relate to, I guess. But her face was a mask of distrust, her eye narrowed now and hard. It told me that she expected everyone she met to abuse her; it was only a matter of how and how bad.

"What's your name?" I asked.

She hesitated and then said, "Ruby." Something about her seemed to soften then, and she opened the door a little wider. I looked past her into the apartment but saw only darkness.

"Nice to meet you," I said, ridiculously.

"Yeah," she said. "You, too."

We stood there awkwardly for a minute, regarding each other.

"If you see him . . . ?"

"I'll tell him you're looking for him."

I wrestled with the idea of giving her some money. I had a couple of twenties folded in my pocket. But something about her made me think it might insult her, as much as she might need it. So I nodded and turned around, walked toward the stairs feeling uncomfortable, guilty as if I were leaving the scene of an accident. I heard her close the door softly and I jogged down the stairs and headed toward the light. Outside, the fat guy had left his perch and stood at the corner with a couple of other thugs who all turned to look at me. He smiled, cruel and wolfish, as though he saw something that confirmed a judgment he'd already made. I turned from him and walked toward home. I squinted against the bright sky and saw Ruby's eye, how hungry it had been and how tired.

NINE

I stepped from the cold into Five Roses, the pizzeria in my building owned by my landlady. The heat offered relief to the red and tingling skin of my face. There were a couple of cops sitting at a corner table eating meatball Parmesan sandwiches, dripping sauce and cheese onto paper plates. The sight of it made my stomach grumble. I'd been walking for hours and the day was fading.

The place was homely, badly decorated, but made glorious by the aromas that wafted from Zelda's magical kitchen. Dreadful faux wood paneling edged the wall, dark and pocked with holes. Fluorescent lights flickered from the sagging water-stained ceiling, casting the space in the worst possible shade of white. There were rickety tables covered by the perennial red-and-white-checkered tablecloths, surrounded by brown vinyl chairs with tufts of foam showing through gouges. A Pepsi cola clock hung crooked above the door. Hundreds of creased, aging photos were taped or thumbtacked to the wall behind the old cash register. My personal favorite was of Zelda beaming up at Robert De Niro, who draped an arm lazily across her shoulders. He smiled that **Cape Fear** smile and held a slice up to the camera. **The best pizza in New York,** he'd scrawled above his signature. Zelda looked over the moon in that picture; she was much younger then, her features had an open lightness to them. She wore a bright red blouse that brought out a blush in her cheeks. Her smile was wide but tentative, as if she never expected it to last, was suspicious of the act itself. In ten years, I'd never seen her smile in person and I'd never seen her wearing anything but black chinos and a black turtleneck, both forever dusted with flour.

I walked over to the counter and Zelda didn't so much as acknowledge me as she shuffled back and forth. She took a pizza out of the oven with one of those giant wooden trays and slid it effortlessly, perfectly into a waiting box. Then with the same quick efficiency, she plucked two slices of Sicilian from a pie underneath the glass case and put them in the oven. I was so predictable, I didn't even have to order anymore. When that was done, she looked up at me.

"That it?" she asked.

"Yes, thanks," I said, and handed her a five. She pressed in digits on her ancient cash register and the drawer opened with an excited **ka-ching!** It was the sound of joyful expectancy.

Zelda was a petite woman with fragile, bent shoulders and small, hawklike features. All the light that I witnessed in the photograph had drained from her, leaving her to sag and go gray. She moved with an aura of resignation, as though her life was no more than forcing herself to put one foot in front of the other. I always imagined that if it were a matter of sheer will, she could lift a ten-ton block of concrete onto those shoulders and carry it as long as she had to. She impressed me as one of those people who saw her life as a prison but wore the key on a chain around her neck.

I used to try to make conversation with her, but some years back I'd given up with no hard feelings. So I stood, waiting for my pizza and staring off into space until she surprised me by talking.

"A man," she said, her beady brown eyes edged with blue fatigue and a million tiny lines, her lips thin and pressed into a straight line. "He look for you."

"Who?" I said, keeping my voice sounding casual as a hole opened in the pit of my stomach.

She shrugged. "I dunno."

"What did he say?"

"He said to call. He said you had the number."

I suppressed the urge to spin around and examine the faces of people on the street. A feeling of dread wrapped itself around me as I noticed that the cops had left. Zelda handed mc my pizza in a white paper bag.

She looked at me sideways. "No good," she said with a definitive shake of her head. "He was no good."

Her words made me go cold inside, and as I left the pizzeria and walked out onto the street, I felt vulnerable and alien. People moved past me, carrying their dry cleaning and briefcases, their backpacks. Someone slid by on Rollerblades; a homeless guy slumped on a stoop across the street. First Avenue was a sea of traffic, honking horns and quick stops emitting brief shrieks of rubber on concrete. The light flashed DON'T WALK. Everything was normal, as it always had been. Except for me.

A little more than a week and a half since

standing on this corner and seeing Justin about to get hit, everything about my life had changed, everything about me felt different. I had walked the few feet from the pizzeria to the door of my building about a million times and never been so aware of the scene around me. I looked at the faces of strangers and envied how they bustled about in their lives, secure in the knowledge of who they were and where they were going . . . or at least where they'd come from. And I sensed a menace beneath the surface of the street noise, as if something dark was waiting, hidden behind the facade of the innocuous scene before me. I felt watched. I moved quickly to the door of my building, opened it with my key and moved inside, feeling the breath of danger on my neck. With the metal clang of the door slamming, I felt a shudder move through me, as if someone was walking on my grave.

Much later that night, when the phone jangled me from an uneasy sleep, I knew it was Ace before I answered.

"I heard you were looking for me," he

greeted me, sounding distant like a stranger on an overseas line. "Bad idea, Ridley."

I didn't say anything, just hung silent on the line. I thought it was funny, though not in a ha-ha way, that my junkie older brother thought he had better ideas about how to handle things than I did.

"What's wrong?" he said after maybe a minute.

"I have to talk to you."

"So talk."

No, I needed to see his face, look into his eyes. He was bad on the phone, anyway. I could never get a sense of him, what he was thinking, feeling. Not that I had much luck with that in person, either.

"I need to see you."

More silence. I could hear him breathing. I could hear the street noise that told me he was on a pay phone. I looked at my caller ID display; the word **Unavailable** glowed there. The word made me feel so lonely, so separate from everyone in my life. I waited. Our phone conversations were generally comprised of these heavy silences.

"Meet me at that diner on West Fourth," he said finally, as if his better judgment had been pinned to the mat, after a lengthy internal wrestling match.

"How long?" I said, glancing at my clock. It was 1:30 A.M.

"Just come now."

"Okay."

I was dressed and out the door in less than ten minutes. I hailed a cab on First and the driver took a left on Twelfth. We glided south on Second; it was quiet and nearly empty, reminding me that Truman Capote had described Second Avenue as having an air of desertion and I had always agreed. We raced by St. Mark's Church, Telephone Bar. People who don't know what they're talking about call New York the city that never sleeps. But it does sleep. Well, it dozes. Windows grow dark; gates come down.

At a light, I watched a middle-aged man in a tweed jacket walk up the avenue. He pulled his jacket tight around him and seemed to huddle against an imaginary wind. He moved quickly, leaning slightly forward, his face blank, eyes straight ahead. Solitary people on the street after a certain hour always seem lost or tired or drunk, rushing toward their destination with an aura of worry. Except for the college students and the people out partying in groups, I always thought of them as people slipping through the cracks, existing on the outer fringes, past concern with early-morning alarms and schedules, deadlines and responsibilities. I always wondered, What leads people to walk the streets alone at night? And here I was, as lost as any of them, albeit in a cab, nursing a bit of a headache. I attributed the dull pain behind my eyes to the bottle of wine I'd nearly finished all by myself.

I hadn't told anyone except my parents and Jake about the notes and photograph, but after Zelda's warning I could no longer carry the burden alone. My mind had been racing as I took the stairs back to my apartment. The man in the stairwell last night . . . was it the same person looking for me this afternoon? I thought of the note I'd found this morning. **They lied.** Did it mean he knew somehow that I'd been to see my parents? And if so, did he have some way of knowing what we'd discussed? Or was it a lucky guess? Or did it mean something else altogether? I thought briefly about checking in with Jake, maybe telling him that someone had been asking about me in the pizzeria. But I wanted to be alone, surrounded by my things, my space safe and familiar.

Lost in thought, I'm not sure how long the

driver had been stopped in front of the diner. A knock on the window brought me back to myself. I saw Ace's face hovering behind the glass. He opened the door for me as I paid the driver and slid out onto the street.

He looked okay, almost healthy if a bit gaunt and gray. His faded denims sagged from his thin frame, but they were clean. He wore a distressed motorcycle jacket over a black turtleneck. He kissed me and I felt sharp stubble on his face; his breath smelled of peppermint. I took this minimum of personal hygiene as a good sign, because, trust me, he didn't always smell of peppermint.

Inside the diner, which was busy with people stopping off after clubs or bars for late-night cheeseburgers or pancakes, we slid into a red vinyl booth. A pie case turned, flirting with me, offering key lime pie, cheesecake, tiramisu. Cigarette smoke, burned coffee, fry grease, maple syrup mingled in the air. Conversations hummed and silverware clattered against ceramic plates.

Ace didn't like it when I looked at him directly for too long. He'd told me he felt like I was inspecting him, and maybe he was right. Looking for signs of an improved or deteriorated condition. Searching for clues of his return to the world, my world, or that he was drifting farther down. I always thought of Ace as existing beneath my life in some secret underworld, as if I had to descend stone stairs to a dungeon and find him by walking through dark corridors and calling his name. So I stole glances at him, looking for new track marks, bruises, lesions, whatever, thinking, How long can he survive? I mean, what is the actual life expectancy of a drug addict? I didn't know.

"So what's going on, Ridley? You look tired."

I told him the whole story, interrupted a couple times by the waitress taking our order and then delivering our cheeseburgers, fries, and chocolate milkshakes. Ace didn't say a word the whole time, just kept his eyes down, first on the gold-flecked gray tabletop and then on the food in front of him, which he nibbled at and pushed around his plate.

"What did Mom and Dad say to you exactly?" he asked me carefully when I got to the part about seeing our parents.

I repeated the conversation for him pretty much verbatim as I remembered it.

"I left there believing them. Feeling pretty foolish, a little unstable."

He snorted a little and nodded. "They

have a way of making people feel like that," he said, his bitterness sharp in his tone. "What's changed?"

I told him about the second note and the newspaper clipping. He was shaking his head when I looked up at him again.

"What?"

"Ridley . . ." He looked off out the window to his side and watched as the tide of traffic ebbed and flowed up Sixth Avenue. "Why are you telling me this?"

"Because . . . I don't know. I'm scared."

He sighed heavily and looked down at his fingers. I tried not to notice the track marks on the back of his hands. I could only imagine what the rest of his body looked like if he'd decided to start using veins there.

"You don't want the answers to these questions. Trust me."

There had been, even in my despair of the last two days, a part of me that believed this all might be some kind of mistake. Like those moments after you crash your car, and the impact has jolted you, those few seconds where you still can't believe it actually happened. I was still in that gap. I had felt such an urgent desire to find my brother, in the hopes that he wouldn't have any idea what I was talking about. I had wanted him to tell me that I was nuts and ask me for money. This had been my last-ditch effort to hold on to the illusions of my life, and it had failed.

"Ace—" I said. But he stopped me by raising his hand.

"Ask Dad about **our** uncle Max," he said, inflecting the word **our** with his typical vitriol. He reminded me that there had always been this weird vibe between Ace and Max. And some strange jealousy about my relationship to him that I never understood. "Ask him, Ridley, about Uncle Max and his pet projects. That's all I have to say about this."

"But—"

"I have to go, kid," he said getting up. My heart fluttered when he stood. My life felt so chaotic right then, I was seized with dread that when he left my sight I might never see him again. And there was anger, too. Anger that he would leave me to face this, whatever it was, alone.

"Ace," I said, my voice sounding desperate, childlike even to my own ears. "You can't just leave me."

He looked down at me and shook his head. His eyes were flat, tired, edged with— dare I even admit it—apathy.

"Ridley, I'm a ghost. I'm not even here right now."

The two girls in the booth behind us had stopped their conversation, and I could sense them listening to ours. I was glad I couldn't see them, because I couldn't stop the tide of tears. That familiar alchemy of adoration and hatred simmered, transforming the flawed man before me into the mythic hero of my imagination. Superman, who had the power to reverse the revolution of the earth to save Lois Lane but refused; Prometheus, afraid of fire; Atlas, who dropped the heavens.

"If you're smart, you'll forget this thing. Just go on with your life. Move, so the person who's doing this to you can't find you."

I nodded, not trusting my voice. I reached into my pocket and handed him the cash I'd brought for him. He took it from me, embarrassed, and looked longingly at the door. He stood there for a second wrestling with something, but then I saw him move away.

"I love you," I said, not looking at him.

"I know you do," he answered. "I just don't know why."

I sat in the booth and watched him walk down Fourth to the corner and make a left. I watched him until I couldn't see him anymore and then I kept looking into the night, thinking he might come back. But he didn't. I put my head down in my arms and let my tears get soaked up in the fabric of my jacket.

"Hey."

I looked up to see Jake had slid into the booth across the table from me. I regarded him for a second. He wore a black denim jacket over a gray T-shirt and an expression I couldn't read. I wiped my eyes quickly, embarrassed that he would see me crying.

"Is this a coincidence?" I asked him, my voice unsteady, my eyes, I'm sure, rimmed red.

"No."

I thought about that for a second. "You followed me."

"I was afraid you were getting reckless, meeting your wanna-be father in the middle of the night."

When I didn't say anything, he said, "I thought you might need some backup."

"You followed me," I repeated. I wasn't sure whether to be scared, thrilled, or pissed. I was a little bit of all three, leaning heavily toward pissed.

"Who was that?" he asked, leaning back and looking out the window, as if he might catch another glimpse of Ace.

I'd never been followed before and I wasn't sure what it said about him. I am not and never have been one of those stupid, hopeless women who think controlling behavior is sexy. In fact, just the opposite. When I sense it, it's pretty much an off switch. So I was a little embarrassed that even though I currently had reason to suspect him of stalking me, part of me was thinking about sweeping the milkshakes off the table and doing him right there.

"Not that it's any of your business," I said. My words came back to me harsher than I intended.

It was suddenly quiet in the diner. I looked around, self-conscious. The after-party crowd had thinned considerably and I could hear the fluorescent lights buzzing. A couple cozied in a booth near the door. Two punks shared an order of fries, their matching orange Mohawks (**so** over) sagging a bit. There was an old man sipping coffee, and the only waitress, a flat-chested, mousy-haired young girl with tragic acne, pretended to read a romance novel but was really listening to our conversation.

"Right," he answered, looking at me quickly and then down at the table. Again I tried to read his expression and couldn't.

"I'll go," he said, getting to his feet. "This

was a bad idea." He walked toward the door and then came back to stand beside the table again. "I'm not a stalker, okay? I didn't mean to freak you out. I just . . . already think of you as a friend; I'm not sure why. I don't make friends easily."

I watched him, trying to figure out if the insurgence in my stomach was from nerves, or from wanting him, or from all the crap I had just eaten.

"Is that what I am?" I asked him.

"What?" he said, showing me his palms.

"Your friend?"

He shrugged, shook his head just slightly, and then looked at me with such naked hunger that I swear I almost gasped. It was so raw, utterly without artifice, a mirror of my own heart. I put twenty-five dollars on the table and followed him out to the street.

In the cold, he took my face in his hands and kissed me softly, just touching his lips to mine. It lit me up inside, as if he had doused me in gasoline and set me on fire. I felt like a teenager, as new to my own sexual desire as I was to his. He managed to hail a cab with me attached to his face, and we fell into the back, where we groped each other like kids on prom night.

At our building, he kissed the back of my neck as I struggled to unlock the street door. He pushed me inside and pressed me against the wall. He was hungry but tender, almost reverent in the way he kissed me. He didn't close his eyes but locked them with my own. I didn't want to stop looking at him. I couldn't. I'm not sure how we made it up three flights of stairs and into my apartment, but we did.

On my bed I straddled him and unbuttoned his shirt. His chest and shoulders were dominated by the tattoo of a dragon in flight, with sweeping, outspread wings, an open mouth bearing sharp teeth and a snaking forked tongue. It was a work of art, every intricate detail elaborately wrought. The dragon was angry, but it was strong and good, wise and fair. Beneath it, though, I could see scars. A four-inch-long gouge in his side, and what looked to be a bullet wound in his shoulder. He lay still as I looked at him, running my fingers along the lines of his tattoo, over the scars. He raised a hand to my face, ran it softly on my cheek, on the line of my jaw. I don't know what he saw in my face.

"Don't be afraid, Ridley," he said.

I leaned in to kiss him. I **was** afraid, not of

him, but of the powerful churning of fear and desire, of the chaos that seemed to be tearing at the edges of my once-very-orderly life. I unbuttoned my shirt and let it drop from my shoulders.

"I'm not afraid," I said.

"This is what you want?" he said, pushing up on his elbows and looking at me. "Because I warn you, I'm not a casual guy. I've been alone, Ridley, for a long time. I don't enter into things lightly."

I felt the full weight of his words. He sat up and I wrapped my arms around him. I whispered into his ear, "Don't be afraid, Jake." He groaned and pulled me tighter.

"There are things you need to know about me," he said into my hair.

"And I want you to tell me. I want to know everything. But not right now."

The light from the hallway snuck into the bedroom and licked at the valleys on his body. His collarbone formed a strong ridge that I touched with my lips. His body, much like his tattoo, was the testament to tremendous effort and attention. Every muscle was ripped, perfectly defined, rock hard beneath the silk of his skin. He shuddered beneath the whisper of my lips. I could feel him growing hard for me, and the knowledge of his need rocketed through my bloodstream.

In the semidark, I could see only half of his face. He kept his eyes open and watched me as I pushed him back onto the bed. His jaw was square and set, his lips unsmiling. To someone who didn't know how to look at faces, he might have seemed hard, almost angry. But I knew that it was the edges of the mouth and the corners of the eyes that told the tale. There again was the sadness I kept sensing, the powerful wanting I could feel with my body, and perhaps the thing that moved me most was the vulnerability of someone who didn't let many people this close, who wasn't sure he could stand the pleasure or the pain of it.

He let me explore his body with my mouth and the tips of my fingers. I wanted to walk the landscape of his physical self, take the winding path. Part of me wanted to engulf him quickly, totally, but mainly I wanted to taste every flavor of him on my tongue. He was patient, but when his low groans became more desperate, I knew his restraint wouldn't last. As my fingers worked the buttons on his jeans, he flipped me over. He was so fast, so strong, I was wrapped in his arms and held looking up at him before

I knew what hit me. For a moment I felt overpowered and flashed on how he'd followed me to the diner. I felt a little jolt, some mingling of exhilaration and alarm.

"You're torturing me," he whispered, his hunger pulling his voice tight and throaty. I smiled then, wrapped my arms around him.

I was lost in a sea of his flesh, floating into his eyes, feeling his strong hands roaming my body. He was feeding on me and I let him take every inch, let him devour me. I'd never offered so much of myself in the act of lovemaking, never relinquished so much to any moment. The nightmares that newly populated my life receded like players exiting a stage, and there was nothing beyond our skin. Maybe a few days ago when I still thought I knew who I was, I would have given less ground. But finding myself suddenly free from the things that had defined me, I had no boundaries to protect. I surrendered to the pleasure created in our communion and revealed myself completely to Jake. In that place, in that moment, I was more real than I had ever been, and the person to most recently enter my life probably knew me better than anyone on earth.

TEN

I never asked for Zack's key back. I'm not sure why; I guess I felt like it would have been adding insult to injury. And ostensibly, we were still close, still good friends. But I thought that it was understood that he was no longer entitled to use it without my permission. Friday morning proved me wrong.

My heart nearly stopped as I stepped from my bedroom into the living space and my sleepy brain registered a form lounging on my couch. I felt the rush of fear to my fingertips and a shriek rise in my throat in the seconds it took me to recognize Zack. He was looking at me with an expression I'd never seen on his face before. It was worry, but it was anger, too, shaded by resentment.

"Zack," I said quietly, raising a hand to my chest. The fear had drained, leaving annoyance in its place. "What are you doing here?"

"What am I doing here?" he said incredulously. "Ridley, people are **worried** about you."

"People?" I said with a frown. "Like who?"

"Like your parents, for Christ's sake. What's going on with you?"

"I just saw my parents the day before yesterday."

"Yeah, ranting and raving like a lunatic about their not really **being** your parents. And then you don't even call to let them know you're okay?"

"Zack, what does that have to do with you?"

I was flashing on something here, something I had always hated about my relationship with Zack—or should I say Zack's relationship to my parents. I often had the feeling that he was a clone they had created for the sole purpose of marrying me and taking care of me in a way that they no longer could. It annoyed me to no end when we were together. And now that we were no longer a couple it was downright infuriating. I felt heat rise to my skin and my throat got tight.

"Zack, you need to go. Right now," I said, continuing on to the kitchen.

"Ridley, talk to me," he said. "What's happening?"

I ignored him as he followed me into the

kitchen. I noted that he wasn't wearing his shoes and this rather threw me over the edge. How could he take off his shoes? What gave him the right to come into my apartment and make himself at home?

"Zack, did you not hear me?" I said, turning to stand and look him in the eye. "Leave."

He looked so hurt then, as if I'd slapped him in the face. What was wrong with me? Why was I being so mean to him? My childhood friend, my former boyfriend, the son of a woman I loved like a mother. It was **Zack.** Why did he feel like an interloper, someone I needed to put out of my apartment?

"I'm sorry," he said, shaking his head. "You're right. It was wrong of me to come here. I was—" He stopped short and looked down at his stocking feet.

I sighed, feeling like a total bitch.

"I know you were just worried," I said as gently as I could, moving toward him. "But this was not a good idea." I put my hands on his arms.

"Ridley," he said, holding my eyes with his icy blues. In the syllables of my name I heard all the ways I'd hurt and disappointed him, all the hope he still held for us. Hope fanned by my parents and his mother, I'm sure:

Let Ridley have some time. She'll come around.

"Zack, I'm sorry," I said. I'm not sure why I was apologizing. He pulled me into his arms and I took in his familiar scent and rested against him for a moment, like we visit our memories. **You're a fool to let that boy go,** my mother had complained. Maybe she was right, as she had been about so many things. But I didn't love Zack, not like that.

"What's up, Ridley?" said Jake, emerging from the bedroom. Zack pulled away from me quickly, as though I'd bit him hard on the neck, looking at me with surprised hurt. For a second they both stood in my line of vision, and the contrast between them was so stark it was nearly comical. Zack: blond, perfectly pressed chinos, white oxford, Lands' End barn jacket slung over the arm of my couch, Rockports under my coffee table. Jake: dark, the giant dragon tattooed across his ripped chest and abs, faded denims, bare feet (irresistible).

Zack's face fell and I felt like a kid caught playing hooky, hanging out with the wrong crowd. My stomach bottomed out for the hurt he must be feeling, but in my rebel heart there was just the smallest twinge of satisfaction.

Let's not forget, he'd stormed my boundaries and was in essence checking up on me for my parents. That was not okay with me.

"Who's this?" said Zack.

"Zack, this is Jake. Jake, Zack."

"Nice to meet you," said Jake, offering his hand.

Zack just looked at him, and after a second Jake withdrew his hand with an understanding nod. Zack brushed past him, grabbed his shoes and his jacket. Guilt and sadness brought heat into my cheeks. I'm not sure why, but it's a feeling I was pretty comfortable with in my relationship with Zack. I didn't say anything as he walked toward the door, carrying his things.

"I need your key, Zack. This wasn't fair."

He pulled the key from his pocket and handed it to me with a half-smile I couldn't read. A strange thought flashed through my mind: **He made a copy.**

"I'm not even sure who you are right now, Ridley," he said.

"I'm not sure you ever did, Zack," I said. The words just slipped from my mouth. I don't know why, since it wasn't something I had consciously considered before. But as I said it, I knew it was true. I knew it was why

I'd left the relationship, because I was never able to be myself without feeling guilty or as if I'd disappointed him. Like a child acting out against a controlling parent, where every independent action causes the parent pain and the child is punished. Subtle, though, not overt so that people would see. Almost imperceptible, in fact . . . except to me.

He left still in stocking feet. I guess the act of putting on his shoes in front of Jake was more than he could bear. I looked out the peephole after I'd closed the door and saw him sit on the top step to lace up his sensible shoes. I felt guilt and anger like a ball of gauze in my throat.

"Everything all right, Ridley?" said Jake from behind me. I liked the way he said it, with concern but with the underlying assumption that I could handle the events of my life. He wasn't jealous or angry. I liked that, too. I appreciated that I didn't have to baby-sit his emotions while mine were in a twister in my chest.

"Not really. Things pretty much suck at the moment."

He nodded and walked over to me.

"Except for last night, right? Don't forget about my delicate ego," he said with a broad smile that was contagious and pulled up the corners of my own mouth. I felt a heat in my belly and his hands were on my shoulders.

"That didn't suck too much," I said, putting my face to his chest and letting him hold me solidly against him. In a minute we were at it again.

I dozed a little after we made love again. When I woke, I didn't open my eyes right away because for a second I didn't think he was next to me on the bed. If I opened my eyes and he was gone, then I'd have been afraid that what had passed between us was nothing more than my fantasy. If he was gone, I was a fool. But after a second, I could smell his cologne. A second later I felt his palm on my belly and it sent a current of electricity through me.

"You're awake," he said.

I opened my eyes to see him looking at me. "How did you know?"

"Your breathing changed."

"You were listening to me breathing?"

He nodded, his lips curling into a sexy, lazy smile. I thought he would say something corny here but he didn't say a word. I liked him more every minute. I felt a flutter of worry at the realization and checked my emotions. **Take it easy, cowgirl.**

"What time is it?" I asked, sitting up and looking at the clock. It was after ten.

"You have work to do," he said simply. I liked that he knew that and it wasn't an issue. Zack never considered my job a real job and viewed any time spent on it when he was around as an infringement on our time together. Jake threw his legs over the bed and got out. I got a nice little show as he pulled on his jeans, grabbed his shirt from the floor. Very nice.

"My studio's on Tenth and A," he said, sitting down on the bed and taking my hand. He put it to his lips. "Come by if you want to see some of my work later. First door on the west side of A between Ninth and Tenth, across from the park. It's red; you can't miss it."

"I'd love that," I said. I felt like sighing but smiled instead. "Around four."

He leaned in to kiss me, lightly but for a long, sweet minute. Then he left without another word.

ELEVEN

After Jake left, I made some coffee and the caffeine buzz got me through the rest of the morning. I talked to Tama Puma.

"Ms. Thurman would be enchanted to meet with you," she said, her voice a warm and self-important purr. Enchanted? Who used words like that in the real world? I imagined her in a boa, with a long cigarette holder dangling from her fingers. Though naturally, Ms. Puma would die before bringing a cigarette to her lips.

I checked in with the accounting department at **New York** magazine on some money they owed me. Check's in the mail, as they say. By noon, the caffeine was wearing off and I could no longer ignore the thoughts that were weighing on me. I felt the familiar tug of guilt—I should call my parents to let them know I'm okay. But I didn't want to. I didn't want to hear their voices, because as soon as I did, I knew I wouldn't be able to hear my own anymore.

I spent awhile on the Internet, searching through LexisNexis for some information on a missing toddler and a murdered mother in the early seventies, but there were too many listings. I narrowed the search to the tristate area, but still there were more than ten thousand hits. The thought chilled me. I thought about my idyllic childhood, how I always felt safe and loved, how the only things I feared were bad grades and embarrassing myself trying to climb that stupid rope in gym class.

I scrolled through the articles, archives from old newspapers and magazines, Web sites with those terrible age-graduated photographs that tell you someone lost a child who was never found. That they had to imagine what that baby might look like five, ten years later, if they were alive at all. It made me realize there is this world, this awful place of pain and violence, where some people have been exiled and the rest of us cannot visit even if we wanted to. I didn't find anything that connected to the partial newspaper clipping I'd received, didn't see any images that matched those sitting on my desk. But I have to admit my search was somewhat half-assed, as my mother would say. I'm not sure how much I really wanted to know then, you know?

I kept a picture of my brother and me as kids on my desk. I picked it up and looked at it. In it I sat on a swing in this park by our house, my brother standing behind me, his hands directly above mine on the chains that held the swing. He rested his chin upon the top of my head and we both smiled for the camera, as red, gold, brown, orange leaves danced around us in a cool, strong wind that was blowing that day. A strand of my hair had drifted up and looked like a thin mustache on his face. I remember the easy days like that, when we were young together, before the circumstances that finally took Ace were even a blip on the radar. I remember walks and parties, vacations and family reunions, where there was no dark specter of my missing brother to shadow our happiness.

My mother likes to tell a story about Ace and me. Or she used to, back when she still liked to talk about Ace, when she still acknowledged him as her son. We were little, I'm not sure how old, about four and seven maybe. I remember the yellow light of Saturday morning leaking in through my blinds and me wak-

ing with the excitement of knowing that Ace
didn't have to go to school and that a morning
of lying on the floor in front of the television
watching cartoons stretched before me. It was
fall and the morning was chill, the floor cold
beneath my bare feet as I padded from my
room through the bathroom and into Ace's
side of the loft. I crawled up onto his bed and
lay beside him, and then, very gently, pried
open one of his eyes. Of course, he was already
awake and only pretending to be asleep. After
the usual grumbling and complaining, he allowed himself to be led down the stairs.

Generally, we began Saturday mornings
by eating giant bowls of Cocoa Pebbles. My
parents were still asleep and would remain so
for at least another hour, so the kitchen was
ours—no one to tell us what to eat and to
turn the television down and to sit back from
the screen. This was a brief, golden universe
where Ace and I made the decisions, an orgy
of sugary cereal and chocolate milk, jumping
on the furniture, and tickle fights where I occasionally wound up wetting my pajamas.

For whatever reason, this morning Ace decided that it was going to be cookies for breakfast. He found a package of Oreos in the
pantry and we took it, along with two glasses

of milk, to our comfortable spot in front of the television.

I think we were about half through with the bag when my mother came down.

"Ace. Ridley. What do you think you're doing?"

We both stopped chewing mid-bite, the next cookie paused halfway to our chocolate-covered lips.

"Give me those cookies right now."

At this point, I reached out my hand to return the cookie to my mother and began to cry. My brother stuck his hand into the package and stuffed as many as he could into his mouth before she reached us.

My mother always told this story with a tone of marvel about how different her children were, even though they came from the same people, were raised in the same home. I remember crying, not because I wanted to eat more cookies—truth be told I was rather sick from what I'd eaten already—but because my mother's arrival marked the abrupt end of the magic time.

I also remember it as the fault line that divides my memory of my childhood and Ace's. My mother and Ace engaged in a full-out battle over the Oreos—my brother cut and ran with the bag, up the stairs and into his room, where he slammed and locked the door, leaving my mother enraged and banging on it like a mad-woman.

"For Christ's sake, calm down, Grace. We're talking about cookies here," said my father, climbing the stairs after them.

But, of course, it wasn't about cookies. It was about control. How she had to have it and how I easily acquiesced and how Ace rebelled. Each of us extracted different people from our parents by our personalities and hence we had different experiences growing up. I wound up sniffling in the arms of my father; Ace earned the stony silence of my mother that generally followed one of her perimenopausal rages.

But my mother turned the incident into a charming and amusing dinner anecdote, drained of the drama of the moment and dis-tilled to illustrate how **quirky** and **funny** kids can be. I always cringed at her retelling, not because I thought of it as a traumatic experi-ence (though Ace certainly remembered it that way), but because I wasn't sure what she was trying to say about me. Did she mean I was weak where my brother was bold? Obedient where my brother was rebellious? Was I to be ashamed or proud? There was a kind of grudging respect in her tone when she spoke about Ace, as though she actually admired him for rebelling against her. But then, of course, she stopped speaking about him altogether. It's strange how memory gets twisted and pulled like taffy in its retelling, how a single event can mean something different to everyone present.

As I sat with the picture of the swing in my hand, memories came marching through my mind like soldiers, things I hadn't thought of in years, sepia-toned by present events. And I couldn't be sure if I was more clear-headed now than I'd ever been, or if I was losing my mind and everything—my recollection of the past, my perception of the present—was distorted by recent events.

My uncle Max was a mountain, a shooting star, a big bear of a man, a piggyback ride waiting to happen, his pockets full of candy and, later money, or whatever the particular currency of our ages happened to be. He was rock concerts, baseball games, he was yes when my parents were no, he was a consolation for every disappointment. He was the embodiment of fun, and the weeks spent with him when my parents were away are some of the happiest memories of my childhood. Ace and I loved him, of course. How could we not? It's easy to be popular with children when you're not the one making the rules, when your only role in their lives is to show them how much fun the world can be.

There was always a woman with my uncle Max, but never the same one. They all kind of run together in my memory, none of them really standing out from the parade of hair dye and silicone, tanned skin, straight silky hair, and high heels. Always high heels, no matter what they were wearing—dresses, blue jeans, bikinis. I do remember one woman, though. It was some party at our house, something during the day; I think it was Ace's birthday. The dining-room ceiling was missing, covered completely by helium balloons—red, orange, blue, green, purple. I remember music, and in my memory it sounds like a carnival ride. Laughter, someone spilling soda on the white rug, a popped balloon and delighted shrieking and a clown doing magic tricks. I remember rounding a corner too fast and running into the bleached denim legs of one of Uncle Max's girlfriends.

"I'm sorry," I said, looking up at her. All I can see now is blue eye shadow, feathered blond hair, and bubble-gum lip gloss.

"That's okay, Ridley," she said sweetly, and

walked off. And all I could see was that she wore the most fabulous red leather pumps. **Candies,** if I'm not mistaken, the very height of sexy-cool. I was breathless in my admiration, wondering how you came to grow up to be like that.

"Really, Max," I heard my mother say from the kitchen, which was where I'd been headed. I knew that tone, heavy as a bag of stones with the weight of her disapproval. "To bring one of them here. To Ace's party. How could you?"

"I didn't want to come alone," he said, something in his tone I didn't recognize.

"Bullshit, Max."

"What do you want from me, Grace, huh? Stop being such a fucking prude."

I didn't have time to be shocked that my mother and Uncle Max were talking to each other this way because suddenly my father appeared.

"There's my girl," he said, picking me up though we both knew I was getting too heavy for him. He carried me into the kitchen. Maybe he didn't see how my mother and Max quickly looked away from each other, carefully morphing their angry expressions into happier ones.

"What are you up to in here?" said my father jovially. "Not putting the moves on my wife again, are you, Max?"

They all laughed at the absurdity of such a notion. And then it was time for cake, which naturally wiped the event completely from my seven-year-old mind.

When the walls of the apartment started to close in on me, I showered, dressed, and left the building. I know what people think about New York City, but I'd never felt unsafe here, not for a minute, until that day. Zelda's warning about the man who'd been looking for me came back to me. I realized that I'd told neither Jake nor Ace about him and I wasn't really sure why. I sometimes had a tendency to treat worrisome things like bumblebees, a kind of ignore-them-and-they'll-go-away philosophy. Maybe admitting that someone was now physically seeking me out, as opposed to just sending mail, ratcheted the problem up to a level where it **couldn't** be ignored. It elevated the threat vector, and I wasn't ready for the consequences, the first of which would be to have my freedom limited. And you know how I felt about that.

I pushed my way through the doors of one of the clinics where my father and Zachary volunteered their services. This one was in midtown; the other was out in New Jersey. My father was putting in more time at these places the closer he came to retirement. Usually at the beginning of the week, he was in Jersey, toward the end in the city, so I had a pretty good idea that I would find him there today. I know you're thinking, Didn't she just say she didn't want to see her parents? It was true, I didn't want to. But my father seems to have a magnetic pull in times of crisis. As much as I swear up and down that I'm not going to call or go to see him when things are bothering me, it's as if he somehow knows and flips a switch somewhere in the universe, magically compelling me to pick up the phone, or show up at his office.

"I'm looking for Dr. Jones. Is he in today?" I asked the young woman working the desk. She had glowing café au lait skin and deep black eyes ridged with lush lashes. I'd never seen her before, though I'd been to the clinic a number of times to visit my dad or Zack. But I wasn't surprised; there had always been a high turnover there.

"Do you have an appointment?" she

asked, not looking up from the file opened in front of her.

"I'm his daughter."

She glanced up at me and smiled. "Oh, you're Zack's fiancée?" she said with a cheerful recognition in her voice.

Something about this annoyed me. We'd ended our relationship more than six months ago now and I'd never accepted his proposal. So, technically, I had never been Zack's fiancée. Before I could even respond:

"And didn't you just save that kid a couple of weeks ago? I saw your picture in the paper."

"Uh, yeah," I said. "That's me."

She looked at me with wonderment in her eyes. "Wow, nice to meet you," she said. "I'm Ava."

"Nice to meet you," I said, feeling impossibly awkward. It was too late to say, "By the way, I'm not engaged to Zack. Really, I never was . . . it's a long story." So I just clammed up and looked away from her.

"Just a second," she said, still looking at me. "I'll page him for you. Have a seat."

I found a chair among the crying babies and toddlers with hacking coughs and runny noses, hoping that my immune system was up to task. A woman breathed heavily beside me, sounding like she had gauze in her lungs.

"Ridley," called Ava after a few minutes. "You can go back. He's in the last office."

"Thanks," I said.

"You know," said Ava as she buzzed me through the door to the right of her desk, "you don't look like your dad."

I tried for a smile. "I've heard that before."

"Your father's a saint. You know that? You kids are lucky, so damn lucky. Don't tell your mother I swear in front of you, okay?"

Uncle Max had said that so many times, it lost its meaning. "You don't know," he would say. "You don't know what it's like to have a father that doesn't love you." And then he'd get that look, the look he had when my mother was around. As if the world were a prom and he was the only one without a date.

I guess Uncle Max may have been the loneliest person I've ever known, except Ace. When I was a kid, I sensed it without completely understanding it. As I got older, I recognized that he had an idea of himself as being alone in the world. But I still didn't quite get why he felt that way; he had my parents, he had Ace and me, he had his parade of Barbie dolls. But I understand now. Loneliness is a condition, an illness. He carried it with him and it infected his life. He could treat it by spoiling us, by loving my parents, with his "girlfriends," with booze. But there was no cure. His disease? It was terminal.

"Ridley," said my father with a sigh. He gave me a pained, glancing look from the corner of his eye. "You've caused us some worry."

"Sorry," I said, closing the door behind me. It was an examining room, really. It smelled, well, you know the smell—Band-Aids and disinfectant. Flickering fluorescents, bad Formica floors speckled with the most awful array of colors: mustard, olive, salmon. Spotless avocado countertops, glass jars filled with cotton balls and tongue depressors still in their paper wrappers.

My father took me in his arms even though I could tell he was angry with me. I loved him for that. My mother, when she was mad, wouldn't even look you in the eye, as though she had ceased to acknowledge your existence until she had forgiven you. I pulled away after a second and pushed myself up onto the examining table, the wrinkle of the tissue paper beneath me reminding me of a thousand visits to rooms just like this for various reasons. And they all seemed just like the same room. Well, not exactly the same. In spite of its cleanliness, there was a seediness, a run-down quality to this room that identified it as a clinic examining room versus some of the opulent private offices I'd been in. It depressed me. It was sterile and clean but ugly, the decor outdated, with hairline cracks in the wall, water stains on the ceiling. As if poor people didn't deserve for things to be modern and pretty. A yellowed poster with ripped corners was taped to the wall: the human musculature system. Pretty. The guy's face looked quite calm, considering he'd been skinned.

"Why did you send Zack to check up on me?" I said.

My father pulled an innocent face. "I didn't, Ridley. I wouldn't."

I was quiet, kept my eyes on him.

"I asked him to **call,**" he said finally. "That's it. I thought maybe you'd talk to him."

"Well, he came to my place and let himself in. I wasn't happy about that, Dad."

"I'd say he's learned his lesson," answered my father, averting his eyes and sitting on a green vinyl chair with metal legs. He leaned back and crossed his arms across his belly. He heaved a sigh.

"God," I said, pissed and a little embarrassed. "What, did he run and tell you everything like a little snitch?"

Did I realize that I sounded like a twelve-year-old? Yes, and I disliked it. But I guess it was part of a problem that I was just beginning to understand. When my parents were around, I **was** a twelve-year-old. And guess what? That's the way they liked it.

"Are you seeing someone, Ridley?" my father asked, forcing his voice to be light and inquiring.

"Dad. That's not what I'm here to talk about."

"No?"

"No, Dad. I want to talk about Uncle Max."

Nobody could ever call my father handsome. Not in the traditional sense. But even as his daughter I could see his sway over women. I've yet to see a woman who did not break into a smile under his gaze. His appeal went beyond the physical. The landscape of his face gave subtle hints at the man who lived beneath its surface. The bump on the bridge of his nose whispered of his tough, working-class roots. His square jaw was a dare to test his resolve once his will had been set. His light blue eyes were a gallery of his every mood. I'd seen them radiate with compassion, glow with love and understanding. I'd seen them grow dark with grief or worry. I'd seen them narrow with anger or disappointment. But never had I seen them the way they looked at that moment. They were utterly blank, unreadable. The pause following my question was a third presence in the room, a ghost that had slipped in under the door.

"Haven't we loved you enough, Ridley?" he said after a few moments. "Haven't we given you everything you needed—financially, emotionally—to thrive as an adult in this world?"

"Yes, Dad," I said, the guilt trip gnawing at me instantly.

"Then **what** is going on? Is this the point in your life where you indict us for all the mistakes that we made in raising you and your brother? I don't expect this from you, Ridley. From Ace, but not you."

There it was again, that crippling comparison. Since he left, Ace had been held up— not always verbally, mind you, but through some kind of emotional osmosis—as an object of disdain in my family, the very ultimate in failure and ingratitude. Any comparison to him in this way let off bottle rockets in my chest. The explosive mixture of shame, resentment, and anger brought color to my cheeks.

"What does any of that have to do with what I just asked you?" I said quietly.

A little flash of surprise lit up his face, as if he hadn't expected me to notice that he'd dragged out the big emotional guns to deflect my question.

"You're telling me that this doesn't have anything to do with what we talked about the other night?" he said with an indignation that didn't seem quite sincere. "Your mother is still upset by that."

"Dad," I said.

He held my eyes for a second, looked away and then back at me again. "What do you want to know?"

What **did** I want to know? Ace had told me to ask Dad about Uncle Max and his "pet projects." But that seemed like such a vague and bizarre thing to ask.

"Were there things about Max I didn't know?"

He shook his head and looked at me with a heavy frown. "Why are you asking me this? Where is it coming from?"

I didn't answer him, just leaned against the wall and kept my eyes on the floor. I heard my father sigh, saw his feet move over toward the window.

"So how long have you been talking to Ace?"

I stared at him. His eyes were edged with sadness now. It wasn't a look I was happy to see, but it was better than the dead, flat look he'd given me just moments before when I asked about Uncle Max.

"A long time," I answered. "But I think you know that already."

The fluorescent lights seemed to get brighter, harsher. I could hear the soft footfall of nurses' shoes scuffling back and forth outside the door. Some chatting, a bit of laughter. I was getting it, finally, that Zack had been giving my dad information about me for as long as he'd known me. The thought made me sick and angry.

My father shrugged. "Better he talks to you than no one. I haven't been able to get near him in years. But why didn't you tell me?"

I felt a little flare of anger. "Tell you? I wasn't allowed to say his **name** after he left," I said, surprised that I had raised my voice and that my hands were now shaking.

My father nodded. He walked over to me

and put his hands on my shoulders. I could smell his Old Spice and remembered how he'd smelled of rain and cologne when he'd come home from work at night.

"I'm sorry, Ridley," he said, forcing me to meet his eyes. "We handled it wrong. I know we did."

"It doesn't matter now, Dad," I said, sliding off the table and moving away from him. "I mean, you know, it's **okay.** I understand." I could feel the undertow of his love. It was subtly pulling me into him and away from the reason I'd come.

"We were hurting, Ridley. Devastated, really . . . your mother especially. We didn't know how to handle it. And we didn't really think about how it was affecting you. That was selfish of us. And we're sorry, both of us."

I felt bad for him, felt guilty again. I sat in the chair he had occupied a moment earlier and put my head in my hands, stared down at my knees. My head ached suddenly and I felt confused. This wasn't the encounter I was expecting to have.

"I'm glad he talks to you, Ridley," said my father again, after a moment. "As long as you're careful to listen selectively to what he has to say."

"What do you mean?"

"Well, Ace has had some strange ideas since he started using. He has a lot of hostility toward Max. A lot of jealousy about the relationship you shared with him. Don't let his anger poison your mind against a man who loved you."

"You think Ace put all this into my head? I showed you the photograph." I could have told him there was more—another envelope, someone in the pizzeria looking for me. But I didn't.

"I know, I know. But I thought we'd put all that to bed. It just seems like if you'd talked to Ace, he might have used the opportunity to spread a little of his poison."

"Why would he think Max had anything to do with this? Why would he tell me to ask you about Uncle Max and his 'pet projects'? That's what he called them."

My father shrugged dramatically, offering his palms in a gesture of helplessness. "How should I know where Ace gets his ideas? He's sick, Ridley. You can't possibly rely on the things he says."

There was a truth to this, I could see, from the outside. I mean, who would listen to a junkie, right? I had faith in Ace because I knew that there was more to him than his addiction. I hope we're all more than the sum of our parts. I thought my father would share that hope, too. But I guess Ace had been lost to him for a very long time.

"You can't think of anything, Dad?"

He sighed. Then: "The only things Max was involved in, other than his business, helped thousands of abused kids and battered women get on their feet."

"You mean the foundation?"

"You remember, don't you?"

He opened a drawer in between us and pulled out a couple of pamphlets. He handed them over.

I read one:

HELP PASS THE SAFE HAVEN LAW IN
NEW YORK STATE
YOUR DOLLARS SAVE LIVES

**The Maxwell Allen Smiley Foundation
A Nonprofit Organization
Committed to the Welfare of Abused
Children and Battered Women**

When I was sixteen years old, my parents took me to a fund-raiser ball at the Waldorf-

Astoria hotel. It was a positively luscious affair, with all the New York City's social elite turned out in glimmering gowns and exquisitely tailored tuxedos. There were towering flower arrangements, legions of champagne flutes, sparkling ice sculptures, and a full jazz band. I wore a pink silk organza gown and my first pair of real heels. The diamond earrings I'd received for my Sweet Sixteen glinted on my earlobes (I chased my own reflection all night long), and my mother's diamond bracelet looked as if it **belonged** dripping off my wrist. Naturally, I felt like a rock star and a supermodel and a princess; I was quite literally flushed and giddy with excitement.

Uncle Max was my date. He walked around with me on his arm, introducing me as his "gorgeous young niece" to people like Ed Koch, Tom Brokaw, Leslie Stahl. I shook hands with Donald Trump, Mary McFadden, Vera Wang. The event was a fund-raiser for the Maxwell Allen Smiley Foundation for the Welfare of Abused Women and Children, and at five thousand dollars a plate, Max was able to raise untold amounts of money that night for the various charities that his foundation supported.

"Your uncle Max initiated the foundation to

help pass the Safe Haven Law in New York State," my father told me now, "which allows women to abandon their babies to safe houses, hospitals, firehouses, or police stations without fear of prosecution and with the knowledge that the infant will be taken care of and put up for adoption."

I looked down at the pamphlet in my hand, flipped through the pages. It had two pictures on the front, one of a Dumpster, the other of a female nurse cradling a sleeping baby wrapped in her arms. **Make the right choice for your child, no questions asked,** it read. It explained the Safe Haven Law and urged mothers not to panic, not to leave their babies in a Dumpster or a toilet, as too many others had, but to bring them to one of the listed safe houses. In an even, nonjudgmental tone, it assured mothers that everything would be taken care of and that after sixty days, if they did not return for the child, all parental rights would be waived and the baby would be put up for adoption and placed in a loving home.

"I never heard him talk about the Safe Haven Law."

"It was controversial," my father said, sitting down again. He looked tired. "Detractors felt that it encouraged young girls to give up their child. Girls, I suppose, who might otherwise have kept their babies. But supporters, like Max and myself, believed that if a mother has an impulse to give up her child, for whatever reason, then that child is better off in a place where he or she can get the love and care needed. And if a frightened, desperate person has a safe alternative to murdering her child, she just might take it. The law passed back in 2000. Now the organization operates as a help line and a public relations office."

Now that he mentioned it, I'd seen the ad campaigns all over trains and on the sides of buses, and had even heard a couple of public service announcements. A deep, mellow voice would intone over the sound of a crying baby: "Stressed out? Can't handle the pressures of parenting? Before you take it out on your kids, call us. We can help." I just never had any idea that it was something my father and Uncle Max had been involved with. It seemed strange to me that I didn't know about it. My dad and I were close and we talked about his work often.

"Why haven't you ever mentioned this to me?" I asked.

"Haven't I? I'm sure that's not true. Maybe you just don't listen to your old father when he tells you things." He tried a smile but it died on his face when I didn't return it. We were silent for a second. I stared at the pamphlet, wondering if this is what Ace meant.

"Your uncle Max's childhood is not a secret to you. He was abused on a level I have rarely seen in my experience as a physician—and that's saying something. Instead of using that as an excuse to throw away his life, he burned it like fuel to drive himself to success. And he used that success to make a difference in the lives of abused children like himself—and battered women like his mother."

I'd heard this speech before. I wasn't sure why I was hearing it again. But I let him go on.

"Getting this law passed was especially important to him," he went on, "because he believed it got babies that were at high risk for abuse or neglect into the arms of people desperate for a child before any real harm could be done. As opposed to after the fact, like so many kids. It was important to him because there were things your uncle Max never got over. Not until the day he died."

I thought about Max, about that sadness deep inside him that nothing seemed ever to reach, even in our happiest moments together.

"Is that what you wanted to know, Ridley?" asked my father.

I shrugged. I didn't know.

"Trust me, kid, there are no dark secrets here for you to uncover. He loved you. More than you know."

I heard something in his voice, but when I looked into his face, I saw only the sweet smile I'd always counted on seeing.

"He loved Ace, too," I said, feeling bad for my brother, wondering why he'd always felt left out.

"Naturally," my father said with a nod. "But you two had a special connection. Maybe Ace sensed that and was envious." He drifted for a second, looked out the window, exhaled sharply through pursed lips. When he spoke again, it seemed more like he was talking to himself. "I don't know. Neither of you ever lacked for love or attention. There was always enough. Enough of everything for both of you."

I nodded. "I know there was, Dad."

"But of course, there's the matter of the money. He may be carrying some bitterness about that, too."

"The money?"

"Yes. The money Max left you when he died."

"What about it?"

"Well," he said with a sigh. "He didn't exactly do the same for Ace."

I shook my head. "I don't understand." I had always assumed that Ace was left an equal amount of money, though I guess I never really considered the logistics of it all. Ace disappeared for a long while around the same time I'd met with Max's lawyer to discuss the terms of my inheritance; I assumed Ace had done the same at some point. We never discussed Max's death or his money, or where he'd been during the months I hadn't talked to him. In fact, we didn't really talk about much except for Ace and his catalog of complaints and perceived injustices. Pretty sad, I know.

"Your trust was unconditional," my dad said. "The money was granted to you upon Max's death. Ace's trust was conditional upon his successful completion of a drug rehabilitation course and five years of clean living. He might be angry about that still."

I couldn't really blame Max. It was a reasonable condition and one obviously designed in Ace's best interests.

"What does that have to do with me?"

He shrugged. "Angry, jealous people do hateful things."

"Are you saying you think Ace has something to do with all this?"

"I'm saying it's not outside the realm of possibility."

"No," I said firmly.

My father gave me the look you would give a kid who still believed in Santa Claus: sadly indulgent.

"No way."

He put a hand on my shoulder. "Food for thought?"

I nodded quickly.

"I have to go," I said, rising. He looked like he wanted to stop me. I saw his arms rise from his sides and then drop again, as if he wanted to reach out for me but changed his mind.

"Call me tonight," he said, "if you want to talk about this more."

"Is there more to talk about?" I asked, looking at him.

"I don't know," he said with a shrug. "You tell me."

I embraced him quickly, not wanting to feel that pull to safety and comfort. Something about it drew me away from myself. I exited the room, leaving more confused than when I arrived. My father's answers led to only more questions. I walked out of the building into the winterlike afternoon.

"Ridley, wait."

I turned to see Zack standing outside the clinic doors. "Wait," he said again. "Can we talk?"

I looked at him and shook my head. The sight of him made my heart thrum with anger; the thought that he had betrayed so many confidences to my father, the mess in my apartment that morning . . . I couldn't deal with him.

"Please, Rid," he said, moving toward me. Through the doors behind him, I saw his mother, Esme, in scrubs with a little bear print on the top. She was a petite woman with a pink complexion, her golden blond hair shaped in a stylish bob. She clutched a file to her chest and cast a worried glance in our direction, then disappeared through another doorway, tossing a sad smile my way.

I didn't say anything to Zack when he stood near me.

"I'm sorry," he said. "About this morning. I was out of line, I know that."

I nodded but couldn't find my voice. His eyes were the palest blue; a light blond stubble shaded his strong jaw. His hand was on my arm. I remembered that not so long ago I thought I loved him. I felt the same pull to him that I'd felt to my father, as if in his arms, all would be well, life predictably safe and secure, and with him I would be cherished and loved. As long as I did what was expected of me, as long as I was the Ridley they wanted me to be.

"It's okay," I said. It wasn't true. I just said it to make us both feel better. "I'll see you later."

I walked away from him without a word and he didn't call me back again. The sliver of sky between the buildings was the same hard slate as the concrete around me. The traffic sang, a cacophony of horns and rumbling engines. I felt loneliness creep into my skin with the cold air that blew in through the cuffs of my coat and made a home in my belly.

TWELVE

I rang the buzzer beside the red door but there was no answer. I gave a dollar to a homeless man pushing a shopping cart filled with doll carcasses and tin cans while I waited, waved to a cop I knew from Five Roses as he and his partner cruised down Avenue A. Some kids were shouting on the playground across the street in Tompkins Square Park. I thought of Justin Wheeler and wondered where he was today. I rang the buzzer again and then tried the knob. I was surprised when the door pushed open.

"Hello?" I called before stepping onto a tiny landing before a steep staircase that led into blackness. When there was no answer, I went back onto the street and looked around for another red door but saw that this was the only one. I leaned back inside.

"Jake?"

I heard a pounding then, the sound of metal on metal. I moved inside again and let the door shut behind me. I felt my way up the dark staircase, the plaster wall cool to my hand, the tall stairway so narrow that if I fanned out my elbows just a little, I could touch both walls. At the top, I stepped onto the floor of a gigantic loft, dark except for the far corner, which was lit by bright artist's lights on giant tripods. He stood there, oblivious to my entry, bringing a large hammer down hard on a smooth arc of metal that stood twice as tall and twice as wide as he was.

Writers are first and foremost observers. We watch. We lose ourselves in the watching and then the telling of the world we find. Often we feel on the fringes, in the margins of life. And that's where we belong. What you are a part of, you cannot observe. I lost myself in the watching of this stranger who'd shared my bed the night before. I watched as the taut, defined muscles on his back tensed and writhed beneath his skin with each hammer strike, as the sheen of sweat on his body reflected the harsh light from the high lamps. I watched the way his fingers gripped the wooden handle of the hammer and how his knuckles were white and swollen, the veins as thick as rope. I felt the vibration, the heavy clang that filled the large space with each blow. I looked around the room and in the black saw dark forms lurking, born from the same hammer. I felt it electric in the air, coming off of him in waves. Anger. He was punishing that piece of metal. He was punishing himself. Something in my belly churned, some combination of fear and desire.

He lifted the hammer and paused mid-swing, let it drop to his side, and turned around. His face was flushed and drawn. He wore a look of interrupted intensity, as though I'd walked in on him making love.

"Ridley," he said, though I wasn't sure how he knew I was there.

I was quiet a second, feeling embarrassed for standing there watching him as I had. "Hi," I said finally, moving toward him. My footfalls echoed loudly off the walls and ceiling.

He wiped the sweat from his brow with his forearm and put the hammer on the floor.

"You okay?" he asked.

"Sure," I said, stepping into the light.

"I forgot to tell you the buzzer doesn't work," he said, looking at me strangely. "I left the door open and hoped you'd give it a push."

I nodded. "I did that."

"I had a feeling you would."

He looked different to me. Something in his face was hard. In the harsh light, there was no mistaking the marks on his body, the line from his neck to his collarbone clearly the mark of something sharp and angry, the starburst of scarred flesh on his shoulder which looked like a gunshot wound, though I admit I'd never seen one before. Who was this guy? Why had I revealed so much of myself to this stranger?

I took an unconscious step back from him, but he reached out for my arm, put a gentle hand on my wrist.

"It's okay," he said, as if he'd read the sudden uncertainty in my eyes. "I go to a weird place when I'm working. I get lost in my head."

I nodded. I understood that, of course. I reached a hand for the scar on his neck and saw him flinch a little. I paused, looked him in the eye, and kept reaching for it. My finger traced the smooth white line. It felt softer than the rest of his skin, like a delicate gauze. I felt him shudder beneath my touch. He closed his eyes. I put my hand on the thick scar on his shoulder; a rubber ball beneath his flesh. There was just one word in my mind. Pain.

I moved into him and didn't care that he

was covered with sweat. I didn't ask him then how he'd gotten those scars. Partly because I wasn't sure I wanted to know and partly because I could sense he wasn't ready to tell me. Asking seemed invasive, seemed to violate an unspoken agreement that he'd tell me the things I needed to know in time. Is it possible to be wary of someone and trust him, too? He tightened his arms around me and held on to me hard, then released me, started peeling off my clothes, his mouth on my neck.

The harsh white light gave me pause as he stripped me down. Not that I resisted. Not that I wasn't tugging at the button on his jeans and sliding them down his hips with as much desperation as he was undoing buttons and clasps to get to my skin. There was no hiding beneath this light. Every flaw, every imperfection would be revealed. But don't we all crave that as much as we fear it? To show ourselves completely, to be loved anyway. He took me hard and deep on the floor on top of the pile of our clothes, the zipper of my coat digging into my back. It was an earthquake.

We lay there awhile, just quiet, looking at each other. Words seemed cheap, unnecessary. I could hear the faintest hum of street noise, could see his computer glowing blue in a little room off the loft that I guessed was his office. I was starting to get a little cold, even though he was beside me. I looked into his face; the softness, the kindness I'd seen there had returned during our lovemaking and I was glad of it.

"Look," he said, taking my hand. "We've got things to talk about."

I hate it when people say that. It's never good.

"Like what?" I said, laughing a little against my nervousness. "Wait, I know . . . you're a Mormon Fundamentalist and you want to take me as your third spiritual wife."

"Uh, no."

"You work for the CIA and you're taking off on a top-secret mission and you don't know when we'll see each other again?"

"Wrong again."

"You really **are** a cabaret dancer?"

"Seriously, Ridley," he said, propping himself up on an elbow. "About your problem, remember? I told you I knew someone who might be able to help you."

I nodded.

"I was going to tell you as soon as you got here but—"

"My tongue was in your mouth?"

"Right," he said with a light laugh. He reached a hand out and pushed a strand of hair out of my eyes. He'd done that before and I liked the way it felt, as if we were intimates already. I looked away from him. I had almost successfully put the whole mess out of my head, and now I braced myself as the waves of fear and sadness came crashing back. They washed over me and in a second I was soaked with dread.

"Well . . . tell me."

"I'd rather show you. Let's get dressed and head back to my place."

THIRTEEN

THE
NEW JERSEY RECORD
YOUNG MOTHER FOUND SLAIN;
TODDLER MISSING

By Margaria Popick

OCTOBER 27, 1972
—HACKETTSTOWN, NJ

Teresa Elizabeth Stone, 25 years old, was
found dead today in her small apartment in the Oak Groves apartment complex on Jefferson Avenue. Police were
alerted when neighbors reported that her
television had been on at top volume for
almost twenty-four hours. This was not
usual for the young, hardworking single

mother who worked as a receptionist at a Manhattan real estate office to support her 18-month-old daughter, Jessie Amelia Stone. Jessie is missing.

Ms. Stone was found brutally beaten to death on the kitchen floor of her apartment. There were no signs of a forced entry and neighbors say she was in an abusive relationship with her boyfriend, Jessie's father. Police had responded to calls of domestic disputes on several occasions since the beginning of the year. Ms. Stone took out a restraining order against him just last month.

Neighbors describe Ms. Stone as being quiet, hardworking, and a loving mother. Maria Cacciatore, Ms. Stone's neighbor, often took in Jessie free of charge while Ms. Stone worked. "We're devastated. I never thought such a thing could happen," she said. "She loved that little girl like crazy. Like crazy."

Police are looking for Ms. Stone's boyfriend, Christian Luna, whom they believe might have Jessie. He is considered extremely dangerous and police urge anyone who sees him to contact the police immediately.

"How did you find this?" I said, looking at the photocopy in front of me. A picture accompanied the article, the same one as in the clipping I'd been sent in the mail. I felt a mild wave of nausea and my throat was dry.

"My friend, the detective, recognized the typeface on the second article, visited the newspaper archives online, and was able to track it down."

"How is that possible?" I said, interrupting him. I looked at the article in my hand. "It's Times New Roman, indistinguishable from a thousand other papers."

"Hey," he said lightly. "You can't argue with results. It took him a couple of hours, but here it is."

"It just seems too easy," I said, and my voice was doubtful, angry, as if I didn't believe my own eyes.

You may ask yourself here why I was being so belligerent. And it's a good question. After all, hadn't I asked him to do just what he did? But I was mad anyway, felt vaguely violated and defensive. I was mad at him for finding the article so fast; maybe I was hoping he wouldn't be able to turn anything up. I remembered all the listings on LexisNexis, how I hadn't had the energy to search through them. Maybe if I had tried harder, I would have found it, too.

I walked over to his window and looked down at First Avenue, Pete's Spice across the street, the Italian bakery that isn't Veniero's. They were the most familiar sights in all the world to me, but I felt as if I were on another planet, distant and cold. Some thugs with do-rags and sagging denims skulked on a stoop, reminding me of my brother's building. I thought about the girl Ruby I had met, my mind wandering.

"What does it mean?" I asked finally. He had seated himself on the couch, waiting patiently for me to figure out what I was feeling.

"I don't know," he said. "Maybe nothing."

Silence. Then: "There's more."

I turned to look at him, then walked back over to the table and seated myself, wrapping my arms tightly across my waist and leaning forward as if I had severe abdominal pain. I wished I did. I wished I would double over and pass out from a burst appendix right there so that I could avoid this whole thing.

"My friend has a contact over at the Hackettstown Police Department, so he gave a call. The case was never solved. Christian Luna was never found, never questioned, and never charged. The little girl, Jessie, was never found."

"What's his name?" I asked.

"Who?"

"This friend of yours who did this for you."

He hesitated just a millisecond. "Harley. Someone I grew up with. He owes me a few favors. I've helped him out a lot over the years."

"He's a detective? With the police department?"

"No, he's a private detective."

I nodded. Why did I care about that? I don't know. Maybe I was just stalling, trying to find a reason why this friend of Jake's was unqualified to have dug up all of this, trying to cast doubt on its veracity. It didn't work. You can't argue with the black and white in front of your face. Well, you can, but you just look like a jackass.

I looked back over at the papers on the table. The printout of the article stared at me. In the picture, the woman and her child were so washed out they looked like ghosts. The yellowed piece of newsprint that I'd received in the mail lay beside it. Someone had kept that piece of paper for more than thirty years. A few days ago they'd decided to part with it and send it to me. I turned that around in my mind, imagining what would inspire **me** to part with something I had clung to for thirty years. The only possible motivation would be the return of the lost thing represented by the cherished item. For what other reason might we cling to objects, old photographs, tarnished jewelry, yellowed letters? They're charms, little pieces of magic. When we touch them, we regain for a second what time has stolen or worn away.

"Christian Luna was born in the Bronx in 1941," said Jake, looking at some notes he'd written in a small black book. "He went to high school in Yonkers, graduated in 1960, and joined the army. He received an honorable discharge after eighteen months. No further information on that yet. He moved to Hackettstown, New Jersey, in 1962 and worked in various locations as a millwright. Never married. One daughter, Jessie Amelia Stone. He was arrested in 1968 for DUI; did three hundred hours of community service. In 1970 he was taken into custody three times after domestic disturbance calls. He was never charged. In September of 1972, Teresa Stone took out a restraining order against him. But that's it. After her murder, he drops off the face of the earth. Driver's license expired in

1974; it's never been renewed. No voter registration, no employment records, no further
arrests. He doesn't profile as someone smart or
connected enough to change his identity, so
either he left the country—probably Canada
or Mexico, since he doesn't have a passport on
record—or he's dead somewhere and no one
ever found him."

"What does that have to do with anything?" I asked ridiculously, still angry, still
copping an attitude. Jake shrugged with a
patient half-smile, oblivious to or very understanding of my shit mood.

"Look," he said, standing and coming over
to the table. He dragged a chair in front of me
and straddled it, facing me. "Either you want
to do this or you don't. Did you ask me to
look into this for you?"

I nodded, feeling a headache make its debut behind my left eye. He put a hand on
my arm.

"Are you still sure you want to know what
this means?" he said, nodding toward the papers on the table. "Because if you don't, we
can work on protecting you, work on stopping the harassment, as opposed to finding
the root cause. That's your choice, Ridley. This
is your life; it's up to you if you want to risk

turning it upside down. I don't think it's too late to forget this ever happened."

He was calm and level. But there was something glowing in his eyes. He was giving me a last chance to keep my illusions intact, and I think he was hoping for my sake that I would choose denial, even though it wasn't what he wanted. Who was it who said that once the mind glimpses enlightenment, it can never go dark again?

"I want to know what's happening. I do."

"Okay," he said slowly, looking at me hard. I noticed only when he released me that his grip on my arm had grown tense. "So if we're trying to figure out who might have sent you the notes and photograph, we have to look at what we've got. We have this article. We have this name, Christian Luna."

"And we have this number," I said, picking up the note.

More silence, Jake's face unreadable.

"Do you think it's him?" I asked. "Do you think it's Christian Luna doing this?"

Jake shrugged. "Well, at this point, that would be assuming a lot."

"But you think it's possible?"

"He seems like a likely suspect. But there are some big questions."

"Like?"

"Like, for starters, where's he been for the last thirty years? And what happened to Jessie? If Christian Luna killed Teresa Stone, and I'm not saying that he did, wouldn't he know what happened to the little girl? But if he **didn't** kill Teresa Stone and he didn't kidnap Jessie . . . who did?"

"What about this number? Isn't there like a reverse directory or something?"

Jake nodded. "There **is** a reverse directory. I plugged the number in."

He walked over to his computer and jiggled the mouse. The black screen bloomed to life and Jake logged on to a site called netcop.com. He plugged the number into one of the fields. A name and address, along with a map, popped up. **Amelia Mira, 6061½ Broadway, Bronx, New York.**

"Whoever is doing this to you is not a professional," said Jake, "and not computer savvy, or we never would have been able to find this so quickly."

"Wasn't Jessie's middle name Amelia?" I asked.

Jake smiled. "You're pretty quick. Sure you never did this before?"

"Yeah. Ridley Jones, writer by day, PI by

night," I said without levity. I wasn't in the mood for jokes. "Okay. So who is she?"

"I don't know. I haven't been able to come up with any information on her."

I sighed, stood up to walk the length of the room and back again. I looked at Jake and noticed again those hands, big and square, how the bulk of his muscles strained the cuffs of his shirt. Something else was bothering me, too.

"Jake," I said. "I don't understand how you got all this information. How you seem to know so much about this."

"I told you," he said.

"Yeah, but you just seem really **comfortable** with it, like you've done it before."

He smiled. "I always secretly wanted to be a detective. And I know a lot of cops. You hang around those guys enough, it starts to rub off." He gave a shrug and pointed toward his notes. "Besides, this isn't me. My buddy got all the info for you."

Distantly something was jangling, something I didn't want to acknowledge. I'd felt his tenderness, his kindness, I'd trusted him with this secret part of myself, felt safe enough to share my body with him. But there was something about him, even about his apartment, that made him seem transient, as though he could walk away from everything in the room, including me, and never look back. I looked around the apartment for something that grounded him, something that made him seem more real, more permanent. A photograph, an address book, anything that made him attached to the space. But it was bare, void of the detritus that makes a place home.

I remembered him saying, **There are things you need to know about me.** He'd said it last night and I'd quieted him and then we'd fucked each other into oblivion. We fucked away each of our pasts, the present. My body, fully electrified by lust and whatever else, was unconcerned about a future. Today again, I'd let desire wrestle all my questions to the floor.

"Ridley," he said, walking toward me, snapping me back to the moment.

He put his hands on my shoulders and looked into my eyes. I saw it there, the thing about him that made me trust him. He put those arms around me and placed a kiss on the top of my head. And then the scent of him unleashed a chemical reaction in my brain. The Japanese believe in a fifth taste sense called **Umami.** When it is ignited by certain foods, it unleashes intense cravings, causing you to eat long after hunger has been sated. I was experiencing the emotional equivalent of that phenomenon. I didn't ask him what he had meant last night.

"So . . . what now?" I said, moving away from him. I sank into his couch, which was about as comfortable as granite.

"Well, the way I see it, you've got two choices. Call the number and see who answers, see how they play it and decide how to proceed based on that. Or maybe I go up to the Bronx and hang out around this address. See what I can turn up. You give away a lot of power if you call. You let them know that they got to you, that you're scared, curious, whatever. They have the upper hand."

Here a kind of mental paralysis set in. To me it felt like choosing how you wanted to commit suicide. Jump off the Brooklyn Bridge or shoot yourself in the head? Slit your wrists in the tub or take a bottle of sleeping pills? Each method had its pros and cons, but in the end you still wound up dead.

"Why you?" I said after a minute. I was suddenly so exhausted it was an effort to voice the question.

He shrugged. "Why not me?"

"Do you have any experience with this kind of thing?" I asked.

He shook his head. "Do you?"

I lay down on my back and looked at him briefly, then covered my eyes with my forearm. It was my "woe is me" position.

"Just forget it," I said, standing up suddenly. "Just forget the whole thing." I left him sitting there and slammed the door as I left.

FOURTEEN

I know what you're thinking: **What a baby!** Here's this beautiful man who went out of his way to help me, though we barely knew each other, who was willing to go up to the Bronx (the Bronx!) to try to figure out what was happening to me. He **cared** about me; I could **feel** that he cared about me in a very real and rare way. So, naturally, I acted like a brat and stormed out of his apartment. My behavior wouldn't have surprised anyone who knew me—just ask Zack. All I can say is that I was scared and confused and suffered some kind of core meltdown, some kind of flight response. "Get away! Get away!" my brain (or was it my heart?) commanded and I obeyed.

How many people can you claim truly care about you? I mean, not just the people in your life who are fun to hang out with, not just the people who you love and trust. But people who feel **good** when you are happy and successful, feel **bad** when you are hurt or going through a hard time, people who would walk away from their lives for a little while to help you with yours. Not many. I felt that from Jake and I wasn't sure how to handle it. Because there's another side to it, you know. When someone is invested in your well-being, like your parents, for example, you become responsible for them in a way. Anything you do to hurt yourself hurts them. I already felt responsible for too many people that way. You're not really free when people care about you; not if you care about them.

I fumbled at the lock on my door and heard Jake come down the stairs. He sat on one and looked at me through the slats of the banister.

"Hey," he said. There was a smile in his voice that told me he found me amusing. "Take it easy."

I leaned my head against the door and smiled to myself.

"You want to go somewhere with me?" I asked him.

"Sure."

Long before I married New York City, I had a passionate love affair with the place. I don't remember **ever** wanting to live anywhere else. The gleaming buildings, the traffic music, the glamorous Manhattanites—everything about it said **grown-up** to me. I always imagined myself walking its streets, wildly successful and impossibly cool. My uncle Max's apartment was the embodiment of everything I loved about New York, every dream I ever had of the city. The penthouse at the top of the Fifty-seventh Street high-rise that he'd developed. Sleek lines, crisply dressed doormen, marble floors, mirrored elevators, plush carpeted hallways. Naturally, at the time I had no concept of what such a place might cost. I figured **everyone** in Manhattan had a sprawling penthouse with panoramic views of the city.

I pushed through the doorway and was greeted with a solemn nod from Dutch, the doorman. He moved as if to get up to push the elevator button for me, but I lifted a friendly hand, tossed him a smile. He looked over a pair of bifocal lenses, the flat gray eyes of the retired police officer. Cool. Level. Missing nothing.

"Good evening, Miss Jones. You have your key?" He gave a long glance at Jake.

"Yes, Dutch. Thanks," I said, my voice bouncing off the black marble floors, the cavernous ceiling.

"Your father was here earlier," he said, looking back down at a paper laid out before him on the tall desk.

"Was he?"

I wasn't surprised, really. We all came here at different times for our different reasons. We visited Max's apartment like some people visit a grave, just to feel close. He'd asked that his ashes be scattered from the Brooklyn Bridge and we'd done that, all of us feeling that a terrible mistake had been made once all that was left of him floated on the air and then into the water below. It was as if we'd given him back, without keeping anything for ourselves. But it was just a moment. We can't hold on to anyone or anything, you know. We lose everything except that which we carry within us.

Max's lawyer kept reminding my father how much Max's apartment was worth, how much the maintenance alone was costing him. But nearly two years after Max's death, it sat just as he'd left it.

"Sweet digs," said Jake as we entered the door and I punched in the alarm code: 5-6-8-3. It spelled love on a touchtone keypad; it was his code for most everything—everything that I had access to, anyway.

All you could see upon entering was a panoramic view of the city. We were on the forty-fifth floor, facing west from First Avenue. You could see to New Jersey. At night the city was a blanket of stars.

"Where are we?" asked Jake.

"This is my uncle Max's place," I said, flipping on the lights that low-lit the art and illuminated the shelves.

"Why are we here?"

I shrugged. "I'm not sure."

I went into Max's office and Jake trailed behind, looking at the gallery of photos hanging on the walls. Pictures of me, Ace, my mom and dad, my grandparents. I barely noticed them as I moved to his desk, flipped on the halogen light, and opened one of the drawers. It was empty of the files I knew were once there. I flipped open two more drawers and found them empty as well. I spun in the chair and looked at the long line of low oak drawers below towering rows of shelves filled with books and some items from Africa and the Orient that my uncle had collected on his travels, as well as more pictures of us. I could see from where I sat that one of the drawers was open just a hair. I walked over and pulled it open slowly. Empty. One by one, I checked the rest of the drawers and found that they were all empty.

I sunk into a thick brown suede couch. Where were the files?

"What's wrong?" asked Jake, sitting beside me.

"His files are all gone," I said.

He frowned. "Since when?"

I shook my head. I didn't know. In all the times I'd come here before and since he died, I'd never had reason to look through his files. I'd just come to lie on his couch, smell the clothes hanging in his closet, look at all the pictures of us together. Same as my mother and father did. Same as Esme had as well. Rumor was that once upon a time they'd had a white-hot love affair, Esme and Max.

"I finally wised up," she told me. "You can't squeeze blood from a stone. You can try, but you do all the bleeding."

She didn't know I knew she was talking about Max. "I'd have done anything for that man," she'd said. She'd told me this when I asked her if she'd ever been in love with anyone but Zack's father, a lawyer who'd died young from a heart attack when Zack was nine.

"Once," she said. "A lifetime ago."

My mother said that Esme would have married Max. "But your uncle couldn't love anyone that way. Not really. He was too . . ." She paused, searching for the right word. "Damaged," she said finally. "And he was smart enough to know it. Her heart was broken but eventually she met and married Russ instead. They had Zack. It was for the best. Or it would have been, if he hadn't died so young. Tragedy. Poor Esme."

Poor Esme. Poor Zack. Me and my uncle Max . . . the heartbreakers.

"Would your father have taken them?" asked Jake. It took a second before his words made it to my brain; I was deep in thought about Esme and Max.

I looked at him. "The files? Why?"

"The doorman said he was here earlier. Didn't you talk to him this afternoon?"

I thought about this for a second. I'd had that conversation with my father and then he'd come over here and confiscated all of Max's files? No. More likely I'd got him thinking about Max and he just came here to sit and be with his stuff, just to visit. Besides, there were drawers and drawers of files; he'd need boxes and a dolly. I told this to Jake.

"His lawyer probably took everything, then," said Jake.

"Yeah," I said, realizing that was probably true. "Of course."

"Where were you just now?" he asked, dropping an arm around my shoulder.

"I was just thinking about Max. I wish you could have met him."

A flicker of something crossed his face here and then it was gone. I wished I hadn't said it. It gave away too much. But he made it all right a second later.

"Yeah," he said, kissing my forehead. "Me, too." Then: "He must have loved you a lot, Ridley."

I looked at him and smiled. "Why do you say that?"

"Look at this place. It's a shrine to you."

"Not to **me**," I said with a little laugh. "To us, to our family."

"Sure, yeah. There are pictures of all of you. But you're clearly the focus."

"No," I said. My eyes fell on the picture on his desk. It was me at three or four, riding on his shoulders, my arms wrapped around his forehead, my own head thrown back in delight. I stood and walked into the hallway and looked at the gallery of pictures there. I'd walked that hallway so many times, seen the pictures all my life. I'd stopped seeing them, stopped looking. They were beautiful prints, some black and white, some color, all professionally matted and framed in thick gold- or silver-painted wood. Looking at them now, I saw myself at virtually every stage of my life. In the bathtub as a little girl with my mom washing my hair. My first day on a bicycle, at the beach, in the snow, prom, graduation. Certainly, in many of them my family was all around me: Ace and me on Santa's lap, my father and me on the teacups at Disney, all of us at my school play. But Jake was right. I'd never seen it.

You two had a special connection, my father had said. I knew it was true, of course. But I'd just taken it for granted, like so many things about my life. It just **was.**

"No wonder Ace was jealous," I said aloud.

"Was he?" Jake asked, coming up behind me.

"Well," I said with a sigh, looking at the picture of Ace and me going down a pool slide together, his arms around my waist. I remembered that a second after that picture was taken we knocked heads as we splashed into the water. I wailed as Ace pulled me to the edge of the pool. "It's okay, Ridley. I'm sorry," he told me. "Don't cry. They'll make us go inside." A few seconds later, Uncle Max lifted me out of the pool. I made his blue shirt damp with my bathing suit and dripping arms and legs as he carried me inside.

"Don't play so rough with her, champ," he said to my brother, not harshly, not with anger. "She's just a little girl."

I remember looking at Ace hanging on the edge of the pool watching us go. I tried to remember his face. Had he been angry, sad, guilty? Had he been jealous? I couldn't recall.

"We never really talked about it," I answered Jake. "But my father seemed to think so." My head was starting to ache again.

"How jealous do you think he is?" he asked.

"Not jealous enough to do this, if that's what you're getting at," I said, pulling the article from my pocket, unfolding it and looking at the picture yet again. Ghosts of a woman and a little girl stared back at me.

Jake didn't answer me. He ambled toward the door. I sensed that he was uncomfortable in Max's place, wanted to leave. I didn't ask him why. I suppose the apartment was intimidating in its opulence. As an artist, Jake must have known that the Miró on one wall, the Dalí sketch on another, were original pieces. Zack had told me once that he felt like he was hanging out in a museum when we were at Max's place, that a guard might come and ask him to take his feet off the couch.

"But jealous enough maybe to fan the flame, to make you think there was more to this than there is?"

I looked at him. Why did everyone always suspect the worst of Ace? Just because he had an addiction, that didn't make him a psychopath and a liar. Did it? Jake lifted his hands, I guess reacting to whatever he saw on my face.

"Just a question," he said. And it was a valid question. If I weren't so defensive about my brother, maybe from years of defending him to Zack, I would have seen that. But at that moment, it just made me feel like I wanted to distance myself from Jake a little bit. Nobody likes people who speak a truth you're not prepared to examine.

On the way out, I asked Dutch if my father had taken anything with him when he left, if Dutch had helped him out with any boxes. Dutch said no, that my father had just come for a while, then left with nothing.

"Why? Something missing?" he asked with a frown.

No, not really. Just a little girl named Jessie. I smiled and shook my head.

I was quiet on the train and on the walk back to our building, and if Jake minded, he didn't show it.

I'd made a decision. I was being tossed around in this situation like a skiff in a hurricane and I was sick of it. All I had so far was the information other people had given me. The mysterious freak sending me mail, my parents, my brother, even Jake. Everyone was telling me his version of the truth, and all of it was different. The only way to make any sense of what was happening was to find out **for myself** what the truth was. So I decided that it was time to head up to the Bronx. I told Jake. He didn't think it was a good idea and tried to be polite about it.

"It was your idea," I said as we stood at the door to his apartment.

"Yes. It was my idea for **me** to go. Not you. Not we. Me."

"Why is this your problem?" I asked. "Why do you care about this?"

He turned and looked at me, put his hands on my shoulders. I could have melted, really, beneath the intensity I saw on his face.

"I **don't** care about this. I care about **you.** A lot. More than I should this soon, I guess." He paused here, sighed, and looked down at the floor. I saw the color come up in his cheeks. "But I can't let you do something I think is dangerous without at least speaking my mind. For Christ's sake, Ridley, someone's watching you. Have you forgotten that? He's been at the pizzeria, in the building."

"Right. So I'm not even safe here in my home. So what difference does it make if I go to the Bronx or not? You can come with me."

Does my logic sound a bit shaky? I guess it was. But I didn't have a lot of experience with this sort of thing. I was just consumed all of a sudden with a desire to know what was happening to me, to find out for myself, not to be told or lied to or manipulated by people with an agenda that might or might not conflict with the truth. I told him this much.

"Ridley, be reasonable."

This made me angry. I didn't like being talked to like a kid. **Be reasonable?** Like just because I disagreed with him that made him reasonable and me unreasonable? How typical.

"No, fuck you. Don't patronize me," I said. Temper, temper.

He sighed. "Okay."

He walked into his apartment and I followed, closing the door behind me. He took off his leather jacket and flung it on the couch. I tried not to look at how the black shirt he wore clung to every ripped muscle on his chest. He sat down.

"You're on your own, then," he said, and looked at me. "I go alone or I don't go at all."

He was bluffing.

"That's it? What's the point of that?"

"I won't willingly put you in a situation that I think might be dangerous for you. If you want to put yourself in harm's way, fine. But I won't be a part of it."

Isn't it just like a man to pretend that trying to **control** you is the same as trying to **protect** you?

His jaw tightened and I could see a muscle throbbing there. He **was** bluffing. I was sure of it. I didn't really want to go it alone, by the way.

"Great. Good. See you later." **I** was definitely bluffing.

But he didn't move, just kept those eyes on me as if expecting me to come to my senses.

So I left the apartment and slammed the door. All the way down the stairs I expected him to come after me but he didn't. Then I was on the street again. I took a left onto Fourteenth Street and caught a bus to the West Side. I took the 1/9 to 242nd Street in the Bronx, out of sheer stubbornness. All the way up there, a long train ride, for nearly an hour I wondered what the hell I was going to do when I got there.

The New York City subway system is pretty mythic, don't you agree? Whether you've ridden it or not, you probably have a picture in your head of what it's like. And it's probably not a pretty picture. When you close your eyes, you probably see these old red cars that rattle and shake their way beneath the streets of Manhattan. In your mind's eye, they're covered with graffiti, lights flickering and going dark around corners. In your imagination, they are likely the habitat for every rapist, mugger, murderer, gang member, and serial killer in the five boroughs. Old New Yorkers, the people I know who grew up on these trains, have told me that once, in the not-too-distant past, that description wasn't too far off. But in my New York, the subway is just another way to get around, probably the fastest way in most cases. The new cars are graffiti resistant and regularly maintained. The most offensive thing about them is the unfortunate beige-and-orange color scheme that seems to dominate. Between the homeless people, the rush-hour crushes, the odd, often inexplicable and interminable delays, and the fact that the stations themselves are not air-conditioned (making them feel like the first layer of hell in the summer), the subways are probably one of the most unpleasant places on the planet. But I've never felt unsafe on the trains.

You can usually count on people all around you, no matter what time it is, but by the time the local 1/9 train passed Ninety-sixth Street and was crawling up to the Bronx, there were only a few people in my car. A young kid in a private-school uniform carrying a bulging backpack listened to a Walkman, rocking to a beat that I could just hear over the rumble of the train. An old woman in a navy wool coat and flowered skirt read a romance novel. A bald (as in shaved, not as in losing) guy in a leather jacket and faded jeans dozed, his head back, mouth agape. By 116th Street I was nodding a bit myself, not sleeping but slipping into a reverie, thoughts of my uncle Max circling my consciousness.

For all his joviality, my uncle Max was a powerful man in New York City, but it wasn't the kind of important that makes much of an impression on you as a kid. When you're twelve it's not a big deal that your uncle plays golf with senators and congressmen or that you see his picture in magazines like **Forbes** rubbing elbows with Donald Trump and Arthur Zeckendorf. Maybe if he'd been hanging out backstage with Bono or Simon LeBon, I might have paid more attention. But real-estate development isn't exactly sexy, if you know what I mean.

Later on, after my first foundation ball, I started to get the idea of the kind of influence my uncle had, the kind of people he knew. He was a major campaign contributor to people like Al D'Amato, George Pataki, and Rudolph Giuliani. The guy was connected in a serious way. He had to be in his business. You had to have a way to part the sea of red tape, a way to get around zoning laws—and if not, a way to see that those zoning laws get changed. There were whispers, too, of other, shadier connections. And if you think about it, as a real-estate developer on the East Coast, there was no way he could do business without associating with the people who controlled the construction industry. The fact that my uncle's business interests sometimes coincided with the business interests of less-than-reputable characters had always stayed in the periphery of my mind. I mean, my uncle's lawyer was Alexander Harriman, a lawyer known for his notorious client list. But I'd never devoted any serious thought to it. Until now.

I always think of him just as **my** uncle Max, never as the man that he was separate from our family. A powerful businessman, rich, influential, lonely, and the only women around him seemed, I don't know, transient, hollow in their affections, going through the motions. Were they call girls? I wondered now. Or were they just gold diggers, women who spent time with him for the gifts he could buy, the places he could take them, the other people he knew and had influence over? **Uncle Max,** I said in case he could hear me, **I'm sorry, but maybe I never knew you.** It's funny how the titans in our lives, the people who have the most influence over our childhoods, over the people we become, never seem like **people,** flawed and separate from us. They're like archetypes, The Mother, The Father, The Good Uncle, existing only as characters in the movie of our lives. When other facets of their personalities come clear and other elements of their lives uncovered, it's shocking, as if they suddenly peeled their face off and revealed another. Does it seem like that to you? Well, maybe it's just me.

The train jerked and rocked and I opened my eyes to find that I was alone in the car with the sleeping man wearing a leather jacket and faded denims. Just one more stop, I knew, and the train would move from the underground tunnel to the elevated tracks. I closed my eyes again. Then I thought, Wasn't that guy all the way on the other end of the car before? The thought made my belly hollow out and my throat go dry. I opened my eyes just a crack and saw that the man was now wide awake and staring at me with a strange half-smile. My breathing came deeper and I tried to keep my chest from heaving. I noticed a long case on the ground beneath his legs. It looked like it might hold some kind of instrument. I felt a little relieved at the sight of it. I've always had this theory that you have nothing to fear from people who have something to carry. The murderer, mugger, rapist, even your random serial killer would not carry anything on his nefarious errands. I mean, think about it, he needs both his hands free. Even a backpack would slow him down.

But that feeling of relief passed as I noticed him inching closer to me. The train flooded suddenly with lamplight as we moved above-ground. I cleared my throat and sat up, opened my eyes. He immediately dropped his head to his shoulder and pretended to be sleeping again.

I stared at him, not sure what to do. My legs felt as if they were filled with sand and my heart was doing step aerobics in my chest. But I forced myself to get up and walk to the front of the car, where I heaved the door open and moved between the cars to the next one. Then I turned around and through the windows looked back the way I'd come. The man sat there looking at me, with that same half-smile, but his eyes seemed dark with menace. I stood staring at him, convinced that as long as my eyes were open, he wouldn't come any closer. I thought about Zelda, about what she had said—God, was it only yesterday?—about someone looking for me, someone who was **no good.** Was this the man she'd seen? Was he following me? I couldn't be sure. After all, there's no shortage of staring freaks and weirdos in this city.

The train stopped at the next station and we were still in a staring contest. But when the doors opened, he got up suddenly, grabbed his case, and left the train. If he came into my car, I was ready to flee through the door to the platform, and move toward the front car, where I knew I would find the conductor. I stood for what seemed like an hour, waiting for him to come in after me. I was all alone, no one in any of the cars I could see from where I was standing and no one on the platform. But then the tone sounded and the conductor said over the intercom, "Stand clear the closing doors." The doors closed. Then jerked open again.

"Hands and bags away from the door," the conductor said over the PA system, sounding annoyed.

I moved to look out onto the platform, but I didn't see the man standing there or walking away. I went back to the window and looked through the train into the other cars but didn't see him there, either. Where is he? I wondered, thinking I should be able to see him on the platform if he'd exited. By now I had so much adrenaline pumping through me that my hands were shaking. Again the tone sounded and the doors closed, then pulled apart again at the last second. I started to move through the train toward the conductor's car in the front. It was so quiet, I could hear only the sound of the heavy doors pushing open and then slamming hard behind me. I kept looking behind me, each time expecting to see the man in pursuit.

"Stand clear the closing doors, asshole," the conductor said loudly. I stopped and looked out the window of the car I was in. Then I saw him, standing on the platform as if he'd moved from behind one of the pillars. The doors finally closed and the train moved slowly away from the station. My body flooded with relief and I sank onto one of the benches, leaned my head back.

"I'm getting paranoid," I said aloud to no one.

Then I opened my eyes to see that he stood staring at me as the train moved past him, one hand raised in farewell, that same smile plastered on his face. I didn't wave back.

I got off at the last stop, still a bit shaken, and walked out onto the landing. Though it was dark, I could see in the glow of the street lamps that Van Cortlandt Park was in high color, its acres of trees painted gold and orange, deep red against the still-green grass of the parade ground to my right. Some kids played handball in the courts next to the staircase as I made my descent to the sidewalk, and their cheers and cries lifted into the air. Riverdale is one of the last nice areas in the Bronx, and that evening it felt safe and idyllic.

At the bottom of the stairs, a black '69 Firebird idled in the street. The engine hummed and rumbled, communicating power like a dog baring its teeth. Jake sat at the wheel. I tried not to smile in relief, kept my eyes ahead and walked past him.

"Hey," he called as I passed by. "I thought you were bluffing."

He trailed me with his car, moving slowly up Broadway, causing the drivers behind him to lean on their horns before passing him by, hurling obscenities.

"Come on, Ridley," he said finally after a few blocks of this. "You win."

That was all I needed to hear. I got into the passenger side and he sped off. The car was cherry inside, leather polished and unblemished, smelling of Armor All. An Alpine compact disc changer was mounted beneath the dash; the knobs on the dash and the gearshift were all new, brushed chrome. It was exactly the kind of car I would have envisioned for him. It was tough, but there was something careful about it, too.

I noticed that we passed the address he found for Amelia Mira by a block before he did a U-turn and got closer so that we could see the row house from the car. After pulling under the large, old branches of some trees beside the park, he handed me a worn blue baseball cap and some Oakley sunglasses, both too big for me, and made me put them on.

"You don't want anyone to recognize you," he said. "That would sort of blow the whole point of our being up here."

I still hadn't said anything and I could tell it was starting to get to him. We sat like that for a few minutes. Finally he said, "Christ. Are you always this stubborn?"

"Yes," I answered. "I really am."

I looked at him then and smiled. He reached for my hand and I took it in mine.

"Ridley, I really didn't think you'd come up here by yourself. I never would have let you walk out if I had thought that."

"I'm sorry," I said. And I meant it because

now that I was looking at him, I could see that I had scared him. The relief on his face was clear, and in his eyes I could read his concern. I felt bad for acting like a brat. Again.

"You know what, Jake? I'm just feeling **manipulated.** Everyone's got a different version of what's going on and I don't know what to believe. I can't do this alone, but I need to see things for **myself.** Do you get that?"

He nodded his understanding. "I get it." I saw something pass across his face, but it was gone before I could put a name to it.

"So what do we do now?" I asked.

"We sit and watch," he said, looking at the scene around us. It was a cold but gorgeous autumn evening, kids still playing soccer in the park, people jogging, walking dogs. It seemed like a strange night for a stakeout, in the middle of all these people living their quiet, happy lives. It should have been raining, with an occasional rumble of thunder and flash of lightning. The park should have been full of thugs, gangs ready to rumble.

"Watch for what?"

"Hopefully," he said with a shrug, "we'll know it when we see it."

I thought about this and what it could mean—hours of just sitting in the car. Sometimes getting your own way is not as gratifying as it should be. He was smiling at me as if he could read my thoughts. My stomach growled and I had to pee.

After making Jake take me to the Burger King we'd passed earlier so that I could get a Whopper and relieve my aching bladder, we parked across the street from 6061½ and watched as people came and went. Dark houses came to life, interior lights began to glow. Some of the houses went dark again as we waited. But 6061½ remained black and still among them.

We didn't talk much, but the silence between us was comfortable. Every half hour or so, Jake would turn on the car for a while to let the heat run and take some of the chill out of the air. I was a little scared and a little uncomfortable, not sure what we were looking for and not sure what we would do if and when we found it. But I wasn't going to give him the satisfaction of complaining aloud. After a couple of hours, I climbed into the backseat and lay on my belly, peering out the side window, just for a change of position. I could just see the top of Jake's head.

"What did you mean, Jake? When you said there were things I needed to know about you."

He didn't answer right away and I wondered if he'd fallen asleep.

"I don't know where to start," he said finally.

I realized that all the talking we'd done in the last few days, ninety percent of it had been about me. I knew a little bit about his art. About where he'd lived before he moved to the East Village. And that was pretty much it. I had the need to look into his face, but something in the air, something about the way he didn't turn around to look at me when he responded, told me that he'd prefer that I didn't. I thought about the scars on his body, and I felt something stutter inside me. This man, for as intimate as we'd become, was still a stranger to me. Somehow I kept forgetting that. I felt as though I knew him in a different way than I'd ever known anyone, that my knowledge of him went beyond his history and straight to the heart of him.

I sat up and snaked my arms over the seat, wrapping them around his neck and putting my face to his. I could just see the outline of him, feel the stubble on his jaw, smell the scent of his skin mingling with the polished leather of the seat. He raised his hands and held on to my forearms.

"Just start at the beginning," I said softly into his ear. "Tell me everything."

"I really wish I could."

There was something dark in his voice, something almost angry. I didn't have a chance to ask him what he meant by that because we both saw the figure of a man making his way up the sidewalk. We'd seen a lot of people tonight, but somehow both of us knew that this was the man we'd been waiting for.

We watched him move quickly, shoulders hunched, a baseball cap pulled down, hiding his face. He had his hands in the pockets of a thin black jacket, which couldn't have been enough to protect him from the cold. There was nothing about him that would cause any-one to look twice: average height, about five-ten; average size, maybe 185. But we both followed him with our eyes, forgetting our conversation as he turned and jogged up the flight of stairs that led to 6061½ Broadway.

We waited another ten minutes in a loaded silence. The house stayed dark.

"Is that him? Is that the man who sent me

the letter?" I'd imagined him bigger, more menacing, this person who'd moved through my life like a wrecking ball.

"It could be."

"What do we do now?" I asked.

"You stay here, watch the front door. I'm going to go take a look around back."

Before I could answer, he slipped quietly from the car and walked up the street away from the house. I saw him in the rearview mirror cross Broadway and then approach the house from the opposite direction, then disappear into an alley. My heart was beating so fast I thought I might be having a panic attack. I waited with nothing but the sound of my own breathing for what seemed like an hour but might have been ten minutes. I didn't have a watch, so I had no way of knowing. Finally I just couldn't take it anymore, so I slipped from the car myself and followed the path Jake had taken.

The dark silence of the park yawned to my right and unlike earlier there was no one around. The lamplights cast an orange glow as I crossed the street. But the west side had no street lamps. Between the convenience store and the first row house was an area of trees. It was a spooky little stretch, the ground slick with wet leaves. Darkness and silence leaked out of the woods like an odor.

I came to the alleyway where Jake had disappeared and peered into its narrow darkness. A light glowed at the end and I made my way toward it, past reeking garbage cans and menacing shadowy spaces where anyone or anything could be hiding, waiting.

I knocked into one of the garbage cans hard with my knee and the metal lid went clanging to the ground. Somewhere close a dog started barking, startling a little burst of adrenaline into my blood. I ran the rest of the way through the alley, which let out into— take a guess—another alleyway that ran along the back of the row houses.

Some of the houses had lights lit in the back, and up above me I could see the glow of interior lamps and the blue flicker of television screens through the windows. I could hear the lightest strains of Pink Floyd's "Money." Someone was cooking pot roast or something meaty, the scent making my stomach grumble (yes, again). It was still dark back here, but at least if I screamed someone might hear me.

I was pretty sure the dark house in the

middle was 6061½. But I didn't see Jake. I managed to continue my way through with a little more stealth and without banging into anything else. I saw a narrow metal staircase that led up to a landing that ran the length of the back of the house. From one of the back windows I thought I caught the movement of light. I climbed the staircase and peered in the window.

He was sitting there on the floor, the man from the street, beside one of those battery-operated lanterns that you can get at Kmart. Leaning against the wall with his legs outstretched and crossed at the ankle, he'd taken off his baseball cap but left his jacket on. I couldn't see his face clearly, couldn't tell for sure if it was the man in the photograph. The light was dim and he was washed in shadows. Beside him sat an old green rotary phone.

He ate slowly from a can of Chef Boyardee ravioli with a plastic fork. Looking intently at the can, he seemed to hold each bite of food in his mouth for a long time before swallowing. I could see the outline of his mouth, full lips pulled down hard at the corners. Sadness, anger, disgust . . . it was hard to tell. But he struck me as the very image of loneliness. Whoever this was, however it was that our lives had come to intersect in this strange way, his loneliness was a contagion and I felt it fill me. Tears welled in my eyes. I don't know why. I had peered into this window of desolation and somehow in doing that I had let what I'd seen into my own heart.

I suddenly felt warm arms around me and a hand over my mouth. I didn't struggle because I knew it was Jake somehow, maybe by his scent.

"What are you doing? Are you crazy?" he hissed into my ear.

He released me and took me by the hand. Together we left and went back to the car.

"Why did we do this?" I said when we were back in the Firebird.

"Because I wanted to see what we were dealing with."

"And what are we dealing with?"

"From what I can see? One lone guy sitting by a phone in an empty house with no electricity."

"So what does that mean?"

"It means that whatever threat he might pose, I can handle it."

My expression must have been blank with my lack of understanding.

"Look," he said patiently, putting a hand

on my shoulder. "You asked me to help you find out what's going on, right? I got some information, found out some background, figured out the address for that telephone number. Before you called, I wanted to know what we were walking into, who exactly we were calling."

"And who are we calling?"

"My bet? That guy is Christian Luna. What he wants, why he thinks you're his daughter, where he's been all these years? I don't think we can find that out without talking to him. So that's the next logical step."

"Call?"

He handed me a cellular phone from his pocket and the telephone number.

"Call."

I paused with the phone in my hand.

"Only if you want to, Ridley. Otherwise, I bust in there, scare the shit out of the guy, and he goes away. I guarantee you never hear from him again. The guy's on the run. He's scared and he's hiding from something or someone, probably the police. He'll slink right back under whatever rock he came out from. And you pretend none of this ever happened."

But it was too late for that now and we both knew it. It took a few minutes of us sit-

ting there in the dark before I turned the
phone on and punched in the number. My
hands were shaking and I felt sweat on my
brow, though it was so cold in the car I could
see my own breath.

He picked up the phone on the first ring.
His voice was deep and had a slight accent I
couldn't make out.

He said, "Jessie?"

I could picture him there on the floor. I
heard the naked mixture of a deep sadness
mitigated by a tentative hope.

"This is Ridley," I said, my voice sounding
a little wobbly even to my own ears. "I'm
Ridley." I felt the need to assert that, at least.
To hold on to that one thing that helped to
claim my life as my own.

"Ridley," he repeated. "Of course. Ridley."

"I'd like to meet you."

"Yes," he said, and it sounded like a plea.

**The benches at the entrance to Van Cort-
landt Park in an hour,** Jake had scribbled onto
a piece of paper. I told him this and he paused.
I wondered if he'd be suspicious of the nearness
to his location, but he agreed after a second.

"You'll come alone?" he asked. And I
agreed, though I was not comfortable lying,
even to this stranger who was ruining my life.

"What's your name?" I asked him.

"I'm your father," he said after another pause.

"What's your name?" I repeated.

"I'll see you in an hour," he said, and hung up.

I ended the call and handed the phone back to Jake.

"Did he tell you his name?"

"No."

Jake shifted in his seat. "I guess I wouldn't, either."

I looked at him, puzzled.

"If I were a fugitive? I told you my name, you could call the police and have a hundred squad cars waiting for me. There's no statute of limitations on murder."

I shrugged. "Then why risk it at all?"

"You'll have to ask him."

FIFTEEN

We waited until he left the row house and watched as he walked toward the park entrance. Jake said he wanted to see him leave to make sure he was in this alone. I wasn't sure who else he thought might be involved but I didn't ask. Jake seemed oddly comfortable with the scenario of waiting and observing, plotting action, making sure things were safe—the whole thing. To me, the situation was surreal, strange enough for me to wonder a few times whether I was dreaming. A couple of times I thought I might actually wake up.

After a few minutes had passed, we trailed behind him in the Firebird. He was hunched again but walking fast. He threw a glance over his shoulder a couple of times, but I don't think he was looking at us.

"He seems so lonely. Lonely and sad," I said.

After a strangely long pause, Jake said, "You can't tell that by looking at him. You only see what he wants you to see."

I thought this was a very odd thing to say and I turned to see Jake's face. But he was totally focused on the dark form in front of us, his eyes trained on the man like a preying owl on a mouse far below.

"You can tell a lot about how someone holds himself when he thinks no one's looking," I said. "I saw him. I saw the sadness."

"I don't believe that. I think we project what we're feeling on the people we see. If you're dishonest, you see dishonesty in people. If you're good, you see only good things when you look at someone's face. Physical cues might tell you if someone's lying or if someone's nervous, but I don't think you can read much about a person, about who they are, by just looking at them."

I considered this for a moment. "So are you saying you think I'm sad and lonely?"

Another pause. The darkness was like a physical substance between us, keeping me from connecting with his eyes.

"Aren't you?"

Denial rose in my throat, indignation pulled my shoulders back. But before I spoke

I realized he was right. That was exactly how I felt. It was how I'd felt from the second I got that envelope in the mail. And maybe on some deep, subconscious level even before that, if I was really honest with myself. I didn't say anything and felt a kind of numbness wash over me as we got closer to the park entrance. Jake reached through the darkness and took my hand and squeezed it hard. I squeezed back and wished he'd never let go.

He drove past the entrance, did another U-turn, and parked the Firebird. We both got out. This time I got a good look at the car. It really **was** mint; an extremely tough, hot car with a shiny paint job. Not exactly inconspicuous.

"You like it?" he said when he saw me looking at the car. I smiled.

"You know what they say about guys who feel compelled to drive a muscle car like this?"

"What's that?" he said, moving into me.

"Overcompensation."

"Well," he said, pulling me close. "You know better than that."

I felt heat rise to my cheeks. "I guess I do."

He placed his lips to mine and kissed me, long and soft, lighting me up inside. He pulled back and placed a hand on my face. His expression had gone from playful to serious.

"It's going to be okay," he said.

"Yeah," I said, nodding an assurance that I didn't feel. "I know."

"You don't," he said softly. "But I do. Let's go."

Jake and I walked into the park about two blocks from where I'd told Christian Luna— or whoever he was—to meet me. Jake hung back in the trees, about a hundred feet away, as I walked up to the path where the man sat on a bench. He turned, startled, when he heard my footsteps on the asphalt, then stood. I stopped walking and he came a little closer.

"Don't come any closer," I said when he was about five feet from me. I was afraid; I wanted him to keep his distance.

He was older and seemed smaller than I would have imagined, but there was no mistaking that he was the man in the picture. It was the dark intensity of his eyes, the heavy brows, the fullness of his lips. We stared at each other, as though we were separated by a sheet of glass and could only see our own reflections. For a moment, I thought I saw something in him that I had never seen in anyone else. The shadow of my own features. I'm not sure it's anything that I could put my finger on, exactly. Something around the eyes, maybe something in the shape of his jaw. I thought, Maybe it's my imagination. Maybe I'm seeing only what I want to see . . . or what I fear the most. Maybe it's the drama of the moment.

"Jessie," he said. Relief, joy, and an intense grief mingled in his tone. He took a step closer and I took one back. He raised his arms slightly, as though he thought he would embrace me. But I wrapped my arms around myself tightly, moved back even farther. I hated him suddenly. Hated him for looking like me.

"Did you kill her?" I said. My voice was an open hand, hard and unyielding, and he jerked as though he'd been slapped.

"What?" he said softly, almost a whisper.

"Teresa Elizabeth Stone. Did you kill her?"

"Your mother," he said, and sat down on the bench as if he'd lost his strength to stand. "No." He dropped his head into his hands and began to sob. It was embarrassing, really, in its intensity, in the depth of its misery. I sat on the bench next to his and waited until he'd stopped crying. I couldn't look at him and I couldn't bring myself to comfort him, but the hatred I'd briefly felt drained away. I leaned back and looked up at the few stars I could see twinkling in the sky. I placed my cold fingers in the pockets of my jacket.

"Are you Christian Luna?" I asked when his sobbing had stopped.

"How do you know all of this?" he asked.

"That's not important," I answered.

Does it sound like I was cold? I was. Hard. Cold. Colder than liquid nitrogen. I have come to regret this. He might have deserved more compassion from me, but I just couldn't afford it at that moment. I was wrecked inside. His face had done it.

"Look," I said after more silence where he seemed to be wrestling with what to say. "What do you want from me?"

I could see disappointment and disbelief in his eyes. Whatever he had imagined of this moment, I was pretty sure he wasn't getting it. And in the state I was in, I took a small, dark victory in depriving him of his fantasy reunion.

"What do I **want**? You're my daughter," he said, sounding incredulous. "My Jessie." His voice and his eyes were pleading with me, but he would have had more luck moving the Statue of Liberty.

"You don't know that really," I said, stubborn, my arms folded across my chest like a judge. Judgment is such a useful shield, isn't it? We can hide behind it, rise above others on its crest, keep ourselves safe and separate.

He laughed then, just a little. "Look at me, Jessie. You see it, don't you?"

I didn't answer. He moved over to my bench and I turned to look at him. I didn't move away from him this time and he didn't reach out to try to touch me.

"If I'm Jessie, then what happened to Teresa Stone?" I said. "If you didn't kill her, who did?"

He sighed. "I've been asking myself that question every day for thirty years." More silence where he looked at me and I looked at anything else. A car sped past, subwoofers booming a dance beat into the cold night.

"I was a bad father," he said. "And I treated your mother badly. But I didn't kill anyone." The youthful indignation and barely repressed rage I heard in his voice caused me to turn and examine his face. He was in his late fifties, maybe early sixties. His skin was brownish, sun damaged, marred with deep lines. He had the worn look of a hard life—bad diet, bad choices, bad outcomes. He seemed to sag beneath the weight of it all but with a kind of determination to shoulder the load regardless. In Christian Luna I had expected to find a villain, someone malicious and menacing, someone powerful with the intent and ability to hurt me. But all I saw was someone tired, someone close to defeat without the sense to cut his losses and move on.

"I **tried** in my way to do right, you know?" he said with that same hopeless laugh. "But I was young. **So** fucked up. I never had a father, so I didn't know how to be a man." He shook his head, remembering, and looked off into the darkness of the park.

It was an interesting admission and it led me to look at him more closely, beyond his physical features. I saw a man who'd lived with regret. Who'd learned his lessons but only after it was too late. It must be the ultimate punishment, don't you think, to finally gain wisdom, only to realize that the consequences of your actions are irrevocable?

"I met Teresa at work; she was a secretary at a real-estate office. I was the building handyman, a millwright with the union. We both lived in Jersey, commuted on the train to and from the city. That's where we first started to talk. I could tell the first second I saw her that she was a good girl. Sweet. Pretty. We went out a few times. I told her I loved her—but I didn't mean it."

I tried to imagine them, based on the picture I'd seen. Imagine what she would have looked like laughing, how she dressed. Maybe she was in love with him, thought he really loved her, too. I'm a writer and I wanted him to tell me the story the way I would have. But I didn't think he had it in him.

"After a few dates, she let me sleep with her a couple of times. Then I lost interest. Stopped calling. You know how it goes."

You know how it goes. I guess I do; I guess most of us have been there at one point or another. You trust someone, you share your body with that person. You think they want to share your life, that physical intimacy is just the beginning. But for the other person, the ultimate goal has been reached and the game is over. Did she cry for him? Was she lonely and hating herself when he'd gone? Did she wish she'd never met him?

He sat silent for a second, I guess waiting for some kind of verbal encouragement, but I didn't say anything. I didn't want anything to be easy for him, not even the telling of this story. I don't know why I felt so selfish and mean, but I did.

"She stopped me one night when I was leaving my shift. It was late, after hours. I hadn't seen her at work in a while. I knew when I saw her that she'd come to the city and waited in the dark just to talk to me. She told me she was pregnant."

I tried again to imagine the scene. Maybe it was cold, a light drizzle in the air, a half-moon glowing behind clouds. Was she afraid, crying?

"Were you kind to her?" I asked hopefully.

"No," he said, lowering his head and sticking his hands in his pockets. "I wasn't."

"Was she scared?"

He shook his head slowly. "She was strong when she told me. I asked her, I'm ashamed to say, how she knew it was mine. She told me she hadn't been with anyone else. I believed her but I pretended I didn't." He was silent and stared at me until I was forced to look at him. The shame was so naked on his face that I looked away again in embarrassment.

"I suggested that—" he started.

"That she have an abortion?" I finished for him, forcing myself to meet his eyes again. It sounded ugly but he nodded.

"She refused. And then she said something that I never forgot. She said, 'We don't need anything from you. I'm just giving you a chance to be a father, to have that joy in your life.'"

He sighed again here, his eyes starting to shine. "Even though I was a shit, even though I'd mistreated her, she wanted me to have the opportunity to know you. I didn't get it. You know? It was a concept that was beyond me then. But even so, I offered to marry her. She turned me down."

"No kidding? After a romantic moment like that?"

He issued a kind of grunt. "Yeah. I was a real prize."

"You must have been around some. There's that picture. The domestic abuse calls. The restraining order."

"What, did you hire a private investigator?"

I didn't answer him. He nodded and looked around him.

"I didn't call the police," I said. "You don't have anything to worry about."

He smiled at me then, but there was something odd about it. Like the way you'd smile at someone who had so little knowledge that it was pointless to try to explain anything. I didn't pay much attention to it then, but I'd remember that look later.

"I was in and out. I gave money when I could. But whenever I showed up to see you, there'd be an argument. I'd go to the apartment, start acting like an asshole. She'd ask me to leave. I'd start yelling. The cops would come and take me away. I don't know, I was, like, all messed up about you. I **loved** you, shit. I couldn't believe how beautiful you were, how the sight of your face lit up my heart. But the responsibility scared me . . . I was a coward. I mean . . ."

He paused, shaking his head as if at the stupidity of someone else. It must have seemed like another life to him, so many years had passed. And maybe he **was** a different man now. He didn't **seem** like the kind of person he described, someone so afraid, so inadequate that he could treat the mother of his child like that.

"Then one day she left you with me. It was an emergency; she had to work and the neighbor who usually watched you was sick. So I came to the apartment and stayed with you—

you were little, not even two. I wasn't paying attention to you, and when I wasn't looking, you pulled a glass of beer off the counter and it shattered all around you. I ran over to you and jerked you by the arm. I was mad, yeah, but I was also trying to get you away from the glass so you didn't cut yourself.

"You started screaming and I couldn't get you to stop. I was scared, didn't know what to do. So I shut you in your room. The neighbor called a couple of times, left a message on the machine, 'What's wrong with Jessie? I never heard her cry like that.'"

He started to cry at the memory. Silently, though, not sobbing like before. "You were still screaming when Teresa came home an hour later. The neighbor called her at work and she rushed home. She could tell right away something was wrong with your arm. She rushed you to the clinic and it turned out I'd broken your arm. She took out the restraining order then. I wasn't allowed to see you anymore."

The night seemed to get colder. He wiped his eyes with the sleeve of his jacket. At this point I managed some compassion for him, even though, according to what he'd said, if it had been up to him, I wouldn't be alive today. He'd abused Jessie as a child, was now ruining my life as an adult. I still wasn't ready to admit we were one and the same, Jessie and I. Still, I did feel some pity for him as he continued.

"A couple weeks later I got drunk and went to the apartment. I was gonna bang on the door until she opened it and let me see you, see that you were okay. I got there, made some noise, but she didn't let me in. Told me through the door that she called the police and they were on their way. I heard the sirens and took off. I drank some more and then went back a few hours later. But this time the door was open."

He was breathing heavily now, tears still falling from his eyes as if there was no end to them, as if he'd been saving them up all these years.

"It was dark in the apartment and I knew something wasn't right. I saw just her one sneaker lying on the floor, lying in a pool of blood. It looked black in the dark, the blood. So thick, almost fake. I flipped on the light and saw her there on the floor. Her eyes were open, blood on her mouth, her neck twisted in a really bad way. The way she stared at me, like it was my fault . . . It **was** my fault; if I'd been a better man, she'd be alive. Maybe we'd be a family."

He stopped again, his breathing ragged. He covered his face with his hands and spoke through his fingers.

"I looked for you, but you were gone. And so I ran. That night I took money I had saved and kept under my bed. I hopped a Greyhound to El Paso and went to Ciudad Juárez in Mexico. I got a flight from there to Puerto Rico. I'd never been, but that's where my grandparents were from and I still had a second cousin there. I stayed on; been working in his garage as a mechanic all these years."

I shook my head. The story was just simple enough and just complicated enough to be the truth. But what was I supposed to do with it?

"So what happened, Mr. Luna? What made you think of me? What made you come back here?"

"I think of you every day," he said, reaching out his hand to me. I moved away from him. "Every day. You don't believe that, right? But it's true."

He had turned those imploring eyes on me

again, but I couldn't give him a touch or a look of compassion. I just couldn't.

"Okay," I said. "So why did you come back now?"

"I saw you on CNN," he said, a wide smile suddenly lighting his face at the memory. "I saw your picture when you saved that kid in the street. Your beautiful face . . . I knew it right away. So much like your mother, **so much** like her, I thought I was seeing a ghost. All these years, I didn't know if you were alive or dead. And then I **saw** you. It was like the answer to every prayer I'd ever had. I had to come and find you, see you alive and healthy."

I didn't know what to say. A cool numbness had washed over me. He was a stranger to me. I was a stranger to myself. What could we possibly have to offer each other? What good could come of this?

"Whose house are you staying in?" I asked. "Who's Amelia Mira?"

He looked at me strangely. I guess it was a weird question, considering everything else I could be asking him. But I wanted to know. Jessie had been given her name and I wanted to know who she was.

"It belonged to my mother, your grandmother. She died last year, left it to me in her will. The city will take it soon, I guess. I can't afford the taxes."

"She knew where you were?"

He nodded.

Jessie Amelia Stone, given the name of a grandmother she never knew by a father who had wanted to have her aborted, then abused her and possibly killed her mother. Poor Jessie, I thought, and realized I was crying.

He did something awful then. He slid off the bench and went on his knees before me, took my hands in his. I have never felt so ashamed or awkward.

"Mr. Luna, please . . ." I bent down and took him by the forearm, tried to get him to stand up.

"Jessie, I don't want anything from you. I just wanted you to know me. I wanted to see you in person."

"Please," I said again but stopped, not sure how to go on. He had so much **feeling** for me; I could see he was sincere, that he really believed I was his Jessie. I just wasn't sure **I** believed it.

"I just don't get it, Mr. Luna," I said, standing and walking away from him, leaving him kneeling on the ground. "Why did you run? Why didn't you look for Jessie?"

He raised his hands in a gesture of surrender. "I wouldn't have had a chance. All those arrests, the restraining order . . . who would have believed that I didn't kill her?"

I sighed and shook my head again.

"You don't believe me, do you?" he said quietly.

"I don't know what to believe."

He stood and moved to me suddenly, grabbed me by the shoulders, and the look in his eyes was one of sheer desperation.

"Please, Jessie. Tell me you believe I didn't kill your mother."

I didn't know what to tell him then. How could he expect me to assimilate all this information and then form a judgment? That's why he'd come, I realized, for absolution. But I wasn't sure I was the one to give it to him. It wasn't for me that he'd returned; it was for himself. Maybe he'd realized his mistakes, maybe even atoned for them in some way, but he was the same selfish man who'd abused Teresa Stone and their daughter, Jessie. He was possibly even a murderer; in the least, he'd run like a coward when he thought he might be accused. Now he'd come to shatter my life in the hope that he might be forgiven, finally, after all these years. What was I supposed to think? How could I even believe anything this man said?

I sat back down on the bench and he sat beside me. I kept waiting for some feeling, as if my DNA might recognize its genesis and send some signal to my brain and my heart. But I wasn't certain of anything. I felt like a kite with its line cut; I was drifting away higher and farther from earth without direction. It dawned on me that the freedom I'd always craved hadn't really been freedom at all but a kind of rooted independence. **This** was freedom and it felt like danger.

I opened my mouth to speak and even now I'm not sure what I would have said. Because one minute I was looking at him and the next minute he sagged beside me as though his bones had turned to Jell-O. I grabbed his shoulder to keep him from falling in my lap, and when I pushed him back against the bench, his head lolled to one side and I could see a perfect red circle between his eyes.

Violence is soft and quiet. Or it can be. In the movies, shots ring loud and punches land with a hard crack. People die with a scream or a moan. But Christian Luna's death was silent. He left the world without a sound.

I shook him. "Mr. Luna? Are you all right?"

Which was a pretty stupid question, but what can I say, shock is the stepsister of denial. It cushions the blow to your psyche when really fucked-up things happen. I felt hands on me then.

"Ridley, holy shit. What the fuck happened?"

"What?" I said, turning around and seeing Jake. "I don't know."

He was pulling me but I was holding on to Christian Luna. My father. Maybe. Jake pried my hands off of him while looking around him, I guess trying to figure out where the shot came from. Then he was dragging me back toward the car. I looked back to see Christian Luna tipped on his side, still on the bench. The full gravity of what had happened was slowly starting to dawn. I felt bile rising in my throat.

"Shouldn't we—" I said. I was going to say "call the police," but I'm not sure I ever finished the sentence because in the next second I was leaning over the railing edging the park and puking onto the grass. I had the sense of

Jake sheltering me with his body, as if he was afraid of more gunfire. He tugged at me, looking behind us. I managed to get moving again.

"The police?" I managed finally. But it came out sounding more like a question.

"We have to get the fuck out of here right now," said Jake, pulling me close to him with his arm around my shoulder. "Walk fast. But try to look normal."

This seemed funny to me and I started to laugh. He smiled, too. But it was fake, forced. **He** was trying to look normal and it wasn't working. The laughter built on itself until I was laughing so hard that I thought I was going to pee in my pants. Then the laughter shifted. Luckily we were in the car by then. Jake was strapping me in and then suddenly I was sobbing with such force that it doubled me over and made my throat hurt. I've never, before or since, felt as powerless against anything as I did against that sobbing. It was like something alive trying to get out of me.

"Ridley," he said, moving his eyes quickly between me and the road, his voice desperate. "It's okay. It's okay."

He kept saying it over and over again as if he thought he could make it true through repetition. At 186th he pulled the car off the

highway and drove up the drive that led to
Fort Tryon Park. It was closed but we pulled
into the parking lot and Jake grabbed me, held
on to me hard while I buried my face into his
shoulder. He held me like that, breathing assurances into my ear. And eventually the sobbing subsided and I was left weakened, my
sinuses so swollen that I couldn't breathe out
of my nose. I sagged against him.

"What happened back there, Ridley?" he
asked when I'd quieted. "Did you see where
the shot came from?"

But I couldn't answer him. I felt like he
was talking to me through water. "I don't
know," I said finally. "I don't know what happened."

I heard him say something about seeing a
shadow on the roof of the building across the
street. But I was caught in some kind of mental loop, where I kept seeing Christian Luna as
his head rolled back, the bullet hole perfect
and red on the middle of his forehead. That
moment played over and over.

After a while, he started to drive and we
took the Henry Hudson back downtown. I
watched the twinkling lights of the city, the
speeding red and white blur of taillights and
headlights rush past us. A kind of numbness

had settled over me and I felt like all my limbs were filled with sand, and that my neck didn't have the strength to support my head.

"What's happening to me?" I wanted to know.

"I'm sorry, Ridley," he said oddly. "I'm so sorry."

I didn't even think to ask him what he meant, why he was sorry.

"I should have taken better care of you, protected you better than that," he said. I wanted to tell him it wasn't his fault, but the words never made it from my head to my mouth.

We went back to the East Village and to Jake's apartment. He put me in his bed and lay beside me, stroking my hair. When he thought I had fallen asleep, he left the room. I could hear that he'd turned on NY1 News and I knew he was waiting for the broadcast about Christian Luna. And I fell asleep wondering, Why didn't he want to call the police?

SIXTEEN

When I woke up, Jake was sleeping beside me, bare-chested but still wearing his jeans. His arm was draped over my abdomen and he wore a slight frown, as if his dreams were troubling him. I smiled, still in that shady place before sleep clears and the consciousness of your life returns. He shifted in his sleep and the features on his face softened, the frown faded. In the dim light he looked, for a moment, peaceful. And I realized what a contrast it was to the dark intensity I normally saw on his face. The thought reminded me that I had so many questions about Jake, and then the events of last night started filing back, flashing before my eyes. Nausea seized me as guilt and grief and fear did battle in my stomach. I lay there, clutching my middle for I don't know how long, trying to make sense of what happened last night.

I slipped from the bed and went out into the living room. The sun was barely making its debut over the horizon and the light that filtered in through the window was a milky gray. I flipped on the television set and turned the volume down low. It was still tuned to NY1 News, the local cable news channel that broadcasts twenty-four hours. I watched a full cycle of news stories: A dog got hit by a car on Second Avenue, was shot by a cop trying to put it out of its misery, was put in a freezer, and lived. Now, **that's** a survivor. Paulie "The Fist" Umbruglia was arrested on charges of fraud and tax evasion. I watched as he was walked from a squad car in handcuffs, flanked by two burly uniformed officers. I did a double take when I saw someone I recognized on the screen. Following behind Paulie was my uncle Max's lawyer, Alexander Harriman. A frost of thick white hair, weekends-in-the-Bahamas tan, glittering Rolex, five-thousand-dollar suit, a smile that could charm you to blushing but that could freeze and become menacing in a heartbeat. My uncle Max had loved him. He always said, "Ridley, you want your lawyer to have retractable claws, a titanium backbone, and flexible morals."

I'd met Harriman many times at charity

functions, dinners at Uncle Max's, even once at a New Year's Eve party my parents threw. As I mentioned, Harriman had a pretty colorful list of clients, but, as with so many of the gray areas in my life, I'd never actually dwelled on it too much. After all, the only time I'd dealt with him personally was to discuss the money my uncle had left me. That was a quick, amicable meeting where he turned over a check to me and offered his assistance in managing the money. I told him that I'd already arranged for it, but thanks.

Something about him had always made me cringe. Maybe it was Max's description of him, which always brought to mind the Terminator, or maybe it was my parents' unspoken distaste for him. My heart always beat a little faster around him, and I always was a little uncomfortable beneath his gaze. As I left his office that day, he said, "Ridley, your uncle Max loved you very much. He wanted to be certain, if anything ever happened to him, that you could always come to me for help. If you ever need anything, have any questions about the law, any legal issues, really **anything,** Ridley, don't hesitate." I shook his hand and thanked him for his concern, secretly wondering how rock bottom you'd have to be to call on Alexander Harriman for help. Sitting on Jake's couch, I wondered if I still had his business card in my Rolodex. I was feeling pretty rock bottom, and thinking that a titanium backbone and retractable claws might be of some use after you'd fled the scene of a murder, because that's precisely what we'd done.

As the local news stories rolled on, with no mention of Christian Luna, I tried to think of a good reason why we'd run. If it had just been a matter of getting ourselves out of harm's way, we could have stopped and called the police when we were safe. But we didn't do that. We watched a man get shot and then we left him there on a park bench.

I took in the cold, industrial room, the absence of personal objects. I thought about the man sleeping in the bedroom. Like I said, I felt as though I **knew** Jake on some instinctive level that transcended my ignorance of his history. But as I sat on his futon and looked around the room for some sense of him, I felt a growing unease. I mean, think about your own living room. Imagine a stranger came into your home and sat on your couch. What would the stranger be able to deduce about you from the things she saw? Aren't there at least some clues about your likes and dislikes, pictures of the people you love and value, a magazine on the coffee table . . . something? Jake's living room offered nothing. It was sterile like a hotel room, had the air of transience. It felt as though he could walk out of that space and never come back, never think on the objects left there again. For some reason this disturbed me suddenly. It made me realize that as much as I felt as if Jake's essence was clear, I was equally certain that he was hiding crucial parts of himself.

His laptop sat on a slim desk in the corner of the room. In the absence of clutter, drawers to poke through, papers to rifle, it double-dog dared me to flip the lid and boot it up. I was always up for a dare, and given my circumstances I was feeling particularly bold. I padded over softly and lifted the lid, pressed the power button. It hummed to life with a couple of unpleasantly loud beeps. A screen presented itself, demanding a password. **Shit.** I thought on the little I knew about Jake and decided that the password wouldn't be anything predictable. That he was likely to be fairly concerned about security. People with something to hide generally were.

"Quidam."

I spun around to see Jake standing in the doorway.

"What?"

"The password. It's 'quidam.'"

He looked at me and I tried to read his expression. He didn't seem hurt or even surprised that I was quite obviously snooping around, or trying to, in his computer files. Oddly, I didn't feel all that embarrassed at having been caught.

"What does that mean?" I asked.

"It's from an epic work by Cyprian Kamil Norwid, a Polish romantic poet. It derives from the Latin word that means 'someone, some human being.' But the hero in Norwid's 'Quidam' is a man looking for a place in his life, someone searching for goodness and truth. 'He was anonymous, without a name— at all orphan, quidam.'"

I walked away from the laptop and back to the futon where I sat earlier and pulled my knees to my chest.

"Is that how you see yourself?"

He shrugged. "I suppose so. In some ways."

He came over and sat beside me. The same shadow of sadness I'd seen cross his face, settle in his eyes for a second, or briefly pull down at the corners of his mouth seemed to find its home in his features. I could see that he wanted to reach out to touch me but wasn't sure if it's what I wanted. Something in the air between us had grown charged. My suspicions, I guess. They kept me from putting my arms around him and kissing all that sadness away, though that's what my heart wanted.

"Why didn't you want to call the police last night?" I asked.

He considered the question. "I guess I don't have a good answer for that except that it would have tied us up in something that I'm not sure would have been good for either one of us."

"We just left him there," I said, and was surprised to hear my voice crack, feel tears rush to my eyes. I put my head to my hand, rubbing at a headache that was now pressing at the back of my eyes.

"He was dead," he said, and seemed to realize that he sounded cold and harsh. "I'm sorry, Ridley." He leaned into me. "I'm sorry it happened. I'm sorry you had to see it. And I'm sorry I didn't do a better job of protecting you. But—I mean—it's not as if we could have helped him. Or even that we knew who'd shot him. The only thing that would have come from calling the police would have been a lot of questions. I just wanted to get you out of there."

I saw him focus on something over my shoulder and I turned to look at the television screen. A young reporter with a blunt blond bob was standing in front of Van Cortlandt Park, police officers milling about behind her.

"An unidentified man was found murdered this morning in Van Cortlandt Park, located in the Riverdale section of the Bronx. Discovered by joggers, the man appears to have died from a gunshot wound to the head," the reporter said with an odd cheeriness to her voice, as if she were reporting on the progress of a parade.

Behind her, I could see a fleet of squad cars, and the place where I'd sat was cordoned off with yellow crime-scene tape. A coroner's van blocked the entrance to the park. I wondered how many people had passed Christian Luna's dead body slumped on the bench before someone figured out he was dead. How many people had jogged by thinking he was just another bum taking a nap in the park? We'd left him to be discovered like that, a man who might have been my father. No matter what he might have done, he didn't deserve that. Did he?

The reporter continued: "Police say that while they can't be certain until ballistics tests have been completed, the bullet appears to have come from a rifle, and the trajectory indicates the shot was fired from a rooftop across the street." The camera panned to the buildings across the street from the park, the residential apartment buildings and row houses we'd sat in front of for hours. "Again, these are just initial reports and cannot be verified without further investigation.

"Witnesses say that a woman and man were seen leaving the park shortly after midnight, but so far no one has come forward with a description. Police say that while these two are not suspects at this time, they **are** wanted for questioning.

"This is Angela Martinez reporting, New York One News."

I got up and turned the television off and stood staring at the blank screen.

"Holy shit," I said, whispering to myself more than anything. "I **cannot** believe this. **What** is happening to my life?"

I spun around to look at Jake. He sat still, looking unbelievably calm. "Did you hear that?" I demanded. "We're **wanted** by the **police.**"

I started walking the length of the room.

"For questioning," he said, as if it was nothing. Maybe it was nothing to him, but to someone who'd never had so much as a parking ticket, it seemed like a pretty big deal.

"Jake," I said, stopping in front of him. "We have to go to the police."

He shook his head. "Forget it. Not an option. Anyway, the police are the least of our concerns."

"What are you talking about?"

"**Think,** Ridley," he said, pointing to his temple. "Who killed Christian Luna? And why?" Actually, believe it or not, in my monumental selfishness, it had not even occurred to me to wonder who had killed Mr. Luna. I was still trying to deal with the fact that a man had been murdered before my eyes. The reasons why hadn't even begun to dawn.

"Nobody knew we were going to meet him," Jake said. "**We** didn't even know until an hour before."

"So maybe it was just an accident. I mean, like something random," I said, reaching, not wanting to even consider the other possibilities.

"A shot like that?" said Jake with a sharp exhale. "No way."

"Then what? Someone was following him? Or tapped his phone?"

"Maybe. Or someone was following **you.**"

"Me?" I said, letting go a little laugh. "Why would anyone be following me?"

You're thinking, Is she nuts? The man in my building, the man in the pizzeria, the man I'd seen on the train. In my frazzled mind, all of these things still remained nebulous and unconnected. But I did think of the man on the train. Remembered his dead eyes and the case he'd carried. Had he been following me? Or was he some random weirdo? There was no way to know.

"Seems like," said Jake, "if someone had been following him with the intent to kill him, they could have done it before they did. When he was walking up the street to the house, for example. If he was the target, it would have been much easier and less risky to hit him when he was alone. But maybe the shooter, whoever it was, didn't know who the target was. Wouldn't know until you led them to him."

"I saw someone on the train," I said. "He might have been following me but he got off before I did." I wondered with a sickening twist in my stomach if I had inadvertently led Christian Luna's killer to him.

"What do you mean?" asked Jake, concerned. "Why would you think he was following you?"

"He was staring at me. He smiled at me," I said. It sounded lame as I described how the man had inched closer to me when he thought my eyes were closed. How he waved as the train pulled away from the station.

"But he got off the train before you?"

"Yeah."

Jake shrugged. "Could have been some freak. It's hard to say."

I sat down beside him again and tried to turn this information around in my mind and draw some conclusions, but I just couldn't get my head around it. Instead, that moment when Christian Luna fell toward me started playing again and I put my head back in my hands.

"Ridley—" he started, putting a hand on my back. But I stood up before he could finish. I walked into the bedroom, pulled on my jeans and socks, grabbed my shoes. Jake slid forward on the futon and looked at me with worry.

"I can't do this right now," I said. He nodded and looked down at the floor. I turned my eyes from him; I didn't want to see how beautiful he was. I didn't want my growing feeling for him to cloud my judgment about what I needed to do next.

"I need to think."

"Ridley, wait," he said, standing. "You need to be careful."

"I will be. I'm just going downstairs for a while." He nodded and sat back down. The look on his face—kind of compassionate and worried, a little hurt—made me feel like a bitch. But I left anyway.

If he had come over to me, put his arms around me, I would have melted into him. Not that it was an unattractive option, but I was starting to see my real self through the fissures that had opened in the fantasy of my life. If I turned to him now, scared and weak, how could I know if what I felt for him was love or just need? And if I turned to him in need, how could I face whatever it was he was hiding from me? Of course, none of these thoughts were fully formed at that moment. The only thing I knew was that I had to get away from him and from this nightmare. As fast and as far as I could.

I went back to my apartment. As soon as I closed the door, everything that happened last night and all the fear I'd felt up in Jake's apartment seemed as though it was behind a sheet of bullet-proof glass. The familiar space wrapped itself around me and for a few merciful minutes I was just Ridley again.

An angry "5" blinked accusingly on my machine. When was the last time I'd checked my messages? Wednesday morning? Thursday? It was Saturday now and I felt like I'd been away from my life for a month. There was a pleasant and then a terse message from Uma Thurman's publicist. The **Vanity Fair** editor wanted to know if I'd been able to connect with Uma and if the article was a go. There was a pleading message from Zachary: Wouldn't I **please** call so we can clear the air about some things? The last message was a hang-up.

A few days earlier, I would have rushed to return all these calls, anxious that I'd been out of the loop, let things slide. But that morning I just lay on the couch, listening to these voices bounce around my apartment, overcome by a kind of emotional lethargy. I felt like I'd left a part of myself in the park where Christian Luna had died, the part of myself that knew how to handle the simple things like returning phone calls. I lay there for a while, my mind reeling so fast that it seemed almost blank. I decided coffee was a good idea, something to get my mental energy up.

After I was properly caffeinated, I called the editor at **Vanity Fair,** thankful that it was Saturday, and left a message saying I'd had a family emergency and would need to postpone the article. I knew she wouldn't like it, and I was not comfortable blowing off such a plum assignment, but what could I do? I called Tama Puma (what kind of name is that, anyway?) and left a similar message. It wasn't a lie. My life **was** officially in a state of emergency; whether it was a family matter or not was still under investigation. I said a brief prayer that I was not flushing my career down the toilet. I mean, the freelance writing thing is hugely competitive and you don't just **postpone** articles you're assigned to write for **Vanity Fair.** Word gets out that you can't be counted on to meet a deadline and all of a sudden those assignments are going to someone else. I'd actually never missed a deadline before; considered it a violation of my personal code. I said another brief prayer that I wasn't flushing my **life** down the toilet.

As for Zack, well, I just couldn't deal with him. Exhausted by my efforts, I lay back down on the couch.

You may be thinking at this point that with Christian Luna dead, my problem had more or less disappeared. And it was true, with him gone there was no one to claim, as far as I knew, that I was not who I believed myself to be. But I couldn't put what I'd learned from Christian Luna out of my head and go on as before. It wasn't even an option. And now there were a gaggle of other questions nipping at me. Most pressing of which was: Who killed Teresa Stone? You probably don't think that's the most pressing question, but bear with me. Here was a young woman, a struggling single mother, working hard and loving her little daughter, putting up with the asshole Christian Luna. Then one night she'd been murdered in her home, her daughter kidnapped. That is, if you believed Christian Luna, and I did on this point at least, that he didn't kill Teresa and that her killer and Jessie's kidnapper was never caught. If Teresa was my mother, and if I was Jessie, I owed it to her— and to myself—to find out what happened to them. Us. Whoever. I felt that beneath my skin. And finding the answer to that question might answer the two others: Who killed Christian Luna? And who the hell was I?

There was a knock on my door then and I sighed. I didn't want to face Jake right now. I didn't want to deal with his puzzles on top of my own. I opened the door and Zelda was standing there. Behind her there were three cops, two in uniform and one in plain clothes.

"Ms. Jones? Ridley Jones?" said the plain-clothes officer.

"Yes."

Let me at this point mention that I'm a very, very bad liar. I can't do it. My face flushes. I stutter. I avert my eyes. In school I'd had a couple of detentions, but as far as being in trouble, that was about it. The sight of a police officer at my door, and basically I felt like I was going to pass out from anxiety.

"We have some questions for you. Can we come in?"

"Sure," I said as lightly as possible.

I stood aside and let them come in. Zelda hung back in the hallway, looking at me sternly. "You're a good girl, Ridley," she said. "I don't want no trouble here."

"I know, Zelda. It's okay."

"The police," she said quietly, making a spitting noise with her mouth that I guessed was meant to communicate her disdain. "Worse than the bad men who come looking for you. Too much trouble, Ridley."

She walked down the stairs shaking her head. I felt eyes on me and looked to my right and saw Victoria peering through a crack she'd opened in her door. When she saw me looking at her, she slammed the door shut. **Had Zelda said bad "men"?**

"Ms. Jones?"

I shut the door and walked into my living room.

"Would you like some coffee?" I asked, sitting down on the couch and curling my legs under me.

"No, thanks," the plainclothes cop said. "Ms. Jones, I'm Detective Gus Salvo. I'm going to get right to it. A man was murdered last night in Van Cortlandt Park up in the Bronx, and witnesses say they saw you talking to this man when he was shot and that you and another man fled the scene shortly after. What can you tell me about this?" I noticed that he didn't say "someone matching your description." He said me.

"Our witness recognized you from the newspaper, Ms. Jones," he said before I could even ask. "From when you saved that kid a couple of weeks ago."

The detective was a lean, rather slight man. It didn't look as if he had a whole lot of muscle to him. But there was something about him that communicated strength. There was a mean narrowness to his face and his eyes were wide open, dark and deep as wells. He had the look of a man who'd heard a thousand pathetic lies, who saw the world in stark black and white, right and wrong, good and bad. Gray areas didn't even **exist** for Gus Salvo.

I didn't say anything for a second. I closed my eyes, and when I opened them, he was still there.

"Look," he said helpfully, "I know you were there. You know you were there. Why don't you just tell me what happened?"

This suggestion seemed so logical that I told him everything, starting with the day I'd rescued the boy and ending with Christian Luna dying on the park bench. I spilled my guts, sang like a canary, whatever it is they call it in those black-and-white gangster movies. I did leave out a couple of things. I left out Jake; I felt very protective of him and didn't want him in trouble because of me. I left out my brother. But I told him pretty much everything else, basically saying that I'd called Christian Luna after a few days of thinking about his notes and agreed to meet him in the park. Okay, so I didn't **exactly** sing like a canary. I actually left out pretty much everything except getting the note and pictures and calling Christian Luna.

Detective Salvo didn't have much of a reaction, just scribbled notes in a small leatherbound notebook as I talked. "Did you talk to anyone about this, Ms. Jones?"

"No," I said, feeling my cheeks go pink. "No one."

He glanced up at me and regarded me coolly for a moment. "So," he said, cocking his head slightly, "you just decided to meet this man in a dark park in the Bronx, in the middle of the night, all by yourself. You didn't tell anyone where you were going. You didn't think it would be a good idea to bring a friend."

I shrugged, shook my head.

"You seem like an intelligent woman. And that doesn't seem like a very intelligent action," he said, giving me a kind of curious half-smile.

I shrugged again. It was a gesture that seemed to be serving me pretty well lately, so I was sticking with it. "Sometimes unusual circumstances cause us to act in unusual ways," I said.

"Hmm," he answered with a nod. He looked at me. I think he was older than I was by about ten years or so and it showed in deep wrinkles around his eyes. He flipped through the pages of his notebook until he found the one he wanted.

"Witnesses say that a few moments after the shooting, they saw a man emerge from the trees. That the two of you left together."

"There was no one else," I said. "I left the park alone and got on the train. Came home." I was proud. I didn't even stutter. He didn't say anything but he turned those eyes on me. He knew I was lying and I knew he knew. The knowledge relaxed me, as if we were just actors playing out a skit and everything we said from here on out was simply lines that had been written for us.

"Why did you flee the scene?"

I shook my head here. "I was in shock. Scared out of my mind. I barely remember leaving."

"Let me see if I can help you with your

memory. Witnesses say that they saw you exit the park with this man. That he seemed to be leading you. That you got into a black sixty-nine Pontiac Firebird."

Christ. It was dark. Who could have seen all this? And didn't the newscaster say that joggers had discovered the body this morning? If someone saw all of this last night, why didn't "they" call the police then?

"I told you I took the train."

I had to think a second about the car. Had Jake parked it in the street in front of the building? No. It was in a parking garage on Tenth Street.

"Ms. Jones," Detective Salvo said, his voice gentle, coaxing. "More than one person saw you."

"Am I responsible for what people think they see?" I said.

He changed tack. "Okay, Ms. Jones. Let's go back. Did you see where the shot came from?"

"No."

"But you said you were both sitting on the same bench. You were turned facing the buildings across the street and he was turned toward you, facing the interior of the park. Is that right?"

"Yes, that's right," I answered. And here I

flashed on something Jake had said about a shadow on the roof of the building across the street. And the newscaster, too, had reported that the bullet might have come from the rooftops. I was no ballistics expert, but thinking on it now, I knew that the shot that hit Christian Luna between the eyes couldn't have come from the roof across the street. It had to have come from the woods . . . where Jake was. I saw a small smile turn up the corners of the detective's mouth, then disappear. I think my face was like a movie screen for him, where he could watch my thoughts flicker in my expressions.

"The car, a black sixty-nine Pontiac Firebird, license plate number RXT 658, is registered to a man by the name of Harley Jacobsen, address 258 West 110th Street."

He looked at me and I tried to make my face blank, shook my head. Harley? someone inside my head asked. Wasn't that the name of Jake's investigator friend? They had the same last name?

"Three assault charges, possession of an unlicensed firearm, breaking and entering," the detective was saying.

I was starting to feel a little sick. But I kept silent.

"I consider myself a good judge of character, Ms. Jones, and this is not the kind of man I would imagine a woman like you spending time with."

"You're right," I said after a second. "It isn't. I've never heard of this man."

Again that small, fleeting smile. "Can I call you Ridley?"

I nodded.

"Ridley, I don't want to see you get in trouble protecting someone who doesn't deserve it."

His words stung a little. I could tell then that I was in the presence of a master. Detective Salvo was a man who knew how to size people up and subtly manipulate them into telling the truth. I wondered if this gift had led him to become a cop, or if he'd discovered it in the commission of his work.

"I don't know who this man is," I said. And that much was true. I had **no idea** who Harley Jacobsen was. Apparently, though, I'd spent the better part of last night riding around in his car. The detective looked back down at his notes and ran down a laundry list of facts on Harley Jacobsen.

"The guy was abandoned into the system when he was five years old. A problem kid.

Was in and out of foster homes until he was fourteen, never adopted. He went to an orphanage in New Jersey then; stayed there until he was eighteen. He joined the Marines. Had some trouble there with fighting, conduct unbecoming, et cetera. His tour ended in ninety-six and he didn't reenlist. Got his New York State private investigator's license in ninety-seven."

There was a loud pounding in my right ear, this weird noise I hear sometimes when I'm under a lot of stress. My mind strained to keep up with what the detective was telling me. Had Jake lied about his name? Was **he** this guy Harley? Or was Harley a friend of his, as he'd told me, and we'd just borrowed his car? I know: duh.

Gus Salvo handed me a piece of paper. It was a copy of Harley Jacobsen's PI license. The picture was poor quality, dark and distorted. But there was no denying that it was Jake. My heart fell into a million pieces, fluttered down into my belly.

Jake had lied about his name. That scared me. Jake had a private investigator's license, which explained a lot of things I hadn't bothered to question. That also scared me. But as for the rest of it, for all I know these were the things he'd been trying to tell me since the night I met him.

"Any of this ringing a bell for you, Ridley?"

"No," I said. "Not in the least."

The detective looked at me long, with hard, seeing eyes.

"Sounds like he's had a hard life," I added, squirming just a little inside beneath those eyes.

"That's not an excuse for breaking the law."

I didn't know what else to say to Detective Salvo. For whatever reason, I was feeling more protective of Jake—or whatever his name was—than ever. Sure, he'd lied about his name. But obviously I'd been lied to about more important things. I **had** been honest about the details of Christian Luna's murder. I really **didn't** know anything else about who had murdered him and why.

"I can't help you, Detective. I've told you everything I know about last night."

"Ridley," he said with a sigh. "I'm just not sure I believe you."

I smiled at him, not in a smart-ass way, but in a way that communicated to him that I was done talking. I guess if he'd wanted to be a hard case, he could have arrested me for leaving the scene of a homicide, but I just didn't get the sense that he was like that. Not that I thought he was giving up, either. He closed his notebook and stood. I told him then about Christian Luna's cousin in Puerto Rico so that his body could be returned to his family. I didn't know the name, but somehow I thought Detective Salvo would figure it out. The two police officers who had stood silent throughout the entire interview moved toward the door. I rose and followed the detective to the doorjamb. As I stood beside him, I realized that he was a bit shorter than I was, but somehow his personality made him seem larger.

"So what did you find out? Was he your father?" asked Detective Salvo.

"He seemed to think so," I answered.

"Any idea who would want him dead?"

I shook my head. "I didn't know him. He was hiding from someone. I thought it was the police. But maybe he had other people to be afraid of as well."

"I think that's a safe assumption," said the detective. "Consider something, will you, Ridley?" he asked, handing me his card.

I nodded.

"It was very easy for me to identify and find you. I was at your doorstep less than twelve hours after Luna was murdered." I didn't say anything, but I felt a chill and my stomach did a little flip. "I'm one of the good guys, okay? I show up at your door and you might get in trouble, but you're not going to get hurt. You hear me? You get what I'm saying, Ridley?"

I'd read somewhere that cops are trained to use your name a lot when they talk to you, that it fosters a sense of intimacy. It was working.

"You're a witness to a murder. If someone thinks you saw something, or wants to eliminate that possibility . . ." He let his voice trail, allowing my imagination to fill in the blanks. "I'm saying watch your back. I think you're in over your head here."

I nodded again, not trusting my own voice. If he had been trying to scare me, he'd succeeded. I remembered what Jake said about the cops being the least of our problems. It sucked that the cops seemed to feel the same way.

"I'll be in touch, Ridley," he said, putting his hand on my arm. "Call me day or night if you remember anything else, need to talk. Call if you're in trouble."

"Okay," I said. "Thanks."

"I'm sure I don't have to tell you that you

should remain easy for me to find." He gave me a look that somehow managed to be condescending and paternal. Then he and the uniformed officers moved down the stairs. I waited until I heard the gate door swing open downstairs and then slam shut before I ran up to Jake's apartment. I knocked on the door but there was no answer. I turned on the knob and pushed at the door but it was locked. I knocked once more but there was only silence.

SEVENTEEN

"Alexander Harriman's office," answered a bright, hard voice. I'd figured someone like Alex Harriman didn't take Saturdays off. And I was right.

"This is Ridley Jones," I said. "Is he in?"

There was a slight pause. "Just a moment."

Rock bottom. Do you think I qualified? I'd just watched a man get murdered, and then fled from the scene of the crime. The man I've been sleeping with was suddenly a stranger who'd lied about or omitted nearly everything important about himself. The police had been to my apartment and asked that I remain "easy to find." Those retractable claws were sounding pretty good.

"Ridley," said Alexander Harriman, his voice warm and familiar as if he'd known me all my life, which I guess he had from a distance. "What can I do for you?"

"I think I'm in trouble."

A pause. "What kind of trouble?" he said, his voice gone from bright to serious.

"I witnessed a murder."

"I'm going to stop you. Don't say another word."

"What?"

"I don't like to have these conversations over the phone. Can you come to my office?"

I showered and pulled myself together. Except for the dark rings around my eyes and the frown on my forehead, I looked fairly normal in my bathroom mirror. I hopped a cab down on First Avenue and headed up to Central Park West to see my uncle's lawyer.

The brownstone office was posh in a subdued way, lots of oak and leather, Oriental carpets, and the same Asian and African art my uncle had always favored. A giant red Buddha stared at me happily from his place in the corner. A tribal mask fashioned from bark and topped with enormous red feathers seemed to recognize the seriousness of my situation and looked down on me gravely from its perch above rows of bookshelves holding law texts.

It seemed weird to be in this much trouble and for my parents not to be around. I don't think I ever got a bad grade without calling my father to lament. I had this feeling of having been cut loose from my life, as if I could drift away, just get smaller and smaller and finally be gone for good.

"I wish we'd had this conversation before you talked to the police," said Harriman, after I told him the whole story, from the first note to my visit with Detective Salvo.

I shrugged.

"In fact," he said, leaning back and looking at me, "you should have called me the minute the harassment began."

"I don't have a lot of experience with this kind of thing." I put my hand to my eyes and started to rub away some of the fatigue that ached there.

"No, of course not," he said, leaning forward in his chair, resting his elbows on the gigantic oak desk. I swear I've seen smaller Volkswagens.

"So what do I do now?"

"My advice? Take a break. Go home and stay with your parents for a while. I'll call Detective Salvo, and any contact you have with him can be arranged through me from now on. I'll handle this from here on out, and if you need to talk to the police again, I'll go with you. You didn't do anything wrong. You're not guilty of anything except some questionable judgment calls."

It sounded easy enough. Downright tempting, in fact. Crawl back into the fold and let the gates come down behind me. Forget it all.

"Seems to me like the source of your problem has been eliminated," said Harriman. "If you want, this can all just go away."

I stood up and walked over to a shelf of photographs to the right of his desk. Outside his window, there was a sprawling view of Central Park and Fifth Avenue. **Eliminated.** Seemed like an odd choice of words for the death of a man who might have been my father.

"He thought I was his daughter. He came to find me and someone killed him," I said, looking out at the traffic on the street below. "How does that just go away?"

He didn't say anything but I could feel his eyes on me. "That man, whoever he was, was not your father. I guarantee you that." He sounded so certain, I turned to look at him.

"I mean, come on," he said with a disdainful laugh. "Give me a break. This guy just emerges after thirty years and claims to be your father? And you believe him? You're a smart girl, Ridley. Too smart for this shit."

I didn't say anything, just looked at him. I tried to think of all the reasons this couldn't have been some kind of sick joke. And I couldn't come up with one.

"Okay," he said, showing me his palms. "Let me do this. I'll get a court order to preserve a tissue sample. We'll do a DNA test."

The thought made my stomach bottom out. Why hadn't I thought of that? Maybe I didn't really want to know. Maybe the question was safer than the answer.

"See?" he said when I didn't answer. "You don't really want to know, do you?"

I looked at the pictures on his shelf and one in particular caught my eye. It was Harriman, my uncle Max, Esme, my father, and a man I didn't recognize. They stood beneath a banner that read:

PROJECT RESCUE,
BRINGING ABANDONED CHILDREN
IN FROM THE COLD

I picked it up and looked at it closely. They all seemed very young and I noticed

Max's arm around Esme's shoulder. Her smile was bright and her arm disappeared around his waist.

"When was this taken?"

He walked over beside me. I could smell his expensive cologne. The watch on his arm probably could have put a kid or two through college. His hands were so tan, it looked like he was wearing leather gloves. He took the photograph from me and looked at it with a smile.

"A long time ago. Before you were born," he said.

"What's Project Rescue?"

"It was one of the ventures of the Maxwell Allen Smiley Foundation. You remember how your uncle lobbied for the passing of the Safe Haven Law?"

I nodded, remembering the conversation I'd had with my father.

"Project Rescue was the group that did all the lobbying, public relations, advertising, soliciting funds, and celebrity support," he said. "Now that the law has passed, they operate a helpline and act as a public relations office, produce those stickers for hospitals, clinics, police stations, and firehouses to put in their windows to identify themselves as Project Rescue facilities where people can leave their babies. They give award dinners honoring physicians who have provided extraordinary assistance to children in need. Max's estate still provides the funding."

He put the picture back on the shelf and turned me away by placing his hands on my shoulders. "Anyway," he said, "that's all ancient history."

I sat down on the couch across from his desk and felt absorbed by it, it was so plush. He sat in a large ornate chair that looked more like a throne with its brocade seat and back, its blackwood arms that ended in fierce lion heads.

"So how about I call you a car to take you home to your parents' place," he said, reaching for the phone beside him. "You can get some rest. I'll deal with the NYPD. A week from today, it'll be like this never happened."

I looked at him. He **could** make it go away. I knew he could. He had that look about him, the look of a man who could give your problem a pair of concrete boots and make it sink into the East River. Just don't ask too many questions about his methods. You don't want to know.

"No," I said. "Don't. I'll take the train."

"Don't be silly," he said, lifting the receiver.

"No, really. I need the time to think."

He paused, holding the phone in his hand, looking at me with skeptical eyes. "But you'll go home to Ben and Grace?"

I nodded. "Where else can I go now? You're right. I need a break."

He put the phone down and I rose.

"My parents can't know about this, Alex," I said. "Not yet. It'll just frighten them."

"Attorney-client privilege, kid," he said, standing up. "Everything we've talked about today stays here. I'll leave a message for you at your place when I've talked to that detective. You check your messages? Check your messages."

"I will."

"Trust me," he said, putting an arm around my shoulder. "This time next week? Never happened. You did the right thing coming here. Your uncle Max wanted to know you'd always be taken care of, you know?"

I nodded, turned, and shook the hand he offered.

"Thanks, Mr. Harriman."

———

I am not a very good driver. Partly from inexperience and partly because of the tendency of my mind to wander. I got into a bunch of accidents as a teenager. Minor stuff, always my fault, leading my father to lament, "Ridley, do you ever leave the house and **not** hit something?" Their insurance went up, the repair bills were not small. But I think their major concern was how much worse it could get. Every fender bender was a reminder of the frailty of my life and how my independence meant that they could no longer be on the lookout for dangers that might befall me. They represented a loss of control.

I rented a black Jeep Grand Cherokee (unbelievably expensive) in the West Village later that day and headed out of the city. I crawled up the Henry Hudson through a gauntlet of construction sites (which I swear have been under way for more than fifteen years) and I finally broke free of the snarl at the exit to the George Washington Bridge. I was headed to Jersey. Not to my parents, as I'd promised Harriman. No. I couldn't have done that, good as it sounded. There was no going home now.

I'm no private investigator, unlike **some** people, but I **am** a writer. Which means I've followed up a few leads, tracked down a few people over the years. I've convinced a few reticent people to talk to me. After leaving Alexander Harriman, I'd returned to my place and sat on the couch with a giant cup of coffee and stared out my window at the concrete wall and dark windows that were my view. I thought about my story. And I asked myself something that I often wondered when I was writing an article or a profile: If I was reading this story, what would I want to know next? What are the big questions left unanswered so far?

I had no intention of going home to my parents or of pretending none of this had ever happened. It wasn't an option. The point of safe return had passed when I agreed to meet Christian Luna in the park. The path back to my old life was closed completely and there was nothing to do but move forward.

I felt unbelievably calm. You'd think I'd have been a complete basket case, but I remember something a psychologist once told me, someone my parents and I saw after my uncle Max died and my father decided we all needed grief counseling. She said that grief is not linear. It's not a slow progression forward toward healing, it's a zigzag, a terrible back-

and-forth from devastated to okay until finally there are more okay patches and fewer devastated ones. The mind can't handle emotions like grief and terror for any sustained period of time, so it takes some downtime, she'd said. I'm not sure that I was in a state of grief, but maybe. Christian Luna, a man who believed himself to be my father, was dead. Jake was a stranger who'd lied to me. And I wasn't sure who I was any longer. But somehow I was transcendent, able to compartmentalize my fear and think about the questions that needed answering in this, the story of my life.

I mentioned that I thought the biggest question was: Who killed Teresa Stone? Like I said, I thought the answer to that question would answer a lot of the others. The way I saw it, there were a couple other biggies. Tell me if you agree. First was: Who the hell is Jake? But I couldn't answer that without talking to him, so the answer was going to have to wait, since PI Jake/Harley was currently MIA. The second question was: Who killed Christian Luna and why? Again, I was at the wall on this one. I had no way of knowing or even beginning to find out. Then last: Did Christian Luna tell the truth? Was I his daughter? And was he innocent of the murder of Teresa Elizabeth Stone?

I read through the article that Jake/Harley had found from the **New Jersey Record.** Maria Cacciatore was Teresa's neighbor, the woman who had taken care of Jessie while Teresa worked. I booted my computer, dialed up the Internet, and went into LexisNexis. Within seconds, I had telephone numbers and addresses for three M. Cacciatores in Hacketts-town, New Jersey. I also found a number for the management company of the Oak Groves apartment complex. "Clean, safe, affordable apartment living!" hailed the Web site. I'd never thought of the words **clean** and **safe** as superlatives to be used in advertising, but I guess you worked with what you had. From the pictures, the complex looked like low-income housing, which I guessed made sense, considering Teresa's situation when she was murdered. I figured if I couldn't locate Maria Cacciatore, maybe someone in the manage-ment company could turn me on to someone who had lived in the apartment complex back in the seventies.

You might think I would have made these calls before heading out to Jersey, but sitting around making phone calls that might or might not be successful did not seem like action to me. I know I was supposed to be careful, but I figured that since Jake/Harley had lied about his name, his profession, and who knows what else, then I was released from the promise I'd made him to be careful. So I headed to New Jersey.

I was the only person in New York City who didn't own a cellular phone. It wasn't really a philosophical decision. It was just that I worked from home and was pretty easy to reach. I didn't drive usually, so it wasn't as if it would come in handy in the event of a breakdown. Cell phones didn't work on the subway, which was the only place I could imagine one being useful, as in "I'm stuck on the train, running late, et cetera." And frankly, if you couldn't reach me, it meant that I didn't want to be reached. My friends and family bitched endlessly. Naturally (you should be getting to know me by now), that only made me want one even less. But I pulled off of Route 80 at the Rockaway Mall and picked up a phone at one of those AT&T kiosks. I could envision a need for one on this errand. I got a tiny red Nokia, barely bigger than a pack of Chiclets. I also grabbed a Cin-a-Bon and an Orange Julius while I was there, which I ate and drank in the parking lot while examining my new toy. God bless America.

I know it sounds like I was pretty solid and clear headed, if a little rash, a little reckless, and I guess I was. I was scared, still rattled from the night before, which flashed with sickeningly vivid clarity. But I felt like, maybe erroneously, I had taken control of the situation. Maria Cacciatore was my only link to a past of which until a few days ago I had been ignorant. If she was still alive and I could find her, then maybe the truth hadn't died last night with Christian Luna. I was infused with hope and the purpose of my mission to find out who killed Teresa Stone, what had happened to Jessie, and what it meant to me.

I knew it was a long shot, but at the same time I had a feeling I was going to find her. The universe conspires to reveal the truth and to make your path easy if you have the courage to follow the signs. And I was long on courage that day. Short on foresight, maybe, but long on courage.

———

When I got to Hackettstown, I pulled into the parking lot of 7-Eleven and started making calls.

The first two calls didn't go well. Maybe it was our alienated, postmodern times, maybe it was all the previous telemarketers that had been fended off before my call. Or maybe the Cacciatores were just a very unfriendly clan. **Martino** Cacciatore suggested that I pull my head out of my ass and stop calling people who weren't interested in my business. I'd interrupted the game show he'd been watching and now he'd never know what the correct price bid for the Caribbean cruise had been. **Margaret** Cacciatore was hard of hearing and after ten minutes of our yelling back and forth to each other, she issued an angry grunt and just hung up on me and didn't pick up when I called back. I dialed the last number.

"Hello?" came the voice of an older woman.

"Hi. I'm looking for a Maria Cacciatore," I said tentatively.

"I'm not interested," she said, and the line went dead. I dialed the number again.

"Hello?" she said, her voice wary and annoyed.

"Ms. Cacciatore, I'm not a telemarketer."

"I know, I know. I've won a sweepstakes for a free two-night stay in Orlando, right? I'm under no obligation to buy anything, right?"

"No, ma'am. I'm really not selling or offering anything."

"Well," she said grudgingly. "What do you want, then?"

"Are you Maria Cacciatore?" I said.

"Yes," she said with a sigh. "Look. What is it?"

"Did you know a Teresa Elizabeth Stone and her daughter, Jessie?"

There was a pause here and I thought maybe she'd hung up. Then I heard her breathing. "Yes," she said finally. "A long time ago. Teresa . . . she died. May she rest in peace."

"I know, Mrs. Cacciatore," I said. "I have some questions for you about her. And about Christian Luna. Can you help me?"

"Who did you say you were?" She sounded upset, angry, as if I had forced her to recall something she would have been happier forgetting.

"My name is Ridley Jones. I'm a writer doing a story on missing children who were never found. I came across your name in an article published in the **New Jersey Record** back in 1972." Okay, maybe I'm a better liar than I said. I was getting a lot of practice. Anyway, it was only a partial lie.

"What publication do you write for?" she asked. Good to know she had her wits about her.

"I'm a freelance writer, ma'am. I haven't sold the article yet."

She seemed to consider that for a moment. I figured she'd probably turn me down. But then she said, "You can come by the apartment if you want. I don't like to talk on the phone."

She told me how to get to her place and that I could come at four o'clock. "It was a long time ago," she said before we hung up. "I don't know how much I'll remember."

"Well, you just do your best, Ms. Cacciatore. That's all anyone can ask."

I had some time to kill and I could see the clerk at the 7-Eleven looking suspiciously at me out the window. I pulled out of the parking lot and drove until I found a Barnes & Noble. I figured it was only a matter of time. Has anyone done any research on that? On how many miles you can drive in any direction before running into a Barnes & Noble or a Starbucks or both? Anyway, I was glad for an iced chai and a comfortable leather chair to sit in while I waited, thumbing though a copy of that day's **New York Times.**

It was a few minutes before the uneasy feeling that had leaked into the periphery of my consciousness got my full attention. I felt eyes on me. I shifted in my seat but didn't raise my gaze from the paper. After a second, I put the newsprint down and stretched, casually looking around. A man stood in the Mystery section to my left reading the back cover of a paperback. He was a stocky guy in sunglasses, as big and solid as a slab of slate, baseball cap over a shaved head, an olive bomber jacket and cleaned, pressed denims. He had on a pair of heavy black boots. He glanced up at me, saw me looking at him. Did he smile, just slightly? He returned the book to the shelf, turned his back, and walked away. There was something ugly about his face. There was a cold meanness to his aura.

It wasn't just some creepy guy staring. The thing was, he looked familiar to me. I'd seen him before. Oh, shit, the thought seized me, was it the same man I saw on the train?

My heart was fluttering. I took my chai and left the store as quickly as I could without running. The baseball cap and the sunglasses made it hard to tell if it was the same guy. Back in the Jeep, I sat breathing hard and watched the door in my rearview mirror, wondering if he'd come out after me. For some reason, I remembered the conversation I'd had with Zelda about the man she told me had been looking for me. I also flashed on what Jake had said and even what the detective had implied, that someone might have trailed me to get to Christian Luna—and that they might still be following me. I pulled the Nokia from the pocket of my coat and called Zelda.

"FiverosescanIhelpyou," she answered. Her voice was gruff and muffled, as always.

"It's Ridley."

"You want a slice?"

"No. Zelda, remember you said someone was looking for me the other day? What did he look like?" I heard the background noise of the restaurant, the **ka-ching!** of the register. I kept my eyes on the rearview mirror, watching the door.

"Akkch," she said. "I can remember? WhatamIEinstein?"

"Zelda. It's important." I knew she could remember every detail about the guy if she wanted to. She just couldn't be bothered. Talking was not her favorite thing to do.

"He looked like trouble. That's what he looked like."

"Was he a medium-sized older man, dark hair, dark eyes, baseball cap?" I asked, hoping she'd say yes and I could go back to thinking it had been Christian Luna asking for me and forget about the B&N skinhead, chalk my fear up to paranoia.

"Nononono. That's not him." I waited for elaboration but none came. "Twelve fifty-five," she said. **Ka-ching!** "Your change. Have a nice day."

"Zelda," I said.

She heaved a sigh. "Big guy. Bald—you know, shaved head. He was a punk, I'll tell you that. Ridley, what kind of trouble are you in?"

My heart sank. "I don't know," I said.

"I don't want any trouble in this building," she said, her voice stern.

"Okay. Bye, Zelda."

I ended the call and slunk down low in the driver's seat, still watching the door. If he came out after me, then . . . I don't know what. Then I was fucked, I guess. I caught sight of myself in the sideview mirrors because I didn't have them set properly. I looked silly, wide-eyed like a spooked horse, hunched down, chewing on the end of my straw. "You're paranoid," I said to my reflection. But just as I was about to laugh at myself, I saw him come out of the double doors and gaze around the parking lot as if he was looking for something. I couldn't tell if it was the guy from the train or not. They looked similar, but that didn't mean anything. He turned and started walking away from the Jeep, disappeared into a crowd of people coming and going from the store. I pulled from my spot quickly while he wasn't looking and left the lot. After driving around for a bit, with adrenaline making me shaky and distracted, I was satisfied that no one had followed me and I went to see Maria Cacciatore.

EIGHTEEN

I guess it was unrealistic of me, but I kept looking out for the Firebird while I was driving with a heart conflicted by hope and wariness. I fantasized ways that Jake could have tracked me. He could be following in another vehicle, not the Firebird, to protect me from whoever it was who might be following me. Maybe he had a way to track my credit-card usage; he'd know I rented a car, bought a cell phone in New Jersey, charged something at Barnes & Noble. PI's could do things like that, couldn't they? But, of course, that was just me being a dork.

I held a picture of Jake in my mind and the memory of our nights together washed over me. Whatever else he'd lied about or omitted, that had been true. There was no way to fake that kind of intimacy. Was there? Does it sound like I was kidding myself? Nor-

mally even the slightest hint of dishonesty and
I walked. But in my new universe, I felt like
Alice in Wonderland. Everything was strangely
off and the usual rules didn't seem to apply
any longer.

When I got to the address Maria had given
me on the phone, I parked the car and looked
uneasily in my rearview mirror for the sub-
way/B&N psycho. I didn't see anyone and
I laughed a little at myself then. I was really
becoming paranoid. There were millions of
stocky guys with shaved heads walking
around, and absolutely no reason for me to
suspect that the man Zelda spoke to, the one
I'd seen on the train, and the B&N freak were
the same. In fact, it was downright preposterous. Right?

I walked along an exterior corridor exposed to the outside, looking at numbers on
the doors. When I came to apartment four, I
knocked. There was a long silence inside and I
wondered if Maria Cacciatore had changed
her mind. I knocked again.

"Hold on, for crying out loud," a muffled
voice called from inside. "I'm coming."

I heard a toilet flush, then water running,
then heavy footfalls on the floor. The door
swung open and a frowning round woman in

a bright blue muumuu and matching turban stood before me.

"Ms. Cacciatore?"

She looked at my face and her frown dropped, was replaced by a look of awe. "Sweet Jesus, Mary, and Joseph," she said, stepping back from me.

I looked behind me to see what she had seen, but when I turned back around, she was still staring at me.

"I'm glad you called me first," she said. "You would have given me a heart attack."

She stepped aside and I walked in. She didn't take her eyes off of me.

"I don't understand," I said, though I think I knew exactly what she was talking about.

"You must know," she said. "You look just like her. You're her very image."

When she closed the door, the room went almost completely dark. The windows were covered by red velvet curtains and the light that came in through them painted the room the color of blood. On every surface there were pillar candles in glass holders painted with the saints—you know, the kind you find in every bodega in the city. In the corner of the room sat a table covered by a dark cloth. It looked red, too. Everything in the room did, even my own hands. There was a chair on either side of the table, a stack of tarot cards, and another candle on top. Wind chimes hung from the ceiling but were silent in the still heat of the room. Somewhere musky incense burned; I could feel my sinuses swelling from the intense aroma.

"You want me to put that incense out? It bothers some of my clients."

"No, it's fine," I said, still looking around me, taking in the space. "Ms. Cacciatore—"

"Call me Madame Maria, dear. Everyone does. Or just Madame for short."

"Oookaay," I said slowly.

"So," she said, sitting down on the couch with a heavy sigh. Her muumuu flowed around her. She repositioned her turban. My eyes had adjusted to the dim light and I could see that she hadn't stopped looking at me. "Why did you lie to me, Jessie? Why would you lie to an old lady who used to change your diapers?" She patted the couch beside her and I sat down.

"I didn't lie. Not about my name. I'm not Jessie. My name is Ridley Jones."

She nodded. "You came to find out about your mother. You want to know what happened to her." She said this as if she had been consulting an oracle, though I'd told her as much already.

"I came to find out about Teresa Elizabeth Stone," I said stubbornly. It's difficult when people think you're someone other than who you are. They call you by a name you don't own, refer to parents you've never met. They're certain of their information, as certain as you are of yours. And it makes your head foggy. It's confusing. There was still no hard proof that I was Jessie Stone, and frankly, even if I had been, I was no longer. I was Ridley Jones. That was my identity and I intended to hold on to that.

"Okay," she said, her tone motherly, knowing. "Ridley. Okay. Tell me what's going on."

I looked around me. "Don't you know, **Madame**?"

"Hey, give me a break," she said with a smile. "An old lady needs to earn a living. Anyway, I just read the cards. People need guidance in this world, someone to talk to about their problems, someone to tell them it's going to be all right. Isn't that why **you** came?"

I didn't answer Maria, tossed around the idea of getting up and leaving. But there was something about the old lady that I liked, in spite of (or maybe because of) her pseudo-mysticism. She had a strong face, lined with wrinkles and heavy with sagging skin around her jawline and eyes. Her body looked soft and welcoming, as if a lot of people had found comfort in her arms. I felt safe in her weird little space. So I told her my story. Unlike I had with Detective Salvo, I omitted nothing. As you can see, it didn't take much to get me to spill my guts. I've never been very good at keeping secrets.

She released a heavy sigh when I'd finished. "You need a cup of tea."

She got up and went to the efficiency kitchen that was just across from the couch. She ran tap water into a cup, put a teabag in, and stuck it in the microwave. She came back over as the microwave hummed and placed a hand on the side of my face.

"You must feel like your head is going to explode, Ridley." Her sympathy made me want to cry but I kept myself together. I really appreciated her making a point to say "Ridley" instead of "Jessie."

The microwave beeped and she retrieved the cup, put in a little milk and honey, and brought it to me. "Your mother—sorry, I mean Teresa—was a good girl," said Maria, sitting back down. "She just made the mistake of getting involved with that loser Christian Luna. I could tell from the minute I met him that he was going to be no good for her. But that was her karma, always involved with the wrong man. Some were rich, some were poor, some were handsome, some were homely. But they all had one thing in common—they were wrong for her." She looked over at me, as if she was afraid her statement had hurt me. I shook my head, indicating that it was fine, that she should say what she felt.

"Anyway, maybe I shouldn't be so hard on Christian Luna," she said thoughtfully, with a small smile. She reached out and touched my face again. "Without him, maybe there wouldn't have been any Jessie. And that baby was the **love** of Teresa's life. The sun rose and set with that little girl." She stopped for a second and put her hand to her chest. "Anyway, now you say he's dead. And I shouldn't speak ill of the dead."

"He said he didn't kill Teresa. Do you believe that?"

"I never believed that he had killed her. I know it **looked** like he did. I mean, he'd been there that night, yelling and screaming. **Everybody** was sure he'd been the one. Especially with him disappearing and Jessie being kidnapped like that. But Christian Luna was a coward. It takes guts to kill a woman and steal her child. And he never wanted the responsibility of caring for Jessie. Not really. Why would he take her?"

"Yeah, but a crime like that is about control, isn't it? You want what you can't have just because someone says it's not yours anymore."

She shrugged. "Maybe. But I didn't see it in him. He would yell and scream, maybe slap Teresa around a little. He broke Jessie's arm, but that was an accident. That's a different personality than someone who murders the mother of his child." She shook her head. "No. I never believed it was him."

"Then who?"

"I don't know," she said. "But I know this: Jessie wasn't the only child in the area to go missing that year."

I looked at her.

"Oh, yes," she said. "There were at least three others that I heard of in the news over the next few months. More over the years."

"Were the parents murdered?" I asked.

She squinted into the distance. "I don't think so. Not that I recall."

"So what happened?" I asked, sitting up. "I mean, the media must have been all over it."

"Not really. It's not like today. Back then you didn't really hear stories like that. The idea of pedophiles abducting children, serial-type crimes . . . people didn't really know that much about it, didn't **want** to know. Plus, these were all poor children from the projects, low-income housing. It's not as though they were rich kids stolen from their homes."

"Yeah," I said, not sure what else to say. The information was hitting me hard for a number of reasons. First of all, it gave a certain credibility to Christian Luna's story, and if he'd been telling the truth about not killing Teresa, then he might have been telling the truth about me. Second, if Jessie was one of a number of local children abducted, and I **was** actually Jessie, what were the implications of that? How did I get from there to here?

Suddenly the wind chimes hanging from the ceiling started to jangle. There were several sets of them, all of them giving off different octaves of tones. The sound was at once eerie and alarming. Madame Maria jumped up from the couch.

"Don't worry," she said loudly, moving behind the counter that separated the kitchen from the rest of the space. "I have a fan set on a timer to go off every hour. It lets me know when a session is over." She disappeared for a second and the fan, mounted in a corner on the ceiling, slowed. The sound of the chimes grew gentler. I was feeling edgy, jumpy, so I got up to leave. I took a business card out of my pocket and handed it to Madame Maria.

"I'm sorry," she said as she took it and put it in her muumuu.

"For what?"

"For everything you've been through. It doesn't seem fair." She looked sad, older than she had when I arrived.

I shrugged. "Life's not fair," I said. But those weren't my words. They were my mother's. It was something I'd heard her say countless times over the years. I did, in fact, believe life was fair. Well, not fair exactly, but balanced. Yin and yang. Good and evil. Right and wrong. Bitter and sweet. One did not exist without the other. When life is bad, you know it's going to get better. When life is good, you know it's going to go bad. If that's not fair, I don't know what is.

She nodded. "Hey, you want a reading before you go?"

"No, thanks," I said with a smile. I wasn't sure I wanted to know what the cards held for me. "Call me, okay? If you think of anything else."

She nodded again and looked like she wanted to say something. I waited. "You know," she said tentatively. "Teresa used to take Jessie to the clinic on Drew Street. They took her insurance and she liked the doctor there. They might still have her records. Little Angels, it was called. It's still there."

I looked at her blankly.

"If you ever want to know for sure. I mean, maybe they have dental records or fingerprints."

She meant if I wanted to know for sure if I was Jessie or not—because both of Jessie's parents were dead and she thought there would be no other way for me to find out. She reached up for me then, took me into her arms, and embraced me. Her arms were as warm and as soft as I imagined they would be.

"Thanks," I said as I stepped back and turned to walk away.

"Be careful, Jessie," she said softly as she closed the door. I think she didn't mean me to hear. I wished I hadn't.

NINETEEN

"Did you know there were three other children abducted from this area in 1972?" I asked Detective Salvo.

I was sitting in my rented Jeep in the parking lot of the Hackettstown Public Library. After sitting in front of the microfiche for more than two hours, I'd been ejected from the building by the librarian, who wanted to go home. She'd let me in just minutes before closing, then let me stay as she finished her work for the night. Finally, she turned out the lights and told me it was time to go. Now, my head ached (yes, again)—eyestrain, probably. It was dark and I was tired, but hopped up on Frappuccinos. It was cold out and the car was taking a while to heat up. I could see my breath.

"I mean, like, literally within a five-mile

radius," I added for emphasis when he didn't say anything.

He was quiet on the other end. Then: "I fail to see what this has to do with my case, Ridley. We're talking thirty years ago in another state."

Now it was my turn to be silent. It had **seemed** important back in my faux-wood carrel at the library. Four children, including Jessie Stone, had all gone missing that year from low-income housing in the Hackettstown area. Two boys, both three years old; two girls, one an infant just nine months old, the other, Jessie, not yet two. Light skinned, one blonde, one redhead, two brunettes. None of the cases were ever solved. I'd taken extensive notes. Now I thought, Why did I call him? Maybe because I didn't have anyone else to call . . . not about this, anyway.

"You know the only thing more annoying to cops than private investigators? Civilians **pretending** to be private investigators."

"Maybe it ties in to what happened to Christian Luna," I said. It sounded lame now, amateurish even to my own ears.

"What, like, maybe he knew something about it?"

"Exactly."

"Ridley, if he knew something that would get him off the hook for murdering his wife, don't you think he'd have brought it up thirty years ago instead of living the rest of his life on the lam?"

I didn't say anything. He had a point.

"Where are you?"

"In Jersey."

"Come on home, okay?" he said, his voice softer now. "I'll look into it. I promise." I couldn't tell whether he was patronizing me or not. He had one of those voices that just sounded patronizing.

"Oh," he said. "One other thing. That friend of yours? Excuse me, the guy you've never heard of?"

"Yeah?"

"Turns out he has a new address. Guess where? Your building."

"How about that," I said. I think I sounded pretty cool. But I had that sick dread you got in your stomach as a kid when you were caught in a lie. Scared, foolish, no idea what to say. Very much inclined to lie again, if pressed.

"Guess what else?" He could barely keep the smile out of his voice. "Guy says he was up in Riverdale last night, a bar up there he likes to hang out at. Jimmy's Bronx Café. Stopped off for a bite at a pizzeria in Riverdale on the way home. But he didn't see or hear anything in the park. And he's never heard of you, either."

"Huh," I said. Keeping it simple. "Well, you know how it is in the city. You can live next door to someone for years and never get to know his name."

"Quite a coincidence, though, don't you think?"

"Certainly is."

"Only I don't believe in coincidences," he said, his voice going flat. "Come back to the city, Ridley. I have a feeling you and I are going to need to talk again."

"I have a lawyer," I said weakly.

"Yes, I know," said Detective Salvo. "He's been in touch. You don't know me very well yet, Ridley. Maybe you think Alexander Harriman intimidates me. Let me assure you that you're mistaken. Just come home."

I did go back to the city but held on to the Jeep, parked it in the same garage where Jake kept his car. I noticed that the Firebird was gone.

I had a lot of new information and no

brainpower to process it. It felt weird going back to my apartment, as if it wasn't really mine anymore. All the memories lingering there were ghosts from someone else's life, someone silly and frivolous. For a second, I thought about turning around and getting back in the Jeep. Going somewhere, anywhere else. But I was too tired. The pizzeria was closed and the street was pretty quiet. I dragged myself up the stairs and into my apartment.

He was there, waiting for me. Of course he was. On some level I knew he would be, would have been disappointed if he hadn't been. He had the light on next to the couch and was lying there, staring at the ceiling. He stood when I entered. He looked so relieved, like he might pass out from it.

"How'd you get in?" I asked.

"You left your keys this morning." It was true. When I left earlier, I'd grabbed the set I'd made Zack return to me when I couldn't find my own.

Anyone in her right mind would have kept her distance, asked him to leave, but I think we've sufficiently established that I wasn't anywhere close to being in my right mind. He came toward me quickly and pulled me into him. I wrapped my arms around him and held on tight. He was so strong and that felt good because suddenly I barely had the strength to even stand. I felt the taut, hard muscles of his biceps, of his thighs. My heart thrummed like an engine in my chest. I couldn't get close enough to him.

"Man," he breathed into my hair. "I don't think I've ever been as worried about anyone as I've been about you tonight."

I looked up at him. There was that sadness I'd seen before and I thought about the things Detective Salvo had told me. An odd vulnerability resided in the features of his face, as if he was unaccustomed to being controlled by his emotions and a little afraid of how it felt. He moved a hand to my face. His touch was tender, though his hands felt calloused.

"There are a lot of things you should know about me," he said softly for the second time since we'd met. This time I was prepared to listen.

"I know," I answered. "Let's start with your name."

The only thing you can give to someone telling a story like Jake's is silence. Silence and your complete attention. We sat on my couch

with my legs draped over his lap. He spoke
very quietly, hardly looking at me except in
quick, shy glances. His speech was halting, as
though it wasn't a story he'd told often. And
when he was done, I felt like he had entrusted
me with something. Something I had to hold
and keep and protect. It bonded us.

"The funny thing is that I remember her.
I remember my mother. Or maybe I just
dreamed her. But I remember what it was like
to feel loved, safe, to be tucked in at night.
Maybe that's why I'm not more fucked up
than I am."

Harley Jacobsen started calling himself
Jake in his first foster home. **Harley** was a kid,
a little boy who wet his bed sometimes and
carried a tattered Winnie the Pooh, the last
remnant of his former life as a child. **Harley**
was someone who couldn't protect himself
against two foster brothers who were bigger
than he was and meaner, more malicious than
wolves. **Jake** fought back where Harley would
have cried and cowered. **Jake** wasn't afraid; he
was angry. And he fought like a berserker, using all his strength and all his will. He had to
because he was small, because it took everything he had just to stand up to people who
were bigger than he was. So one day, when his

two foster brothers started taunting him in the small backyard of their New Jersey home, after months of beatings and verbal abuse, Harley went away and Jake took up a big, sharp stick. When the older of the two boys grabbed for him, Jake took the stick and drove it into his eye.

"I can still hear him screaming," said Jake. "It makes me sad now. But back then, it was the sound of victory. It was the sound that let me know I didn't have to be anyone's victim anymore."

He was, of course, removed from that foster home and labeled as a problem kid, disturbed. One shrink noted in his juvenile record, which Jake later gained access to, that he had a disassociative disorder because he'd started calling himself Jake.

"But I wasn't disassociating. I knew who I was. I just had this sense that I had to get real hard real fast or I wasn't going to survive. Harley was a little kid's name, to my seven-year-old mind. Jake, which I got from the first syllable of my last name, was a man's name. I knew that's what I needed to be."

The rest of his childhood was a veritable carnival of abuse. In one home, he was made to sleep in a sleeping bag under another child's bed. "They called it a bunk bed," he said with a short, hard laugh. In this home, he ate cheese sandwiches for every meal for about three months. "It wasn't bad, though. Looking back, it was probably the best of all of them. No one bothered me." Eventually they turned him back over to the state because he kept wetting his bed and was sick often, coming down with cold after cold. The abuse he endured in subsequent foster homes ranged from neglect to physical violence, and he had the scars all over his body to prove it. There was the foster mother who made him kneel on the broken glass of a window he'd broken while playing ball in the yard. And the man who burned him with a cigarette when he discovered Jake had finished off the last of a carton of milk. There were knife fights and fistfights at school, nearly every week.

"My foster home 'tour of duty' ended when I was fourteen," he said, glancing up at me. I held his eyes for a second and he seemed to find what he needed there. I was riven by what he was telling me, shredded. I wanted to climb inside his skin and comfort him on a cellular level, erase all memory of his suffering. But of course you can never do that for someone, and it's a folly to imagine you can. Besides, he seemed whole, solid. A man who'd walked through the gauntlet, survived, and healed his own wounds. He was strong.

"My foster father, a man named Ben Wright, shot me. He seemed okay at first. I mean, really like a nice guy. He took me to a couple of baseball games at Yankee Stadium. His wife, Janet, was cool, really pretty. I was their only foster kid. It was a pretty good gig for a while.

"I was really big by then. I mean, ripped. I worked out every day. It served a couple of purposes. I think I was channeling my rage without really knowing it at the time. And it made me look hard. People stayed away from me. I think I looked more like sixteen or seventeen. I had a couple of tattoos by then; some pretty nasty scars. People had stopped fucking with me. I think everything about me said, **Stay away.** Of course, the flip side of that was that I didn't have an easy time making friends, either.

"Then Janet got pregnant. I thought, Great, I'm so out of here. But she said no, I could stay as long as I wanted.

"The thing was, Ben, I guess, was sterile. Only Janet didn't know it. She'd fucked around and got herself pregnant, not realizing.

Ben went nuts. Got it in his head that it was **me** who knocked her up."

"You were fourteen," I said.

He laughed without any humor. "Yeah, I know."

"I was sleeping one night and woke up to see Ben standing over me tapping me on the head with a gun. He goes, 'You fuck my wife, punk?' I said, 'No, Ben. No way.'

"And I remember feeling so sad in that moment, more than scared. Because Ben had been nicer to me than anyone had ever been. And it made me feel bad that he'd think I'd do that to him. I said to him, 'Don't send me away. I like it here.' It just felt so unfair. They'd been kind to me. I'd been better behaved because of it. I was doing all right in high school, getting good grades, and still everything was going to shit.

"Anyway, I tried to sit up and he shot me in the shoulder. He meant to kill me but he missed."

The rest of his adolescence was spent in an orphanage for boys. And it was there of all places that he found a mentor and a friend. A counselor by the name of Arnie Coel.

"He taught me how to face my demons, express my anger in healthy ways. He made me keep a journal and then discuss the things I wrote with him. He taught me about art, encouraged me to get in touch with the creative part of myself. Paid out of his own pocket for me to take classes in metalwork and sculpture when I expressed an interest. He'd grown up in the system as well. And he used to say, 'Just because people treat you like shit, just because you may feel like shit sometimes, doesn't mean you **are** shit. You can make something out of your life. You can give of yourself in this world to make it a better place.'

"He was the one who suggested I enlist, so that they'd pay for my education. It was a hard road but I think the right one for me. Without that discipline after I left the orphanage, I think I might have headed down some wrong roads. Isn't that what they say about soldiers, if they weren't in the armed forces, they'd be in prison? I moved to the city when my time was up, went to John Jay College. I liked the idea of law enforcement, but I didn't like the NYPD."

"That's why you got your PI license?"

He nodded, looked at the floor.

"The police were here. A detective told me everything," I said. And he nodded again.

"Why didn't you tell me about it?" I asked.

He shrugged. "It doesn't define me. I'm more defined by my art. The more money I made with my sculpture and the furniture, the less PI work I did. I primarily did insurance fraud investigation, checked up on some cheating husbands, did some work for the NYPD following around people on probation for DUI."

He paused a second, rubbed his eyes. I wasn't sure how well this answer sat with me. It seemed incomplete, a little vague. But he seemed frayed from the telling of things and I didn't want to push him for more and better answers. I had a lot of other questions, too, but it didn't seem like the right time for asking them. There'd be time for that later, I thought.

"I felt like as a private investigator I could right some wrongs and still play by my own rules," he went on when I didn't say anything. "So I got my PI license in ninety-seven. But it felt low. You catch somebody cheating on his wife, or some poor slob trying to make ends meet while on worker's comp, and then you fuck up his life. I don't know. Maybe I had a fantasy about what it would mean to be a PI. Thought I could use those skills to find out what happened to me, what happened to my parents. But I never got very far with that, either."

He sighed, looked up at the ceiling. I saw the tension in his shoulders relax a little.

"I stayed close with Arnie until he died a little over a year ago. Colon cancer. He was the one always pushing me to find out about my parents. But when he died . . ." He let his voice trail off. He was finished talking; I could see that. He leaned back and looked at me, as if trying to decide what kind of impact he'd had on me. He looked a little uncertain, as if he thought I might ask him to leave. I crawled into his arms and we stayed holding each other like that for a long time. I could hear his heart beating in his chest, and the sound made me feel an overwhelming wash of gratitude. In spite of all the things and all the people that had tried to break it, even stop its rhythm, it was strong.

"I'm sorry," he said after a while. "I've never really told anyone all of that. Except for Arnie. It was too heavy to lay on you. Especially with everything you're dealing with."

I sat up. "I'm stronger than I look," I said with a smile.

"You look pretty strong," he said, smiling back and looking relieved. He reached out to touch my hair, but I took his hand and placed his palm to my mouth. I kissed him there and he closed his eyes.

"Thank you," I said to him.

He shook his head and frowned. "For what?"

"For sharing yourself with me, for telling me that."

"I—" he said, and stopped. "I don't want you to feel sorry for me. That's not why I told you."

"Believe me, Jake," I said, looking at him dead in the eye. "That's the last thing I feel for you. You're a strong man who was dealt a shitty hand and came out a winner, anyway. I admire you. I respect you. I do **not** feel sorry for you."

When you start to really know someone, all his physical characteristics start to disappear. You begin to dwell in his energy, recognize the scent of his skin. You see only the essence of the person, not the shell. That's why you can't fall in love with beauty. You can lust after it, be infatuated by it, want to own it. You can love it with your eyes and your body but not your heart. And that's why, when you really connect with a person's inner self, any physical imperfections disappear, become irrelevant.

Loving my ex-boyfriend Zack was, I think, looking back, a decision. He was handsome, funny, he displayed the characteristics most women found desirable in a mate. I liked him. He was close to my family. I **decided** to be in love with him, to form a relationship with him. It was a good idea, praised by many. Falling in love with Jake, though, was just that . . . falling. There was no choice involved. It rushed through me in a white-water current, and if I'd tried to fight it, I might have drowned.

The way he looked at me in that moment, I could tell he was there, too, in the same mighty rush. He saw me, the shimmering essence of me beneath my skin. I felt recognized. And I was so grateful, because I'm not sure I would have even recognized myself at this point. I knew who I was; don't get me wrong. I just didn't know what to call her anymore. Maybe that's all love really is, just seeing each other. Seeing beyond the names and all the external things we use to define and label ourselves. It didn't matter if he was Harley or Jake, if I was Ridley or Jessie. Maybe it never had.

He stood then and pulled me to him, pressed his mouth to mine. In a minute, we were devouring each other. There was more to say but there were no more words, just this ravenous physical need. I made him take me upstairs to his apartment; I couldn't relax in mine with all of my ghosts hanging around watching. And in the gray nothing of his apartment we disappeared into an ocean of warmth and pleasure, giving everything and asking for nothing, but finding ourselves sated just the same.

TWENTY

The next morning, he made me Sunday breakfast, pancakes with strawberry jam since he was out of syrup, and rich, strong cups of coffee. We ate in bed and I filled him in on the day before. It didn't seem possible that it hadn't even been forty-eight hours since I'd watched Christian Luna die. I told him about Detective Salvo, Madame Maria, and what I'd found at the library.

"Detective Salvo's partner came to have a little chat with me and wound up taking me down to the Ninth Precinct," Jake said. "I wasn't as cooperative as you were, I guess. But they had to let me go after a couple of hours. I had the feeling they would have liked to hold on to me longer. Anyway, they impounded my car."

"He told me they'd talked to you."

"When?"

"I called Salvo to tell him about the missing kids in Hackettstown."

"Why did you do that?" he asked, and for a second I thought I heard something more than curiosity in his voice. Was it worry?

"I don't know." I shrugged, considering the answer. I wasn't really sure myself. "I felt like I needed an ally." Then I added, "I wasn't sure who I could trust."

He nodded. "I know," he said quietly. "I'd lied to you. You weren't sure you could trust me. I'm sorry for that."

I shook my head dismissively. It didn't matter anymore.

"What did he say? About the kids?" Jake asked after another minute.

"Nothing. Just told me he'd look into it, I think more to placate me than anything. Told me to give up my new career as private investigator and come home."

"That's not bad advice."

I rolled my eyes at him.

"Jake," I said after some more coffee and a few bites of pancake. "What happened when you tried to look for your family?"

I wasn't sure if this was an okay question to ask, but I was operating under a new policy of saying exactly what I was thinking, and it had been nagging at me since we'd made love the night before. He'd fallen asleep and I'd lain awake thinking about what he'd told me earlier. I remembered what Detective Salvo had said, his exact words that Jake had been "abandoned into the system." Jake had told me that he remembered his mother, nothing more.

He stopped chewing and didn't look at me right away. He shrugged. "I looked more or less nonstop from the time I got my PI license up until Arnie died. Like I said, it was one of his big things. He thought I needed to solve the mystery of my past before I could build a future. Maybe, if I'm honest with myself, it's the whole reason I became a PI."

"And . . ."

"I'm not much closer than I was five years ago," he said with a shrug. He cleared our empty plates off the bed and took them into the kitchen. I let him go and didn't follow, in case he was looking for some space from the question. He came back and sat beside me and continued.

"They say she left me without any documents, no birth certificate, no vaccination records. If I told you I didn't believe that, that I remembered being loved by the woman whose face I still see in my mind, that I don't believe I was abandoned like that, would you think it was just a little kid's fantasy?"

I shook my head. His eyes were bright and he was looking at me hard. I could see that it was important to him that I give him my faith. And I could do that honestly. "I wouldn't think that, no. I'd tell you to follow your gut. Sometimes it's the only thing we can trust."

He nodded and looked away from me. "Arnie did a lot for me on the sly. That's how I got access to my juvenile record, could see how they labeled me early on in the system that made me undesirable to couples looking to adopt. Not that the odds were good, anyway. I was too old; people want infants."

"Where were you found?" I asked, thinking that would be a logical place to start the search.

"There's no record of that," he said. "My intake file was lost."

It seemed pretty grim—no parent names, no birth records. I thought of his password, "quidam." It made sense to me now.

"Anyway," he said, slapping his hands down on his legs as he stood. "This is my ongoing crusade and we have more pressing things to worry about right now, mainly **your** ongoing crusade." He was working hard at lightening the mood. It wasn't really working, sorry to say.

"Our crusades are eerily similar," I noted, trying and failing to keep the sadness out of my voice.

"Indeed they are," he agreed. "Except people I talk to aren't being assassinated and I'm not being menaced by a skinhead."

We laughed then. Like people laugh at funerals, letting off some steam, aware that there's nothing to laugh about at all.

Jake and I spent the rest of the day trying to locate the parents of the missing children in Hackettstown, using the same story I'd used to get Madame Maria to talk to me. I sat on Jake's couch with a Morris County phone book, one in a collection of phone books he had in his closet for his work as a PI, and his telephone. He sat at his computer and used the Internet, called on some of his police contacts using his cell phone. By the end of the day, we'd learned through family members and newspaper and police reports that except for one, they were all dead.

Jake was able to find much of the information we sought on the Internet archives of a couple of different Jersey papers, the **Record** and the **Star-Ledger.**

Sheila Murray, mother of Pamela, who was nine months old when she was abducted, died in 1975 in a DUI wreck for which she was responsible. Three years after the unsolved abduction of her only child, she ran a red light and collided with another vehicle carrying three teenage girls, all of whom also died at the scene. According to articles written after Pamela was snatched from her crib while Sheila slept, Sheila apparently hadn't been sure of Pamela's paternity and was raising the child alone.

"Dead end," said Jake after we'd exhausted both papers of their articles on Sheila and Pamela Murray.

"Literally," I said.

Michael Reynolds, father of Charlie, who was three when he went missing, had been left to raise his son alone when his wife, Adele, died from injuries incurred in a fight at a local bar. The article we found in the **Record** reported that the family was survived by Adele's mother, Linda McNaughton. When there was no listing in the phone book, a quick search in the online phone directory located a telephone number for the woman, who still lived in the same town.

In a terse, uncomfortable conversation with Linda McNaughton, I learned that Michael Reynolds was a heroin addict who died less than a year after Charlie was kidnapped from their one-bedroom apartment.

Ms. McNaughton said something chilling during my conversation with her, something that stayed with me for the rest of the day, long after our conversation had ended. "She was my daughter, may she rest in peace, and I loved her," she said. "But she never wanted that boy. Tried to give him up a couple days after he was born, but she went back for him. Couldn't take the guilt. And Michael, he never wanted anything but the needle. You ask me, alive or dead, the kid's probably better off."

Jake was staring at the computer screen as I ended my call with her.

"Anything?" he asked absently, not taking his eyes off the screen.

I told him what she'd said. He didn't respond, just kept tapping his right finger on the mouse, scrolling through an article I couldn't see from my place on the couch.

"Doesn't it seem odd that all these people are dead?" I asked.

"It's very odd," he agreed, seeming distracted by his computer screen.

"Look at this," he said. I walked over to him to read over his shoulder.

Marjorie Mathers, mother of Brian, age three when he disappeared from his bed in the middle of the night, was currently serving a life sentence for the murder of her husband. She'd killed him three weeks after Brian had gone missing. They'd been entrenched in a vicious custody battle over their child, and she claimed that he'd hired men to abduct him. Her lawyers claimed that she was half-mad over her missing boy and that, in combination with suffering years of abuse from her husband, was teetering on the edge of sanity. They said that she hadn't meant to kill him but had gone to accuse him of abducting Brian to punish her for leaving him. The gun, she claimed, had accidentally discharged in the struggle. But evidence supported the prosecutors' claim that she'd shot him in the back while he slept. She would be eligible for parole in the year 2020.

"Well, let's see if we can find a way to talk to this woman," I suggested.

"I don't know if that's such a good idea, Ridley," said Jake, swiveling around to look at me.

"Why?"

"Because she's obviously a nutcase."

"Why would you say that?"

"Um, because she murdered her husband?"

I shrugged and moved back over to the couch. "Just because she killed someone doesn't mean she doesn't have information that might be helpful. She's the only parent alive."

Jake sighed. "I just think it's irresponsible at this point to dredge up the past for this woman without more pointed questions. It's going to be a painful conversation, if she agrees to see us at all. The woman is spending the rest of her life in prison; her son was abducted and never found. Try to imagine that. Do you really want to cause her more pain?"

He was right. And I felt like a shit, someone so selfishly in pursuit of my own answers that I'd lost compassion for someone else's suffering.

"Then where do we go from here?"

"I don't know," answered Jake.

Around eight o'clock, Jake went out to get

us some dinner and I sat flipping though my notebook trying to figure out why it had seemed so important to me to find these people. What had I hoped to learn? Where did I expect it to lead me? I thought about what Linda McNaughton had said. I flipped through the pages of my notes, found her number, and dialed again.

"Ms. McNaughton?" I said when she picked up.

"Yes," she said, fatigue and annoyance creeping into her tone as she recognized my voice.

"This is Ridley Jones. I'm so sorry to bother you again, but I had another question about something you said."

She sighed. I heard the click and hiss of a butane lighter and she inhaled sharply. "This is not easy for me, Miss."

"I know and I'm sorry," I said as gently as I could, remembering Jake's words. "But please, just one more thing."

"What is it?"

"You said that your daughter tried to give Charlie up after he was born."

"That's right," she said, sounding defensive. "I tried to stop her. But we were all struggling financially. She thought it would be best for him."

"So . . . she took him to an adoption agency?"

"No," she said, and another sharp inhale was followed by a long pause. "You have to understand, with Michael being an addict and all, she didn't think they'd be good parents."

"I understand," I said. "But where did she take Charlie?"

"She . . . left him at one of those places."

"What places?" I asked. My blood was thrumming in my ears.

"One of those places that take your baby, no questions asked. You know, they don't want people to leave their babies in a Dumpster, so you can drop them, ring a bell, and take off. You have three days or something to go back if you change your mind."

"Ms. McNaughton," I said, "did she take Charlie to a Project Rescue facility?"

"Yes, that was it. That's what it was called. But like I said, she went back and got him. They were kind to her, gave her some counseling. She felt better after talking to them, like she could handle being a mother to Charlie. But you ask me, he knew she didn't really want him. Colicky like you read about, screamed his head off night and day."

But I barely heard the rest. All I could

think about was Ace and what he had said to me that night. **Ask Dad about Uncle Max and his pet projects.**

I thanked her and hung up the phone. What did it mean? I had no idea. But I kept flashing on the brochures Dad had given me, seeing the images of the cold, filthy Dumpster and the warm blanketed arms of the nurse.

A thought danced through my mind, one that I immediately pushed aside as preposterous. But it kept pirouetting back and forth and I was unable to still it.

"What's wrong?" said Jake, entering the room with aromatic bags of Chinese food from Young Chow's. We were just out of range of their delivery service, but Jake and I both agreed they had the best garlic prawns in the East Village, well worth the walk.

"Nothing," I lied. "I'm just zoning out. I feel pretty wiped."

"I bet," he answered, looking at me. I think he knew I was holding something back, but he let it go. I wasn't ready to tell him what I was thinking. Hell, I wasn't even ready to **think** it.

"Find anything else out?" he said, nudging a little, I thought.

"No. Nothing." I rose and walked over to

the table, started unpacking the takeout containers.

He walked into the kitchen and after a few moments returned with plates, silverware, napkins, and, under his arm, a bottle of white wine.

"Let's eat," he said, pulling out a chair for me. "Everything seems better after a good meal and a good bottle of wine."

I smiled at him, hoping he was right.

TWENTY-ONE

Looking back at things now, I'm amazed at myself, really. I know they say hindsight is twenty-twenty and all that, but honestly, there were so many things about my past that I just accepted on face value, never questioned, never even wondered about. It's mind-boggling. On the other hand, doesn't everybody accept the life they're dealt at face value? Shouldn't they be allowed to? There were signs, though, I think. I'd always internally slagged on my mother for her dogged denial of anything and everything that came close to disturbing her concept of herself and her life, like her ability to pretend that Ace had never existed. But it was a trait I had inherited from her without even knowing it.

Is it strange that I have never once in all this time thought back on the last night I spent with my uncle Max? His death was so shocking that all the events following the phone call to our house announcing Max's car wreck had taken over all other memories of that night.

It was a perfect Christmas Eve. A light snow fell and all the houses on the street were glittering with tiny white lights. (It was a town ordinance that no multicolored-light strands could be used; that's how precious it is there.) All the neighbors had been saving their gallon milk and water jugs for weeks, and now they lined the streets, filled with sand and votive candles. The effect was magical, roads lined with glimmering white candles, protected by the plastic containers. After dinner, families would take to the streets, where the gaslight street lamps had been dimmed for the evening, and stroll off their heavy meals, stopping to chat with neighbors and friends amid the candlelight. It was nice. Even a hip, jaded New Yorker like myself had to admit there was simple beauty to it.

Nobody except me seemed to notice that Uncle Max showed up drunk. Well, maybe my parents noticed but nobody acknowledged it. Are you starting to get how it is with my family? I am, finally. Ugly or worrisome things are ignored. It's such a Waspy cliché. Not that we're actually Wasps. But the ignorance of these things was so deliberate, so total, that mentioning or discussing them would be tantamount to setting the house on fire, met with alarms and pandemonium. Denial, she's a fragile bitch, isn't she. So brittle and self-conscious, she can't stand the sight of herself.

Uncle Max was a practiced, functioning alcoholic. Maybe if you didn't know him, you wouldn't hear the lilt in his voice, see the glitter in his eye, the teeter in his gait. We had a house full of guests. Some of the young doctors my father worked with and their spouses, as well as Esme. Zack was also there; we were at the beginning of our relationship; it was still new, still promising, and though not thrilling, exactly, at least pleasantly tingling. Some of our neighbors had joined us. My mother had slaved to make everything perfect, from the flowers to the food. She was running around like an overstrung wind-up doll, marshaling the perfection, her face a grim mask of concentration among the sea of flushed and smiling ones. I remember Zack saying to me, "What's up with your mom? Is she okay?" I looked over at her. The tension was coming off her in waves as she straightened and served, moved quickly to and from the kitchen. "What do you mean?" I asked over the din of carols and conversation. "She's always like that." In that moment I really didn't see the problem. My mother was a basket case in her frenzy to have everything perceived as perfect; any flaw in the evening would be seen as a disaster and would be met with her total emotional withdrawal from everyone around her. And that seemed absolutely normal to me.

Looking back, I realize my father stayed as far away from her as possible. I remembered her scolding him for removing an hors d'oeuvre tray from the oven with a dishrag instead of an oven mitt, for overfilling the coffee filter, making the coffee too strong, any number of minor things. She'd scold him quietly but in a tone sizzling with white-hot disdain. By a certain point, he'd just learned to stay out of the line of fire. Again, none of this seemed odd to me. My obliviousness was total and I was having a perfectly lovely time.

Max blew in like a gale-force wind, all smiles and arms full of shopping bags filled, I knew, with impossibly extravagant gifts. He was a magnet and all the partygoers swirled around him like metallic dust. I don't know if it was his personality or his money or the powerful alchemy of those two things that drew so much attention to him, but from the minute he entered the room, he was its center and the joviality level increased tenfold. His booming voice and laughter could be heard over all the other auditory confetti. Even my mother seemed to relax a bit, the attention drawn away from her performance as hostess.

Zack and I disappeared into the kitchen and sat at the table, eating from a box of cookies someone had brought as a gift to my parents. From our position, we could still see all the party activities but we had stolen ourselves a quiet spot to sit alone and talk. We ripped open the decorative red cellophane and found these luscious little bow-tie cookies filled with raspberry jelly and dusted with sugar.

"Man, your uncle can put it away," Zack said.

"Hmm?" I said. "What do you mean?"

He looked at me. "I mean he's had five bourbons and he's only been here an hour."

I shrugged. "He's a big guy."

"Yeah, but, Jesus, it's barely had an effect on him."

I shrugged again, intent on the cookies in front of me. "That's just Max."

That's just Max. As if I even knew him.

A couple hours later the house was quieter.

Esme and Zack had left. My father had led a group out for the annual neighborhood candlelight stroll. My mother stayed behind, was furiously scrubbing pots in the kitchen, rebuffing all of my attempts to help her with the implication that no one could do it the way she could. Whatever. I wandered into the front room in search of something sweet and found my uncle Max sitting by himself in the dim light of the room before our gigantic Christmas tree. That's one of my favorite things in the world, the sight of a lit Christmas tree in a darkened room. I plopped myself next to him on the couch and he threw an arm around my shoulder, balancing a glass of bourbon on his knee with his free hand.

"What's up, Uncle Max?"

"Not much, kid. Nice party."

"Yeah."

We sat like that in a companionable silence for a while until something made me look up at him. He was crying, not making a sound, thin lines of tears streaming down his face like raindrops on glass. His expression was so unlike anything I'd ever seen on him, almost blank in its hopeless sadness. I think I just stared at him in shock. I grabbed his big bear-claw hand and clasped it in both of mine.

"What is it, Uncle Max?" I whispered, as if afraid that someone would see his true face exposed like this. I wanted to protect him.

"It's all coming back on me, Ridley."

"What is?"

"All the good I tried to do. I fucked it up. Man, I fucked it up so bad." His voice was shaking.

I shook my head. I was thinking, He's drunk. He's just drunk. But he grabbed me then by both of my shoulders, not hard but passionately. His eyes were bright and clear in his desperation.

"You're happy, right, Ridley? You grew up loved, safe. Right?"

"Yes, Uncle Max. Of course," I said, wanting so badly to reassure him, though at a total loss as to why my happiness meant so much to him.

He nodded and loosened his grip on me but still looked me dead in the eye. "Ridley," he said. "You might be the only good I've ever done."

"What's going on? Max?" We both turned to see my father standing in the doorway. He was just a black form surrounded by light. His voice sounded odd. Something foreign had crept into him, something dark and unrecognizable. Max released me as if I'd burned his hands.

"Max, let's talk," said my father, and Max rose. I followed him through the doorway and my father placed a hand on my shoulder to stop me. Max continued and walked through the French doors that led to my father's study. His shoulders sagged and his head was down, but he turned to give me a smile before disappearing into the room.

"What's wrong with him?" I asked my father.

"Don't worry, lullaby," he said with a forced lightness. "Uncle Max has had a bit too much to drink. He's got a lot of demons; sometimes the bourbon lets them loose."

"But what was he talking about?" I asked stubbornly, having the sense that I was being shut out of something important.

"Ridley," said my father, too sternly. He caught himself and softened his tone so quickly, I believed I'd imagined the harshness just a moment before. "Really, honey, don't worry about Max. It's the bourbon talking."

He walked away from me and disappeared behind his study doors. I hovered there a minute, heard the rumbling of their voices behind the oak. I knew the impossibility of listening at those doors; I'd tried it many times as a kid. Those doors were thick. You had to stand with your ear against them, and the people inside had to be yelling to hear anything. Plus, I'd run into my favorite aunt in the hallway. You remember her, Auntie Denial. She wrapped her arms around me and whispered comforting sentiments: **Just the bourbon. Just Max's demons talking. You know Max. Tomorrow he'll be fine.** As fragile as she is (she can't take a direct assault, you know), she's just as powerful when you cooperate with her, when you let her spin her web around you. Yes, as long as you don't look her in the face, she'll wrap you in a cocoon. It's safe and warm in there. So much nicer than the alternative.

That's the last time I saw my uncle Max. His face still wet with tears and flushed with bourbon, his sad smile, his final words to me. **Ridley, you might be the only good I've ever done.**

Oh, God, I thought now as I watched the ebb and flow of traffic down on First Avenue from Jake's window. What did he mean?

Jake was loading the dishwasher in the kitchen and I could hear him humming something. I loved that he got dinner and did the dishes. Zack had been such a mama's boy. Esme had always done everything for him, even picked out his clothes every morning until he went off to college. With a man like that, even if he'd learned at some point that not all women existed to tend to his needs, there was still the scent of resentment wafting off of him when he was doing something he secretly believed was beneath him. Jake knew how to take care of himself and didn't mind taking care of others. Maybe even liked it a little.

You're probably wondering, When is she going to bring up the things Detective Salvo told her? First, Jake's criminal record, and how the shot that killed Christian Luna came from the park where Jake had been hiding and not from the rooftop, as Jake implied that night. No, I hadn't forgotten about those things. And I knew I'd waited long enough to ask the questions to which I wasn't sure I wanted answers.

I felt him come into the room, rather than saw him, since I was staring out the window. He moved in close to me and wrapped me up in his arms. I waited for him to ask me what I was thinking, but he didn't.

"Detective Salvo says you have a criminal record," I said quietly.

He exhaled close to my ear but didn't release me from his arms. "You tend to get in trouble when you do PI work. It's not like the movies; cops don't like PI's. You get in the way, they bring you up on charges. None of it sticks. Anyway, I don't actually have a **record,** per se. It's not like I've done time, for Christ's sake." I could hear the laughter in his voice and it made me smile.

"You like the bad boys, huh?" he said, kissing my neck.

"You're my first one."

I was about to ask him about the shot fired in the park when I felt him stiffen and go quiet suddenly. I turned to look at him, wondering what I'd said. But he wasn't looking at me. He was looking out the window. He nudged me gently to the side.

"What do you see?"

"That guy standing in the doorway over there. Is that the man who's been following you? He was there when I came back from getting the food. And he's still standing there."

I peered over his shoulder and saw a form looming in a dark doorway. But I couldn't see a face, could make out only a leg and a black boot.

"I don't know," I said, feeling that flutter in my chest. "It could be anyone."

"I have a strange feeling."

"Yeah, shady people lingering in doorways in the East Village . . . that's really weird. Not normal at all."

"I'm going to go check it out. Stay here."

He'd grabbed his jacket and keys and was gone before I even finished saying, "What do you mean, check it out? That's ridiculous."

I heard him hammering down the stairs. I figured by the time I put pants on (I was wearing one of Jake's T-shirts and a pair of white socks) and followed him onto the street, he'd be back. So I stood in the window and watched the man across the street.

TWENTY-TWO

Before Jake reached the avenue, I saw the form move from the darkness and take off down the street. It wasn't the man from the train and Barnes & Noble. It was my brother.

What was he doing there? Waiting for me? I opened the window and yelled his name but the traffic noise took my voice away. I hurried to get dressed, and as I pulled on my jeans, I heard an odd ringing, muted as if coming from beneath layers of fabric. I realized it was coming from beneath the pile of my clothes on Jake's bedroom floor. I dug through it until I found it in the pocket of my coat—my new cell phone. I fished it out and looked at the number blinking on the screen. I didn't recognize it. I hesitated, wondering if I should bother answering it since no one I knew even had this number. Finally my curiosity got the better of me.

"Hello?" I said tentatively.

"Ridley Jones?" Gruff voice, older man. I recognized the voice but couldn't place it.

"Yes?"

"It's Detective Salvo." **Crap.**

"How'd you get this number?"

"You called me, remember? I saved the number on my cell phone."

"Oh." Another reason not to have a cellular phone.

"Listen, Ridley. I've got some bad news for you. We found the rifle that we believe killed Christian Luna," he said. My heart started thumping. Why was he telling me this?

"We found it up in the parking lot beside Fort Tryon Park in the Bronx. It was registered to your friend, Harley Jacobsen."

My mind started racing as I thought back to that night. Jake rushing from the darkness, pulling me from Christian Luna. I remembered his arm around me, ushering me quickly to the car. I remembered him driving to Fort Tryon Park and parking in the deserted lot, letting me sob into his shoulder. I didn't remember a rifle. I would have seen it. Wouldn't I?

"I just want to make sure you stay away from him tonight. We're going to be taking him in. I don't want you to get hurt."

"I told you I don't—"

"Spare me, Ms. Jones."

He was right. It seemed kind of silly to keep insisting that I didn't know him when it was obvious that I did. Still, I felt the need to stick to my story.

"If you think I'm his friend, why would you warn me that you're taking him in and risk my tipping him off?"

He paused for a second and I heard him release a breath. "Because I think you're a good person who has put her trust in someone that doesn't deserve it. And frankly, I don't want you caught in the crossfire. Don't make me regret giving you this break," he said, and hung up the phone.

Jake entered the apartment then and closed the door behind him.

"He took off," he said, shedding his jacket and throwing it over the chair. "He wasn't there when I reached the street."

I stood there with the cell phone still in my hand, not sure what to say or do. "Did you get a look at him when he ran?" I'd forgotten all about Ace. I must have looked strange staring at him, my mind rushing to process the information Detective Salvo had given me.

"What?" he said, his brow knitting.

Then I thought I could hear the sirens faintly, off in the distance. He didn't really seem to notice. It's not as though it's an unusual sound in the city night. "They're coming for you, Jake," I said.

"Who?"

"Detective Salvo just called me," I said, buttoning my jeans and looking at him now.

"He called you?" he said, looking at me hard. "How?"

"On my cell phone. He had the number from when I called him yesterday." I moved closer to him. "That's not important. They say they found the rifle that killed Christian Luna."

"Okay, good," he said with a shrug. "What does that have to do with me?"

"They say it's registered to you, Jake."

He paused as the weight of my words hit him. "Oh, shit," he said, reaching for the nearby chair. "That's bullshit, Ridley."

"They're coming for you right now." I was putting on my tennis shoes and tying the laces. I could hear the sirens growing louder now. I put on my coat.

"No," he said, shaking his head. "That's not my gun. And there's no way they can prove it is."

What can I tell you about how I was feeling at that moment? I could hear that odd rushing sound in my right ear; my hands were shaking a little. I wasn't sure what I believed about Jake. I guess mostly I was just in shock. I had no frame of reference for this kind of situation, so I was flying blind.

"That shot. They say it came from the trees where you were hiding, not from the rooftop," I said.

He looked down at the floor and then back at me. "I don't know where the shot came from, Ridley. But it didn't come from me."

Jake looked scared, as scared as I felt. He grabbed his jacket and started moving toward the door.

"Ridley, I want you to get yourself someplace safe. Right now."

His words made me go cold inside. "What are you saying?"

I moved to follow him. His face was pale as he came close to me, put his hand gently on my arms.

"Listen to me carefully, Ridley. I want you to go back to your apartment, get some things, and check into a hotel. Don't tell anyone where you are. No one. Not your parents, not your friend Zack. Do you understand me?"

"I'm coming with you." I couldn't even believe the words had left my mouth. Was I really considering joining him in his flight from the authorities? The answer is yes. I was so unrooted from my life, so disconnected from my former version of reality, that it seemed like an actual option.

The sound of the sirens was louder still. I could start to see the flashing red lights reflecting on the building across the street. He kissed me lightly on the lips and looked at me with that expression I couldn't read.

"I won't do that to your life, Ridley."

"Jake . . ."

"Just **promise** me you'll do what I say. Swear you won't tell anyone where you are, and pay for the room with cash. That's important. Cash only."

"Why, Jake?" I wasn't sure what was happening, but I was realizing, maybe since I'd talked to Linda McNaughton, that there was something much darker, much bigger, at work here than the manipulations of Christian Luna.

"You're in danger, Ridley. We both are. So promise me."

"Jake, I don't understand. What are you talking about?"

"Ridley, I'll explain everything. You have

no reason to trust me, but I'm asking you to do that now. Just tell me you're going to do what I say."

I could hear the banging on the metal door downstairs. "I promise," I said.

"I'll find you. Don't worry."

I nodded and he moved toward the door. I felt my stomach twist with the fear that I was never going to see him again.

"I didn't kill Christian Luna. I want you to know that, Ridley."

And then he was gone. I waited a second and listened to the police shaking the door downstairs. When I entered the hallway, I could hear Zelda yelling downstairs and Jake was nowhere in sight.

"Hold on, hold on!" Zelda's voice carried up the stairs. I heard the creaking of the door and pounding footsteps on the stairs. I ran up one more flight and pushed out onto the roof. The cold air hit me hard and I stood in the dark, wondering what the hell I was going to do up here. I half expected to see Jake racing across the rooftops. But I didn't see him anywhere. I wasn't sure how, or if, he'd made it out of the building.

I threw my leg over the back ledge and stepped down onto the fire escape. The dogs were going crazy below me, barking their heads off as I climbed down to my floor. With a little bit of rattling, the window opened and I climbed into my apartment. It was dark and I tried to be as quiet as possible.

I heard loud voices in the hallway, the sound of police radios crackling and beeping, the heavy footsteps of big men wearing hard boots. I heard Zelda yelling, "Hey, you gotta warrant to come in here? Are you listening to me?" I looked out of my peephole and didn't see anyone on my floor, so I opened the door a crack. I wondered briefly if I could just walk down the stairs and exit through the rear of the building. But I'd seen enough cop shows to know they'd be crazy not to have covered both the front and back entrance. As I was about to retreat, I noticed Victoria's door was ajar and I could see her eye, wide with terror, peering back at me. I felt bad for her, thinking how terrified she must be, but I also wasn't in any position to help her. I closed the door quickly and quietly, sat with my back against it. I was breathing hard, thinking, I'm hiding from the police right now. I have officially walked off the edge of my life. I am falling, limbs flailing, into the dark unknown.

I heard footsteps on the stairs. "She's not

here. I told you. She went out before and she didn't come back." It was Zelda barking at someone.

"Where'd she go?" Detective Salvo. I could hear their footfalls on the tiles outside my door, their voices getting closer.

"Hey, whatdoIlooklike, her mother?"

Detective Salvo banged hard on the door and I braced myself because I was still leaning against it. "Whatareyou, deaf?" yelled Zelda. I held my breath in the silence that followed and then he banged again.

"Ridley. Do yourself a favor if you're in there and come out. Talk to me. Don't make me issue a warrant for your arrest. Aiding and abetting, failure to cooperate with a police investigation. I don't want to fuck up your life, Ridley. But I will."

I sat as still and solid as a stone. I couldn't go out there now. I'd tipped off Jake; I'd fled the apartment and I'd been hiding from the police. I had no choice but to hold my ground. The phone in my apartment started ringing and I held my breath. The machine picked up after two rings and I heard my father's voice.

"Ridley," he said, sounding stern and worried. "Your mother and I have had a disturbing call from Alexander Harriman. We're extremely concerned and need to speak with you right away. Call us." The line went dead.

So much for attorney-client privilege. He couldn't do that, could he? Call my parents? How much had he told them? I wondered. Shit.

"You got a key for this apartment?" Detective Salvo asked Zelda outside. I closed my eyes and said a prayer.

"You got a warrant?"

"Don't make this difficult for yourself, Mrs. Impecciate."

"You got a warrant?" she repeated levelly. I loved her so much right then.

"No, I don't."

"Then I don't got a key." Zelda was lying for me and protecting me. She knew I was in the building. I think she knew I was sitting behind that door. For someone who'd barely spoken a civil word to me, she was really going to the mat for me. I wondered if it was because she'd secretly really liked me all these years, or because she really hated the police.

"What are you doing?"

"I'm calling her cell phone," he said. "I just talked to her."

I fumbled in my pocket for the phone. I

heard the long beep as he pressed **Send** to make his call. I felt around in the dark for the power button and managed to turn it off before it rang.

"Voice mail," he said, half to himself. "Goddammit, Ridley." They walked off without any further conversation. I'm not sure how much longer I sat there. I just listened until the chaos upstairs melted away, listened as heavy footfalls disappeared down the stairs and out onto the street, until I didn't hear the police radios and the booming voices. I sat there for so long that after a while, I think I might have dozed a bit. My phone kept ringing, but whoever was calling hung up on the machine. I still hadn't moved from my crouch by the door when I heard the softest knock.

"Ridley," came a whisper at the doorjamb. I jumped slightly and became aware that both of my legs were painfully asleep. I held my breath, not sure what to do. "Ridley," the whisper came again. "It's Zelda."

"Zelda?"

I opened the door a bit. "Come on," she said. "I show you the way out of here so the police don't see. They're waiting outside for you to come back. That cop said he was getting a warrant for your apartment."

I didn't know why Zelda was helping me and there wasn't time to ask. I followed her down the three flights of stairs, through the restaurant kitchen, out into the courtyard. We walked through the crowd of barking dogs, who jumped at us in greeting. Zelda bent down and, with a heave, swung open a pair of metal doors in the ground that led to the basement. I followed her down the stairs, ducking my head to keep it from banging on the low ceiling. She led me through dark rows of shelving that held bottles of olive oil and cans of crushed tomatoes, huge containers of spices, paper plates and napkins, crates of garlic. The aromas of these things mixed with the musty smell of the underground space, and the effect was not unpleasant.

At the far corner of the room, she unbolted another metal door. It led into pitch darkness. Zelda disappeared through the door and I followed her, feeling my way along the wall. We were in some kind of a tunnel. It was damp and cold and the air was so moldy there, my sinuses started to swell.

"This tunnel lets out on Eleventh Street," Zelda's voice sounded through the dark. "I don't know why it's here, but it runs along the back of the Black Forest Pastry Shop. There's a door that leads into their basement, too." Just as she said that my hands touched what felt like a metal doorway. The whole situation had taken on another layer of nonreality to me and I felt laughter rising in my throat, a punchy, hysterical laughter that I knew, if released, would immediately turn to sobbing. I quashed it and kept moving. After another few minutes, I heard Zelda unhinge some bolts and then a door opened onto Eleventh Street, the crisp, fresh air feeling good on my skin. The night sky seemed as bright as day compared to the pitch-dark tunnel. I walked past Zelda and turned to her from the street.

"Thanks, Zelda." She looked at me and seemed to consider saying something but then clamped her mouth shut.

"Be careful," she responded. Her mouth tried a smile but it didn't take. Something unidentifiable glittered in her eyes. She closed the door with a heavy clang.

TWENTY-THREE

Was he smirking? It was hard to tell in the darkened room, which smelled faintly of beer and garbage. Ace hadn't been happy to see me when I showed up at his door.

"What are you doing here?" he'd asked through the same crack I'd spoken to Ruby through a couple of days ago. I'd just stood there, not knowing how to answer, not having an answer, anyway. Where else could I have gone? Not to my parents, certainly. It was only a matter of time before the police got in touch with them, if they hadn't already. Not to Alexander Harriman. He was scary, and there was something about him I didn't trust (and hadn't even before he ratted me out to my parents). Part of me had the urge to go to Zack but I quashed it. It was selfish to go running to him when I was in trouble, especially after everything that had passed between us over the last few days. Finally, after an uncomfortable thirty seconds of silence, Ace had opened the door. I'd followed him inside. It was as filthy and awful as you would imagine it to be. Ruby lay akimbo on a tattered old chair with a faded floral pattern and its stuffing coming out. I'd have thought she was dead if I'd seen her on the street. The tiniest line of drool traveled from the corner of her mouth down her chin.

"Is she all right?" I asked.

"As right as she could be," he answered coldly. "Now tell me what's going on."

I had butterflies in my stomach and my throat was dry.

"Why are you always such an asshole?" I asked him. "Do you think I'd come here if I didn't need to?" I started to cry then. Not that same sobbing I experienced after Christian Luna died, but close. I sat on the bed and he sat beside me, let me have it out with his hand on my back. When I was calmer, wiping tears and snot on a deli napkin he happened to find on a nearby pile of junk, he said, "Just tell me what's going on, Ridley. I'll do what I can for you." **Which isn't much,** he didn't say, but was the implied ending to his sentence. I told him everything that had happened since we last saw each other.

"Ben and Grace must be wigging out," he said with a light laugh. "Perfect little Ridley on the run from the law. They're probably having a conference with Zack and Esme right now about what to do about it."

There was so much bitterness in his voice, it would have hurt less if he'd slapped me. I could see it now, the jealousy, the resentment. I'd never really seen it uncloaked like that before. I thought about what my father had said, and what Jake had implied, that maybe Ace had something to do with this. I saw my brother for a second the way everyone else in my life seemed to see him: low, untrustworthy, someone willing to hurt me. It made me so sad. How can I tell you? So, so sad.

"I saw you," I said. "Waiting outside my building a little while ago. What were you doing there?"

He shrugged, leaned back on his elbows. Looked at the wall behind me.

When I first moved to New York and started seeing my brother, I used to have this fantasy about him, that he was secretly watching out for me, shadowing me, in case I ever got into any trouble. I had these elaborate daydreams about my being mugged in some alley somewhere and my brother leaping out from behind garbage cans to save me. He'd take me back to my dorm room and take care of me until I felt better. Then he'd go back to his life and I could go on with mine, secure in the knowledge that he'd always have my back, always be watching out for me. In another daydream, we'd go home to our parents and there would be this tearful reunion and everyone would live happily ever after. Pretty sad, I know. But little girls are raised on fairy tales. Is it any wonder we all crave the happy endings to the dark things in our lives? No one ever tells you that sad things stay sad, some people die angry and unforgiven, and some things are lost and never found.

"Are you going to answer me?" I asked.

"I was waiting for you. I needed money. But your goon came down after me. I bolted."

"My goon?"

"Your new boyfriend or whatever. You better watch out for that guy. I bet he's not who you think he is."

He looked at me, smug and unkind. I wanted to slap his stupid face.

"What do you know about him? What do you know about **anything**?"

He shrugged again, didn't answer me.

"You didn't always hate me, did you?" I asked him. "I remember you loving me when we were kids."

The smirk (yes, he **was** smirking) fell from his face and he looked at me with surprise. "I don't hate you, Rid. I've never hated you."

I held his eyes until he looked away.

"There's so much you don't understand," he said, shaking his head slowly.

"I think I do understand," I said. A terrible anger was simmering in my chest. "It's about Max, right?"

He looked at me, startled. "What do you think you know, Ridley?"

"About the money he left us."

He released a breath and rolled his eyes. "You mean left **you**."

"To you, too, if you'd pull yourself together, Ace." I didn't like the way that sounded, as if it was so easy, but I guess a part of me believed that Ace had chosen this life. Maybe the drugs had their claws in him now. But if it's a choice to start using, then it's a choice to stop. The road is long and hard, riven with obstacles both internal and external, but the first step is a choice, isn't it? He had the resources. The help was waiting for him.

"Who told you that? Dad?" he said, rising.

"What difference does it make? It's true, isn't it?"

"Per usual, you have no idea what you're talking about. You're just living in your own little world. **Ridley World,** where everything is black and white, right and wrong. It's all about choices, right? Making the right choices?"

Did you think you were the only one who had been subjected to my lecture on choices? As you can see, Ace totally missed the point. I got up and moved toward the door. I was shaking from anger and sadness, my stomach was in full revolt. I'd come for help and for some solace, but I could see he had neither to offer and might have even withheld it, if he did. I wanted to get away from him. I wanted to run to him and throw my arms around him, hold him as tightly as I could. I hated him. I loved him.

"Life's not that simple, Ridley."

I didn't know how to answer him; I didn't trust my voice. And before I could stop them, the tears started to fall again. I'd never said life was simple. I've never believed that.

"Go turn yourself in, Ridley. Call Mom and Dad. It'll all turn out all right for you. It **always** does."

Such vitriol from this man I've loved since he was a boy and I was a little girl. My brother. I'd just loved him so long without question, I'd never realized he hated me. But maybe he just hated himself. Esme's words about Max came back to me. **You can't squeeze blood from a stone. You can try, but you do all the bleeding.**

I left then and slammed the door behind me, feeling its vibration in the floor beneath my feet. I ran down the stairs and out onto the deserted street. I didn't know which way to turn or where to go. I took a seat on a bench inside Tompkins Square by the bandshell. The universe was trying to tell me something. **You're on your own, kid.**

I went to the West Village. I did something kind of weird first. I took the train uptown to Ninety-sixth Street and then went out onto the street and hailed a cab. I took the cab to the

Barnes & Noble kitty-corner from the Met, walked in the entrance on Broadway, and then exited another door. I went to a cash machine and took out a few hundred, as much as the machine would let me. Then I hopped another cab. All the while, I kept watch for the skinhead, the cops, or anyone else who looked suspicious. I don't think anyone followed me. But I was new at this. Jake's warning before he fled the police was ringing in my ears, and I don't mind telling you that I was scared, scared to the verge of tears.

I checked into a crappy hotel I'd passed a couple of times off Washington Square, one of those places that in spite of attempts to renovate still looks like what it is, a place for transients, people who want to pay for their rooms with cash in advance. The clerk was an old man wearing a denim shirt with a stain on the breast pocket that looked like ketchup. His face, as wrinkled and clenched as a fist, looked like he was wearing a rubber mask. He never even glanced at me, just took my cash and handed me a key.

"Room 203. Elevator to your right. Stairs to your left."

He couldn't have picked me out of a lineup, I'm sure. This was probably a job requirement, I thought. Strangely, I wanted him to look at me. I wanted him to acknowledge that I wasn't a ghost in this world.

"Have a nice night," I said, lingering at the desk. He didn't say a word. Just turned his back and walked into an office.

The room was reasonably clean, but there were chipped tiles in the bathroom, water marks on the ceiling, drapes stained yellow with cigarette smoke. Lying on the bed that night, looking out the window at the street-light's orange glow and listening to the outside noise, with no one knowing where I was or what was happening to me, I had never been so completely alone. I felt like someone had neatly punched a hole through my chest and the wind whistled through it, making a hol-low, mournful sound that kept me up the whole night.

TWENTY-FOUR

Monday morning. After a sleepless night, I took a cab over to the lot where I'd left that rented Jeep and headed back out to New Jersey. On my way, I stopped at an Internet café on Third Avenue and, using MapQuest, got a map that led directly to Linda Mc-Naughton's doorstep. It's kind of crazy, if you think about it, that any stranger can enter your address into a computer and get step-by-step directions to your house, but as it was working to my advantage at the moment, I wasn't really in any position to complain. I used my credit card here. Didn't have a choice. Anyway, the events of last night were starting to seem surreal and I had achieved a strange mental distance from everything. So much had happened since I'd called Linda McNaughton. My brain was taking a little break from the fact that my boyfriend (he was, wasn't he?) had fled the police (so, for that matter, had I) and my brother hated me and obviously had for years.

Once I was on the highway, I called my father from my cell phone.

"Ridley," he said, managing to fit anger, worry, relief, and love into the two syllables of my name. "You tell me what's going on. Right now."

"Nothing. Why?" I asked.

"Ridley."

"Dad, everything's fine," I lied. "I just need you to tell me about Project Rescue."

There was a pause on the line. "Ridley, you need to come home right now. We've talked to Alexander Harriman. The police were here this morning."

It's sad when your parents give you orders that you are too old to obey. It represents a disconnect between who they think you are and who you actually are. They hold on to this concept of you as a small being within their control and it takes a lot of time before they get the fact that it's no longer the case.

"I can't come home, Dad. I need to know what's happening to me. Tell me about Project Rescue."

"Project Rescue? Ridley, what are you talking about?"

"Dad, tell me!" I yelled this. I'd never really yelled at my father before and something about it felt good. He was quiet for long enough that I wondered if he'd hung up or if the line had gone dead. Then I heard him breathing.

"Dad."

"It was the group responsible for getting the Safe Haven Law passed," he said. His voice sounded strange and his words had a canned quality to them.

"No," I said. "It's more than that." I realized then that I was driving really fast and couldn't afford to get pulled over. I slowed down, pulled into the right lane.

He sighed. "Well, let's see. Early on there were safe houses, Project Rescue safe houses. Usually at churches or clinics, sometimes at cooperating orphan facilities. It was before the law was passed, so while it wasn't illegal, it wasn't exactly state sanctioned and it was privately funded. We always thought of it as kind of an underground railroad."

"Who funded it? Max?"

"Yes, and others." He sounded tired and I thought his voice was shaking just slightly, but it could have been the cell phone reception.

"So what happened at these places?"

"The same thing that happens now. A parent could leave her child safely, the child would be held and cared for for seventy-two hours. If before that time the parent changed her mind, she could come back for her baby. She'd receive counseling and any other kind of assistance she needed."

"And if she didn't come back?"

"Then the baby was absorbed into the child welfare system."

"And you were involved?"

"Not really. Though some of the clinics where I donated my time over the years were Project Rescue sites, and when there was a baby or child abandoned, I'd provide health care just like I would for any child."

"But were you breaking the law?"

"Not in any real sense. There was no law to say that you couldn't provide health care to a needy, abandoned child, as long as that abandonment was reported within seventy-two hours."

"So you were just flying under the radar."

He released another sigh. "In the best interests of the children, of course."

It made sense that my father would work the angles of the system to help children. I could see that in him. But the logic seemed slightly faulty to me. I mean, why go to all this trouble to get children away from potentially abusive situations, just to put them into the child welfare system, which was rife with flaws and abuses of its own? I thought of Jake's childhood experiences.

I was missing something and I knew it. The answers were right in front of me but I wasn't seeing them. I was tired and the whole thing was too much. It's like when you start out on a big project, like cleaning out your closet. You've got everything you own on the floor and on the bed, the closet is empty, and then lethargy sets in. You think, Why did I even start this? I don't have the energy to finish. But you can't just walk away, it's too late for that. I knew there were a million questions I could be asking my father, but I couldn't think of one.

"What do I have to say to get you to come home?"

I thought about it a second. "Tell me there's nothing I need to know, that I've got myself wound up in something that has nothing to do with me and that I've lost my perspective."

There was just the slightest hesitation. Then: "Ridley, there's nothing you need to know."

I don't know how, but I knew with a cool certainty that my father was lying to me. I heard my mother in the background: "Tell Ridley her room is ready. Alex can handle everything and she can just stay here until it all blows over."

"I'll call you, Dad. Try not to worry."

I heard his voice as I took the phone away from my ear and ended the call. It sounded small and tinny, farther away than it had ever been. There was officially no one I could trust in the world.

I found Linda McNaughton living in a double-wide trailer in a well-kept mobile-home park off of Route 206 in a town called Lost Valley. It was a pretty nice trailer, with casement windows and aluminum siding, across the street from the public library. She came to the door with a smile on her face, but only opened the door partway. I hadn't called to announce my arrival, thinking that she might refuse to see me.

"Can I help you?"

"Hi, Ms. McNaughton," I said brightly with a Girl Scout smile. "I'm Ridley . . . we talked on the phone last night."

The smile dropped quickly. "What are you doing here?"

"I was in town doing research on my story and I was just hoping to talk to you a bit more. Actually, I was hoping that you had a picture of Charlie you might be willing to loan to me."

She narrowed her eyes at me in some combination of suspicion and anger. "I don't have a picture and I don't have anything left to say to you. Please go." She then closed the door on me. Hard.

"What if," I said through the door, pretty sure she was still standing behind it, watching me through the peephole, "I told you that there's a chance Charlie might be alive?"

I heard a gasp from behind the door and immediately felt bad. After all, I didn't have any proof that Charlie might be alive. But while I was lying on that strange bed last night, all night, thinking about what had happened to me, about the things Christian Luna had told me, what I'd learned about the other missing children, my uncle Max, what Ace had said, the germ of something had taken hold and now, especially after the conversation with my father, was spreading like a virus.

The door opened again and Linda's face

had softened. She opened the door the rest of the way and stood to the side, offering me passage.

In her parlor, I sat on a stiff beige sofa covered in plastic and sipped the coffee she'd offered me. It managed to be weak and bitter at the same time. Linda wore a gray sweat suit that exactly matched the gray of her short-cropped hair. Her face was a landscape of lines and sagging skin, but she had sharp blue eyes that shone with attention and intelligence. She sat across from me and watched me now. We were surrounded by turtles—turtle figurines, turtles painted on pillows and platters, stuffed turtles, turtle mobiles.

"You know," she told me when she saw me looking around, "I don't really have any special fondness for turtles. Just this one year, my husband bought me a gold turtle pendant after we'd been to that turtle farm in the Caribbean. I made such a big deal about how much I loved it that from then on, everyone started buying me turtles. And it's just gone on like that."

She looked at me almost apologetically and laughed awkwardly. I smiled at her, placed the coffee cup down on the table. She got up and walked toward a bookshelf on the far side of the room. When she returned she held a small photograph in a pewter frame. She handed it to me. It was a couple with a small child. The little boy, about two, wearing a red-and-white-striped shirt and denim shorts, sat on top of a pony. The man, thin and bearded, stood to one side of him with a tentative smile and a protective hand on the child's thigh. The woman, mousy, emaciated, looked on, her shoulders hunched in as she laughed, a bright smile on her face.

I don't know what I expected of Michael and Adele Reynolds. All I knew of Michael was that he had been a heroin addict. Adele was a woman who'd sought to abandon her child. But in the photograph, I saw two people who looked a bit used, a bit worn maybe, but who were enjoying a day with their son. The image seemed incongruous to the judgment I'd unconsciously formed. It surprised me. I'd imagined them cold, selfish, abusive, neglectful. And maybe they'd been that in some moments. But in others maybe they'd been loving, happy, protective of their child. Maybe when Adele had tried to give up Charlie, she'd just been fearful that she was not up to the responsibility of raising a child, afraid that he would have been better off in someone else's care. I had always been so angry at Zack for judging Ace by that one aspect, by his addiction, and I had unconsciously done the same thing to Adele and Michael.

"When there are so few good times, you remember them more clearly, I think," said Linda. "I remember that day. We were all happy—Charlie's second birthday. My daughter, Adele, was dead a month later. Then Charlie was gone. Then Michael. Within eighteen months, I lost them all."

I felt my heart clench for her, imagining blow after blow like that and how it must have felt like the world had gone dark on her. I looked at her, expected to see her eyes filled with tears or her face to have changed with her grief. But she just gazed at the picture with a sad half-smile, as if all that remained was a sad resignation that things could not be changed.

Even Linda I'd judged. I'd imagined her as someone who didn't love Adele enough, who **chose** not to help her in the crisis of not being able to care for Charlie. Because of the way I was raised, in a house where there was more than enough money and enough love to go around, I always thought that everyone had access to the same unlimited resources. I hate to admit it, but it wasn't until that moment, surrounded by Linda McNaughton's turtles, that I realized poverty was not an abstract concept, that sometimes people just didn't have enough love or money to care properly for a child. You can't judge people for what they don't have to give, can you?

"Do you know for sure?" she said suddenly, looking at me with an expression I couldn't read. "Do you have **proof** that he's still alive?"

I could see a slight shake in her hands, as though the hope was filling her with a kind of agitation. "No," I admitted, returning her gaze. "Not yet."

She sat down again with a sigh and looked away from me. I looked at the picture in my hand. The image was nebulous, the faces unclear and yellowed with age.

"I'll try not to get my hopes up. Like I did last year."

"Last year?"

"A young fellow came. About your age. Said he was a detective working on cold cases. That's what he called them. He contacted me a couple of times with questions like who was Charlie's pediatrician, did he ever go to the emergency room, how often. I told him what I could. But after a while he stopped calling. I called once and he said he was still working on it, promised he wouldn't forget to call if anything came up, but I never heard from him again. Funny. Just the other day, I thought of calling him."

"Why?"

"I came across Charlie's birth certificate in a stack of old files. Thought it might be helpful to him."

"Actually, Mrs. McNaughton, can I take a look at that?"

"Sure," she said, getting up and walking over to a desk nestled in a corner of the room.

I leaned forward on my chair. "The man who came to see you—do you remember his name?"

"Well, I have his card right here with Charlie's birth certificate. I can't read without my glasses."

She handed the card to me. I felt my stomach hollow out as I looked at the cream stock business card, embossed with black type. **Jake Jacobsen, Private Investigations.**

Some of our moments together came back in flashes. I remembered his strange tone when I told him about the other missing kids, how he hadn't seemed surprised at all. I thought about how he'd found so much information about the parents on the Internet. I also remembered how quickly he'd determined the origins of the clipping Christian Luna had sent. How he'd seemed alarmed when he learned I'd told Detective Salvo what I'd found. Tiny seeds of dread started blooming in my chest. He knew, I thought. He knew about the other missing kids already.

"Miss Jones, you all right?" I must have just been sitting there staring at the card as she held a piece of paper out to me, I don't know how long.

"I'm sorry," I said, taking the paper from her hand.

"Charlie's birth certificate. It's a copy; keep it."

I glanced at it and folded it, put it in the inside pocket of my jacket. I looked up to see Linda watching me still.

"You didn't tell me why," she said. "Why do you think Charlie might still be alive?"

I paused a second and then answered as honestly as I could at the moment. "Because I am."

She shook her head, not understanding.

"Some other children went missing that year, Mrs. McNaughton, and at least one of them might be alive and well. My hope is that the same is true for Charlie."

She looked at me and I saw a cautious happiness in her face. It made me feel guilty. "I hope so, too," she said, and clasped her hands together as if in prayer.

I got up and took her hand, thanked her for her help. I promised to return her photograph and not to leave her only with questions. She stood at the door and held her hand up in a wave as I got into the Jeep and pulled up the gravel drive toward the highway. I was thinking that hope is not always a gift.

As I pulled onto Route 206, in the rearview mirror I saw a black 1969 Firebird with tinted windows approaching. My heart did a little dance and I pulled over to the side of the road, expecting to see the car pull up behind me. But it didn't. It passed by, the engine revving as it did. Relief and disappointment duked it out in my chest. As I watched the car disappear around the next turn, I remembered then that Jake had said the police had impounded his car. I wasn't ready to face him anyway, not with these new suspicions tugging at my pants leg. If he already knew about the other missing kids, then that meant he knew about Jessie Stone. He'd known before he even met me. I tried to think about what that might mean, and a thick curtain came down in my mind. I didn't want to deal with it.

I pulled back onto the highway and drove toward Skully's Mountain, on my way back to Hackettstown. In the absence of any better ideas, I thought I'd head to the clinic where Teresa Stone had taken Jessie. What was I going to do there? I didn't really know. I was going to have to get creative. I was operating under a faith that the universe conspires to reveal the truth, that lies are unstable elements that tend toward breaking down.

The sky above me had gone a moody gray black, threatening snow. As I moved under a canopy of trees, it grew dark enough that I had to turn my headlights on. I drove through a small town center and turned off the main drag onto a smaller road that wound up Skully's Mountain. It was a dark, narrow pass, and as I pulled over a small one-lane bridge at the base of a steep incline, I saw that it was edged only by a wooden guardrail protecting against a drop into a wide rushing river.

That was when I saw the Firebird again in

my rearview mirror. How it had wound up behind me, I wasn't sure. I couldn't make out the
form of the driver, but something went dark
and cold inside me. I put my foot down hard
on the gas and the Jeep burned a little rubber
as I took off up the incline.

But the Jeep couldn't compete with the
muscle of a Firebird. In a second, it was on top
of me, its high beams reflecting blindingly in
my mirrors. I felt a heavy thud as the car
rammed me from behind. In the movies,
when people get hit from behind, it never
seems to be especially jarring. It felt to me like
the earth below my car had shifted, as my
head knocked forward and then snapped back
hard. I was jolted and involuntarily let go of
the wheel for a second. The Jeep veered sick-
enly toward the edge before I could grab the
wheel again. I overcorrected and wound up
swerving to the other lane and just pulled
back as another car came around the bend, its
horn wailing in alarm as it flew past.

Mortal terror slows everything down and I
felt like I was in a time warp as the Firebird
rammed me again. All I could hear was the
sound of my own ragged breathing as we came
up on the next hairpin turn. I pushed my foot
down on the gas but the Firebird was too fast;

it came up on me again harder than before. Tears sprang to my eyes, casting the road in a wet blur.

"Stop it!" I screamed at no one.

Another jolt sent the Jeep swerving into the oncoming lane. I hit the mountainside guardrail and saw sparks fly as the Jeep bounced off it. The Firebird pulled up quickly beside me so that I couldn't get back over. I looked over and saw nothing but the tinted black window. Suddenly anger cleared the fog of fear that was clouding my brain. I didn't know who was driving that car and I didn't care. I turned the wheel sharply, slamming the side of the Jeep hard into the Firebird. They don't call them muscle cars for nothing; it felt like I'd hit a stone wall. The car swerved a bit but held its ground. I was really pissed then. I slammed it again, harder, not caring if I took us both over the side of the mountain. We drove like that, racing, the chassis of our vehicles joined in a horrible screech of metal on metal. Then I saw the glow of approaching headlights just past the curve.

The Firebird wouldn't give ground. I leaned on my horn, hoping to alert the on-coming driver that I was in his path. I knew if

I slammed on my brakes on a curve like this, I'd flip the Jeep or still wind up in a head-on collision with the approaching car because I wouldn't have time to get back over to the right side. I leaned on my horn again, praying that the driver heard me and would slow, but just then the Firebird gunned its engine and took off. I jerked the wheel and moved back into the right-hand lane, I swear, two seconds before a red Dodge truck came fast around the corner. The truck flew past me, an angry horn reprimanding me for my careless driving. I watched as the Firebird disappeared around the next curve.

I slammed on the breaks and sat there, my hands gripping the wheel, my teeth gritted, every muscle in my body on fire with adrenaline. I was shaking uncontrollably. I wept into the steering wheel until I saw a car approaching from behind. Then I drove shakily up the rest of the mountain and when I got to the other side pulled into a Burger King drive-through and got myself a chocolate milkshake and fries. Having almost been murdered on a mountain road, very possibly by the man I'd been recently sleeping with, I figured I owed it to myself. I sat in the parking lot quaking, crying, and shoving greasy French fries into my mouth as fast as I could without choking myself.

The thoughts in my brain were spinning. I found that I couldn't really process what had just happened to me, what I was supposed to do next. I wasn't able to identify the driver of the car, but it had to be Jake's car. Had it been him at the wheel? Why would he want to hurt me? If not him, then who? How did they get his car? And over and over the same question: Why was any of this happening? As I sat sipping the milkshake, still shaking, that horrible feeling of aloneness settled in the marrow of my bones. But I'd stopped crying. I was beyond that now. I was out of tears.

When you discover that the foundation of your life has been constructed over a sinkhole and every wall has begun to crumble, what do you do? Where do you go? My mind drifted as thoughts that had no relevance to the moment presented themselves for consideration, as if to give my frazzled brain a little recovery time. For some reason, I thought about my mother.

Back in the years after I graduated from college, I took the 4/5 train every Wednesday and Friday to attend a yoga class on the Upper East Side. It was at a hideous time, six to seven-thirty in the morning, but I found that, if I could make it, it significantly improved the quality and productivity of my day. On a particularly cold February morning, I walked to Fourteenth Street in the early darkness and descended into the Union Square subway station. Still half asleep when the train arrived, I got on and sat down. The train paused in the station and I looked out the window. Fluttering there was a monarch butterfly. It seemed to hover beside the window as I stared at it in wonder. I thought, How could it be here, in this dark, underground place in winter? How could it survive in the cold? But there it was. I looked around the train to see if any of the other passengers noticed, but they were all dozing or reading. They all missed it, this tiny miracle. And when I looked back, it was gone. The doors closed and the train pulled from the station.

It occurred to me, not then but now as I sat in the parking lot in the likely totaled Jeep, that that was how I loved my mother. Behind glass in a train that was always leaving the station. My mother was someone you admired for her beauty, for her charm, for the strength of her character. But like that monarch butterfly, she was ultimately distant and elusive.

Something to be glimpsed but not held. It might have been different if she hadn't lost Ace. Because I think we all knew on some level that he was her one true love and that when he abandoned her, she never quite recovered. That for all the fire and conflict in their relationship, she adored him. There was a light that shone from within her when she looked at my brother. When he'd gone, the stage went dark. And we were all left to fumble around, finding new roles in her production.

I guess I hated her a little for that, as much as I loved her. In my most secret heart I always believed that if she could have chosen to lose one of us, it would have been me, that she would have traded me to have Ace back in a heartbeat. Maybe it wasn't true, but I believed that through most of my adolescence and into adulthood.

Anyway, life doesn't work like that. You can't make trades. Or so I thought.

TWENTY-FIVE

The damage was extensive. I could tell by the way drivers were passing me in the lot, giving me a wide berth and craning their necks to look back at me, that the Jeep was really looking bad. I got out of the vehicle and walked around it. It looked as though it had narrowly escaped the compactor, both the passenger and driver side severely scratched and dented where it had alternately hit the Firebird and the mountainside guardrail. I was glad that I'd invested in the extra insurance.

I suppose I should have called the police, or maybe even driven to the nearest police station and given up this quest. I mean, clearly that was the message, right? If that driver had wanted me dead, he wouldn't have pulled off at the last minute, allowing me to return to the proper lane and avoid the collision with the oncoming car. The intention was to terrorize me, to scare me off my errand, and I **was** terrorized. But I was also angry, angrier than I had ever been in my life. And more determined than ever to find out what was happening to me.

The other big question at this point was: What was I doing exactly? Remember, this all started because I felt the need to leap in front of an oncoming van to save a child who'd wandered into its path. That act had set into action a series of events that led me to question my identity. But now I also found myself driven to know what had happened to the other children who went missing the same year as Jessie Amelia Stone. Sometime after I'd finished my milkshake and before I'd finished my fries, I'd made a decision. You know how in the safety instructions on an aircraft they tell you to put on your own oxygen mask before you offer assistance to anyone else? It was like that. I couldn't answer the question of what happened to Charlie, Pamela, or Brian until I knew what happened to **Ridley.** And because of the events of my recent life, I had to know more about **Jessie** to figure that out. So I started the car and continued to drive to the clinic to which Maria Cacciatore told me Teresa had taken Jessie, the Little Angels Children's Health Clinic. I thought of a few different lies I might tell that could get me access to her files, if they even still existed. But in the end, the truth was the key.

As I walked through the automatic doors, I noticed a Project Rescue sticker on the glass. Its logo was the impression of a pair of cradling arms, the image of an infant nestled there, below which it read, **This Is a Safe Haven.** Quite a coincidence. I remembered how Detective Salvo didn't like coincidence. I decided I was with him on that one.

"I need to see the person in charge," I told the young man who sat at the reception desk. He was cute, with a round, earnest face and just the hint of stubble on his jaw.

"You mean, like in charge of all the doctors?"

"No. In charge of the whole place. In charge of the files."

"Oh, you need your medical records."

"Yeah, sort of."

"You just need to see that lady over there and she can help you." He pointed over toward a humorless-looking old woman manning a giant desk. I could see immediately that I wasn't going to get anywhere with her.

"It's not going to be easy that way. I don't have any identification."

He looked at me grimly and started to shake his head. "Uh . . ."

"Can you just get me the person in charge? Please," I said, offering him my sweetest smile. He smiled back. It is my opinion that as a reasonably attractive young woman, you can talk your way into almost anything. Maybe I'm right. Or maybe it's just the confidence that gets me what I want. Either way, I needed something to work today.

"Okay," he said, giving me a conspiratorial look. "Have a seat."

I waited a while, flipping through an old copy of **Parenting** magazine. The debate on spanking is alive and well, as is the new debate over vaccinations. I vote no on spanking, yes on vaccines. Why did people even **want** kids, considering all the ways you can screw them up?

"Can I help you?" A warm baritone broke into my thoughts. I looked up to see an extremely large black man with a shining bald head and gold wire-rimmed spectacles. There was the lightest dusting of gray in the stubble on his jaw. He wore a physician's white jacket over a royal blue oxford and a tie with an Escher-type print of the Grateful Dead Dancing Bears. I stood and offered my hand, which he clamped in his gigantic bear claw. He held on to my hand for a second.

"Do I know you?" he said, looking at me with a cocked head.

"I don't think so."

"Yeah," he said, a wide grin splitting his face. When I first saw him, I put him in his late fifties. That megawatt smile shaved about fifteen years off his face. "You're the one that saved that kid. Amazing. Good work."

"Oh, yeah, that's me," I said, smiling back. "Ridley Jones. Thanks."

"Dr. Jonathon Hauser." He kept smiling and nodding for a second. Then: "What can I do for you, Ridley?"

"Is there someplace we can talk? It's kind of a long story."

He looked at me, his brow wrinkling in benevolent curiosity. "Sure," he said, glancing at his watch. "Come with me."

We sat in his plain but neat and well-lit office and I told him the whole story, omitting anything questionable or illegal, which basically eliminated all mention of Jake. I also didn't tell him about the whole getting run off the road by a mysterious driver in a '69 Firebird thing. My hope with the good doctor was that his Dancing Bear tie communicated a kind of hippie, rule-breaking center. That he might be the type of person who would be willing to sidestep regulations in the interest of justice.

"That's a hell of a story, Ridley," he said quietly when I'd finished. "But without proof of your identity, I'm sure you realize that I can't release Jessie's records."

"But you think you might have them here?"

"We do have them. And I know this because about a year ago a young man, a private investigator, was here asking for the same thing. Said he'd been hired to revisit some cold cases, children who'd gone missing back in the seventies. Jessie Amelia Stone was one of those kids. We dug up the records, which were still in the basement of this building."

Jake had been here, too. I guess I wasn't really that surprised.

"Were the other children patients at this clinic?" I asked, trying to stay focused.

"I'm not able to reveal that information," he said, leaning forward. "Of course, had I never heard of them, I'd be able to tell you **that.**"

I nodded my understanding. "Did the investigator gain access to any of those files?"

"As much as I would have liked to help

him, I told him that he'd need a court order to have those files released."

"And?"

"And I never heard from him again."

I sighed and leaned back in the chair. I hadn't realized but I'd been sliding forward toward him, my shoulders tensing. I felt like you feel at the DMV, powerless against a system as unyielding as a stone wall, forced to play by the rules or not play at all. I appealed to that Dancing Bear center.

"Dr. Hauser, I'm **not** a private investigator. And there's a possibility that I may actually **be** one of those children. Isn't there anything you can do?"

He looked down at the leather blotter on his desk and I could hear him release a breath. "What do you even hope to find in these records? How is seeing them going to answer any of your questions?"

I shrugged and said truthfully, "I don't know. But I can't think of any other place to go from here."

He looked at me for a long moment, his hands steepled in front of his face. He gave his head a little shake and stood up. "Give me a second, okay?"

"Okay," I said. And he left the room, closing the door quietly behind him.

I stared at the wall behind his desk. Degrees, photographs, and newspaper clippings hung against the dark faux-wood paneling. I got up and walked behind his desk to take a closer look. An undergraduate degree from Rutgers University caught my eye. Class of '62, the same year my father graduated from college before going on to medical school. I gazed over the other myriad degrees and awards. Another caught my eye; it was a plaque from Project Rescue awarded to Little Angels for their "Excellence in the Care and Service to Children." I remembered the decal I had seen on the clinic's doors and for a second some bells started ringing in my mind. Little Angels Health Clinic—had I heard that name before Maria Cacciatore told me about it? I went back to the chair and sat down, racked my brain, and came up with nothing.

The doctor entered the room again and he had a file in his hand.

"Listen, Ridley. I'm a medical professional bound by very strict rules and regulations. Any violation of those rules could cost me my career. Do you understand that?"

"Yes," I said, still turning the clinic name around in my mind.

"That said," he went on, "I helped that investigator and I'll help you. I'll tell you what I told him, at least."

I leaned toward him, offered a grateful smile.

"The investigator, his name was Jake, was also a child of the welfare system and his mentor, Arnie Coel, was a good friend of mine," he said. "Aside from the investigation, he had his own reasons for wanting to know what happened to those kids." He released a sigh here.

"As much as I'd like to, I really can't tell you what's in these files," he said, "but I happen to know that the doctor who attended Jessie Stone is still practicing in New Jersey. He's close to retirement, but he might be willing to talk to you. You may even convince him to petition the Medical Association to release this file. Since Jessie was his patient, he's the only one that can really do that for you."

I nodded. "Thank you," I said. I wasn't sure if it was going to be any help, but I guessed it was better than nothing.

"His name is Dr. Benjamin Jones. I'll give

you the number for his private practice." He chuckled a bit then. "Quite a coincidence, you having the same last name. But I guess it happens to you all the time."

Dr. Benjamin Jones. My father.

I heard the distant beat of drums and the room seemed to darken and spin. I was afraid that I might be sick in his office. "Yeah," I said, the fakest smile I have ever worn threatening to shatter like glass. "Happens all the time."

TWENTY-SIX

I got out of there as fast as I could. Looking back, I realize there were a thousand questions I should have asked Dr. Hauser—a real private investigator wouldn't have freaked the way I did and bolted—but I didn't know how long I could hold that fake smile and nod my thanks for his help. I felt like there was a siren going off in my head and I was walking on one of those fun-house floors that jolt and tilt. So as soon as he handed me the number, I left. I didn't ask him about Jake, about Project Rescue.

I yanked the crumpled door open on the Jeep (it still opened and closed but not without effort) and climbed inside. I sat there a minute in the cold. It was growing dark outside now and the snow that had started to fall was growing heavier. I turned the engine on and realized as I reached to put the car into reverse that I didn't have any idea where to go next. I fished my cellular phone out of my coat and dialed.

"Salvo." He answered before the second ring, his voice gruff, tired but officious.

"It's Ridley Jones."

A sigh, then silence. "You tipped him off. And now he's gone."

I didn't respond to his statement. I wasn't going to incriminate myself, but I didn't feel like lying anymore, either. "Is his car still impounded?" I asked instead. That was the reason I'd called, or one of them. I had to know whether Jake had tried to kill me.

"What?"

"The Firebird," I said, sounding a little snappish, tense. "Is it still impounded?"

He was quiet for a minute. "We never impounded his car, Ridley."

My heart sank a little further in my chest and I fought back tears of disappointment and fear.

"I'm in trouble, Detective Salvo. Someone tried to kill me." My voice sounded odd, even to my own ears, tinny and strained. Even then, I didn't want to say it. I didn't want to say, **I think Jake tried to run me off the road in his Firebird.**

"Come in to the station. I can't protect you if I don't know where you are." He sounded calm and concerned, gentle. But I didn't trust him, either. Maybe he was just trying to coax me.

"I need to find out what's happening to me," I said, trying to sound firm and together. "Did you look into those missing kids I told you about? Or were you just humoring me?"

I heard some papers rustling in the background. "I did some nosing around, just because I said I would. All the parents are dead . . . except for Marjorie Mathers, mother of Brian. She's serving a life sentence for murder at Rahway State Penitentiary for Women."

"Doesn't it seem odd to you?"

"What? That all these kids went missing and were never found? Sad to say, it happens more often than people want to admit."

"Okay. But then most of the parents die?"

"Well, I mean, these are what we call high-risk people. You know, their lives and habits put them in dangerous situations. Drug addicts, right? Drinkers who don't think twice about getting into a car. People who get in bar fights. I mean, think about it. People like you, Ridley, are low risk. You obey the law—up

until now, anyway. You're responsible to yourself and the people around you. You're less
likely to meet with a violent and early death
because of your choices. If you'd had too
much to drink, you'd probably choose to get a
cab or call a friend than get behind the wheel.
A choice, which, poorly made, might result in
your death and the death of three teenage
girls . . . or not."

Choices. We were back to that, the things
that determine the course of your life. Was it
that simple? Some of us are high risk and some
of us low? Some of us made bad choices and
some of us made wise ones? And these choices
determined whether we were happy or miser-
able, healthy or unhealthy, loved or unloved? I
had to wonder, What informed these choices?
The obvious answer is our parents, the people
who loved or didn't love us, raised us well or
poorly. There were other factors, of course.
But did it just come down to whether someone loved us enough to teach us how to make
the right choices for ourselves?

No. It's not that simple. Life never is. I
mean, look at Ace and me. We were raised by
the same people in the same house. Totally
different outcomes; we've made totally differ-

ent choices in our lives. Like I said, how you were raised **is** part of the big picture. It's one important factor in a million. But in the end, it's not just the big and small events that make you who you are, make your life what it is, it's how you choose to react to them. That's where you have control over your life. I believe that.

"So what about these kids? Their parents were poor—high risk, as you say. Everyone who might have loved them is dead. No one ever figures out what happened to them. And, oh well?"

I heard Detective Salvo sigh again on the other end of the phone. "It was thirty years ago. I'd say the trail has gone cold."

"If someone was alive to love those kids, they'd still love them even thirty years later."

"Now you sound like Marjorie Mathers."

"You talked to her?"

"I told you I'd look into it."

"And?"

Another heavy sigh. Or maybe it was that he was smoking, releasing these sharp exhales. "She says two men dressed in black with masks over their faces came in that night and took her boy. She thought her husband had hired them because they were duking it out over custody. She claimed he abused the kid and she was gunning for full custody and supervised visitation only for the father."

He paused and cleared his throat. I heard him sifting again through papers.

"Thing was, you know, she didn't call the police until the next morning. Claims she was knocked out by some drug and didn't recover consciousness until the next day. But there was no evidence of that. The police didn't believe her story. So both she and her husband were suspects. And she wasn't very credible—had a history of depression and suicide attempts. Says in the report that she was hysterical."

I laughed a little. "Wouldn't you be?"

"So she killed her husband 'by accident,' trying to find out what happened to her son. But she got murder one, anyway. Jury didn't buy it. And that was that."

"Brian got lost again."

"Yeah, I guess he did. They had the case open for another year. I can see from the file that they followed procedure."

"For all the good it did," I said. "What did she say when you talked to her?"

"She's a little nuts," said Detective Salvo unkindly. "I talked to her on the phone. She's sticking to her story, anyway. Says a day doesn't go by she doesn't cry for her little boy, wonder where he is. She swears he's still alive."

"Let me ask you. Did she mention that a private investigator had been to see her awhile ago?"

The detective was quiet a minute. "Yeah, she did. How do you know that?"

"I've been following this trail and he's been everywhere I've been so far."

"Harley Jacobsen?" he asked.

I didn't answer.

"What does that tell you?" he said.

I didn't say anything. The last light had gone from the sky and I was sitting in the dark. The air blowing from the vents was tepid at best. I knew the car wouldn't really warm up until it was moving. The dials on the dash glowed orange and green. The radio was turned down low, but I could hear a low murmur of voices coming from the speakers.

"Well, it tells **me** something," he said when I didn't answer. "It tells me you were the last stop on that trail, Ridley. That he followed it to you and he's using you to get what he wants."

The words hit me hard. I hadn't really thought of that. It made sense now. Made sense like a lead boot in the stomach. I thought of him coming to my door that night, just after I'd received the letter from Christian Luna. I thought of the invitation I found at my doorstep, the bottle of wine and apology. Thought about the way I'd told him everything that first night. The man on the staircase. The second note and the newspaper clipping that he was so quick to identify. **They lied.** That's what the note had said and I had wondered how anyone could know what my parents had said to me. He knew because **I'd told him.** My mind struggled with it all. I thought of Christian Luna. He was real; I knew that much. But who had killed him? Jake? Why would he do that? Why would he lead me to him and then kill him? It didn't make sense.

"What does he want?" I said, more thinking aloud than really asking.

"I don't know, Ridley," said Detective Salvo, startling me. I'd forgotten I was on the phone with him. "But let me help you, okay? Just come on in and we'll figure everything out."

Gus Salvo was a nice man. He was a good cop, and though I didn't doubt that he wanted to help me, my gut told me that he couldn't, that I was on my own if I wanted to find out the truth. I was swimming in an ocean of lies and my instincts were the only thing keeping me from going under. So I hung up on poor Detective Salvo without another word and pulled out of the Little Angels parking lot. I drove the battered Jeep back to the city, watching out nervously for the Firebird and for cop cars all the way home.

I returned the Jeep to the after-hours drop-off lot, left the keys and the documents in the cup holder. I began walking out of there and the attendant, a young black woman with ironed hair, red and purple bejeweled nails, and the biggest gold hoop earrings I've ever seen, looked at me as if I'd lost my mind.

"You're going to have to **pay** for that," she said. "That car's **damaged.**" She grabbed the paperwork from the car and started marking up the little diagram of a car with a red pen.

"That's fine. You have all my information," I said. I couldn't care less. Before all of this I would have felt bad if I'd left a cigarette burn on the seat of a rental car, would have felt terribly irresponsible, but that seemed like a very long time ago and a very different Ridley. Now all I could think about was lying down. I went back to the hotel on Washington Square. I didn't do any transportation acrobatics. I just walked; it wasn't far from where I'd left the car.

I walked into the dingy lobby and got into the small elevator, exited on the third floor, which smelled like mold and mothballs even though it looked as if it had been newly renovated. I let myself into my room and climbed onto the stiff mattress with its scratchy comforter. I lay there in the dark for a second, my mind totally blank, my body numb. And then I fell into a black, dreamless sleep.

TWENTY-SEVEN

Carl Jung believed in a shadow self, a dark side to each of us that we learn to hide. Within this darkness dwells our forbidden appetites, our secret beliefs about ourselves and the world around us, the ugly traits and flaws that we hate and seek to bury. But Jung held that there was no denying this part of ourselves, that the more we tried to hide it, pretend it didn't exist, the more audaciously the universe would conspire to reveal it. He maintained that this shadow craved more than anything to be recognized and embraced. Only when we have forgiven it can we truly be whole, truly be free.

I awoke with a start in my hotel room. It took a few seconds to orient myself and then another few for everything that had happened to me in the last few days to come back in an ugly rush. I flipped on the light by the bed and half of me expected to see Jake sitting in the chair by the window. But he wasn't. I was alone.

For the first time since leaving Dr. Hauser's office, I allowed myself to reflect on what he'd told me. My father was Jessie Amelia Stone's pediatrician. He knew her. Could it be a coincidence? Carl Jung would say that there is no coincidence, only synchronicity, the forces of the universe colluding to introduce us to our shadows. In this moment, lying in a space that was completely sterile and that offered me no comfort whatsoever, I now had to fully face what I think, on some level, I had always known. That my life up until the moment when I received the note from Christian Luna had been a series of beautiful lies. Beautiful lies that had made me happy, provided me with a good life, lies that were told no doubt out of love, but lies nonetheless.

I still hadn't quite fit the pieces together, the why and how and who of what had happened to me. But it was clear that Ridley Jones was born on the night that Teresa Stone had been murdered in her home. And that my parents (of course, I still thought of them that way) must have had knowledge of that fact but were invested enough in hiding it that they had feigned ignorance on three separate occasions.

I also deduced that someone else, someone separate from them, was equally invested in preventing my discovery of these things, invested enough that they would have me followed, kill Christian Luna, and try to run me off the road to deter me from pursuing the truth. Why did I think this? Because I **knew** my parents. For all their flaws and mistakes, for all their lies and half-truths, I knew they loved me, would rather die themselves than see me hurt. Whatever it was they had to hide, they would never sacrifice **me** to hide it. I was in real danger and the only way I could escape it was to wrap myself back up in those beautiful lies, pretend that all of this was a terrible dream, and go back to sleep. But, of course, I couldn't do that now. Once you've started down that road to self-discovery, no matter how treacherous the path before you, you can't turn back. The universe doesn't allow it.

And where did Jake fit into this? Was he friend or enemy, lover or assassin? I didn't know. He had lied to me, yes. I believed that he knew who I was before I ever met him. And in thinking on it, I was sure that he had sent

that second envelope. The first had come from
Christian Luna, but the second one had come
from Jake. Still, I couldn't forget the way he
had looked at me, the way he held and made
love to me. I couldn't forget the way he had
laid the ugliness of his past before me, made
himself vulnerable to me in that way. For all
the lies, there was something real there, too.
But for all I knew I might never see him again.
He might be gone for good.

It was two in the morning when I left the
hotel room again. There's a hush over the city
at this time of night, like a breath drawn and
held. The street was quiet, dozing, but the city
seemed restless. Or maybe it was just me. I
smelled bacon and coffee as I walked past an
all-night diner. I could smell wood burning
from someone's fireplace. The air was cold,
and a slight wind snaked down the collar of
my shirt. I was tired to the core, my eyes
heavy, and I had that nausea that you get from
lack of sleep.

I walked up the stoop and pressed the
buzzer. Once. Twice. Three times.

"Hello?" A tired voice, alarmed.

"It's Ridley."

"Holy shit, Ridley," he said, and pressed the
buzzer to let me in.

I waited for the elevator. I had come to the only person who knew me and my parents. The only person I thought might have some answers. Zachary.

He stood waiting for me at his apartment door in his boxers and his Rutgers University sweatshirt, his blond hair tussled, his face creased with sleep. He embraced me and I let him take me into his arms, even though I didn't lift my arms to him. It felt good to be held, even by him. He led me inside and took my coat. I sat on the couch while he made me a cup of tea. Then he sat beside me on his couch while I drank it, not saying a word. Finally:

"Ridley, are you going to tell me what's going on?" He was gentle and looked at me with such worry. I remembered how harshly I'd treated him the last time I saw him and I felt bad (but not too bad—he had been **way** out of line). Well, you know by now how prone I am to spilling my guts. The story came out in a tumble. I told him everything but omitted a lot of the stuff with Jake. I didn't want to hurt him any more than I already had.

When I'd finished, he leaned back and shook his head. "Whoa. You've been through the wringer, Ridley." He put a comforting hand on my shoulder. I had pulled my shoes off and was sitting cross-legged beside him. It was nice to be somewhere familiar and comfortable that had never been mine. The leather couch, the big-screen television, the clutter of Knicks paraphernalia, the bar lined with his collection of beer cans.

"Yeah," I admitted. "It's been a little rough."

"Listen," he said. "Why don't you take my bed and try to get some sleep. I'll sleep out here on the couch. And in the morning, when you're rested, you take a fresh look at some of this stuff. I think things are going to seem a lot different after you've had some sleep."

"What?" I said. "No, Zachary. I can't sleep right now. I need answers. That's why I'm here."

He looked at me with that same expression of worry, and instead of being comforted by it, I wanted to punch him. Suddenly it didn't look like concern as much as condescension. He leaned forward and rested his forearms on his thighs, steepled his fingers. I felt a lecture coming on. "I want you to consider something for a moment, Rid."

"Consider what?"

"I know you've had a hard couple of days. But I want you to stop for a second and ask yourself if any of this seems reasonable to you."

"Reasonable?"

"Yeah. Has it occurred to you that this whole thing is just bullshit? That the psycho who started all of this and your 'friend' Jake were lying? That this whole thing is just some kind of scam?"

It struck me as a ridiculous thing to say and I was amazed that he could even suggest it. "A scam? What would any of them have to gain? Have you been listening to me?"

"Yes, I have been," he said slowly. "Have you been listening to yourself?"

I shook my head in confusion. He didn't believe me.

"I mean, what makes you so ready to listen to these total strangers over your own father?" he asked.

"Zack, I just **told** you that he was Jessie Stone's pediatrician."

He shrugged. "So what, Ridley? Your father has been doing clinic work for longer than you've been alive. He's probably seen thousands of kids at these clinics. And yeah, some of them have probably gone missing or died from illness or neglect or abuse. But that doesn't mean he had anything to do with it."

I just looked at him. I felt this veil of confusion fall over my thoughts. If you ques-

tioned the basic truth of what had happened
to me, then every single one of the events that
had occurred in the last few days could be explained away as the elements of a very complicated lie, some kind of plot to make me
question my identity. I entertained the idea
for a second, the way you might daydream
about winning the lottery or moving to the
Caribbean. Sitting in the warmth and comfort
of Zachary's living room, I could almost be
convinced. It would be so easy to let him convince me that I had been deceived and manipulated, suffered from a kind of temporary
insanity. I could check into someplace plush
in the country for a little "rest" and recover
from my nervous breakdown. And when I got
out, I could marry Zack and have children
and we'd all be one big happy family. We'd forget all about poor Ridley's little "episode."

I lay back on the couch, closed my eyes,
and tried it on. Was it possible? But the question "Why?" was the one that couldn't be answered. Why would anyone do this? Even Ace,
who maybe did have reason to hate me, to be
consumed by some kind of irrational jealousy—what would he have to gain?

Zack rested a comforting hand on my forehead. I opened my eyes and looked at him. He wore a relieved smile.

"Just rest awhile," he said. "This is all going to look different in the morning."

He grabbed the oversize chenille Knicks blanket I'd given him for his birthday last year and pulled it over me. I could almost imagine doing it, lying there and letting him take care of me. He'd sit with me awhile, until he thought I was sleeping. Then he'd go in the other room and call my parents, tell them I was all right and that he was going to take care of me. It would have been the easiest, most familiar thing for me to do.

"Tell me about Project Rescue," I said.

The relief dropped from his face, the smile faded. Annoyance took its place.

"You need to move past this, Ridley," he said. "You can't believe someone like Christian Luna over your own father."

At another point in my life, I might have missed it. It might have slipped past me. But that Ridley was gone. I smiled at Zachary. I imagine it was a sad, angry smile because that's what I was feeling. I sat up and threw the blanket off of me.

"I never told you his name," I said quietly.

"What?"

"Christian Luna. I never said his name."

"Yes, you did, Ridley," he said, looking at me sadly.

But I hadn't and I was certain of that. In fact, I had purposely omitted the name for reasons I couldn't have explained at the time. He could pretend that he thought I was insane but I knew that I wasn't.

"Ridley. Please."

I looked at Zachary then and realized that there had been more than just wanting my freedom, more than just not loving him enough, that had led me to leave him. It was something about him that I had intuited but had never had proof of, something that had disturbed me on a subliminal level. I had caught a glimpse of it when he'd let himself into my apartment that day. I was feeling it now but still couldn't put into words exactly what it was. I stood up slowly and reached for my coat. He stood with me, and when I looked into his face again, he was someone I didn't recognize.

"If you leave here, I won't be responsible for what happens to you." His voice cracked when he said it but his eyes were flat and cold.

"What's Project Rescue, Zack?" I asked, and I heard my voice quaver. I was scared of him, I realized. Physically afraid. I started backing toward the door.

He heard the fear in my voice, too. He looked surprised by it, as if I'd slapped him. And for a second he was the man I had loved once. "Rid, please. Don't look at me like that. I would never hurt you. You know that."

But I didn't want to see any more lying faces, any more masks.

"What is it, Zack?" I was screaming now.

"Calm down. Stop yelling," he pleaded, looking past me down the hall. "Project Rescue is exactly what your father told you it was. It's an organization that gives frightened mothers an alternative to abandoning their babies in the street. It's nothing more than that."

"You're a liar."

"No. It's the truth."

I didn't say anything and he sighed and sat down on the couch. "The child welfare system wasn't always what it is today. Now, whatever its flaws, at least it errs on the side of safety for the child. But in the seventies, it wasn't like that. It was hard to get a kid away from an abuse situation. Physicians a lot of times had a front-row seat to the systematic neglect and abuse of a child that would eventually end in that child's death. Their hands were tied."

"What are you saying?" I asked. But I was starting to see. I was starting to understand. The missing piece I'd sensed during the conversation with my father.

"I'm saying that there were some people that couldn't stand by and watch. They couldn't live with themselves."

"People like my father and Uncle Max."

"Among others. Including my mother," he said, looking up from the floor and meeting my eyes.

I remembered Esme saying, **I'd have done anything for that man.** The words took on a different meaning. I wondered what she had done for Max.

"That's enough, Zack." The voice made me spin around. There was Esme in a pink pajama-and-robe set. I remembered how she sometimes stayed on the futon in Zack's study when her work kept her late in the city. I used to love the nights when she was there and we'd all cook dinner together and rent a video, make popcorn.

"Ridley," she said softly. "You're making a terrible mistake, honey."

I looked at her. "What mistake am I making?"

"Dredging up the past like this. It won't be good for any of us."

"I haven't dredged up anything. It's coming up on its own."

She shook her head, seemed about to say something but then clamped her mouth shut.

"Do you know who I am, Esme?"

"I do, Ridley. I do know who you are. The question is: Why don't you?"

She wore a sympathetic smile that didn't do much to hide frightened eyes. I looked to Zack, hoping to see something in his face that I recognized.

His face was pale, his eyes filled with anger and something else. It was a look I recognized from my years with him. It had never been directed at me before, but I had seen it when he talked about certain patients he saw at the free clinic where he worked once a week with my father. It was usually accompanied by a comment like "Some people don't deserve to have children." I used to mistake it as passion, a passion for his work, a love for children, a sadness that so many of them fell through the cracks of the system. But now I saw it for what it was: judgment, a lack of compassion, arrogance.

"If you'd stayed with me, none of this would ever have happened," he said petulantly. "You never would have had to deal with any of this."

He was right, of course. If I'd stayed with him, I'd probably have been in his bed that morning or he in mine. I never would have left my place to meet him. The chances of my being on that corner at exactly the right second were slim to none. But who knows, maybe it was time for my shadow to reveal itself and nothing would have stopped it. Maybe every choice I made, the little ones, the big ones, those choices I thought had so much influence over the course of my life, maybe they weren't choices at all. Maybe it was just my shadow whispering in my ear, quietly leading me to myself, to the truth, to wholeness.

"Yeah, Zack. Maybe I could have lived out my whole life never knowing who I really am."

"Has it been so bad . . . your life?" asked Esme. There was something close to bitterness in her voice. "Have you considered what the alternative might have been?"

I looked at her. She seemed small, even fragile. But there was a terrible anger in her eyes.

"How could I have? I didn't even know there **was** an alternative."

She laughed a little. "Well, now you know. Happy?"

I turned from them and ran out of the apartment. "Ridley," I heard Zack yell after me, his voice sounding desperate. "It's not safe."

I had no idea where I was going but I ran.

It is not the strongest among us who survive. Nor is it the most intelligent. It is those among us who are the most adaptable to change. I don't remember who said this, but it has always struck me as being quite brilliant. And it kept playing in my mind. I ran for a couple of blocks, then I got winded and limped for a while, clutching my side against the cramp that had seized me just minutes after I fled Zack. Don't you just love it in the movies when normal people run for miles, scale chain-link fences at the end of alleyways, leap onto moving cars? Those kind of acrobatics weren't an option for me; I couldn't even remember the last time I'd worked out. If someone started chasing me right then, they would have caught me pretty easily. I kept looking over my shoulder for the Firebird or the skinhead. Zack said it wasn't safe and I had every reason to believe him. I

moved fast but I had no direction. I couldn't
go home. I couldn't go back to that grim,
lonely hotel room. I couldn't go to my parents.
So I walked.

I was fractured. Damaged but not broken.
My mind was a jumble of disconnected
thoughts and questions, but I wasn't insane. I
knew that much at least. I walked east toward
the river through a city that was starting to
wake, the sky fading from black to blue velvet.
I went to Jake's studio but found the door
locked tight. I rang the buzzer, knowing the
futility of it even as I did so. He wasn't there.
For all I knew, he was gone for good. And
maybe I was better off for that, considering
that he'd possibly tried to kill me.

The sun was still at least an hour from rising but already traffic had picked up. I passed
a man pulling his coffee cart up the street. I
walked through an already bustling China-
town, fresh fish markets opening, fluorescent
lights flickering on in shops. On Chambers
Street, parked Lincoln sedans were already dis-
charging early-bird lawyers and judges onto
the sidewalks, where they walked quickly
toward the giant, dirty-white court buildings.
I was tired, more tired than I had ever been.
But I kept walking. I thought of that footage

you always see of those people climbing Mt. Everest. They're at twenty-six thousand feet or something, at subzero temperatures, barely getting enough oxygen, but they just keep going. They just keep putting one foot in front of the other. They know if they stop, they'll die. That simple. I don't know if it was that simple for me. But I felt like I had to keep moving or the weight of my thoughts and my fears was going to crush me. Finally I stood at the base of the walkway that leads over the Brooklyn Bridge. I started up the wooden slats. If I could make it to the other side, I knew I could find a hotel there. Maybe I could check in and sleep for the next week and a half. Or maybe I would just keep going until I walked off the edge of the earth.

I want to say that I always knew there was something fractured about my life, but I don't think so. I do think, though, that there was a feeling that had always dwelled in the periphery of my consciousness, a specter that never quite came into focus. Esme had asked me, **Has it been so bad . . . your life? Have you considered what the alternative might have been?**

I told you, I just have to close my eyes and my childhood comes back to me in a rush, the scents and feelings. Not specific memories, really, but the essence of memory. Johnson's baby shampoo and burned toast, birthday parties and cut grass, fireplace embers and Christmas trees. I was loved. I grew up feeling safe, knowing I wouldn't go hungry. I was never afraid in my home. Was it perfect? I'll ask you: What is? Were there things I didn't know or ignored? Obviously. But it was a good suburban American childhood full of minivans and football games. From what I could see, the alternative might not have been as good. I might have been abused by my father, my mother might have been afraid of him, he might have been cruel to her. Who can say who I would be if I had been raised as Jessie by Teresa Elizabeth Stone? I would never know. And I couldn't say I was sorry. But that didn't mean that what had happened was right. Someone had murdered Teresa Stone and kidnapped her child. I'm sorry, but I'm just not one of those people who think the end justifies the means.

"Hey."

I spun to see him standing close behind me.

"You can't keep walking forever," he said. "Eventually you're going to have to stop and face what's happening to you."

I felt a rush of emotion at the sight of him, this train wreck of love and anger and fear that I thought might just run me down.

"And I suppose you're going to help me do that?" I said, unable to keep my voice from shaking.

He nodded slowly. "If you're ready to hear the truth."

TWENTY-EIGHT

"I guess you don't see the irony in that," I said, backing away from Jake. I hated my voice and hands, mutinous in their shaking, betraying the emotion coursing through me. He just looked at me. To his credit, he didn't say anything. The sky was lightening around us and the traffic below on the bridge was starting to pick up, filling the air with the white noise of tires on asphalt, punctuated by the sudden sharp blast of a car horn. He was standing very still, as if he were approaching a bird he was afraid to startle. And I was ready to fly.

"I know everything," I said, pulling my shoulders back and looking him right in the eye.

"No," he said with a slow shake of his head. "You don't."

In that second he became every person in

my life who had lied to me. And I wanted to rage at him, pummel him, break a hole in the universe by the sheer force of my anger and grief and throw him through it. But incredibly I held my temper for a few more seconds, which felt like holding on to a Rottweiler with a piece of dental floss.

"I know that your moving into my building wasn't an accident. I know that you followed a long trail that eventually, somehow, led you to me. I know that you wrote that second note."

"Ridley." It sounded like a prayer.

"Stay away from me," I said. Meltdown. The tremors in my voice and hands spread to the rest of my body and I was shaking uncontrollably. "Don't come any closer."

"I would never hurt you."

I laughed a short, hard laugh that sounded a little unstable even to my own ears. "You know," I said, my voice starting to raise a couple octaves. "I keep hearing that tonight. Seems to me like when people feel the need to assert that, there might be a problem."

Some of the color had drained from his face and he looked tired, black circles shadowing his eyes.

That crazy laugh rocked me again. It didn't

feel like me. Sounded hard and strange. "You're such a fucking liar. You almost killed us both yesterday. What were you trying to do?" I was yelling and looking around me. In New York City, you can never be alone, there's always someone around. Except when you're scared; then the city has a way of being the most deserted place on earth. There was no one else on the bridge.

"What are you talking about?" He was convincing, I'll give him that. He'd perfected the look of innocent confusion.

"The car!" I screamed, my throat going sore from it. "The fucking Firebird. Were you driving it when it almost forced me into a head-on collision?"

"What?" He shook his head, his eyes glistening. "No. God, Ridley. Are you okay?" He moved a step closer and I moved back again, as if we were dancing.

I had never been sure it was him, you remember. In fact, on an emotional level, I had been nearly sure it wasn't. But in that moment on the Brooklyn Bridge with the sun rising on a new day, I couldn't trust what I had felt, what I had seen, or what I had been told five minutes ago, a day ago, thirty years ago. I could operate only in the present tense. I was afraid and angry in equal measure, and that was literally the only thing I knew for sure.

"Listen to me," he said slowly. "The Firebird is gone. It's been stolen."

I shook my head in disbelief. "Do you think I'm an idiot, Jake? You told me yourself it was impounded and I know for a fact that it wasn't." A hard, cold wind gusted off the water, blowing my coat open. I pulled it tight around myself.

"Okay," he said, raising a hand. "I know what I told you. I was wrong. I assumed it had been impounded, but I have since learned that it wasn't."

I thought about that for a second, weighed the likelihood of what he'd said and found it pretty weak. "How could you learn that? You couldn't exactly call up and ask. You're a fugitive, wanted for the murder of Christian Luna."

He nodded as if he understood my skepticism. "I still have friends with connections."

"Who would do that? Who would steal your car and then try to kill me with it?"

"The same people who would leave a rifle registered to me in Fort Tryon Park for the police to find."

I looked at him hard, as if I was expecting

to squeeze the truth from him with the very force of my gaze. "Oh, so now it's some kind of conspiracy?"

"What do you want to call it?"

There was too much information for me to process about too many different people and circumstances. I started to feel that fog fall over my brain again, everything suddenly nebulous, dark forms moving behind a veil of smoke.

"I need to know everything that's happening, Jake. No more lies. Are you prepared to tell me everything? No omissions."

"I'll tell you everything I know. There's no more reason to hide anything from you," he said softly. I was quiet a minute, thinking of all my million questions as they jammed up against one another on the way to my mouth. I could come up with only one.

"Did you find what you were looking for?" I said as the sadness finally pushed its way past the anger and showed its face. The tears came then, too. Silent, heavy, sent directly from my bruised and mangled heart. "After all of this? Murder and lies and manipulation. Did you at least get what you were looking for?"

He sighed and turned his eyes from me,

cast them down to his feet, and his body seemed to sag a little beneath the weight of my words. "I haven't found what I was looking for, no." His voice was quiet and he raised his eyes back to me as he moved toward me. "But I found something I never even knew existed."

"Oh, please," I said, hating him for saying what I wanted to hear. "Don't even pretend you ever cared about me. You know what? Fuck you, Jake." I turned my back and started moving away from him.

"Ridley, please."

He moved quickly, too quickly for me to get away. He held me hard while I fought harder. I'm not talking about little girlie slaps and halfhearted punches. I kicked him in the shin. Pounded on his back. He didn't release me.

"Let go of me. You're a liar. I fucking hate you." Screaming like a maniac. Between blows to his back, which by the way felt like granite, he said, "I'll let you go when you promise to **hear** me."

I tried to bring my knee up into his groin, but he deftly blocked me with his leg. Finally I just leaned against him in exhaustion, like boxers seem to do in the ring, holding each other, delivering painful blows to the kidneys. I released a long breath and rested my head against his neck. "Okay," I said. "Okay."

He kept his word. But I didn't. The minute he released me, I took off like a shot heading to Brooklyn. "Ridley, Jesus!" he yelled. I was running with every ounce of strength and speed I had left in me, but he was on me in a heartbeat. I told you I wasn't very fast. Now he had me from behind, my arms locked to my side. I tried to kick back at him; I thrashed and screamed like a kid throwing a tantrum.

"You're right, Ridley!" he yelled over my screaming. "I lied to you. Let me explain."

I don't know how long this went on, but eventually exhaustion, coupled with the knowledge of Jake's physical strength, led me to just collapse against him. "Okay," I said finally. "Let me go. I won't run. I'm too tired."

"Please," he said, his breathing heavy. "Don't. I'm too tired to chase you." After another second, he released his hold on me and I moved away from him. I walked over and leaned on the railing. The morning was almost pretty, a moody gray-blue sky, whitecaps on the gray water below us.

"Tell me it wasn't you," I said, looking off into the distance. "Tell me you didn't kill

Christian Luna. Tell me it wasn't you driving that car."

To be honest with you, as far as what was between Jake and me, even with all the lies and manipulations, those were the only deal breakers, the things for which there could be no forgiveness, no explanation. He moved in next to me, slipped an arm around my shoulder, and lifted my chin with his hand until I had to look into those eyes.

"It wasn't me."

I think if he had tried to say more, I might not have believed him. But he let me look into his eyes and I could see it was the truth. I nodded.

"How did you find me?"

"What do you mean? Right now?"

"No. I mean, I know how you found out that my father was Jessie Stone's physician. But how did you find me?"

He laughed a little. "The same way Christian Luna did. Thank that **Post** photographer."

I sighed. "God, I hate that guy."

He hung his head a bit at that and I could see that I had hurt him a little. I didn't say anything to make it better.

"You're sorry you met me," he said after a while.

"Let's just say you've got a lot of talking to do."

We stood there for I don't know how long, looking down into the river of traffic rushing beneath us, the smell of exhaust rising, feeling black and gritty in my throat. Neither one of us said a word. My fears and questions were a coil of razor wire between us. We might get through them, but it was going to hurt like hell.

We found a diner on Montague Street in Brooklyn. We'd walked there in silence. He had a lot to say, I know, and I had so many questions, but it was understood between us that we needed to find someplace safe and quiet to talk. He wore a sweatshirt with a hood over his head and the bill of a baseball cap covered his eyes. I kept my distance and walked quickly. With the sun coming up, I felt as if we were both exposed and needed to get inside.

We slid into a red leather booth and ordered coffee. We were quiet, not looking at each other. Neither one of us was sure where to start, I think.

"How did you find me?" I asked. "Right now, I mean."

"I was watching the studio from Tompkins Square."

I nodded. "You knew I'd come looking for you?"

"I didn't know. I hoped."

More silence.

"I went to see Zack," I said after a minute.

"Yeah? Why did you go there?"

"Where else was there for me to go?" I shrugged. "I thought because he knew my father, he could help me see things more clearly."

"But?"

"But . . . he tried to make me believe I had imagined all of this. His mother was there, too. And then I realized."

"Realized what?

"Project Rescue. That whatever it is, they're part of it."

He nodded as though he already knew it, which he probably did. I reached into my pocket, withdrew the copy of Charlie's birth certificate and the photograph of Charlie, Adele, and Michael. I placed them on the table, slid it over to him.

"You're Charlie, aren't you?" I said quietly.

How did I come up with this? While I'd been on the phone with Detective Salvo, I'd been looking at the birth certificate and noticed that Charlie's birthday was July 4, 1969. The first night I'd met Jake, I'd wanted to know his sign; he told me Cancer. I looked at the fuzzy picture of the toddler on the pony and I couldn't be sure then that it was him. But something about his face on the bridge had made me think of the photograph again. And my subconscious had been shifting around pieces of the puzzle. I wasn't surprised when he nodded, looking down at the items in front of him. "Yeah," he said. "I think so. Or I was once, anyway."

"What happened?"

"I still don't know exactly. I don't know how I wound up abandoned in the system. All I know is that Charlie was kidnapped from his home when he was three years old. What happened from there is still unclear."

"But you were right about your mother. She loved you."

"She tried to abandon me."

"But she came back for you. She was young and scared. Her husband was a junkie. It doesn't mean she didn't love you."

He gave a shrug and a halfhearted nod. God, aren't we all just little kids who so badly need to know that we were loved by our parents?

"And you found your grandmother. Why didn't you tell her?"

Another shrug as he looked into his cup of coffee, which he turned between his palms.

"I don't understand," I said when he didn't respond. "Isn't that what you were looking for? Your family?"

"I thought so," he said. "But when I found Linda McNaughton . . . I don't know. It didn't seem right. The boy she loved was so long gone. Her daughter, too. I couldn't bring myself to tell her. I thought I'd go back when I figured out what had happened to me. I still don't know."

We were quiet for a minute. Then he said, "There's only one person left who knows what happened to both of us for sure. Why and how we were taken, what happened from there."

"Who?"

"Your father. He was the attending physician for all four of the children that went missing that year. And who knows how many others."

"There are others?"

"I think there are many, many others."

"Project Rescue . . ." I said, more thinking aloud than anything. I couldn't see the connection between what had happened to Charlie, Jessie, and the others and Uncle Max's organization, but I knew there was one, like you know an island connects to the ocean floor though it may be miles below the surface of the sea.

"That's why you sought me out?"

He released a long breath and looked at me. "To be honest, I was kind of at a dead end when I saw you on the cover of the **Post.** I'd seen Dr. Hauser and I knew about your father. But I didn't know how to get close to him. It's not like I could just walk up to him and ask about Project Rescue. Then Arnie died. All my other efforts to find out about the organization failed. And I was just lost for a while, grieving, walking around like a zombie, working on some cases to bring in money.

"Then I saw your picture in the paper. You looked **so much** like the picture of Teresa Stone from the **Record,** I had to wonder. I mean, it was jarring. I thought I was losing my mind, becoming so desperate for a lead, so obsessed with this quest that I was seeing things that weren't there. Then I read that you were Benjamin Jones's daughter and it just felt like fate. I thought by getting to know you I could find a way closer to your father."

"So you used me, basically."

He reached for my hand and I didn't pull it away.

"It started out that way, Ridley. But . . ." He didn't finish his sentence and I was glad, because I didn't want to hear how he'd never expected to have feelings for me. I think on a cellular level I knew what had happened between us. Words would just make it less than what it was.

"So if you're Charlie and I'm Jessie, what about the other two children who went missing that year? Who are they?"

"I don't know. I've never been able to track them down. These kids all **disappeared.** I mean, take yourself, for example. You have a different name **and** a different Social Security number. There's a birth certificate in the name of Ridley Jones. It's the same with me; I have a birth certificate for Harley Jacobsen. Charlie, Brian, Pamela, and Jessie don't even exist anymore. Most of their biological parents are dead."

It didn't seem strange to be talking about

Charlie and Jessie in the third person. Neither one of us, I think, quite identified yet with the missing children. I didn't feel as though I had ever **been** Jessie. She was someone whose fate was intimately connected to mine, someone whose story I needed to unravel before I could understand what had happened to me. By the way Jake was talking, it seemed as though he felt the same way.

"I still don't understand. These children were taken from their homes and somehow wound up in other homes with different names and Social Security numbers. Why? And how could this have happened?"

"A network of very powerful people with a lot of money and a lot of influence," he said without any hesitation, as if he'd been thinking about it for a while. "The level of organization and corruption it would take to accomplish it is nothing short of astounding."

"But why?" I asked again. "Why would anyone do this?"

"When I first started looking into this, it was just about me, what had happened to me. At first I thought it was some kind of black-market thing. I thought, Okay, kids were abandoned at the Project Rescue sites, many of them probably left without birth certificates, Social Security numbers. There has to be a system in place for getting abandoned children new identities, right? Maybe the healthy Caucasian children were snatched from the system somehow and sold to wealthy people who wanted children but couldn't conceive."

"But your mother went back for you. You weren't actually abandoned."

"Right. And when I learned about the other children who went missing in that area, I found that they were never abandoned, so it kind of blew my theory."

"But they'd all been patients at the Little Angels clinic."

"That's what they had in common."

"And the Little Angels clinic is a Project Rescue facility."

"That's right."

"So? What does that mean?"

"The other thing they had in common was the number of visits to the clinic. When a child has too many visits to the doctor for certain kinds of injuries or excessive illness, they're flagged by attending physicians as possible victims of abuse. Jessie's arm was broken. Charlie was abandoned. Brian was brought in for a broken leg, a blow to the head. Pamela had her arm pulled out of the socket. These are not normal injuries for toddlers."

"How do you know that? Dr. Hauser said he didn't give you the files."

"Well, you wouldn't expect him to tell you that he'd violated clinic policy because of his friendship with Arnie."

I smiled inside. I had been right about Dr. Hauser and his Dancing Bear tie. The inner hippie had won out in the interest of doing the right thing, even if it meant breaking the rules.

"So you're saying that someone believed these children were the victims of abuse."

"Not someone, Ridley. Your father."

Jake seemed to be looking past me, his brow knitting, and I turned to see what he was looking at. There I saw what he saw, the Firebird, as stealthy and menacing as a shark.

He reached over and grabbed my head and pushed it down on the table. He lay his head next to mine and yelled to the waitress, who was the only other person in the diner, "Get down!" She responded as if she'd been trained to do so, immediately dropping into a crouch behind the counter.

It was then that the windows of the diner

exploded in a crystalline blizzard of glass. The sound of automatic gunfire and shattering glass was deafening, easily the most terrifying sound I'd ever heard. The whole world was a kaleidoscope of deadly shards and blinding light. Jake dropped under the table and tugged on my legs for me to do the same, and together we crawled behind the counter, where the frightened waitress was weeping on the floor. I was too stunned to even be afraid.

"Is there a back door?" Jake yelled above the sound.

She nodded and crawled into the kitchen. A back door stood open through which the cook must have fled. We exited on all fours.

By the time we were in the back lot, the sound of gunfire had ceased and we heard the burning of rubber on asphalt. The Firebird engine revved and rumbled off into the distance. Jake pulled me to my feet.

"Call the police!" he yelled at the frightened woman, who huddled against a concrete wall, weeping. "Ask for a Detective Gus Salvo."

In the cold, bright morning, Jake took my hand and we started to run.

We ducked into a church on Hicks Street. My ears were ringing from the violence of the sound and my heart had burrowed itself into my esophagus, where it stayed, making it difficult for me to breathe. I gripped Jake's hand like a vice, only noticing how hard once I let go and felt my fingers cramp.

The church hummed with silence. An old lady in a black kerchief prayed in the front pew. The morning light washed in through the stained-glass windows, those bright colors dancing on the floor like butterflies. Votive candles flickered in the alcoves. It felt very safe. Who would try to kill you in a church?

Jake dragged me into a confessional. A small sign announced that confession would begin at four P.M. I was glad. I wouldn't even know where to begin. I sunk onto the red velvet cushion that was so worn, its stuffing had started to show through. I touched the leather Bible and took away a fingertip black with dust. Jake stood peering through the curtain.

"Who is trying to kill us?" I whispered fiercely.

"Ridley, we're deep into something. Someone doesn't want us getting any deeper. But at this point, you know as much as I do," he answered softly.

"But I don't know anything."

He gave me a look that I couldn't read and then turned back to keep his watch outside the confessional. I noticed a gun, a semiautomatic, cold and menacing in his hand. I realized I'd never seen an actual handgun before. It made me sick.

"What are you going to do with that?" I asked stupidly.

"Protect us . . . if it comes to that."

Do you think you go straight to hell for shooting someone in a church, or does God understand that sometimes there are extenuating circumstances? I leaned my head against the wood wall and felt the most powerful wash of fatigue. "I don't know anything," I whispered again.

I thought about those foundation dinners, those glamorous events filled with New York City's elite in business, broadcasting, medicine, society. I thought about all that money being funneled into Max's charitable fund. I thought about all the people that money had helped. I thought about Max's driving passion to save abused children and battered women in a way he and his mother had never been saved, how it had become a kind of salve for his own pain. I thought of how frustrated he and my father were sometimes over a system that failed so often, a system that bound the hands of physicians from helping children in danger. So many nights over dinner they had discussed these issues. So many times I over-heard their impassioned debates in the study. So many times as a child I wondered why they became so angry and sad.

What would have happened if Max and my father had decided to take certain cases into their own hands? What if providing safe haven for abandoned babies was just one arm of Project Rescue? What if there was another Project Rescue? One with which the social elite of New York City wouldn't be so eager to have their stellar names associated. These thoughts ran like liquid nitrogen in my veins.

"So you don't have any idea **how** these kids were taken and **why**? You don't have any theories?" I whispered to him.

"I didn't say that."

He moved away from the curtain and sat beside me on the small bench so that we were squished in next to each other. He stuck the gun in his waistband and wiped a sheen of sweat from his brow, then dropped his arm around me.

"We'll stay here for a while, okay?"

"And then what?"

"I don't know. I haven't thought that far ahead."

I noticed for the first time just how dog tired he looked.

"What are you going to do, Jake?" I said softly, my lips so close to his ear that I could taste him.

"What do you mean?"

"When you figure it out? When you know all the answers about what Project Rescue is and what happened to us, what are you going to do?"

He looked at me blankly with a slight shake of his head, as if the thought had never occurred to him, as if he'd been questing for an object he couldn't identify. We're all so lost, aren't we? Always looking for something elusive, something we think is crucial, never knowing exactly what it is.

"I just need to know who I am," he said.

"You know, don't you?"

"I need to know what happened to me. These other kids wound up in homes, I think, like you did. What happened to me? How did I wind up in the system? Don't you want to know for sure, Ridley, what happened to you? Don't you want to know the truth?"

We were still whispering. It was a good question. The truth is always held up as this Holy Grail, the thing for which all must be sacrificed. Everyone's always talking about how it will **set you free** and how nothing bad can come of **facing it.** I strongly suspected, in this case at least, that the truth was going to suck completely, that all my beautiful lies had been so much better. But I knew enough by then to know that the universe doesn't like secrets, that it lays snares you can't avoid. I was a fox with my leg in a trap. The only way to escape now would be to chew off a limb. And I'd lost too much already. I didn't realize that I was crying (yes, again) until Jake reached over and gently wiped a big fat tear from my cheek.

"I'm sorry, Ridley. I'm so sorry for all of this," he said, kissing me. His breath was hot in my ear as he whispered and goose bumps raised on my arms. "I could have squashed this for you but I didn't. I fanned the flame. I led you to Christian Luna. It was so selfish. I just—"

"Didn't want to be alone in this anymore?"

He nodded. I understood that. I remembered how alone I'd felt lying in that dark hotel room wondering who I was and where I came from, who was trying to hurt me. Jake had felt like that all his life. And in the last year, this searching for his family and for answers to what happened to him, his only friend gone. How lonely he must have been. The thought of having someone sharing his questions, sharing his quest, must have been irresistible. After all, beneath the surface of it, isn't that what we're all looking for? We may say we're looking for love, following dreams, chasing the dollar, but aren't we just looking for a place where we belong? A place where our thoughts, feelings, and fears are understood?

"I'm sorry," he said again, pulling me into his arms and holding me. I wrapped my arms around him as best I could in the small space and held on tight. I couldn't get close enough to him.

"It's okay," I said. "I understand it now."

"What?"

"Quidam."

He looked at me then, some combination of disbelief and gratitude in his eyes. I could taste the salt of my tears on his lips.

While we were hiding in the church, Detective Gus Salvo arrived at the scene of the shooting. I would find out later that, standing amid the glass confetti on the floor of the diner, he took from the shaken waitress the description of the two people who had fled the scene. He shook his head as she told him what she'd seen. It was another misshapen piece in a puzzle that made less and less sense the more he learned. What had started as a random shooting in a dangerous park was taking on dimensions he hadn't intuited when the case first landed on his desk.

Gun laws in New York State were pretty strict. If you wanted to legally obtain a weapon, there's a gauntlet of checks and balances, a long waiting period, etc. Harley Jacobsen had observed these laws in obtaining his Glock nine-millimeter and another smaller five-shot .38 Special Smith & Wesson, a gun cops often used as their off-duty piece. He was legally licensed to carry both. The rifle used to kill Christian Luna, however, had been purchased in Florida, where laws were much more lenient, employing only a three-day waiting period. In fact, in Florida, you could buy a weapon legally without registering it. Now, Detective Salvo could understand driving to Florida, buying an assault rifle, and driving back to New York City to use that weapon in the commission of a murder. What he couldn't understand was why Jacobsen would have **registered** it. Salvo obtained the documents that Jake had signed, compared them to the signature he had on file for Jake's PI license, and discovered that they were not even close.

He had been true to his word to me and was looking into the cases of the four missing children, following pretty much the same trail Jake, and then I, had taken. But Gus Salvo was a very single-minded man. He didn't have all the distractions and personal agendas that Jake and I did. And he never lost sight of his goal, to discover who had killed Christian Luna and why.

Luna was believed by police to be Teresa Stone's murderer. The fact that he hadn't been caught meant that the case was still open. But according to the files Detective Salvo had been poring over, no one had looked into any other possibilities. Teresa Stone didn't have any family to press the investigation, so after a year or so it had fallen into Cold Cases, more or less finished, gathering dust in a file deep in a basement somewhere in Jersey. Good news for whoever killed her. So the fact that Christian Luna had resurfaced and asserted his innocence to a woman he believed to be his kidnapped daughter, and who happened to have an entirely new identity now, must have seemed like pretty bad news and a very big problem to someone.

So Detective Salvo had come to the conclusion that Christian Luna had been someone's loose end. The fact that Jake had been digging around in the same graveyard made him a loose end, too. And I, for that matter, looked to be doing a bit of dangling myself.

He looked around the diner, littered now with shattered glass. The sidewalk outside was riven with rounds from an automatic weapon. What the fuck, he wondered to himself, was going on? And I might have known this sooner if I hadn't stubbornly turned my cell phone off when it started to vibrate in my pocket and I saw his number blinking on my caller ID.

TWENTY-NINE

You're driving on the highway and an eighteen-wheeler in front of you kicks up a little rock, which hits your windshield with a surprising, loud snap. That stone, probably no bigger than the nail on your little finger, leaves a tiny, almost invisible chip. And even though at first you can barely see it, eventually it's going to spider. That minuscule rupture has created fissures that compromise the stability of the whole. Eventually everything you see through it will become fractured and broken, and another blow, however small, might cause the entire thing to collapse in a deadly, slicing rain.

Through the compromised windshield of my memory, I saw things that I hadn't thought about since childhood, if I'd thought about them at all. They were rushing back to me, these moments that had been recorded but buried. How many things have we seen once and then never thought about again? I think, as a kid, when you see things you don't understand, maybe you file them away in your subconscious, and only when you have the language and the knowledge to finally process them do they surface in your memory again. I'm not talking about repressed memories. I'm talking about nuances, subtleties, those delicate moments that can change meaning.

I remembered an afternoon in winter when my school closed early. I was eight maybe, in the third grade, and we all gathered at the jalousie windows to watch the snow fall, coating the playground impossibly fast. The sky was that blizzard color, a kind of blackish gray. Our school was dismissed in shifts generally, the kindergartners and pre-K's all released at noon and the rest of us at three, so there weren't enough buses for all of us to go home early on that day it snowed. Mothers were called and the drive leading past the entrance to the school was a parade of station wagons and minivans. I remembered this feeling of guilty excitement, happy to be going where it was warm and cozy to watch the cold, wet world grow ever whiter from a window near our fireplace, eating grilled cheese sandwiches and drinking hot chocolate. We were all bundled and waiting by the aluminum-and-glass doors, and every time the doors opened, a flurry of snowflakes and cold wind blew in so that our noses and cheeks grew pink in the waiting. I was one of the last children to be picked up. I saw our familiar car approach, but at first the woman driving didn't look like my mother. Her face was gray, her expression hard and drawn. Her hair looked tousled, and her eyes were narrowed in an angry squint. My mother was a beautiful woman, always impeccably maintained. I don't recall ever seeing her "undone," as she would say. The woman who had seen us off that morning, though still in her red silk pajamas, had been perfectly groomed, face washed, hair brushed, wearing a matching black velvet robe and slippers. She was in costume and playing her role as mother perfectly.

The woman at the wheel of the black Mercedes looked anxious, annoyed, and deeply, deeply sad. She stared ahead into the snow as if the weather were the most crushing disappointment to her. I remembered a flutter in my heart that I'm not sure I would have been able to explain. In that moment, I think I saw my mother without her mask.

My teacher, Miss Angelica, said, "There you go, Ridley. There's your mom."

I looked away from the woman at the wheel and shook my head. "That's not my mother, Miss Angelica."

My teacher looked again, peering through her glasses into the snow. "Why, sure it is, Ridley." She gave me a confused, benevolent smile.

When I looked back my mother was there, smiling and waving. I felt a little jolt of surprise and then moved out into the snow. My mother leaned over and pushed the door open for me. I climbed in beside her and smelled her perfume, L'Air du Temps, the one that came in that frosted glass bottle with the little bird on the stopper. She brushed the snowflakes from my hat.

"Snow day!" she said cheerfully. "Let's go pick up your brother from the middle school. Then we'll go home and have some hot chocolate."

I was still looking for that ghost woman.

"What is it?" she said with a smile when she saw me staring.

"You didn't look like yourself," I said. "When I saw you from the door. You looked different."

She gave a little laugh, as if I was silly or playing a game. But her smile twitched a bit.

"Did I?" she said. Then she turned and made a face, sticking out her tongue. "Do I look like myself now?" I dissolved into giggles.

What am I trying to say? What am I trying to tell you? I guess that it's not just the big things that were lies—some of the little things were, too.

I remembered again that day, that birthday party when I overheard Uncle Max and my mother talking in the kitchen, how I couldn't believe the tones they were using with each other. So angry. I realize now, so intimate. Because, think about it, you don't talk that way to polite strangers, even to your husband's best friend, even if over the years he's become your friend, too. There was so much emotion in their words. As if there was a whole layer to their relationship I hadn't suspected.

To bring one of them here. To Ace's party. How could you?

I didn't want to come alone.

Bullshit, Max.

What do you want from me, Grace, huh? Stop being such a fucking prude.

My maternal grandmother always said with such pride about my mother and her siblings, "Oh, they never, ever fight." And for the longest time I thought this was the hallmark of a good relationship, a lack of conflict. And then, one night, when my grandmother made the remark, I heard my father whisper under his breath, "Yeah, they never fight because they never **talk.**"

"What was that, Benjamin?"

"Nothing, **Mother.**" He called her that, as if it tasted sour in his mouth. He called his own mother Ma.

I remembered how my parents never fought—except about Ace. That I knew when she was angry at him—he was never angry with her that I saw—because of the silence and the darkness. When my mother was in a good mood, all the lights would be on in the house, the fire lighted in winter and autumn, the sound of a television or a stereo some-where. When she was angry, she sat quiet and alone in the dark until she was appeased. That's how I knew when things were not good.

"You doing all right?" asked Jake, putting a hand on the back of my head.

"Yeah. Just remembering," I answered. He nodded as if he understood.

The cab we had hailed on Hicks Street had come to a stop in front of Ace's building. I won't say I was thrilled about seeing him again; I was still angry and hurt from our last encounter. But honestly, there was nowhere else to go for answers. He knew more than he'd told me. His passive-aggressive hinting around told me that. And he was going to be honest with me, for once. I wasn't leaving without answers. Not this time.

The stoop was empty, and though it was just after 4:30 P.M., the sky was nearly dark. We'd waited in the church for a while, considering ourselves safe because no one had followed us there. We dozed off in the confessional, leaning against each other, holding hands. Both of us were so tired, it felt as if we'd been drugged. We awoke during an afternoon Mass and remembered that the sign said confession began at four. When the Mass ended, we filed out with the faithful and got a cab right in front of the church, told the driver to head toward the Lower East Side. Jake watched out the back window, and when he was satisfied that we hadn't been followed, asked me to give the driver the address. Now we stood in front of the building.

"This is where he lives?" he asked.

"If you can call it a life."

As we walked into the building, Jake put his hand to the gun at his waist. Like before, that awful odor—garbage, human rot, something chemical—drifted up into my sinuses. But tonight the building seemed quiet, deserted, and there was no sunlight fighting its way in through the dirty windows.

"It's okay," I told him, taking his hand.

"I don't like dark like this," he said. I thought about all the awful things that had happened to him in the dark and I understood. I squeezed his hand tighter. Our eyes adjusted as we climbed the stairs, the wood creaking beneath our weight. When we came to the apartment door, it stood open and my heart fell like a stone into my stomach.

"Ace?" I said. But there was no answer.

Jake drew his gun and stood to the side, guiding me gently over toward the wall. He pushed the door and with a creak it opened. There was a figure slumped on the bed; I could see the outline in the dark. The thin, frail shadow seemed to shake slightly. Then I heard the sound of low sobbing.

"Ruby?" I said, moving closer to her. Jake reached for my wrist but I shook out of his grasp and walked toward her.

"They took him," she said quietly between sobs.

"Who took him?" I asked, kneeling beside

her. I couldn't see her face but I could smell the cigarettes on her breath.

"I don't know," she said. "Two men in masks. They slammed through the door. One of them hit me so hard in the jaw." She reached her hand up and rubbed her face. "I blacked out. When I woke up, they were gone and so was Ace."

"Are you okay?" I said, trying to inspect her jaw in the relative darkness.

She nodded and looked at me, her eyes wide and full of tears.

"They didn't say anything?" said Jake from the door.

She nodded. "They said to tell you to let it go."

"To tell **me**?" I said, incredulous.

"Both of you. They said, 'Let it go and we'll let **him** go.'"

I didn't say anything for a second because there was something lodged in my throat that kept all the words bottled in my chest. I had that nightmare feeling again, that moment where you look at things around you and hope that something is going to remind you that you're dreaming.

"It's my fault," she was saying. "I told him

to help you. I told him he had to tell you the things he knew, that he had to protect you from them."

"Protect me from who?"

"He knows," she said, nodding toward Jake. "He knows who."

Jake just shook his head and raised his shoulders. "No idea," he said when I looked at him.

"The men who took you, Ridley," she said, looking at me earnestly. "The people responsible for everything that's happening to you."

"Who, Ruby? Who's responsible?"

She started crying again. I had dueling impulses: One was to embrace her, the other to slap her.

"I don't know. He wouldn't tell me," she said as she cried harder. "For the same reason he wouldn't tell you. He thought it was too dangerous for us to know."

Was this girl just a crazy junkie? Did she have any idea what she was talking about? I didn't know what to say to her.

"They left this telephone number," said Ruby finally, sitting up and handing me a piece of paper. She kept suspicious eyes on Jake. It was dark in the room but there was enough light that we could see one another's faces. The smell of cigarette smoke was like a presence. I pulled the cell phone from my pocket and turned it on. With a beep and a flash of green light, the screen announced that I had three messages. I had no idea how to retrieve them. I looked over at Jake.

"Should I call?" I asked him.

He moved in closer to me. "What choice do you have?"

I should have been panicked, crippled with fear over what had happened to Ace and what was happening to me. But I was calm. The only hints of my fear were the persistent rushing sound in my right ear, the dryness in my throat, and the slight, barely perceptible shaking of my hands.

I dialed the number and we all waited while it rang.

"Ridley. That didn't take you long at all. You always were a smart girl."

I recognized the older man's voice but couldn't place it. It was smooth and educated but edged with malice.

"I thought we agreed that you'd go home to your parents, Ridley."

The tumblers of recognition fell into place with a sick snap, unlocking the door to a tiger's cage. It was Alexander Harriman.

"I don't understand . . ." I said.

"I knew the minute I saw that picture of you on the cover of the paper that there was going to be trouble." His voice was casual, lilting, as if we were old friends.

"What do you **want,** Mr. Harriman?"

"I just think we need to get together and talk some things over, clarify some misunderstandings, set a plan for the future. And when that's all taken care of, we can talk about your brother, getting him the help he needs."

I realized he was being careful about what he was saying on the phone.

"I could go to the media with what I already know, Mr. Harriman. I could call the police since I know you have my brother."

He didn't miss a beat. "You could. But there would be consequences. I think you're starting to realize that the truth doesn't always set us free. For many of the people I know, it's quite the opposite. For many of the people you know as well."

"Are you threatening me, Mr. Harriman?"

"Certainly not," he said with mock indignation. My mind was racing. I didn't know how to play this game. I felt like a mouse in the paws of a hungry house cat.

"I need to know that Ace is okay." I know,

it was lame. But I couldn't think of any other demand to make. Plus, I just wanted to hear his voice, know that he was safe and that it was within my power to help him still.

"As long as you and I can reach an agreement, then your brother and the rest of your family, not to mention your friend Mr. Jacobsen, will have no concerns. You have my word."

"That's not good enough," I said weakly.

"Look, Ridley," he said, impatience slithering into his measured voice. "You're not holding any cards here, so let's stop fucking around. Be at my office before the end of the hour. I'm extending you a courtesy because of Max's love for you. But I'm not a sentimental man by nature and you've become a terrible inconvenience."

He hung up then. After all, he'd said everything he needed to. I took the phone away from my ear and stared at it as if it were a murder weapon. I felt a shudder move through my body, thinking about how his courtesy so far had involved a drive-by shooting and a bad case of road rage. I wondered what happened when his sentiment ran out. I looked over at Jake and he moved in to me and took my shoulders.

"Who was it, Ridley?"

"My uncle's lawyer, a man named Alexander Harriman."

"As in mob lawyer Alexander Harriman?"

I hadn't really thought of him like that, but I guess once you've defended a mobster, then you're a mob lawyer. I sat down on the bed beside Ruby, who was now looking at me with desperate eyes.

"I love him," she told me. She was a wreck, so thin I could see the knobs in her shoulders and elbows, mascara streaking down her face. Her hair was fried from too much bleach. But there was a prettiness to her, a sweetness, something about her that I wanted to protect.

"I do, too," I answered, a catch in my voice I hadn't expected.

"So what does he want?" asked Jake.

"He wants to see me in his office, inside the hour."

Jake shook his head. "That's not a good idea."

"What's the alternative?"

We looked at each other for a second, but neither of us came up with an answer.

"Well, you're not going alone," he said.

"You can't trust him," Ruby said, grabbing my arm and turning a fearful gaze on Jake. She seemed desperate but not crazy.

"Why, Ruby? Why would you say that?" I asked her, looking at Jake. He just lifted his palms. She pulled me close to her and I could smell the cigarettes on her breath. She whispered fiercely, "He killed your uncle Max."

The words chilled me. "Ruby, my uncle drove himself off a bridge. He was drunk. It was icy. He wasn't murdered."

I looked over at Jake, who stood still and silent. I wished I could see his eyes, but all I could see was the slow shake of his head.

"You don't have to shoot a gun to kill someone," she said, looking right at Jake.

Jake stepped into the light so that I could see his face and he sighed. "Sometimes," he said, "all you have to do is tell them the truth."

"What? What are you talking about?"

I remembered how my uncle Max cried that night. I remembered his words. **Ridley, you might be the only good I've ever done.** And then I understood what Jake meant.

"You met him," I said to Jake. "You told him what happened to you."

He nodded. "I was in a dark place when I met Max. Like I told you, I had learned about the other missing kids, about your father. But I didn't know how to move forward with the investigation. Then Arnie died. I had so much anger in me that I couldn't sleep at night without drinking.

"When I learned about the Maxwell Allen Smiley Foundation and how it funded Project Rescue, I knew I had to talk to your uncle. You asked me about my theories? My theory was that the Little Angels Clinic and other places like it across the state that had been designated as 'Safe Havens,' places where scared mothers could leave their children, had a different function as well. Certain physicians were acting as 'Guardian Angels.'"

He sighed again here, as if it was painful for him to go on.

"They were watching over children who they thought were being abused?" I asked. I thought about Jessie with her broken arm. I thought about how my father, so concerned for the welfare of children, must have felt while treating her.

"Yes, and flagging them," said Jake.

"What do you mean?"

"In the seventies, it was very difficult to get a child out of an abusive situation."

"So you think there was a system by which these abused children were identified by certain clinic physicians . . . and what?"

"They were abducted," he said. "Maybe."

"By who? And then what happened to them?"

"I didn't know those answers when I went to see Max and I still don't know for sure."

"What happened?" I asked.

"I tried to see him at his office but I couldn't get an appointment with him, so I followed him for a couple of days and figured out the places he went to drink. I waited for him at the Blue Hen, not far from where your parents live, Ridley."

"On Christmas Eve?"

"No. A couple weeks before that. He'd already been drinking when he arrived and everyone there seemed to know him. I waited at a corner table, nursing a Guinness until he sat alone. Then I joined him. He was a friendly guy, bought me a round. I hated him, hated his guts." Jake's voice had gone cold and I was hearing something there that I hadn't suspected. I heard the anger he'd described and realized that it was still alive and well within him. Maybe it would be until he could understand his past.

"I said, 'Do you know who I am?' He looked at me, curious, a little suspicious. 'No, son. I have no idea.' I said, 'Let me tell you about myself.' And you know what? He was

kind to me. He listened to my story, he engaged, shared a little bit about his own history
of abuse. But I didn't care about his kindness.
I just wanted answers. After I'd finished and
we'd shared another beer, I said, 'Mr. Smiley,
what can you tell me about Project Rescue?'

"He stopped being kind then and started
looking a little gray. 'Who are you, son?' he
wanted to know. 'That's just it. I have no
idea,' I answered. He got the check then and
wanted to leave but I followed him outside.
He could have made a scene, got any of the
guys in that bar to work me over, or called the
police, but he didn't do that. In the parking
lot, I told him my theory about Project
Rescue. 'I think I was one of those kids, Mr.
Smiley. But something went wrong and I
wound up back in the system.'

"He told me I was crazy, that I didn't know
what I was talking about. 'Project Rescue is
about saving abandoned infants, that's it. You
need help, son.'

" 'You're right. I do need help. I need you
to tell me the truth about Project Rescue.' We
were standing so close to each other that we
were almost whispering. 'I've told you the
truth. I can't help you.' He got in his car then,
but before he closed the door, I flicked a copy

of my card onto his lap. I could see by the shine in his eyes that I'd upset him, unnerved him. I thought if he knew more, that his conscience would eventually get to him one day. And maybe it did. Maybe that's how he came to drive off that bridge on Christmas Eve. And if I killed him, then that's how."

I braced myself against the wave of grief I felt for my uncle Max. Even after all of this, it still hurt to think of him dying with all that sadness. The sadness had stalked him every day of his life, thieved every possible joy from him, led him to do unspeakable things. It had won.

"How did Ace know about this?"

"Your uncle told him," said Ruby. "A few days before he died, he came looking for Ace. He wanted to make things right with Ace, help him to get clean, pay for rehab. He told Ace that the past had come back on him and he had to fix some of the things he'd broken. I guess he thought Ace was one of those things."

I remembered my last conversation with Uncle Max and I wondered what he would have told me that night if my father hadn't stopped him. I thought about what my father told me, about Max leaving Ace's inheritance in a trust available only after he'd been clean for five years. Was he trying to make things right by Ace in doing that?

I looked to Ruby, who seemed not to know what else to say. She just stared at Jake, chewing on what was left of her nails. I guess the only thing that rivaled my fear at that moment was a crushing gloom that so much harm had been done, that so much had gone so irreparably wrong. Did I blame Jake for Max's death? No. He had a right to seek his truth. Did I blame Max for what had happened to Jake? I still didn't know. And I wasn't sure blame was really all that important now.

"We have to go," I said to Jake. "It's been a half hour since I called."

He looked at me in surprise, as if waiting for a reaction he didn't get. Then he gave a quick nod. "Let's go."

On the way down the stairs, my cell phone vibrated in my pocket and a glance at the screen revealed that it was Detective Salvo. I didn't dare answer. But it gave me an idea.

THIRTY

Anyone who has watched an execution will tell you that it's an anticlimax. Families of murder victims, after raging for years, waiting through endless trials they hope will bring the killer to justice, death row appeal after death row appeal, finally come to gather in a sterile room. They watch justice behind a sheet of glass. They watch the killer die. All those years they've looked to that moment as the time when pain ends and healing begins. They imagine a weight will be lifted from their hearts, that their sleep will be free from the nightmares. But once it's done, they'll tell you the pain doesn't go away. They are not relieved of suffering. Their grief is just as hot and bright as it was the first day, not mitigated in the least by the death of the perpetrator.

Maybe it's because the concept of punish-ment is a false one, because through good or

evil action everything around us is altered ir-
revocably. We are changed by the things we
experience. The big things, the small things
have their impact and can't be undone. To
judge those experiences, to hate the things
that have happened to us is to hate who we've
become because of them. I guess that's why I
didn't feel angry as we sped in a cab toward
Harriman's office. I was afraid, I was grieved
by the things that had happened, but I wasn't
cursing the day I leaped in front of that van to
save a little boy. I didn't hate my father for
"flagging" little Jessie Stone, if that's what he
in fact did. I didn't hate Jake for confronting
Max. I couldn't muster a feeling of righteous
indignation. Because it's like I told you, I believe in balance, in karma. That for every good
there is a bad, for every right there is a wrong.

Of course, in that moment I wasn't thinking of any of that. Every nerve ending was
alive with fear for my brother, for my family,
for what Alexander Harriman wanted from
me. Once again, I found myself in a situation
for which I had no frame of reference. I leaned
forward in my seat, willing the cab to move
faster, the traffic to clear. By the time we were
in front of the Central Park West brownstone

that housed Alexander Harriman's office, I was suddenly stuck to the vinyl upholstery with dread.

"It's okay," said Jake, paying the driver and nudging me out onto the sidewalk. "If he wanted to hurt you, you'd be dead already."

I had to admit there was a logic to this, but it didn't make me feel much better. We rang the buzzer and I wish I could say I was surprised when the skinhead freak opened the door for us. He smiled as he patted Jake down and took the gun at his waist. He didn't look as scary as he had come to seem in my memory of him. He had stubble on his jaw and his eyes were rimmed with girlishly long lashes. He smelled of cheap, heavy cologne.

"Nice," the bald man said, turning the weapon in his hand, then removing the magazine and the round in the chamber with two quick maneuvers. He handed the empty gun back to Jake.

He looked at me and smiled that wolfish grin I'd seen once before. "I feel like we know each other," he said.

"We don't," I answered, trying for cold and tough but just sounding like a scared kid. His smile didn't waver. Do things like this happen to people? I was wondering, feeling that dreamy wobble to my consciousness again.

The last time I'd been in Alexander Harriman's plush office, I'd been a different person . . . though it was only a few days ago. Everything looked different to me—the plush carpets, the leather furniture, the portrait of his wife and daughter hanging on the wall over the wet bar. What had once seemed elegant and comforting seemed tainted now.

"I am going to give you something, Ridley, that no one ever has," said Harriman as we entered the room. His thug for hire left and closed the door behind us, but I imagined he wouldn't go far.

"And what's that?"

He was standing, leaning on the edge of his monolithic oak desk with his arms folded across his belly. He was handsome, seemed almost benevolent if you failed to notice the glint of steel in his eyes.

"The truth," he said, raising his eyebrows and showing us his palms. "I'm going to give both of you the truth."

"Why bother?" asked Jake. "Why not just get rid of us. It's not like you haven't tried."

"Well," Harriman said with a placating laugh, "I wasn't trying to kill you, exactly. Just turn you off. Sometimes these things . . . You ask someone to do a job for you and they get a little carried away."

"Anyway," he went on with a dismissive wave of his hand, "I'm going to tell you what you both want to know, and then I'm going to insist that it stays here, between us. I've given it a lot of thought and I believe it's the only way to get you to stop nosing around, short of actually killing you."

"And why would we agree to this?" asked Jake.

"The knowledge of consequences. Ridley, if your brother turned up on an East Village sidewalk tomorrow, dead from an overdose, can you think of anyone who would be surprised? If your friend here disappeared without a trace, who—other than you—would miss him? Would you like me to go on or do you get the point?"

I got the point like a blow to the solar plexus. I nodded to communicate that.

"Where's my brother?" I asked him.

"He's quite a bit safer than he was when we found him. Sit down, Ridley. The sooner we get this over with, the sooner you'll be reunited with Ace."

I sunk into the leather sofa, more because

I felt like I couldn't hold my own body weight than out of an urge to obey Harriman. Jake stayed by the door.

"What I am going to give you," he said dramatically, "is what they call in law enforcement 'the fruits from a poisonous tree.' You'll have the knowledge you seek, but you won't be able to use it to bring justice—just as if it had been obtained in an illegal search and seizure. Your questions will be answered, but you'll have to be content with that. Shall I continue?"

I thought about it for a second. Maybe, even after all of this, I didn't want to know. What would I do with the knowledge if I couldn't share it, couldn't pursue it, couldn't endeavor to put wrong things right? Maybe I was better off not ever knowing what had happened to all of us. But I nodded my assent.

"Max was a **crusader.** He saw a wrong, a system that was failing, and he sought to correct it. But reforming a government system is slow work indeed, and in the meantime, children were dying. Children were being abused, neglected, fucked up in a hundred different ways by people who neither loved them nor wanted them or didn't know what to do with them even if they did. Meanwhile, other

couples were desperately seeking children, unable to conceive for whatever reasons, on long
waiting lists for adoptions. Through his foundation, Max encountered many of these
people, knew their desperation, knew what
loving, affluent homes they could offer needy
children. He was deeply frustrated by that
knowledge, seeing these people as wasted
resources.

"Max conceived of a way to help these
kids, and he convinced others to help them as
well. He called his endeavor Project Rescue."

I couldn't take my eyes off Harriman as he
pushed himself off the edge of his desk and
began pacing the floor like a trial lawyer giving his closing arguments. Jake stayed by the
door and kept his eyes on the older man as
well. His face was a mask; I couldn't even
imagine what he was thinking.

"Project Rescue had two different facets.
One was the group lobbying to pass the Safe
Haven Law in New York State, which would
allow mothers to abandon their children to
places like hospitals, clinics, fire departments,
whatever, no questions asked. Those children
were absorbed into the child welfare system . . . totally above board. But the other was
a more nebulous function, whereby cooperat-

ing medical staff at clinics that serviced the poorer communities were able to anonymously notify Project Rescue about certain children who were being abused and neglected. Many of these physicians and nurses did so quite innocently, thinking that Project Rescue had some special pull with the government agencies that investigated child abuse cases."

"But in fact," interrupted Jake, "they were marking them as children in need of rescue."

"That's right," said Harriman. "Now, while the **concept** behind Project Rescue was quite noble, the **execution** was a little less so. Someone actually had to remove the children from their homes. And this was something with which your uncle was not eager to be involved."

"And that's where some of your other clients came in handy," said Jake.

"Very good, Mr. Jacobsen."

"What?" I said. "I don't get it. What do you mean, other clients?"

Harriman gave me the kind of smile one might deliver to a slow student who, in spite of her best efforts, was still very behind in class. "I'm sure I don't have to tell you the kind of people I deal with on a daily basis."

"So . . . what?" I said, disgusted. "You brokered some kind of deal between Project Rescue and the **Mob**?"

Harriman cringed dramatically. "Please, Ridley. I said no such thing. And if I were you, I'd never say that again."

I stared at him, deciding that he was a monster, utterly without morality. He cleared his throat, then continued on. "For a while things went quite smoothly. Physicians and nurses were reporting abuse to Project Rescue. Removals were 'hired out.' Children were going to good homes; no one with clean hands was involved directly with anything questionable. And money was being made. A lot of it."

"They were **selling** the children?" I asked, my disgust and horror mounting.

Harriman shrugged. "This was an expensive operation. And not everyone was involved for the 'good of the children,' if you know what I mean."

He was so level, so unemotional about it all, it was hard to believe the things he was saying. He was telling me that Max colluded with organized crime to abduct children from their homes and families and sell them to strangers. Wealthy, important strangers. I thought of those foundation dinners glittering with star power, and I wondered how many of those people had **bought** their children from Project Rescue.

"The most important thing to your uncle was that no one got hurt. So when Teresa Stone was killed during the removal of her child, Jessie, Max was furious. At this point, he wanted to close down the operation, but by then it was bigger than him. The people involved were making a lot of money and no one was eager to give that up."

Harriman sat down across from me, poured three glasses of water from a tray that held a sweating crystal pitcher and matching glasses. "You look a little pale." He held out a glass to me but I didn't take it from him. He placed it back on the tray.

"Max was afraid then that they'd created something he could no longer control. And he was right."

"How many children were there?" asked Jake, moving to stand behind me.

Harriman shook his head. "There's no way to know," he said with a laugh. "I mean, it's not like anyone kept a log."

Jake looked like a statue, cold, paralyzed by anger. I wasn't sure he could open his mouth again if he wanted to. "What happened to Jake?" I asked. "We know his mother abandoned him and then went back for him. We know he was abducted. How did he wind up back in the system?"

Harriman showed me his palms. "I'm afraid I don't have an answer for that. All I can say is that people who think they can **buy** children probably don't have a crisis of conscience when it comes to returning their merchandise. I mean, think about all those people who buy purebred puppies and bring them to the pound when they bark too much or shit on the carpet."

I cringed at the comparison. But Harriman was right about something. It shouldn't be as easy to get a child as it is to get a puppy. I looked over at Jake. His face was pale, his mouth a thin line. Anger was coming off him in waves.

"So you think I was 'removed' by Project Rescue from my home because Dr. Jones thought I was being abused, but the family I was **sold** to decided I was too much trouble and then abandoned me at a Project Rescue site?"

"It's possible," said Harriman, looking at Jake. "I'm sorry, son. I really don't know. There's just no way to know these things."

"Wait a minute," I said. "Are you telling me that my father was a part of this? That he knew?"

"I don't know if your father knew about the other side of Project Rescue."

"He was the doctor to all four of those missing children, Ridley," Jake said gently. He came to sit beside me, put a hand on my leg.

"Fine. But that doesn't mean he was the one who 'flagged' the children. It could have been anyone at that clinic. Any nurse or any other doctor."

Jake looked at me sadly. "Then how did he wind up with you?"

We all sat there silent for a second. Then I turned to look at Harriman again. "Am I Jessie Stone?"

He looked at me, and I thought I saw the glimmer of compassion in his eyes. "Yes," he said. "You are. And I only know this because your case was special."

"Special how?"

"I have an agreement with Ben and Grace, Ridley. You need to speak to them."

"Are you telling me that my parents **bought** me?" I asked.

"I didn't say that, Ridley. You need to talk with Ben and Grace."

"But I'm asking you," I said.

I thought about the man I had always thought was my father. I knew his face, his hands, the feel of his arms around me so well. I thought that I came from that place, that his skin was my skin. But he bought me, like a house or a new car. Our family, everything about it a false front, pretty from the outside, hollow and empty at its core.

"What about Ace?"

"Ace," Harriman said slowly. "Ace is not a Project Rescue baby."

"What? I don't understand. I thought . . ."

"Again, Ridley, you'll have to discuss that with Ben and Grace." I noticed he never referred to them as my parents.

I didn't know how to feel. I was floating, suspended in the air, wondering what the ground was going to feel like when I hit it hard, when the reality of this situation brought me down.

"Is it still happening?" asked Jake, breaking my thoughts.

"I have no knowledge of any such enterprise. As far as I know, it ended when Project Rescue stopped participating."

"How can we believe that?" I said, feeling a strange desperation. "You said yourself it had grown beyond Max."

"It's not my concern what you believe, Ridley," he said, standing, his voice going cold. "All that concerns me is that you keep your fucking mouth **shut.** Don't make me fail in my promise to Max. Don't make me silence you."

Jake got up and walked toward Harriman and I pulled at his hand. But he shook me off and in the next second his powerful fist connected with Harriman's jaw. Harriman issued a kind of **"Oof,"** and stumbled back. I thought he would fall but he caught himself against the edge of his desk. I jumped up and grabbed Jake's arm before he could go after him again.

"Stop it. There's no point," I said, but he didn't look at me, kept his eyes on Harriman. Coolly, Harriman pulled a handkerchief from his pocket and dabbed at the blood that made a line down his jaw.

"Feel better now?" he asked Jake. "I'm going to do you a favor and not hold that against you. You've had a rough time." I felt Jake tense, as if he was going to throw another punch, but I held on to him tight.

"There are no guarantees in this life, kids. Loved or not loved, abused or cherished, adored or neglected . . . We don't choose what happens to us, we only choose how we react to it. Jake, you've had it rough. Ridley, you've had it pretty good. But you're both here, alive and healthy. And you've found each other. Make the most of it. It's more than a lot of people have."

There was a Ridley who wanted to lie down on the couch and sob. There was a Ridley who wanted to throw herself at Alexander Harriman and pummel him with all the strength of her anger and her sorrow. There was a Ridley who wanted to run from this man and never think of him or what he'd told her ever again. There was a Ridley who wanted to go to the police and the media and fuck the consequences to her, to Ace, to her parents, to Jake, and to all the Project Rescue babies out there living their beautiful lies.

He was right about all this information seeming like the fruits from a poisonous tree. What could we do with any of it? I felt dead inside. I searched for more questions for him, knowing that this was the last chance I would ever have to ask them. But I couldn't think of one.

"My father would never be a part of something like this. Never."

I looked at Jake. More than anything, I wanted him to believe that. But I looked in his face and saw that he didn't.

Harriman shrugged. "It would be hard to convince the authorities of that, given his position, all the work he did for the legitimate arm of Project Rescue, his relationship to Max, and his possession of you."

I didn't know what to say to that. The word **possession** threw me.

Finally I managed, "What are you saying?"

"I'm saying that Max is gone. If this comes out, someone is going to have to answer for Project Rescue. You're the only link between the criminal and legitimate arms of Project Rescue. What do you think that will mean for your father? To his career? To all the good he's tried to do in his life? It'll ruin him, at the very least."

I was numb. I looked at Jake, who seemed to have softened a little, as if an acceptance that he might never know the full story had washed over him and given him some small peace. He came and sat beside me. I moved in close to him and he pulled me into his arms. "I'm sorry," I whispered to him.

"It's all right," he said into my hair. "It's okay. Let's get out of here."

"Where's my brother?" I said, remembering with a start.

Harriman walked to a door toward the back of his office and opened it. In it there was a large conference table and several desks. On a long leather couch lay my brother. He wasn't beaten or bound, just completely passed out. He was pale except for his eyes, which had blue canyons beneath them. He was sprawled there, an arm draping on the floor. He looked like a corpse.

"His girlfriend put up more of a fight than he did," said Harriman. "Today he winds up on my couch. Tomorrow it's an alley on the Lower East Side. Today he's alive. Tomorrow . . . up to you."

I wish I could tell you that something miraculous happened here, that by some tremendous act of heroism we were able to outwit Alexander Harriman. I wish I could tell you that the cavalry came in and we were all saved and justice was done. But all we could do was pull Ace to his feet and drag him toward the door.

Alexander Harriman was right about something else. I'm not sure how he knew me so well. The knowledge of consequences was a powerful deterrent. Even if he hadn't threatened Ace's life, was I really prepared to bring this down on my father? Was I prepared to ask him to pay for what he might or might not have done? Was I strong enough to expose Project Rescue? Righteous enough? In that moment, the answer to all those questions was no.

Remember how we started this, though, talking about the little things. How they can affect the course of our lives more profoundly than any of the major decisions we make. More than where you went to college, more than who you married . . . or didn't, more than what you chose to do with your life. In this case, it was that cell phone.

As I hesitated in the cab on arriving at Harriman's office, I did something silly and desperate, something straight out of the movies. Just me being a dork again. I pressed the call button on my phone and stuck it in my pocket. I knew it would call the last person who'd called me, Detective Salvo. I didn't know if it would work, if he'd be able to hear anything or if he'd be able to use it to figure out our location. It was just the last-ditch effort of a frightened person way out of her league. It turned out not to be so silly after all.

In the bits and pieces of conversation he

was able to pick up through the fabric of my jacket, some of the foggy places in his investigation started to come clear. And as Jake and I emerged from Harriman's office onto Central Park West, Ace unconscious between us, the street was a sea of squad cars. Detective Salvo stood waiting on the sidewalk, leaning against his unmarked Caprice.

"Ms. Jones, Mr. Jacobsen, good to see you both healthy. Who's your friend?"

"He's my brother," I answered defensively. He was, after all, and always would be, blood or no blood.

He nodded. "Mr. Jacobsen, I'm going to ask you to place your weapon on the ground and kick it out of your reach, please. Then place your hands on your head."

Jake did as he was told, while I held the bulk of Ace's weight. Two paramedics emerged from an ambulance that I hadn't noticed when we first stepped out into the night. I released Ace to them and they placed him on the gurney.

"Is he hurt?" one of them asked.

"Yes," I answered. "I don't know. He's high, I think."

I looked down at my brother and just felt so sad for him. Then I glanced up to see Detective Salvo watching me. "Rough couple of days, Ridley," he said quietly.

"How did you find us?" I asked.

He held up his cell phone. "Nice work," he said. "It wasn't an accident, was it?"

I shook my head.

"You two need to come with me," he said. "We have a lot of talking to do."

"Are you arresting us?" asked Jake.

"Not at the moment. But it's in your best interest, I think, to cooperate. Otherwise I can do that. I'll charge you with the murder of Christian Luna, Mr. Jacobsen. And Ridley, I'll charge you with aiding and abetting. Shall I read you your rights?"

I looked at Jake and shook my head. "We'll come with you," I said.

"Good thinking," said Detective Salvo.

"How much of that did you hear?" I asked, realizing suddenly what I'd done by making that call.

"Enough," he said as he led me to his car, Jake right behind us.

"Then you know I can't tell you anything."

"I heard enough that you don't have to," he said.

I thought, If Detective Salvo knows everything I'm not supposed to tell the police, then

what's going to happen to Ace, to my parents?
I stopped walking then. I felt as if I had lead
in my chest, thinking about my brother who
wasn't my brother and my parents who weren't
my parents and what was going to happen to
all of us because of the choices **I** made. I
thought about my uncle Max and what he'd
tried to do . . . and what he'd done instead. I
thought about him dying, knowing the horrible consequences of his good intentions.
None of it could be undone. Justice would not
be served. Where was the balance I had always
believed in? And then, just for a second, I **did**
wish I had never stepped in front of that van.
With all my heart and soul, I wished for ignorance again.

I was suddenly having trouble taking in air
and all I could hear was my own labored
breathing. I heard Jake say something. Detective Salvo's voice sounded worried and far
away. There was a light show of stars in front
of my eyes, white noise in my brain, and then
everything tilted and went black.

I regained consciousness for a second in the
back of an ambulance, my head pounding. I
reached up to touch it and felt a bandage. My

fingers came back damp with blood. Jake was there. Detective Salvo, too.

"What happened?" I said. But I didn't stay awake long enough to hear the answer.

In the hallway of a busy hospital, young people in green scrubs rushed back and forth. I could hear a voice over the intercom, smell bandages and disinfectant. Jake was holding my hand, looking at me. He looked so worried. "What's wrong?" I asked him.

"You passed out," he said. "I didn't catch you in time and you hit your head on the sidewalk hard. You have a . . ."

But then he faded away.

When I woke up again it was dark and quiet. I could hear the soft beeping of a heart monitor and it took me a second to realize that it was **my** heart being monitored. Scratchy, sterile-smelling sheets, hard mattress, metal guardrail. Light shone in from beneath the door, and as my eyes adjusted, I saw a form sitting in a chair across from me. I'd recognize him anywhere.

"Dad?"

"Ridley," he answered, getting up quickly and walking over to me. "How are you, lullaby?"

"My head hurts."

He placed a gentle hand on my forehead. "I bet," he said.

"What happened?"

"You passed out, and before anyone could catch you, you hit your head on the sidewalk. Gave yourself a nasty concussion and lost a lot of blood."

I tried to remember falling and, in doing so, all the events of the day came back to me in a rush: the diner windows exploding in a shower of glass, the church, finding Ace missing, Alexander Harriman's office.

"Dad," I said, releasing a sob. "So many lies."

My father sighed and pulled a chair over to the bed. He sat heavily and rested his head on one hand. When he lifted his face to me again, I could see that he'd been crying. The sight of it frightened me. The face I'd always looked to for comfort was shattered.

"Dad. Who am I?" I tried to sit up and realized by the warbling of the room that it wasn't going to happen.

He shook his head slowly. "You're Ridley. You're **my** Ridley. You'll **always** be that."

There was truth in this that I recognized. But it wasn't the whole truth and we both knew it. "No more lies, Dad."

"It's not a lie," he said, nearly yelling. "You couldn't **be** any more my daughter."

I knew if he could, he'd try to pull his cloak of denial over us both. But it was no use. It didn't fit anymore. I'd outgrown it.

"I am Ridley, Dad. But I wasn't always Ridley. Once I was Jessie Amelia Stone, daughter of Teresa Stone. A woman now dead because of Project Rescue."

He looked at me blankly for a second. There were lines around his eyes I hadn't seen before. The skin on his hands looked dry and papery. They were the hands of an old man. He rested his head in them.

"No," he said through his fingers.

"Did you know, Dad? Did you know what they were doing?"

He shook his head vigorously. "No," he said firmly. "I told you everything I knew about Project Rescue. If they did what that detective thinks they did, I had no idea. You know me, Ridley. You know I would never do that. Don't you?"

I didn't know if I could believe him. That was the worst thing about all of this. There was no one I could trust. Everyone had an agenda, good or bad, a reason to hide the truth from me.

"Then how did you wind up with me, Dad? If you didn't know, how did I become Ridley Jones?"

He looked at me with profound sadness. It mimicked perfectly the expression I'd seen on Max's face the night my father closed the study door on him.

The door to my hospital room pushed open then and in came my mother. She looked stronger than my father, more reserved. Her eyes were dry and she wore a faint, sad smile on her face. I didn't know how long she had been listening and I didn't know how much she knew to begin with. I looked at her and thought of the butterfly at Union Square. She came to stand by my bed and put a cool, dry hand to my head, as if in some motherly instinct to check my temperature.

"It's time, Ben. Ridley's right. No more lies." She kept her eyes on my face but I couldn't read her expression. All I could think was how different she was from me. There was nothing of my face in hers.

"No, Grace. We made a promise," he almost whispered.

"Max is dead," my mother said harshly, the word **dead** like a stone that she threw. My father looked startled by her tone. "I don't want to keep this secret anymore. It's caused too much damage already. If we'd have been honest from the beginning, Ridley would never have been vulnerable to this kind of nightmare in the first place."

My father seemed to sink down in his chair. He shook his head slowly.

"Maybe you're right," he said.

THIRTY-ONE

I thought they were going to tell me about Project Rescue, that they'd colluded in Max's plan, had been a part of it in some way. I thought they were going to tell me how I was taken from Teresa Stone and that they bought me and raised me as their own. I thought they'd tell me all the reasons why it was okay, why I was better off for the way things had been. But those weren't the secrets they'd kept.

"First, Ridley, I want you to understand that your father had nothing to do with Project Rescue," said my mother. "I don't care what that private detective says. You have to believe that he would never knowingly be a party to abduction and murder, no matter what. He may have treated those children, he may have noted the potential for abuse, but he would never be an accessory to such a scheme."

I didn't say anything. I wanted to believe

her. And it didn't mesh with anything I knew about my father. But it was hard to imagine that he didn't have at least some idea what Project Rescue was all about. Then, of course, there was the fact that both of them had lied to me for my entire life. I just wasn't as certain of them, their beliefs, their judgments, as I had been a week ago.

"Ridley." My mother wanted me to agree with her. So I nodded my head, just so she would go on. "That's not how you came to us."

"Then how?"

"There was always a parade of women through Max's life, and at first no one thought Teresa Stone was any different. A pretty young woman who worked at the reception desk in Max's Manhattan office; it was only a matter of time before he took notice of her and asked her out. And of course, she would say yes. No one could resist Max, his charm, his money, the way he had of making a girl see stars.

"Truth be told, I never even bothered to remember their names most of the time. I think Teresa was the only girl, other than Esme, that he saw more than once."

"I knew she was different right away," my father interjected. "There was a goodness to her that attracted Max, a decency. She wasn't like the others."

My mother gave him a look that told him he'd interrupted her. "Sorry," he said.

They saw her first at a Christmas party, then he brought her to dinner at my parents' house; a while later he brought her to a performance of **La Bohème** at the Met and they all had dinner afterward at "21."

"She was quiet," my mother remembered, "clearly intimidated by the evening. The box seats at the Met, Max's special treatment at '21.' I don't know; I liked that about her. She didn't take it for granted or have the usual air of pampered entitlement that so many of Max's friends seemed to have." She leaned heavily on the word **friends,** effectively communicating her disdain.

"Anyway, we thought, Well, maybe this is it. A **real** girlfriend; not one he's hired— literally or figuratively." My mother always has been a bit catty. "But then she was gone. We didn't see her again. I asked about her, though that was a big no-no with Max. He said they didn't share the same interests . . . or something vague like that. But it was more than that. You and I have talked about it, Ridley."

I remembered our conversation about Esme and the things my mother had told me about Max then.

"A man like Max," my father said, "so broken and lonely inside from all those years of abuse, from the things he'd endured and seen, can't really love well. He was smart enough to know it. It's why he never married."

I thought of Max's parade of call girls, his aura of loneliness, the way he always looked at my mother and father with that strange mixture of love and envy. The misshapen pieces of my life, the ones I had always ignored, were fitting themselves together.

"What are you telling me, Dad? That he knew Teresa Stone and allowed her child to be taken from her, anyway?"

My parents exchanged a look.

"Not exactly," my mother said, looking down at her fingernails.

I managed to push myself upright with great difficulty. My father jumped up to help me. My head felt like a helium balloon; the room had an unpleasant spin to it.

"Max and Teresa went their separate ways," my mother said. "Eventually she left the office, went on to other employment. And

I never saw her again." She released a heavy sigh and walked over to the window.

They were stalling. But I didn't push. I'm not sure I was any more eager for them to get to the point than they were.

"But a couple of years later, she showed up at the Little Angels clinic with a baby. A little girl, almost two," my father said. "I remembered her, but she didn't remember me. I didn't want to embarrass her, so I didn't say anything about my relationship to Max. Over the next few months, there were incidents that caused me some alarm."

"He broke Jessie's arm. Christian Luna."

My father nodded. "So you know."

"He told me before he was killed." I fought back tears and a wave of fatigue.

My father nodded with a heavy frown. "I had a conversation with her," he said. "She promised me that Luna wouldn't have access to her any longer and I let the incident go."

"But you mentioned it to Max?"

My father shook his head. "No. I didn't. Couldn't have. It would have violated her doctor-patient confidentiality."

"But he found out somehow," I said.

"I don't know, Ridley." He shrugged,

looked away from me. "All I know is that he showed up at our house a few weeks later. With little Jessie Stone." He paused, put a hand on my arm. "With you."

"With me?"

"Ridley," my father said, his voice hoarse and his eyes getting glassy. "I'm not your biological father; that much you know. But neither is Christian Luna. He may have believed he was. Possibly Teresa led him to believe it."

I shook my head. "Then who?"

"Ridley, honey," my mother said, standing. "You're Max's daughter."

I looked at her and saw that she was telling the truth. I heard Max's voice in my head. **Ridley, you might be the only good I've ever done.** And I started to cry because I finally knew what he meant.

Max came to them late in the evening, after midnight and unannounced. He came with a little girl in his arms. His daughter, he told them, by a woman he hadn't seen in years. The little girl clung to him, wept quietly, her dark eyes wide, taking in all the unfamiliar sights and sounds.

"Oh, my God. This is Teresa Stone's little girl," my father said, taking her from Max's arms. "I've treated her at the clinic."

Max looked at him, his face blank, a sheen of sweat on his forehead. "You knew I had a daughter?"

"No, of course not," he said. "I didn't realize she was **your** daughter, Max."

Max drifted into the kitchen, rubbing his temples with his hands. He sat at the table. Little Jessie pulled at my father's earlobe, made a light cooing noise.

"Something terrible has happened to Teresa. She's dead, Ben. Murdered in her home." His voice was little more than a whisper. The little girl started to cry and my mother took her into her arms, brought her into the other room to comfort her.

"What? When?" my father wanted to know, shocked.

"What difference does it make?" Max snapped.

"What difference does it make?" my father repeated, incredulous. "Max. What's going on?"

"I can't raise this child, Ben. You know that."

"Wait a minute, Max. Let's go back. How did you get this little girl?"

"The police called me. Teresa had my name

on the birth certificate. I picked her up from Child Services a little while ago."

"But that was a lie," I said, interrupting my father. "Teresa Stone was murdered that night and Jessie was never found."

He nodded. "You're right. Max wasn't on the original birth certificate. She'd left the father's name blank. There was no way the police would have known to call Max. But by the time we realized that, it was too late."

"What do you mean too late?"

My father shook his head. "We took you from Max that night. We accepted what he told us without question."

"We'd been trying for eighteen months for a second child and your arrival just seemed like the answer to our prayers," said my mother. She was sitting across the room from me now. It was dark; I couldn't see her face.

"So when you figured out that Max had lied, that Jessie was a missing child, that no one knew who'd murdered her mother, you just kept quiet?"

"We fell in love with you right away. And by the time we realized that there was so much Max hadn't told us, we'd already bent some rules," my father said. He almost looked sheepish.

"What kind of rules?"

"With the help of some of Max's connections, we processed you like a Project Rescue baby, like a child who'd been abandoned without documents. We created a new birth certificate and Social Security card."

"And that's how you became Ridley Jones," said my mother with a smile, as if she were telling me the happy ending to a bedtime story.

"And Jessie Stone disappeared," I said. "Until I saved Justin Wheeler from his fate."

Nothing about their story rang true. There was a false note to it that could not be denied and there were so many questions. Like how could you just take a child in the night from your friend and ask no questions? Didn't it seem like a huge coincidence that Jessie, Max's daughter, would wind up being treated by Dr. Benjamin Jones, Max's best friend? If Ben didn't realize Jessie was Max's daughter and Max's name wasn't on that birth certificate, how did Max find out about Jessie? And did he arrange to have Jessie taken that night? Did he arrange to have Teresa Stone murdered? But these questions seemed to dam up against one another, and for a minute I couldn't bring myself to ask them. The answers were so potentially ugly.

They each had their eyes on me. And I wasn't sure what to say to them.

"So you took this child, promised Max you'd raise her as your own. You falsified documents so that you could keep her true identity a secret from her for the rest of her life. You never asked any questions about what happened to her mother, how she died?"

"Well, we all thought Christian Luna had killed her. He was on the run. The child had no family except for Max." He ended with a shrug. "What would have happened to her if we hadn't taken her? She would have gone into the system. Been adopted by strangers."

"If Max had kept her, she would have been raised by nannies," said my mother.

They'd had a lifetime to justify their actions to themselves. Not that I was inclined to judge them. How could I? If they'd lied and broken the law, if they'd looked away from everything suspicious about my arrival at their doorstep, they'd done it for Jessie. They'd done it for me.

"Why not just tell me the truth? Why not just raise me as an adopted child? People do it every day; it's not exactly taboo."

"Max was adamant that you never know he was your father. He never wanted you to know that he didn't have what it took to raise you. He never wanted you to think he didn't want you."

"And he never wanted me to start looking into my past. He never wanted me to know what happened to Teresa Stone. And he never wanted me asking any questions about Project Rescue."

"Project Rescue doesn't have anything to do with this," my father said sternly.

I don't know how he could say that. But I could see that he believed it. That he needed to believe it. But the first of many ugly questions pushed its way through the dirt.

"If Max's name wasn't on the birth certificate and the police never called him, how did he wind up with Jessie that night?" I asked.

They looked at each other and then at me.

"Did he have something to do with her murder?" I asked, my voice cracking.

"No," said my father. "Of course not."

"Then how? How did he know about me? How did he wind up with me that night?"

They were both silent. Then my mother spoke, quietly, almost in a whisper.

"We never asked those questions, Ridley," she said. "What would have been the point?"

Denial: my family heritage. If you don't

ask the questions, the truth will never inconvenience you.

I tried to process the information but my
exhausted brain wouldn't allow it. Ben and
Grace weren't my parents. Max was my father.
My mother had been brutally murdered.
Possibly, maybe probably, Max had something
to do with it. And I had been more or less abducted. My birth certificate and Social Security card were falsified documents. I got it. But
the information was having no impact on me
whatsoever.

You'd expect me to have raged, lambasted
them for all the lies and all the mistakes—
crimes—they'd committed. But I didn't do
any of that. I slipped back down on the bed. I
didn't have a tear left in me. I was numb.
Maybe it was the painkillers. I wondered if I
could get some more. Like a lifetime supply.

I looked at the people before me and tried
to imagine that they weren't my parents. It was
impossible to comprehend. It made me think
that it's not blood that binds us, it's experience. Teresa Stone was a stranger to me, a sad
stranger who'd met a heinous and unjust end.
I felt a pain in my chest for her and all that she
had endured. But she was as distant and faded
as the old photograph that had started all of

this. As for Max, I would need some time to recast him as my father, my failed father. He was the good uncle, a man I loved dearly all my life. Incredibly, I couldn't muster any anger at him for the things I knew he'd done and for the things I suspected. Not then anyway; there would be time for that. Max, for all his joviality, operated from a place of terrible pain; for all his wealth, he was an emotional pauper. Can you judge that? Feel contempt for what a person doesn't have? Well, maybe you can. But I don't have it in me.

"What about Ace?"

"What about him?" my father said.

"Is he your son?"

My father nodded. "Ace is our son, our biological child."

I thought about it a second. "Does he know I'm not your biological child?"

My father nodded. "He overheard your uncle and me talking one day. We were careless and he got an earful. But the problems with Ace started long before that day. In fact, I think he was in my office trying to steal some money when Max and I entered and shut the door. He hid behind the desk and heard everything."

I had to give a little laugh. "Well, what right does he have to be so fucked up, then?"

"Ridley," said my mother, who'd visibly stiffened at the sound of Ace's name. "Watch your language."

Watch my language. Can you believe that? They can never stop parenting, can they? Ben and Grace were my parents, and they always would be. There was no changing that.

"Where is he?"

"They've got him in rehab. They can't keep him there, though, so if he wants to leave, they have to let him go."

I nodded. Normally, I would have felt desperate and worried about him, wondering if he would stay or go back to the streets. But part of me had let Ace go. Not that I didn't love him as much, or that I didn't want him to be well. But I'd finally gotten the clue that no matter what I did I couldn't control him. All this time, that's what I'd been trying to do. Hoping if I just loved him enough, helped him enough, he'd learn to love himself, help himself. Maybe it was the little bit of concrete to the skull; it knocked some sense into me.

My father sighed. "I think he felt we favored you, Ridley. Me and Max. But it was never that, you know. There was always enough love for both of you. Enough of everything."

He'd said the same thing to me in his office. It was like a mantra he was repeating to comfort himself. "You were always just easy, Ridley. Easy to please, easy to love." He didn't say "easier," but I heard it in his tone.

"Let's not get into this," my mother said to him. Yes, let's not get into who was whose favorite and how that's communicated in all sorts of nonverbal ways, I thought but didn't say. I threw my mother a look and she looked away.

My father was sitting beside me on the bed with his hand on my arm. I looked at him and I saw shame on his face. I wasn't sure what it was exactly that he regretted; it seemed as though there was a lot to choose from. I didn't have a chance to ask. The door opened softly and Jake walked in. I was washed with relief at seeing him. He paused in the doorway, seeing me with my father. "Everything okay?"

"Yeah," I answered. "These are my parents, Ben and Grace." My mother rose, clutched her purse to her side, and started moving toward me.

"We've met," Jake said. "We had a long talk."

I looked over at my father and he nodded. My mother made some kind of small sound to communicate her disapproval. She came over and kissed me on the head.

"Get some rest, dear. This will all seem less awful in the morning."

Just like that. I could tell by the way she'd squared her shoulders and held her head high that she believed it. That she would make it so. I envied her. I knew nothing was going to seem less awful in the morning. That the road ahead of us was dangerous and uncharted. And that there were miles and miles to cross.

My father rose and kissed my head. "I love you, little girl. I'm sorry for all of this." That apology sounded so simple, as if it was all just some silly misunderstanding that we'd all soon laugh about.

"I love you, too, Dad," I said, more from reflex than anything. I did love him, of course. He was right about one thing, I couldn't be any more his daughter, biology or not. He left quietly, picking up his coat from the chair and moving past Jake with a cool nod. He seemed old and stooped, as if the heavy burden he'd carried all these years was finally weighing him down.

"I'll see you tomorrow," he said, looking back at me from the door. "We'll talk everything out, Ridley. It'll all be okay."

"Okay," I said. But I wasn't sure about what tomorrow held anymore. I could tell he didn't want to go, didn't want to leave me with the truth and not be around to spin and control it. He cast a long gaze at Jake, the truth-sayer, and I could see anger on his face. I think he felt unseated by Jake, as if Jake had taken a place in my life that he'd never expected anyone to fill, the place I looked to for the truth. No parent ever wants to give that place up in their child's eyes, but they all have to sooner or later, don't they? He left then and that's when the tears came again. (Who knew I had so many?)

Jake pulled the chair beside my bed closer and took my hand, let me cry, comforted me only by touch, spared me all the platitudes.

"Are **you** okay?" I asked Jake when I'd finally pulled myself together.

"I'm okay. I feel like a shit for not catching you when you fell."

"That's not what I mean."

He shrugged and squeezed my hand. "I know. I don't know what I'm feeling right now. There's too much to work through. It's going to take time."

I tried for an empathetic smile but it made my head hurt. I told him all the things my parents had revealed.

"I'm so sorry for all of this, Ridley—all the lies, all the mess," he said when I was done.

Like Jake, I still had to sort through what

had happened to me. I definitely didn't know what the future held. And my life as I knew it had literally been shattered. But I was still there, still me. And there was something comforting about that. There's something comforting about knowing that when all the things that you think define you fall away, you're still standing.

"I'm not sorry," I said.

He looked at me, confused.

"On the bridge," I said, putting my hand to his beautiful face. "You asked me if I was sorry I met you. I never answered you. Well, I'm not."

He smiled, leaned in, and kissed me on the lips, so softly, so gently, sending off starbursts of pain behind my eyes. He whispered in my ear, "I love you, Ridley Jones . . . or whatever your name is."

We laughed then because as sad and awful as the truth was, Alexander Harriman had been right. We were alive and healthy and we had each other. Like he said, that was more than a lot of people had.

THIRTY-TWO

I don't believe in mistakes. Never have. I believe that there are a multitude of paths before us and it's just a matter of which way we walk home. I don't believe in regret. If you regret things about your life, then I'll bet that you're not paying attention. Regret is just imagining that you know what would have happened if you took that job in California or married your high-school sweetheart or just looked one more time before you stepped out into the street . . . or didn't. But you don't know; you can't possibly know. I could have spent a lot of time thinking about what would have happened if I hadn't seen Justin Wheeler toddling into the street that day. And I did spend a little time thinking about that—but not much. You could drive yourself crazy thinking that way.

They were eager to get rid of me at Mount

Sinai Hospital. I had only a "catastrophic" health insurance policy (private insurance is **expensive** and I never get sick) and there was some debate over whether hitting your head on a sidewalk after passing out from what amounts to a panic attack was exactly catastrophic. There was some debate over the meaning of the word and whether it was the incident or the result of the incident that had to be life threatening in order to be covered. Since the less than twenty-four hours I had spent in the hospital was already costing me over two thousand dollars, I figured I could recover more cheaply somewhere else. Jake had gone downstairs to hail a cab and I was washing my face, looking pale and funny in the mirror with a bandage on my head, when Detective Salvo walked in.

"They spring you?" he asked.

"Yeah, they're sick of me already."

He smiled and sat on the vinyl chair by the door. He looked tired. I noticed he was wearing the same clothes he'd been wearing the day before.

"The charges against Harley Jacobsen have been dropped," he said as I sat back down on the bed. He told me about the signatures on his gun registrations and how they hadn't matched the rifle registration. That and the fact that there hadn't been any fingerprints on the gun meant that there was no legal basis for charging him.

"That's good news."

"For you and Mr. Jacobsen. For me, I've still got a murder to solve and no leads."

We sat in silence. I could have suggested that he start investigating Alex Harriman's client roster, but I wasn't going to do that. I couldn't do that.

"Something interesting, though," he said, looking at me. "Some of the shell casings found at the scene of the diner shooting match a gun used in another crime, a shooting up on Arthur Avenue in the Bronx last week. Guess who the prime suspect is."

I shrugged.

"A thug named Angelo Numbruzio, a known associate of Paulie 'The Fist' Umbruglia. Does that name ring a bell?"

"I guess it does. I've heard about him on the news."

"His lawyer is Alexander Harriman."

I looked at him. "That's quite a coincidence."

"I thought it was information you might like to have. I mean, somebody who was looking to draw connections between things might find it interesting."

Jake appeared in the door then and the look on his face told me that **he** found it interesting. I felt my stomach do a little flip. Was he still looking for justice, for answers?

"I've made all the connections I need to make," I said. "Is there anything else, Detective?"

He stood up as I made my way toward the door and followed me into the hallway. "If there is, I'll give you a call. I have your number."

"I'm getting rid of that cell phone."

He laughed then and I smiled back at him. He was a good man but I knew he wasn't going to let this thing go. And I couldn't afford his questions, not with Alexander Harriman's threats still echoing in my battered head.

Are you disappointed in me? Did you expect me to begin a crusade to find all the Project Rescue babies in the world and reunite them with their possibly abusive parents? Ask yourself, if you'd lost everything, if you were barely clinging to the shreds of what was left of your life, if the lives of the only family you had ever known had been threatened by a lawyer who represented people with names like Paulie "The Fist," what would you do? Really. What would you do?

In the cab on the way downtown, I leaned against Jake. I wasn't wearing any shoes because somehow my Nikes had gotten lost between my arrival at the hospital and my departure. So I'd left the hospital in stocking feet.

I watched a sunlit Central Park roll by. The trees were losing their leaves; people were jogging, Rollerblading, walking dogs. Such a normal day for everyone else.

"There's no proof of any of it, you know that?" he said, as if thinking aloud. "They were so careful. There's no proof that any of it ever happened."

"Except that those kids are missing. Except that you're Charlie and I'm Jessie."

"Yeah, but there are kids missing all over the country and all over the world. Unsolved cases like Charlie, Jessie, Brian, and Pamela. We could never trace it back to Project Rescue."

It was true. They'd left no evidence. They'd managed somehow to change the Social Security numbers and birth certificates of the children, to give them new identities altogether. The children, they were . . . ghosts. Maybe they were better off, maybe not.

"Unless . . ." said Jake, looking past me out the window.

"Unless what?"

"Unless we could get someone to talk."

"How are we going to do that?"

"I don't know," he said, looking at me. "We don't have to think about it now. Let's just get you home."

"Jake, my family—"

"I know, Ridley. Don't worry. Forget I said anything."

I didn't respond. I was still feeling pretty groggy and all I wanted to do was lie down. But I had this uneasy feeling in my shoulders, and that noise I hear when I'm stressed, the blood rushing in my right ear. And I knew it wasn't over.

THIRTY-THREE

We had dinner with injustice sitting between us. It drank a glass of wine and ate heartily while we pushed pasta around our plates and picked at salad. We had been crushed by fear and it sat with us fat and victorious, untouchable.

We barely talked through the meal. As Jake cleared the plates I sat on the couch and looked out onto First Avenue, thought about where I would move. I couldn't even stand to go into my apartment. Jake had promised to go down for me and retrieve some clean clothes, shoes, and toiletries after we'd finished eating. I turned the television on and pressed the mute button and zoned out on the silent images flashing on the screen.

After a while, Jake came to the futon and sat beside me. I leaned into him and we sat in silence for a while, listening to the street noise outside. There was so much hanging between us that the silence was not comfortable. I could hear the wheels in his mind turning and I'm sure he could hear mine.

"Can you walk away from this?" I asked him finally. "Can you settle for what we know and move on from here?"

He was quiet for a minute. "Can you?"

"I think I have to," I said, even as uncertainty tugged at me. "You said it yourself. There's no proof. No trail to follow."

"Unless we can get someone to talk; someone to admit what happened. Unless we can get someone to take responsibility for Project Rescue."

"Like who?"

"I've been thinking. Your father is adamant that he had no knowledge of the other side of Project Rescue. But someone was flagging those kids. Someone who worked with him, maybe?"

I turned to look at him. He had his eyes down as if he didn't want to see the expression on my face.

"Hasn't your ex's mother worked with your father for years?"

"Esme?"

"I saw her name on every one of those files."

I thought of Esme, that night in Zack's

apartment, the conversation we'd had about Max. **I'd have done anything for that man,** she'd said. What **had** she done?

"Maybe, Ridley, maybe she'd talk to us. Maybe because of her love for you, she'd tell us what she knows about Project Rescue."

I remembered how she acted at Zack's. Not like a woman prepared to talk about the past, that's for sure.

"You want to risk all our lives for this, Jake?" I asked.

He shook his head but kept his eyes on the floor. "You have a life, Ridley," he said softly. "I don't."

I felt inexplicably hurt at that statement. I guess part of me thought we had a life together, a possible future, and that would have been enough for me to move forward and leave all of this behind. But I guess the difference was I knew the answers to my questions. I knew what happened to Jessie and Teresa Stone. I knew what happened to Christian Luna. I knew who I was then and who I had become. Jake was still an orphan, still quidam. His place with me was not enough.

I saw the choice I had to make. If I chose Jake, I had to choose the truth no matter how painful, no matter how ugly, no matter the

risk involved. If I chose to keep silent and protect my family, I chose the beautiful, familiar
lie, where everything was a false front. I would
have to choose a place where my past would,
over the years, become like the Loch Ness
monster or Bigfoot, a creature that someone
claimed to have seen once, but one in which
no one quite believed.

You don't have much faith in me, I'm sure.
I haven't exactly made the noblest choices up
to now. It's been Jake pushing me along the
path, coaxing me to ask the questions that led
us here. I felt his eyes on me then, and when I
met them, I knew. We had already allied ourselves in this world. The day I stood here and
held his hand, we began our trek to the edge
of my reality. And at the precipice, there was
nothing to do but jump.

"She was there that night, at Zack's. She
knows what happened, I think. She told me
that I was dredging up things that wouldn't be
good for anyone."

Jake leaned forward. "How much do you
think she knows?"

"I really don't know. She didn't say much.
But she was clearly in the loop. I think Zack
knows something, too. She stopped him from

telling me everything he knew about Project Rescue."

"If she was the one doing the flagging, she'd at least know who she flagged for Project Rescue," said Jake. "And she might know how Max found out about you."

"You mean she might know if Max was responsible for Teresa Stone's murder."

Jake was looking at me intently. Then suddenly he got up quickly and moved past me. I realized then that he hadn't been looking at me but at the television that was on behind me.

"Notorious mob attorney Alexander Harriman and an unidentified associate were found murdered execution style in his Central Park West office today," said the grim-faced newscaster when Jake turned up the volume. In the background, I could see the entrance to Harriman's brownstone office, where we'd just been twenty-four hours earlier. Someone was being rolled out on a stretcher, in a body bag. "So far the police have no information on any suspects."

"Mr. Harriman had no shortage of enemies," said a homicide detective at the scene to the reporter. "We have our work cut out for us."

Jake turned to look at me. His face was a mirror of my own heart, stunned, afraid.

"Our deal was with Harriman," I said slowly.

"I have a bad feeling the deal is off."

We wouldn't have gone back to my apartment at all except for the small problem of my not having any shoes, remember. I'd gone from the hospital to the cab to our building in socks and couldn't stand to enter my apartment on my way up to Jake's. So I changed into a clean pair of Jake's socks at his place and left it at that. I was regretting it as Jake pulled on his jacket and handed me mine.

"We are most definitely not safe here. We have to go."

"Where?"

"Someplace we've never been before."

I looked down at my feet.

"Shit," he said, moving toward the door. "Okay. Wait here."

"No way. We go together or we leave like this."

He sighed and disappeared into his bedroom. He came back with the gun I'd seen before. He shoved it in his waistband and zipped his jacket up over it.

"Okay, let's go."

We moved quickly and quietly down the stairs and onto the landing that led to my apartment. At the door, Jake motioned for me to be quiet as I handed him my keys.

"Ridley!" A sharp whisper startled us both. I turned and saw Victoria's one eye peering out from the darkness of her apartment. I put my finger to my lips and moved toward her. I couldn't help but think, She does know my name!

"Victoria, it's not safe. Go back to your apartment and close the door."

She huddled in the crack, staring at me with fear. Her wig was forgotten and a few gray strands on her bald head were caught by a breeze and stood nearly on end.

"There's someone in there. In your apartment."

"How many?" asked Jake, coming up behind me.

"Just one," she said, and closed the door. I heard the turning of three locks in quick succession.

I was ready to make a run for it without

my shoes, but Jake was moving toward the
door. He gave it a push and realized there was
no need for a key. It was open. He walked in
slowly, gun drawn, staying close to the wall.
He motioned for me to stay back but I followed behind.

The desk light behind the screen that separated my "office" from my bedroom was on
and we could hear the sound of someone shuffling through papers. A bulky shadow moved
there. We didn't enter the room but stayed behind the cover of the wall.

"Put your hands where I can see them and
step out from behind the screen," said Jake.
His voice boomed; he was downright terrifying. Something clattered hard to the floor and
I hoped it wasn't my laptop. The shadow
stood frozen.

"Put your hands where I can see them or
I'm just going to unload, asshole." His voice
was flat and hard and I had to look at him to
be sure it was actually coming from his
mouth. He sounded like a stone-cold killer.
We waited a moment and then I watched as
Jake's finger started to tense around the trigger.
I have no doubt he would have opened fire,
but then two hands reached above the screen.

"Don't shoot," said a voice I recognized.

The shadow stepped out where we could see him. The tension of the moment drained. Fear, anger, and relief vied for their positions in my chest.

"What are you doing here, Zack?" I asked from behind Jake, surprised that my voice sounded so steady.

"I'm trying to save your life, Ridley."

"How's that?"

"There are people looking for you . . . people who are very curious about what you know. I'm trying to figure it out before they do."

"The same people who killed Alexander Harriman?" I asked.

He nodded. "You're in real trouble. Both of you. But I can make it all go away. I can make it so both of you walk away from this safely."

His face was a mask of earnest benevolence. I wanted to believe that he was trying to help us, but I was having a hard time trusting people. Imagine that.

He moved closer to us. Jake and I backed up. "Stay where you are," said Jake, and Zack froze.

"Okay, okay," he said. "Just hear me out."

"We're listening," I said.

"All Jake has to do is disappear. No one will look for him if he stops digging around, if he stops making inquiries. There's money for him to set up somewhere and start over, anywhere in the world. Just not here."

He nodded over to a duffel bag that lay on my bed. "Go ahead," he said. "Take a look." I walked over to the bag and pulled the zipper. It was packed with bricks of cash. I couldn't even guess how much. A lot, seriously.

"Unmarked. Untraceable," said Zack.

I saw Jake's eyes rest on the cash for a second. I tried to read his face but it was hard and expressionless. He kept the gun on Zack, who still had his hands in the air.

"And what about Ridley?" Jake asked. I felt my stomach flip at the question. Was he considering the offer?

"They just want **my** word that she's not going to pursue the matter, that she's going to come back into the fold of the people who have loved and cared about her, and as long as it stays that way, she has nothing to worry about. She'll be fine. Her family will be fine."

"So why will they take your word?" Jake wanted to know.

He laughed a little. "Because I'm in this so

deep, they know they own me. And my mom, too. She's been in this since the beginning. You've probably figured out as much."

"So it still exists. Children are still being abducted and sold."

"Don't make it sound so **sinister,** Ridley," said Zack defensively. "We're **saving** children that are being neglected and abused. Turn on the fucking television—every day you'll hear about some animal who killed his girlfriend's baby because it was crying too much, or some crazy bitch who thinks God wants her to save her children from sin by drowning them in a bathtub. **We're** not the criminals."

"You don't have the right to make these choices," said Jake. His voice was shaking. "We only get to make the choices for one life, our own."

"Wrong," said Zack. "If everyone thought like you, Ridley might be dead right now. Killed by her mother's boyfriend. Even you, Jake, even you might not have survived your childhood."

"My mother loved me," said Jake. "I was **loved.**"

"That's not enough," said Zack. "Lots of people love their children and fail to protect them from harm. Lots of people claim to love their children and hurt them, neglect them, or murder them, anyway."

There was a logic to the argument and I think we all heard it, even Jake. But it didn't make any of it right. It didn't make the fact that children had been abducted from their homes and sold to wealthy families the right thing. All the children who may have been helped didn't make what happened to Teresa Stone or what had happened to Jake okay. Life's not like that. We don't get to make those kinds of bargains. No one has that right.

We stood in an awkward triangle. Jake looked at me and I was sad to see that he was wondering what my choice was going to be. I could see that if I chose to return to "the fold," he would let me go and wouldn't judge me. He would let me be safe if that's what I wanted. Even though he'd said it last night, I knew in my heart at that moment that he loved me. I walked back over to him.

"I'm sorry," I told Zack. "I can't live with this."

He looked surprised and sad.

"What about your family, Ridley? What about my mother? She's always treated you like her own daughter. What do you think will happen to them if people find out about Project Rescue? Do you think anyone will believe your father wasn't involved?"

I couldn't answer. I couldn't be concerned with the consequences of choices other people had made. Right now I could worry only about the consequences of my own choices. And the way I saw it, I was in a lose-lose situation. I couldn't go back into the fold. It wasn't an option for me; I'd seen everyone and everything too clearly. We've already talked about how you can't go dark again. If I left with Jake, the consequences were impossible to predict. I could hurt a lot of people I loved. I could be hurt myself. I walked over to the closet and got a pair of sneakers, sat down on the bed next to that pile of cash, and laced them up.

"Let's go," I said to Jake, rising.

"Are you sure?" he asked. "It's not safe. I don't know what we're up against and if I can protect us."

I nodded. "I know."

"If you leave here, Ridley, I can't be responsible for what happens to you," said Zack. All the concern had left his voice and there was just a petulant anger there. I wondered if he realized that it was the second time he'd said that to me in two days. "Even if you're not interested in protecting your family, I'll do what I have to do to protect my mother."

Jake and I left Zack standing there with his arms outspread. In the hallway, Jake took me in his arms and kissed me hard on the mouth. I clung to him for a moment, and when I pulled back I could see the relief in his eyes. He wasn't alone anymore and he knew it. We ran down the remaining flights of stairs and Jake headed toward the front door. I pulled at his arm.

"There's another way out of this building," I told him, and showed him the way to Zelda's tunnel.

THIRTY-FOUR

I was clever but not clever enough. We had made it east to Avenue C before we sensed rather than saw that we were being followed. The silent street around us seemed to darken with menace as we passed an abandoned lot filled with garbage, a burned-out car, some junkies huddled in a corner with a pipe glowing between them. I think we felt rather than heard the low rumble of the engine of a car that was following us without headlights. Jake took my hand and we started to run. We ran hard, expecting at any second to hear the sound of gunfire, but there was nothing. The only sound I heard was our footfalls and our breathing. The city seemed to draw a breath and hold it.

On Avenue D we turned the corner. We looked around and there was no one in sight. We ran up the front steps of a condemned apartment building and slipped through the triangle of space where someone had pushed back the piece of plywood that acted as the door. Inside, we peered through the window that was black with soot from some long-ago fire and saw a Lincoln Town Car come to a stop on the avenue. Men wearing ski masks emerged from the vehicle and I swear my heart almost stopped. I felt as if the city was an alien world where all the rules had changed. It was like **Escape from New York** or something, only there was no escape. Jake put his hand over my mouth against the cry of panic he must have sensed coming.

"Stay with me, Ridley. Stay calm, girl."

I nodded and together we made our way through a ruined foyer that reeked of smoke. I pulled my shirt up over my nose to keep myself from breathing in the filthy air so I wouldn't cough or sneeze. We passed a mustard couch that lay on its back beside a rusted file cabinet with no drawers. We started to climb a crumbling staircase that groaned in protest beneath our weight. On the next level, we again looked out the window and saw the men, four of them, walking the street looking for us, climbing front stoops, peering in windows.

The building was only three stories high, and at the top we could see that something from the roof had fallen through all the way to the bottom, leaving a gaping hole in the ceiling above us and in each floor below, so that we could clearly see the ground-floor entrance to the building from our perch on the third. We sat on the floor and Jake took out his gun, lay on his belly, and trained it on the door below us. We sat listening to the men call to one another on the street below us, and then everything went quiet. We waited. Then it started to rain. We were unprotected in the downpour.

"I'm so sorry," he whispered after a few minutes. He looked up at me.

I shook my head. "You have nothing to be sorry for."

"I did this to your life, Ridley."

"No," I said, shaking my head.

"Yes. If I hadn't left that second note . . . if I had let this all go away for you, we wouldn't be sitting here right now."

I shook my head. There was no point in thinking like this; it was way too late. There was only moving forward now, hoping to survive this night.

I put my hand on his shoulder. "It was my

choice to be here with you tonight. I chose."
And that was the truth. He nodded and I
leaned in to kiss him. But then he was firing
his gun at something behind me. The night
fractured in a gale of light and thunder and we
were falling.

I fell only one floor, but Jake went all the
way down to the ground level. I heard his
body hit the floor so hard, I felt it in my own
bones. I think I had a split second of uncon-
sciousness before the sound of voices brought
me around.

"What the fuck? Where did they go?"

They'd come from the roof of another
building, I realized.

"Watch out, you fucking moron, the
floor's not solid." I heard a heavy thump and
watched as more debris fell through the hole.
I couldn't see the men above me and hoped it
meant that they couldn't see me.

"Don't fire until you see one of them, for
Christ's sake. This building is going to crumble like a pile of shit."

I looked down to see Jake lying below me.
He wasn't moving and I felt a shock of fear
and dread like I'd never felt before. I began to
crawl when a white-hot pain in my leg rocketed through me, so intense, I held back

vomit. I couldn't see what was in my leg, only the tear in my pants and the sticky, hot, wet feeling of blood. There was something lodged in there and any movement made me want to scream. But my desire to get to Jake was greater than my physical pain and I dragged myself to the staircase, pulled myself up on the banister, and managed to make it to the bottom before they rained bullets on me again.

I pushed myself against the wall and watched the bullets shred the floor and walls around me. Jake lay still on the floor, unresponsive to the noise and the danger. I heard a heavy thud and a sudden crashing followed by a groan.

"Angelo! Are you all right?"

"Yeah," a voice with a thick New York accent responded. "I fell through the fucking floor."

I used this distraction to make it to Jake before the bullets started to rain again.

THIRTY-FIVE

"Six," he whispers.

"What?"

"You have six bullets left."

I nod to him and keep my eyes on the staircase. I've heard Zack's voice, so I know he's one of the men coming after us, and I just can't get my head around this. He would kill us to keep his secret, then pretend to grieve at my funeral. This is the man my father wanted me to marry. My hands are shaking with pain and fear and rage. White lights have started to dance in front of my vision.

"We can make this right," he calls, though I still can't see him. I know they're close; I can hear the stairs groaning. At the instant I see a leg, I fire and miss. The sound is so loud and the kickback so powerful that I let out a little scream of terror. My ears are ringing. When I look back, the leg is gone. Maybe I can hold them at bay for a while like this. Now there are five bullets and four men.

"Don't waste the bullets on impossible shots," Jake whispers. "Wait until you can shoot center mass. You'll never hit otherwise." I look over at him. He's lying so still it seems as if he can't move, and I can see he's in so much pain.

"Ridley, please," calls Zack. "It doesn't have to end this way. My offer stands. You loved me once. Can't you trust me now?"

I look at Jake and he looks at me. Jake puts a finger to his lips and points up. I can see the men above us with their guns pointed down. Zack is just trying to get me to talk so that the men know where to fire. I smile grimly and stay silent.

"Fuck it," Zack says finally.

When they start shooting, I fire back. Their shots spit and bounce off the walls around us and one even hits the couch, but it doesn't come through the frame. I keep waiting to feel metal pierce my skin. I can feel Jake trying to protect my body with his. The smell of gunpowder fills my nose, and my ears are ringing so loudly, everything else seems muffled. The situation takes on a nonreality and I am not as afraid as I should be. I think this must be what combat feels like, surreal, so terrifying that your mind's ability to perceive danger and your capacity for fear diminish. With one of my shots, a man falls heavily to the floor with a groan, but there are three more and the shooting doesn't seem to end. I aim with each remaining bullet as best I can, but soon the gun is empty and the other men are still firing on us. In the movies, I would have hit them all with my few bullets, but I learn that I'm not a very good shot. When the gun is empty, I drop it to the floor and cling to Jake, thinking we are going to die here tonight. And the one thing I can say for sure is that I don't have any regrets. I'm glad he didn't have to face this alone.

I close my eyes and think I'm dreaming when I hear the chopping blades of a helicopter and see the room flood with light.

"Drop your weapons!" roars the voice of God. "Get down on the ground and put your hands behind your heads."

In the chaos of light and sound, the gunfire ceases. I can feel Jake's arms strong around me, holding me.

"Ridley," I hear God calling me. "Ridley Jones, are you okay? Are you down there?"

And from fear or pain or sheer relief everything goes black.

THIRTY-SIX

It's like I said before. The universe doesn't like secrets. It conspires to reveal the truth, to lead you to it. As easy as it might have been for me to accept Alexander Harriman's deal and walk away, the universe just didn't allow it. Harriman had said Project Rescue had grown into something Max couldn't control. Turned out it had grown into something Alexander Harriman couldn't control, either.

Closure. We all seek it. We seek the end of things and also the beginning of new things. Those things we can't find closure on, they haunt us. They pop up in our dreams, they creep into our thoughts in idle moments, like a mind-bender that's beyond our mental capacity, a mystery that just won't be solved. I think about Teresa Stone, my biological mother, fighting to save her child and losing her life in the process. I think about Christian

Luna with his thousand regrets and failed attempt at redemption. I think about Max, my father, and all the crimes he committed in his quest to heal himself through "helping" others. I think about all the rest of those parents, their children's faces on the back of mailers and milk cartons. Those awful age-graduated composites, what they'd look like five, six, ten years after they'd gone missing, showing up in mailboxes, in cafeterias. Maybe some of those people deserved to lose their children, maybe some of them didn't. But I'm willing to bet that for every Project Rescue baby out there, there's a haunted soul. For Jessie, it was Christian Luna. For Charlie, it was Linda McNaughton.

If I had done as Harriman asked, the people responsible for that pain would have continued on with their days; people like Zack and Esme would continue making judgments and playing God with strangers' lives, never having a moment of guilt or pain. But my life would have been populated with the ghosts of the people I'd failed to help, Jake chief among them.

Speaking of helping people, it was Gus Salvo who saved us that night in the condemned building. He'd had a tail on Angelo

Numbruzio because of the shell casings they found at the scene of Christian Luna's murder. When the cop watching Numbruzio discovered that he had contacted Zack and was headed for my building, Detective Salvo put the pieces together . . . a little on the slow side maybe, but just in time at least.

In the fall, Jake had broken his right leg and left arm and punctured his lung. He'd severely strained his back but all the vertebrae were intact. The bullet that had pierced my thigh had missed the major artery. It's the little things, remember? A fraction of an inch and I wouldn't be here to tell you what happened to us.

When I regained consciousness at St. Vincent's Hospital, Gus Salvo was the first thing I saw. Not pretty, but better than a lot of things I'd seen recently.

"Where's Jake?" I asked, my heart filling with panic, remembering the last moments we were together.

"He's fine," he said kindly. "Well, he'll **be** fine."

He pulled his chair close to me and held my hand. He told me the extent of Jake's injuries and that he was within hopping distance of my hospital room.

"Don't worry, Ridley. It's all over now."

I looked at him and knew it wasn't true.

"Then why are you here, Detective Salvo?"

He sighed and looked past me. "I should wait till you're feeling better, Ridley, I know that. But . . ."

"But?"

"I have to know where you come down on this. The men who chased you tonight are in custody. I believe that one of those men killed Christian Luna. Remember I told you about Angelo Numbruzio, how I was able to tie him to the shooting at the diner? We have him on a surveillance tape from the gun store in Florida that sold the assault rifle that killed Christian Luna.

"We can't prosecute him without your testimony, not effectively. And if we move forward with it, everything about your past, about Project Rescue, is going to come out. I know you're afraid for your family, but I have to tell you Zack and Esme Gray are making a deal with the DA. It's all coming out, anyway."

I didn't say anything, just looked past him to the hallway. Alexander Harriman was dead. Obviously, the deal I had with him was not going to be honored by the people who killed him. They'd already tried to kill me. I knew I didn't have any power to protect anyone any longer. Maybe I never did.

"I'll testify, Detective Salvo. I'll testify for Christian Luna. But I can't testify about Project Rescue." We looked at each other. "I can't testify against Max or Esme."

He nodded. "Ridley, you were only a baby. You shouldn't have to testify if that comes to trial. You're the **victim** in that case, not a witness."

The fact hit home hard. Detective Salvo held my hand and let me cry. I cried for Teresa Stone. I cried for Christian Luna. I cried for Max. And, yes, I cried for all the pieces of myself that I had lost.

Later that night, I hobbled from my room trailing my morphine drip (which was probably the reason I was able to hobble at all) to find Jake. The duty nurse was helpful rather than mean and officious. She put me in a wheelchair and took me to him herself. He was groggy but lifted his good hand to me as soon as he saw me.

"You're beautiful," he said to me, his words slurring a bit. Doubtful. I could taste my own teeth.

"You're high," I said, and started to giggle. I was a little high myself, but through it I was starting to feel the dull throb of my leg.

His right leg and left arm were both in casts. His face was bruised, his muscular chest wrapped tight with bandages. I'd never seen anyone more gorgeous in my life.

"You should go back to bed," he said, taking my hand.

"I will," I said. "I just wanted you to know that you weren't alone anymore. I'm with you."

I kissed his hand then and he touched my face. He smiled and I could see one tear trapped in the corner of his eye, but he blinked away at it hard.

"I love you, Jake . . . or whatever your name is."

He started to laugh and then groaned at the pain it caused. I stayed with him until he fell asleep, which wasn't long. And then the nurse wheeled me back to my room.

THIRTY-SEVEN

You might remember I made a promise to Linda McNaughton. But it was more than a month before Jake and I had our legs under us again. And a bit longer after that before I was able to convince Jake to help me keep it. Jake's leg was still in a cast when we rented a car and headed out to Jersey. The Firebird was gone; it never turned up again. The guy who'd probably taken it and then tried to kill me with it—or **scare** me, as Alexander Harriman had said—had a bullet in the back of his brain. There was no way to know where he had dumped it.

"Come with me," Jake said, looking pale when I pulled in front of the trailer.

"You don't want an audience," I said. "Give yourself a few minutes alone with her and then wave me in."

He nodded and left me listening to "Roxanne" by the Police on the radio. I watched as he made his way on crutches up the walk, as she opened the door for him and he disappeared inside. I closed my eyes and imagined him surrounded by turtles, telling Linda McNaughton that he was Charlie, her grandson lost so many years ago. I could see her, gray hair and matching sweat suit, covering her mouth, tears springing to her eyes. I could see her throwing her arms around him and him holding her awkwardly. I wanted to be there with him. But it was their moment, alone. I wanted them both to have that.

About a half hour later I saw him in the doorjamb waving for me. I looked for joy on his face and I didn't really see it there. But he looked happy enough, a little flushed as I approached. It was bitterly cold outside, the ground frozen hard, the trees black and dead around the trailer park. But it was warm inside. Linda sat teary on the couch, clutching the photograph I'd taken from her and sent Jake to return. She stood and embraced me.

"I didn't think you'd be back," she said. "Either of you."

We stayed for a while. What can I say? It was awkward. They were strangers to each other. She talked about his parents and he listened, attentive and present. She told him a bit about his early years, how he'd walked and talked early, how he'd had a plush frog that he carried with him everywhere. He smiled and made the appropriate responses. There wasn't much he could share about his years growing up that wouldn't have caused her pain, so he glossed over it, gave her vagaries about his life. We drank tea with her. Then:

"Mrs. McNaughton," he started.

"Please call me Grandma," she said, looking shy. "Or at least Linda."

I could tell he wasn't comfortable saying it but he did. "Grandma," he said with an uncomfortable laugh, "we have to go now."

We didn't really but I stood with him and nodded.

"Oh, of course," she said, and I detected a little relief there. "Perhaps you two could come this Sunday for dinner. We don't have much family, but I have a sister who'd love to see you."

"I'd like that," he said. He hugged her and I saw her tear up again as she held on to him. She stood in the door and watched us leave, the same way she'd watched me when I left her the first time, her arm suspended in the air in a wave. Back in the car, he was quiet as we pulled away toward the highway. I placed a hand on his thigh. "How was that for you?"

He sighed. "I don't know. Not like I expected. I guess I hoped to feel more **connected** to her."

"You will," I said. "Give it time."

I've come to believe, as I said, that it's not blood that connects us but experience. For everything we'd been through, for all the lies, for all the wrongs done by my family, they were still my family. I never once stopped thinking about them that way; they never became strangers to my heart. And even though the ideal I had held in my imagination proved to be completely false, it didn't change the way I felt about them. They could be only what they were. That had to be enough.

We pulled to a stop in front of my parents' house and sat for a minute. There it was, that picture postcard of my childhood. The house was decorated for Christmas with pretty wreaths in each window, those plug-in candles glowing. I could see the tree with its white lights and tiny red ribbons glinting through the bay window. I didn't want it to seem like a false front. But it did. I hoped it was a feeling that would pass.

"They don't want to see me, I'm sure," said Jake.

"Why would you say that?"

He gave me a look. "I blew the roof off of your life. And theirs."

"I don't see it that way," I said, opening the door and stepping outside.

We made our way carefully up the front walk, worried for the icy patches and Jake's crutches. My father came out to help; my mother waited, arms folded at the door. We all went inside, had hot chocolate by the tree.

I'd stripped away the script of our lives. Doesn't it feel that way in your family? Everyone has his role, and as long as everyone keeps true to the part that has been cast for him, things go on as they always have. You laugh about the same things, fight about the same things, harbor all the same old resentments, share the same memories, good and bad. But when one person starts to improvise, starts to write her own lines, the whole script has to be thrown out. Everyone else misses cues, there's an awkward silence, then chaos. Then, if you're lucky, you all create a new production together. One based in the present, based on honesty, one that's fluid and malleable to change. We were in the awkward-silence stage. Lots of uncomfortable pauses. Lots of shared memories, especially those involving Max, that didn't seem appropriate to mention any longer.

"I want you to know, Jake and Ridley," my father said during one of those silences that had been precipitated by my noticing an ornament given to my mother by Max. It was a silver ballerina with a delicate crystal tutu, inspired I think by the Degas painting. "I want you to know that I never suspected for a moment the true nature of Project Rescue." He was silent for a second, not looking at either of us but down at the cup in his hand. "What we did with you, Ridley, was wrong. We're guilty of a lot of failures with you even beyond that, but I can never be sorry for taking you that night. I can never regret having the chance to be your father. Still, it's important for me to let you both know that I never would have been a part of the abduction and selling of children. Not for any reason."

Jake nodded politely, but I knew he wasn't convinced. I chose to believe my father. I knew him well and really couldn't see him being a part of it. Jake didn't know him as well and was having a hard time swallowing it.

"It was Esme Gray, then?" asked Jake. "She flagged the kids she thought were in danger? She was the one who told Max about Jessie?"

That was one of the big unanswered questions for me. Alexander Harriman said that the murder of Teresa Stone was an accident, the point at which Max realized he'd lost control of Project Rescue. But who had arranged for Jessie's abduction that night? And how had Max wound up with her? There was a big piece missing here. And Esme, the only person who might have answers, wasn't talking about any of it.

"I don't know," my father said after a long pause. "I really don't know, Jake."

"And you don't want to know," said Jake, holding his eyes.

My father sighed and looked away. "I'm sure there are more answers coming. An investigation is under way, as you well know."

I heard the resentment in his voice then. And I saw it in my mother, who sat quietly on the far corner of the couch, present but distant, a fake half-smile on her lips. She was **enduring** this visit, not participating. Jake was the truth they didn't want to face, the spotlight they couldn't extinguish. And he was here to stay. They both wished that none of this had ever happened. If they could turn back the clock and keep me from stepping in front of that van, they would. They would choose to go dark again.

You're probably wondering, What about me? What was my wish? Would I turn back the clock? I can't answer that. Like I told you, I don't believe in mistakes or in regret. We don't know the other road, the one we didn't take, or where it leads.

Epilogue

Quidam, the stranger, the anonymous passerby. The man walking in the rain on the street after midnight. The sound of a violin through your apartment wall. The homeless man asking for change on the steps of a church. The old woman next to you on the bus. Disconnected from your life but joined to you by a moment in time. All the choices and events of his life and the choices and events of yours have led you to be in the exact same place at the exact same time. Think about it.

I am writing this from my new apartment on Park Avenue South, across from the 4/5-train station. It's an artist's loft, big and breezy, washed with light, overlooking downtown Manhattan. The floors don't sag and there's no aroma of pastry or pizza, which I really miss. Those little quirks of East Village living.

There's enough room for both our offices, though Jake still keeps his studio downtown. I actually have a room where I write now, not just a corner divided by a screen from the rest of my bedroom. We wanted a new place, where we could start all over again together. New life, new apartment. Makes sense, right?

Jake and I are getting to know Linda better. She's starting to feel like family. Little by little, Jake is getting to know his parents, too, or at least Linda's memory of them. They were flawed people to be sure, but aren't we all? In learning about them, Jake is learning about himself. For the first time in his life he says he doesn't feel **quidam,** like a stranger in his skin, disconnected from the world around him. And I like to think I have something to do with that.

Ace is still in rehab, nearly three months now. I see him on Thursdays. I am really getting to know him for the first time. As a child, he was my hero; as an adult, he was the part of me I was always trying to save. Now he's just Ace, my brother who I've known all of my remembered life but who has been a stranger to me, partly because of his addiction and partly because of my addiction to an idea of him. We're in counseling together. He has told me that he believed I had always loved an idea of him and that I'd never really seen the true person there. Just my memories and my dream of him. I suppose he's right. Isn't that so often true with family, that we see them through the filters of our own fears, expectations, and desire to control? He's struggling with this thing. I don't know if he'll succeed, but I know now that I can't help him. Only be present for him, be honest with him, and love him for who he is rather than who I want him to be.

He never had anything to do with what happened to me. He's guilty only of never telling me the truth that he knew. And he kept it from me only because he knew the pain it would cause. He did love me, after all. He did want to protect me from the bad guys.

Ace and my parents have begun to tentatively negotiate a new relationship. It's a series of fits and starts. There's so much anger there, so many years of hurt. Each meeting so far has ended in yelling and tears, or so I'm told. But at least they keep meeting. That's something, isn't it?

Ruby's gone. She came to see Ace once a few weeks after he'd been in rehab when visitors were allowed. He tried to convince her to try to get clean. I offered to pay for the private facility where Ace is being treated, but she refused. And Ace was smart enough to know you can't help someone who doesn't want to be helped. We haven't seen her since. At Ace's request, I went to the Lower East Side one Sunday with Jake to look in on her, to tell her that Ace was asking after her. But she had gone, packed her things and moved on. Ace is hopeful that he'll see her again.

Hope is good. Without it, well, you do the math. But hope has to be like a prayer. Putting it out there to something more powerful than yourself. If the last few months have taught me anything, it's this: We don't have control, we have choices. The little ones, the big ones, these are the points on which our lives pitch and pivot. All we can do is make the best **choices** we can with what we know, and **hope** that things turn out the way we want.

My parents and I are muddling through in our new relationship. There have been a few screaming matches; all that rage and sadness I didn't feel during our first confrontation have come to the surface more than once. But no one's walked away or severed ties, no one has given up. The big stuff hangs between us. But we love each other, and we're learning how to be together in this new life where there are no secrets and no lies between us. I have faith that when the hurt fades, our relationship will be stronger for being based on honesty. And I hope that my parents can find a way to love Jake, too, though I know in their hearts they blame him for all of this.

Christian Luna's murder trial still looms. I will testify to what he told me and how I watched him die. The prosecutors will use that to prove motive for Angelo Numbruzio and the people from whom he takes his orders. Depending on the outcome of the trial, state prosecutors will decide how to proceed with the Project Rescue case. And that will determine Zack and Esme's fate. My father will probably have some questions to answer. I know he's frightened and so am I.

I haven't spoken to Zack or Esme. Zack is in custody, charged with attempted murder. I try not to think about him the way I last saw him, about the fact that he tried to kill me and Jake. I try not to think about what has happened to his life. He and Esme have been advised by their lawyers not to speak to any of us. The deal they've made with prosecutors in the Project Rescue case prohibits it. Not that they'd **want** to talk to us. But I'd like to talk to Esme. I'd like to know who she was then and what she knows about the night that Teresa Stone died and about the other children who passed through the Little Angels clinic and disappeared. I think she's the link, that she has the answers Jake and I still need. What do you think? Anyway, we may get those answers yet, as the investigation unfolds.

The media has already begun to feed. A show about Max and his alleged involvement in Project Rescue has already aired on **Dateline.** They made him seem like a monster. And to some people, I'm sure he is. But not to me. Project Rescue was ill conceived and the ramifications unspeakable. But he's still Max. And more than that, he was my father. I've tried to recast him in my memory as that. But I can't; not really. Not yet. As my father, he was flawed, guilty of some terrible errors in judgment at best. As my uncle Max, he was perfect, this bright star in the memory of my life. Is it wrong to want to keep that?

I don't know what happened that night when he brought Jessie to my parents. I don't know what his involvement was, if Teresa Stone's murder was an accident. I may never know if my father was responsible for the murder of my mother. Whether the terrible legacy of abuse and murder Max spent his whole life trying to flee had caught up with him just the same. I remember often what he said to me that last night. **Ridley, you might be the only good I've ever done.** He was in so much pain. The demons he'd battled all his life had come for him. Later that night, they took him home.

The **Dateline** people called me, too, but I, of course, don't do interviews. Not anymore. It will take all my courage and all my strength to talk about the things that have happened during Christian Luna's murder trial when the time comes.

There are no villains here. Not really. If you think about it, there are no true villains in life. Only in fiction do we see distilled versions of good and bad. In life, there are only good and bad **choices.** And sometimes even choices can be judged only by their consequences. And sometimes not even then. I guess if you want to see Zack as a villain or Esme, you can. Maybe you think Max is the villain. But I think they all believed that they were doing right, right for the children, right for one another, right for me. No matter how wrong-headed their thinking was, it counts for something, doesn't it?

What about all those children, all those

other Project Rescue babies? I heard that a hotline has been established for people who suspect that they might have been one of those children. But my suspicion is that most of them don't have the first clue about what has happened to them. I suspect that not many would **want** to know. I can't imagine many parents stepping forward to say they'd obtained their child through an illegal adoption, if they weren't forced to do so. But who knows, the truth can be a powerful lure to the shadow side. Maybe the universe will lead some of those children kicking and screaming to their truth, as it did for me.

From the moment Jake and I stood standing in his apartment, our hands locked, we have been allies. Yes, there have been lies and moments of doubt between us. And though those moments have been more **extreme** for us than for others in a new relationship, I don't see it as being all that different. Don't we reveal ourselves slowly, in parts, to the people we are starting to love? Don't we pick and choose what we want them to see and when? Aren't we afraid to be judged or rejected because of who we are, at least a little at first, until we grow more intimate, feel safer beneath each other's gazes? Now Jake and I have a policy of total honesty between us. And that's not always **easy** (as in, "Do these jeans make me look fat?"), but it's always **real.** And I'll take real any day over lies, no matter how they glimmer and shine, no matter how beautiful.

THE BEGINNING

Acknowledgments

My most heartfelt thanks to . . .

. . . my agent, Elaine Markson, and her assistant, Gary Johnson, for their unfailing support and enthusiasm. They are absolutely my lifeline in this business. I can't imagine where I'd be without them.

. . . Sally Kim for her wonderful and loving editing and for giving me such a beautiful home at Shaye Areheart Books. What a total love connection!

. . . Shaye Areheart for welcoming me with her warm and open arms. I feel so blessed to be a part of her universe, as it is infused with light and benevolence. Also, my thanks to Jenny Frost, Tina Constable, Philip Patrick, and Doug Jones for their tremendous energy, enthusiasm, and support. With them on my side, I feel like anything is possible.

. . . Whitney Cookman, Jacqui LeBow,

Kim Shannon, Jill Flaxman, Kira Stevens, Tara Gilbride, Darlene Faster, Linda Kaplan, Karin Shulze, Alex Lencicki, and everyone in the Shaye Areheart Books/Crown family who made my first visit seem like a homecoming. What a privilege to work with such a bright and talented team of people.

. . . the wonderful network of family and friends with which I have been blessed, most especially: my husband, Jeffrey, for **way** too many reasons to list here; Heather Mikesell for her tireless reading of drafts, endless enthusiasm, and invaluable input; and my parents, Joe and Virginia, for their unflagging cheerleading and shameless bragging.

About the Author

LISA UNGER lives in Florida with her husband and is at work on her next novel.